CW00515001

A Confusion of Crows

Susan Handley

Published by Sunningdale Books

All rights reserved
© Susan Handley, 2018

Susan Handley has asserted her right under the Copyright, Designs and
Patents Act 1988 to be identified as the author of this work.

Without limiting the rights under copyright reserved above, no part of this
publication may be reproduced, stored in or introduced into a retrieval system,
or transmitted, in any form or by any means (electronic, mechanical,
photocopying, recording or otherwise) without the prior written permission
of both the copyright owner and the above publisher of this book

This book is a work of fiction and any resemblance to actual persons, living or
dead, is purely coincidental.

A CIP catalogue record for this book is available from the British Library

To John – for believing in me

Prologue

Jamie clambered up onto the old weir. It was worn and dilapidated; a thick carpet of moss shrouded its uneven surface. He peered down, drawn by the violent noise of the river and felt the first wobble of his legs at the prospect of the drop. The narrow ledge was the only thing between him and the swirling, turbulent water below, angry and swollen after several weeks of summer storms. Nervous now, he cast a longing look back at his friends. They screamed and shouted at him, goading him on from the safety of the river bank.

Jamie's legs grew even weaker and before fear could force him to fail, he pulled his shoulders back, held his head high and launched off the ledge, somersaulting into the inky liquid.

His breath exploded from him and the cold water sucked him under. He kicked and thrashed, the little air left in his lungs growing stale, until eventually he burst through the bubbling white froth, coughing and spluttering. He gulped greedy lungfuls of air, while the river carried him through green fields dotted with grazing cows, away from his friends and the weir. As soon as he had breath enough to spare, he spent it cursing.

Spotting a felled oak jutting into the water, Jamie stopped muttering and started to scull towards it. Close now, he reached out a hand and grabbed at the tree's long limbs. Whip-thin tendrils of bare branch sliced his palms but he tightened his grip, determined not to let them slip from his grasp. Finally, he came to a stop, content to let the water continue its journey without him.

Using the branches for support, Jamie began to pull himself through the chest-high water towards the bank but the silt sucked at his feet like a mat of leeches. Suddenly seized with the enormity of the task, he felt his chest constrict and his vision grew swimmy with tears. He sniffed hard and snorted back his self-pity.

With a fresh determination he reached up and wedged a foot between two branches, took a hard, angry hit of air and hauled himself clear of the water. He clambered onto all fours and stared down the trunk's rippled surface, checking out the makeshift bridge.

But the wood had been rotting for some time and a branch beneath his foot gave way with a loud cracking, snapping sound. Terrified of falling back in, he flung himself forward and wrapped his arms tightly around the trunk.

And that's when he saw it, trapped below the splintered cream bones of a broken branch.

Oblivious to the rough bark, which grated his young skin, or the trip hazards posed by the twigs beneath his toes, Jamie scrambled down the length of the trunk onto solid ground, where he started a lung-bursting sprint up the steep and muddy bank. But no matter how hard or fast he ran he could not outrun the memory of that face, its features swollen beyond recognition, straining at skin pulled taut and shiny. A single eye bulged out as though looking to make its escape, its neighbour already gone; the empty socket white and cavernous, picked clean by the river's livestock.

One

Cat climbed out of the car and surveyed the scene. The sound of the river rushing by and the smell of newly baled hay brought back memories of lazy afternoons spent under cloud-dotted blue skies. She could almost hear the whoops and hollers of her friends, carefree and laughing, with sun kissed shoulders, gangly limbs and impish expressions. And when it had got too hot, there had always been those cool, clear waters.

She shivered.

A cloud had slipped in front of the low sun and hung there, as though keen to keep the warmth-giving rays to itself.

Jolted out of her sentimental mood by the sudden drop in temperature she checked her watch and looked towards the road beyond her car. Still no sign of him. Turning back, she spotted a uniformed officer heading across the field towards her.

'Any news?' she called.

'The photographer's finished and the divers are ready to start, so if you want to go and take a look for yourself...'

She hurried down towards the water's edge, but the ground was boggy and difficult to navigate and the heavy wet clay made staying upright a challenge. After nearly losing her footing for the umpteenth time she finally put caution over curiosity and retreated to her vantage point at the top of the hill.

She was still standing watching the extraction exercise when she heard an approaching vehicle. Turning, she raised a hand and waved at the car that pulled to a stop next to hers.

'Bang goes my budget,' Alex said, climbing out.

'The divers?' Cat asked.

'The overtime.' He slammed the car door shut. 'Murder

investigations always cost a bloody fortune.'

She felt a stirring of excitement.

'How do you know it's murder? You only just got here.'

'Why else would she be here?'

'Suicide?'

Alex scanned the scene and shook his head.

'No.' He sounded confident.

Her excitement tightened its grip. So far, after nearly a year in CID, she'd scored a couple of frauds and a job lot of robberies. This would be her first serious crime. Her first chance to really prove her worth.

Alex stared across the field down to the river. The divers were sliding around as they struggled to pull their quarry from the water. He looked back at Cat and then down at her shoes, which were thick with mud.

'Give me the run down. Start with who found her.'

'A fourteen-year old lad. Been messing around with his mates upstream. He jumped off the weir, a bet or a dare or something like that. The current caught him and he ended up down there. He dislodged the body while he was trying to climb out. His mother called after he arrived home in a state.'

Alex nodded. 'What about Tony? Did he find anything of any interest?'

'Tony?'

'The photographer. You did speak with him before he left?'

She looked at him anxiously.

'No. Should I have done?'

'If the photographer gets to see the scene close up before you do then it's always worth a chat. Don't just wait for the glossies.'

'Sorry, I didn't think.'

'You'll know for next time.' Alex looked around. 'What about access points?'

At least she knew the answer to that one.

She gestured to a small brick arch that spanned the river some hundred yards away.

'There's that road bridge there. She could have jumped from that. Or been thrown over,' she said, remembering Alex's assessment.

He glanced at the small stone bridge.

'It's not suicide. Not off a bridge like that. It's way too low.'

'What if she couldn't swim?'

When Alex didn't reply Cat continued, 'It's possible she entered the river further up and floated down. I'm sure we can find out when the sluice gates were last open. Or I suppose she could have already been dead or sedated and then carried down from somewhere around here. But I'm not so sure about that. There are no obvious vehicle tracks and carrying a body over terrain like this certainly wouldn't have been my choice.'

Alex nodded but said nothing and for a while they stood in silence, watching and waiting until the divers finally hauled the limp and lifeless form out of the water. Cat steeled herself as they headed over to take a look.

Two

'Don't bother taking your coat off. We're going straight out,' Alex said as soon as Cat arrived at the office the next morning. He threw her his keys. 'You drive.'

'Where to?' she asked, starting after him.

'The mortuary. It must be a quiet time of year; the PM starts in half an hour.'

Cat frowned.

'The post-mortem,' Alex explained.

She could feel herself colouring.

'I know what PM stands for.' She sounded defensive even to her ears. 'I just didn't understand what you meant by quiet time of year.'

'They've pushed it through quickly. Sometimes it can take days.'

'Really? Even with a suspicious death?'

Alex ignored her question. That would be a 'yes' then.

Little was said on the journey there. Not that Cat minded; she made the most of the time, trying to fit together the few facts they had, to form some sort of preamble to the story that would follow.

The roads were thick with commuter traffic and despite taking a direct route there, by the time they arrived the procedure had already begun. Cat waited while Alex consulted with the receptionist.

'The doc's got some students in, so we'll watch from in here,' he said, opening the door to an observation room.

After making themselves comfortable, Cat quickly became mesmerised listening to the smooth, rich baritone of the Oxford-educated pathologist as it emerged from the speakers into the confined space. Speaking a secret language of those schooled in the art of medicine, the professor reminded his students of their theoretical studies as they gathered around the cadaver, like children watching a show and tell.

'Immersion artefacts occur in any corpse immersed in water, irrespective of whether death was from drowning or the person was dead on entering the water.' He raised his voice. 'This is an important point, as it therefore means that immersion artefacts do not contribute to proof of death by drowning.' He paused to let his audience absorb this information before booming out a challenge. 'Who can give me any of the common examples of an immersion artefact?'

His question was met with silence. He looked from student to student before pointing a finger at a tired-looking, skinny youth.

'You, Jones, give me two examples of an immersion artefact.'

Jones paused before venturing an answer.

'One symptom is cutis anserina, known as goose skin due to the fact the pimpling of the skin looks like a plucked goose. The second example is skin maceration. That is a swelling and wrinkling of the skin.'

'Spot on. Notice here and here.' The professor pointed towards the skin on the corpse before them. 'I'm sure you will all have remembered a third type of immersion artefact? Adipocere – the transformation of the fatty layer beneath the skin into a soap-like material. Let's see if you can be as lucky a second time Jones. How could adipocere help us with the particular knotty problem of identifying time of death?'

Bolstered by his success so far, Jones replied in a confident voice.

'Adipocere is a process that takes weeks or months to occur. If the body exhibits signs of it, it's evidence it has been immersed for some significant time.'

'Correct!' The professor gave a nod of approval in Jones'

direction before addressing the rest of the group. 'Everyone gather round and take a good look. As you will all observe, there are no signs of adipocere.'

They all leaned forward to get a better view as he eased up the layers of skin to expose the tissue beneath it.

'So, who wants to have a bash at estimating of the time of death?' the professor asked.

'Late Saturday,' Cat said, sounding confident in their enclosed cubicle.

Alex remained quiet.

Cat turned in her seat to face him.

'What do you think?'

'I don't know. That's why I'm waiting for the expert to tell me.'

Cat turned her attention back to the viewing window in front of her, aware of the pinpricks of pink that were colouring her cheeks.

Despite most of the students' off-the-mark guesses, misled by the disfigured appearance of the bloated body, the professor pronounced the time of death as somewhere between midday Saturday and the same time on Sunday.

Cat tried not to look too pleased with herself but clearly failed.

'Alright smart arse, just because you've got a degree in biology.'

From the corner of her eye Cat thought she could see him smiling. Maybe he was just ribbing her. She opened her mouth to reply but thought better of it and for a change took a lead from him and said nothing.

The post-mortem continued along the same lines for some hours. Questions and answers were frequent and accompanied a thorough and well-tested routine. Each statement was illustrated through various stomach-churning cuts, slices and extractions. And even though she was interested, Cat couldn't concentrate. The pronouncement that the young girl – probably no more than eighteen – had been garrotted before being dumped in the river infuriated her. Soon her head was spinning with ideas of what should be done to whoever had turned what had once been a living, breathing person into nothing more than a teaching instrument.

Eventually the procedure drew to a close and the class dispersed. Alex and Cat joined the professor in the main examination room.

'Hi Larry. Can you spare five minutes?' Alex asked.

Without looking up, the professor asked, 'What do you want to know?'

'The murder weapon – you talked about the size and depth of the marks on her neck but you didn't say what could have made them. Any ideas?'

The professor turned and seemed about to answer, but stopped short and gave an enquiring look in Cat's direction.

'Detective Constable Caitlin McKenzie, Professor Lawrence Jarrett,' Alex said.

'Cat. Everyone calls me Cat,' she said, holding out a hand. But instead of reciprocating, the professor glanced down at his blood-stained gloves and gave her a bemused look. She quickly withdrew her hand.

The professor turned back to Alex.

'Hmm, the murder weapon, good question. First impressions are that it was something strong and thin, like nylon, maybe fishing line or garden wire, but not that thick plastic-coated stuff. Once we've had a chance to take a closer look at the wounds under the microscope, I should be in a better position to comment.'

Cat was watching a technician stitch up a long incision running the length of the young girl's slight body when she noticed the livid lines across her neck.

She turned to the professor.

'Could she have hung herself and then slipped from the

noose?' she asked.

'Absolutely not. The force was applied backwards and down. She was definitely garrotted.' The professor ripped off his gloves and dropped them into a nearby bin. 'Anything else?'

'No, that's everything,' Alex said, fixing Cat with a warning glare.

'Fine. The report should be with you within the next day or two. The tox' screens will take a couple of weeks.

'And don't forget the dentals,' the professor called to them as they reached the door, reminding them to pick up the negatives from the office on their way out.

Three

After the post-mortem, during the journey back to the station, Cat could feel Alex's energy rise. He drove fast with tight, precise movements, hardly speaking, and once there he jumped out of the car and set off across the car park with a confident stride.

He kept the pace up all the way to their office, where he pushed the door open with more force than was necessary. It banged noisily into the wall causing everyone to look up from their desks.

'Post-mortem confirms it. We've got ourselves a murder investigation,' he announced.

Around the room people broke into excited conversation. Not at all the response Cat had expected: sadness maybe or anger partnered with a determination to catch the killer, but excitement? She realised then that it wasn't just her newness on the job that was making her stomach flip.

'So how are we getting on here? Have we got an ID yet?' Alex asked.

The chatter suddenly stopped. Cat looked around at expressions that had become as empty as the murder board.

Alex turned to a scruffy-looking man.

'Bob?'

'Nothing yet boss,' replied the senior detective.

'Nothing at all?'

'Both the door-to-door and missing persons have drawn a blank so far.'

'How can someone not be missed since Saturday?' Cat said.

Bob looked at her, a slight sneer appearing on his lips.

'Shall I fill Mary Poppins in on life in the twenty-first

century?'

'Bob, don't start,' Alex said. He turned to Cat, 'Some teenagers are cut a lot of slack. And if the parents are divorced sometimes no one realises that the kid isn't where they're supposed to be. And don't forget this girl could be as old as seventeen or eighteen. She might live on her own, in which case there could be no one to miss her.'

'So what do we do now?' she asked.

Without answering, Alex walked over to the murder board and grabbed a marker pen from the attached tray.

'For those of you that weren't on duty yesterday, say hello to our new Jane Doe. The teenager, a red head, was found partially submerged in the River Wen, near to the basin by Cox Hill.'

Jotted on the board were the few scant details they had. Alex added a few more garnered from that morning's post-mortem.

JANE DOE

Victim:	White female. Red head. Aged 16 to 18
Found:	3pm 6 Sept by Jamie Wilkins, local 14-yr-old
SoC:	River Wen, partially undressed
ToD:	12:00pm Sat 3 Sept to 12:00pm Sun 4 Sept
CoD:	Ligature strangulation – thin wire
Other:	Birth mark on right thigh

'Not a lot to go on is it?' Alex said, returning the pen to its holder. 'As well as the photos from the scene we've got some taken at the PM. Not ideal, but they'll have to do until we get a positive ID.'

He passed a handful of glossy prints to a young woman in jeans and a denim shirt who began to tape them down the left side of the board.

'Sir,' Cat said, putting her hand up.

'Cat?'

'I thought it was worth pointing out that the shoes she was

wearing were strappy sandals, you know, the sort that–'

'Jesus wept. It's not a fucking fashion show,' Bob interrupted. 'There's more to a murder investigation than the victim's taste in clothes.'

Cat took a deep breath. She'd known her arrival on the team was going to ruffle a few feathers but she hadn't been prepared for the level of resentment that some of her colleagues exhibited.

Alex silenced Bob with a single look.

'Cat, perhaps you could tell Bob why he should give a toss,' he said, his expressionless stare still fixed on the older detective.

'Because they're the sort of shoes teenage girls wear to go clubbing. As it's possible she was killed on Saturday night maybe it was a date rape that went wrong, or maybe someone picked her up in a club. It could be worth talking to the pubs and nightclubs that were open?'

'Good idea,' Alex said.

Bob leaned back in his chair and crossed his arms.

'Well give her a gold fucking star,' he muttered under his breath, but loud enough for Cat to hear.

If Alex had heard he ignored it. Addressing the room once more he clapped his hands in a business-like gesture.

'Right, now to everyone's assignments. Cat: I want you to follow up on the dentals. Spencer: go back through the missing persons now we've got a better handle on her age and time of death. And while you're at it, trawl the databases for any similar deaths that have happened in the last eighteen months. Bob: I want you with me; we need to get something together for the press. As for the rest of you, sorry, you get the short straw. You and our uniformed colleagues get to carry on with the house-to-house enquiries. Don't forget, there's a prize for whoever brings in the first solid lead.'

They all knew the prize was just a pint over at Mickey's at the end of the case. It always was, but it managed to energise the room nonetheless.

Cat walked over to Alex, who was still standing next to the murder board. She looked at the photos that lined its edge.

'You're going to the press already?' she said.

Alex looked at her.

'We've got to find out who this girl was.'

Bob joined them. Cat kept her attention on Alex.

'But that could be the first time someone realises their daughter is dead. Isn't that a bit, well, brutal?'

'Unless we get something from the dentals, we haven't got much choice,' Alex said.

A hint of a smile curled Bob's lips.

'Maybe you've got a better suggestion?'

She paused and gave it some thought before shaking her head.

'No, not really.'

It turned out Alex was right to push ahead with the release. The responses from the public started to come in minutes after the first appeal was aired on the local TV and radio news. A slow trickle at first but by the following morning things were looking up.

'How long's this woman's daughter been missing for?' Cat asked as Alex navigated his way through the town's tortuous one-way system.

'She last saw her on Saturday.'

'And she's only just thought to call?'

'Apparently the daughter was supposed to be staying at a friend's house.'

'Oh. Fair enough.' She tried to think of other questions Alex might be expecting her to ask but failed, in the end resorting to, 'Is there anything else I should know?'

He gave her a quizzical look.

'Like what?'

'I don't know. I just thought... What about when we get there? Do you want me to ask any questions or shall I just observe?'

'Cat, just treat this like any other investigation. If you think of something useful to ask, then ask it. You're not coming along just for the ride.'

'Just thought I'd check.'

She put his sour mood down to the traffic. The journey should have only taken twenty minutes yet they'd already been on the road for thirty. Five minutes later, though, they had finally left the ring road and were heading out of town along what had once been an affluent tree-lined avenue. But the elms were no more, sacrificed to make space for bus lanes fringed with signs advertising accountants, osteopaths and dentists, the grandiose pre-war homes of the local gentry now host to a plethora of private practices.

The roads here were clear and they soon reached the Coney Estate. Created in the seventies, it was a rabbit warren of Lego-like houses, pre-fabricated carbon copies of one another, each with the character of a shoebox. For years the local press had been reporting on the rot setting in but the deterioration had accelerated of late. And as the level of criminal activity soared, the law-abiding residents had left in their droves. Now only delinquents and the poor sods who couldn't afford anywhere else remained to tough it out in streets pock-marked with graffiti, smashed-up bus shelters and burnt-out cars on blocks.

'Hey! Slow down,' Cat said, trying to make out the worn and rusted numbers screwed to the front doors. '166, 168, 170... there, it's the next one, on the left by the street lamp.'

Alex brought the car to a stop directly outside number 172, an abandoned-looking house. He swung the door open and stepped out.

'Shit!' he said, stepping carefully over a pile of fly-infested kitchen scraps that had spilled out of an empty black bin bag that lay nearby.

Cat was already at the small wooden gate that separated the scruffy, weed-filled front garden of number 172 from the rest of the street. The gate, once painted black, now virtually bare and warped, hung by a single pin from its post. It creaked loudly as Cat lifted it up and pushed it open. She stepped gingerly onto the concrete path that peeked out through a layer of moss and damp leaves. Alex ignored the slip hazard and marched to the front door, which he assaulted with three hard bangs of his fist. He never did have much finesse, and the little he'd possessed had been worn down over the years, eroded by the grittiness of the job.

After a short wait, the door trembled slightly and then started to shake in its frame. Suddenly it flew open to reveal a thin, spindly woman who looked worn out from her efforts.

'Bloody door. Never does open properly once it gets a bit damp. I keep telling them I need a new one.'

She was tiny, all skin and bone, with an untidy cloud of grey hair that surrounded her deeply lined, sallow-skinned face. She pulled a blue knitted cardigan tightly around her chest and focused her gaze on her two visitors. Cat was transfixed with this bird-like woman, who twitched and fidgeted, pulling at a loose thread that hung from what looked like a cigarette hole in her cardigan. The woman looked down, following Cat's gaze, before looking back up at her with a challenging stare.

'Mrs Pat Joseph?' Alex asked.

The woman looked at him sharply. 'Who are you?'

'We're police officers, Mrs Joseph. You called to report your daughter missing earlier today.'

She eyed them suspiciously.

'I told them on the phone everything I know. Besides, I said it didn't matter. She'll come home when she's good and ready.'

'I'm sure you're right but we have to be thorough and there were just a couple of things we weren't quite clear about. We'd like to come in and talk to you.'

Mrs Joseph turned on her heel and retreated into the house.

'You can't stay long. I need to get to the shops.'

They followed her into the small front room. Cat's eyes took a moment to adjust to the gloom, daylight having been reduced to a grim half-light by the dirt on the windows and the nicotine-stained net curtains. Shadows grew into shapes as her eyes adapted and she was astonished to see how much had been crammed into the tiny space, including two sagging high-backed armchairs and a threadbare three-seater. Without offering either of them a seat, the woman made straight for an armchair. It was positioned within arm's reach of an old boxy television set and as soon as the weight was lifted from her legs, her attention drifted onto the daytime soap that filled the screen.

Alex brought the conversation back to the purpose of their visit.

'Mrs Joseph, could we just go over a few of the facts you gave to the officer on the phone earlier today?'

'Go on then,' she said, amicably enough.

Cat was beginning to think that this strange old bird wasn't entirely all there. She waited for Alex to begin, but to her surprise he gestured for her to start the questioning. After a moment's stalling, she stammered out a hastily concocted introduction before outlining the reason for their visit.

'You said your daughter, Mary, went to stay with a friend on Saturday.' Cat paused to look at her notes. 'And you have had no contact with her since.'

'That's right.'

'And she's not at her friends now?'

'No.'

'When did she leave?'

'She didn't.'

Cat was confused for a moment until she thought it through. 'So she never actually got to her friend's. Is that right?'

'No. At least that's what she said.'

'Who said?'

'Stacey.'

'Stacey is the friend that she was supposed to stay with?'

'Yes. I just told you that.'

Cat took out her notepad and jotted the name down.

'Sorry, Mrs Joseph, I was a little confused there. So, Mary was supposed to be staying with her friend Stacey but you have since spoken to Stacey, who told you she didn't turn up.'

But she didn't get a response. Cat realised that the TV was winning the battle as she saw the woman's eyes flickering about as she tried to focus on the screen. Cat repeated the question, drawing the distracted woman's attention back to her.

'Yes, that's right. I told all this to the woman on the phone like she told me to.'

'Like who told you?'

'Stacey. She told me to call you lot. Said she saw something on the news and gave me the number to call to find out where Mary was. But when I called, they didn't know where she was. I'll tell her what for when I see her though. She normally does the shopping on a Thursday. I'm going to have to go myself now.'

Cat looked at the face of the woman that sat in front of her, so heavy with wrinkles it looked as though she had deflated with age.

'Mrs Joseph, how old is Mary?'

'Fifteen. No, sixteen. It was her birthday a few weeks ago. Not that she looks it. They don't these days, do they, with all that make-up? Old before their time, I reckon. When I was her age things were different. There was none of this cavorting around...' her words slowly dropped away and she let her gaze fall to the floor, before looking back at Cat with her brow furrowed and her lips pinched. 'I was nearly thirty when I fell with Mary. Ten years... ten years we were together. And then the bastard upped and left me for some tart as soon as she was born.'

Bitterness peppered every word. But her indignation fell on deaf ears, as Cat was still reeling from the realisation that this worn-looking woman had yet to reach fifty.

'How do Stacey and Mary know each other?' Alex asked.

'They were at school together. Mary left last term.'

'And what does she do now?'

'Stacey?'

'No, Mary. What does Mary do now she's left school?'

Pat Joseph coughed; a phlegm-ridden explosion that ricocheted through her chest. Cat looked down at the ashtray on the floor by the woman's chair, half full of the butts of slim hand-rolled cigarettes. She couldn't help but screw her nose up.

'Does she work or go to college?' Alex asked.

The cough became a laugh and a trace of amusement crossed the heavily lined face.

'She does a few nights at the club for a bit of extra cash. Not that I get to see much of it; a bit of housekeeping now and then.'

'Weren't you worried when she didn't come home at the end of the weekend?'

'Not really.' She shrugged. 'She's a popular girl. I'm sure she's got lots of friends.'

'Can you give us the names of any friends?' Alex asked.

'She talked about a lot of people. I'm not very good with names. I told you about Stacey.'

'What about a boyfriend?' Cat asked.

'They don't have boyfriends these days. It's all one-night stands. Not that Mary's like that.' Her expression softened a little. 'She's a good girl really, just a bit wayward. But aren't they all?'

'Has she ever brought a boy home to meet you or talked about anyone in particular?'

'No. Don't ask me why not, it's not like I'd mind.'

Her eyes flicked back to the TV screen as the soap returned after the adverts. Once again, she appeared to forget her guests.

'Mrs Joseph, what is Stacey's last name?' Alex asked, raising his voice to be heard above a rowdy argument that had broken out on the screen.

The woman's rheumy eyes looked away from the TV. She

stared up at the ceiling, her mouth pursed in concentration.

'Gould.' A smile puckered her wizened cheeks. 'I knew I knew it.'

Cat scribbled the name down in her pad.

'I don't suppose you've got a phone number?' she said.

Pat Joseph gave her a vexed look.

'No. Anyway, I already told you, she doesn't know where Mary is.'

'What about an address? It's possible Stacey knows more than she's told you. We will need to speak to her.'

'Church Road. I don't know the number. It's the white house. Everything's white: white fence, white windows, white door. Are we nearly done yet?'

'Just one more thing. Do you have a recent photograph of Mary?'

The woman gave a heavy, impatient sigh. The request meant that she would have to leave the comfort of her seat. She crossed the tiny room and headed towards a sideboard that nestled tightly between a wall and the settee. It was crammed so full of trinkets and knick-knacks it was difficult to distinguish one item from another. Cat found herself surprisingly touched, seeing a lifetime of memories in that collection of random objects. She was aware that many people, Alex included, would have considered them little more than the worthless hoardings of cheap presents and free 'gifts' from cereal boxes. She figured the truth was probably somewhere in between.

They watched as the worn-looking woman reached for a cheaply framed photograph that had been resting on top of the unit, partially hidden behind a scratched biscuit barrel that heralded 'Greetings from Dorset'. Without saying anything she passed the picture to Cat and returned to her chair.

Cat looked down at a smiling red-haired teenager. She looked across at Alex and gave a shrug. The pretty girl in the picture was so far removed from the bloated body they had seen on the mortuary slab that, even if her face had been intact, Cat wasn't sure she could confidently identify her from the photograph.

She looked back down at the picture. It showed the teenager smiling, standing next to a scruffy-looking man.

'This guy here; is he a friend of Mary's?'

'You've got to be joking,' Mrs Joseph said. 'He's a celebrity. That's why Mary insists we have it out on show. He's the only famous person she's ever met.'

Alex walked over and took the photo from her. He scrutinised it silently.

'I thought he seemed familiar,' Cat continued. 'He was in that reality TV show that was all over the papers last summer. He won it, didn't he?'

'Mrs Joseph,' Alex interrupted. 'I'm afraid I need to ask you one more question. When you telephoned earlier, they asked whether Mary had any identifying marks. You mentioned a birthmark on her thigh. Could you describe it for me, perhaps you could point to whereabouts on Mary it is?'

There were no tears.

For a moment Mary's mother's eyes misted over, maybe as a memory of happier days crossed her mind, nudging an emotion from somewhere deep down, but then it was gone. As they announced their departure, she rose to her feet, giving Cat the impression that she was going to show them to the door. Instead, she picked up a glass tumbler from the floor next to her chair and headed toward the sideboard; she reached in and retrieved a large green bottle.

Not looking back to where her two visitors stood, she poured herself a generous measure of its contents and knocked it back in one hit. She poured herself a refill before returning to her seat, taking the glass and bottle with her.

Cat looked at Mary's glassy-eyed mother, and at the nicotine-stained walls, and the photograph with the Z-list celebrity and suddenly she felt a swell of emotion at the thought of the girl who had no hope of ever knowing anything different.

A girl whose death, it would later transpire, had a much bigger impact than her life ever had.

Four

Broadheath Comprehensive was an impressive-looking building. Georgian styled in a deep russet-red brick, it stood head and shoulders above the houses that flanked it. As with much of the area, its grandeur spoke of better, more affluent times. Sadly, the same couldn't be said of the scraped and stained interior. Battleship grey walls and windowless corridors lent a stifling and claustrophobic feel, seeming more fitting for a turn of the century asylum than an Ofsted-rated 'good' school. Even the kids' colourful artwork that adorned the walls did little to enhance the ambiance.

Not that Cat had time to ponder any of that as she and Alex followed the school secretary down corridor after corridor of the labyrinthine layout. A short and stocky woman with a thick thatch of grey hair, she had met them on their arrival and after the briefest of introductions set off at a brisk trot. Eventually she slowed as they approached the end of a corridor where a single door denied them any further passage.

The secretary turned to them.

'Please wait here.' She gave a short knock and, without waiting for a reply, entered the room beyond.

'Have you been laying a length of yarn? I think this is the equivalent of the gingerbread house,' whispered Cat. She pointed to an inscribed brass plate on the door: Miss Hand, Head Teacher. 'Which I suppose makes her the witch.'

Alex ignored her.

Cat ambled over to a row of chairs that formed a line along the corridor wall. 'These must be the naughty seats, where they send kids to get their punishment.' She eased herself into one of the chairs, her adult frame looking at odds against the seat's child-sized proportions. 'When I left Uni, I thought about becoming a teacher.'

'Really?' Alex said.

Cat was about to quiz him on why he should sound so surprised when the door swung open and the secretary called them in to meet the formidable Miss Hand.

Elizabeth Hand was younger than Cat had expected, only just forty, and strikingly attractive. Smartly dressed in a classically tailored navy suit she was the image of modern efficiency.

'Please, call me Beth,' she said, greeting them with a gentle but firm handshake. She guided them into the inner sanctum of her office and poured them tea while they settled into a couple of stylish easy chairs.

Sitting back in her seat, Beth Hand listened to the reason for their visit. She seemed genuinely saddened.

'I didn't know Mary very well,' she admitted. 'She wasn't a particularly strong student. But she wasn't a bad student.'

'What about Stacey, is she the same?' asked Alex.

'Oh no, Stacey is an excellent student. She has a real chance at getting to university. I just hope this doesn't change things for her. Teenagers can be so sensitive.'

'If only the same could be said for Mary,' Cat said.

'I didn't mean...' A tint of pink flushed across the head teacher's neck.

'I'm sure DC McKenzie didn't mean that to sound at all critical,' Alex said, giving Cat a warning look.

'No, I'm sorry, that came out quite wrong.' Cat pressed her lips together to stop any more stupidity slipping out.

'Would it be possible to speak to Stacey now?' Alex asked.

'Of course. I'll arrange for someone to go and get her. You can use this office,' Beth Hand said, having regained some of her previous composure.

Stacey was evidently where she was supposed to be, as within five minutes they heard a quiet knock at the door. An attractive girl; she had long, dark hair that caused her pale skin to look almost translucent, giving her an ethereal quality, which, in the circumstances, made her appear even more fragile.

She smiled politely at the two officers, before turning her attention to the head teacher.

'Miss Hand, Mrs Pullman said you wanted to see me.'

'Stacey, these two police officers would like to talk to you about your friend Mary Joseph.'

Stacey turned back to face them, minus the smile.

'Hi Stacey, I'm DI York and this is my colleague DC McKenzie. We just want to ask you a couple of questions about Mary. Please, sit down.' He gestured to a chair across the small coffee table.

The teenager complied, nervously.

'I'm sorry but am I supposed to know what this is about? Has something happened to Mary?'

'That's what we want to talk to you about. Mrs Joseph called us concerned about her daughter.'

'She did? Really? I didn't think she would.'

'Well she did. She called, on your advice. Can you tell us why you were worried enough to suggest it?'

'Well I wasn't really. Not worried, I mean. I was more annoyed. When I went round on Sunday it was only to have a go at her. Mary, I mean.' Stacey hunched forward in her seat. Her gaze settled somewhere around her knees. 'She's been such a...' She stalled and looked across at the two detectives. Cat could imagine her searching for a safe expletive. 'Such a pain,' Stacey continued. 'She's got a dumb job in town and just wants to hang out with her new friends. Since term started, she just keeps messing me around. I guess I'd had enough.'

'What had she done?' Cat asked.

'She was supposed to be staying over at my house. She was going to get the bus back from town when she finished at ten but she never showed. It wasn't the first time but at least before she's tried to make up for it. She normally phones the next day and apologises. Only this time she didn't. I was so angry.'

'So that's why you went round,' Cat said. 'You must have been surprised to find she hadn't been home. No wonder you suggested her mother report her missing.'

Stacey looked timidly towards the floor.

'I didn't. Not at first. It was only because I happened to see the news last night. It said that you were looking for people who may be missing. It gave me a reason to go around a second time. To be honest I thought that she'd be at home, but even when she wasn't, I never...'

Stacey looked from the head teacher to Alex and then to Cat, who could see that the young girl was begging to be reassured that everything was all alright. Cat ignored the unspoken plea and carried on with her questions.

'If it's okay I'd like to go back to Saturday night. You mentioned that Mary had a new job.'

Stacey nodded.

'In a bar in town. The Exit. It only pays peanuts but she's always raving about it... *it* and *the girls*.'

'The girls?' Cat said.

'There's a group of them that work there. They go out sometimes. I figured that's what happened on Saturday.'

'Do you know any of their names?' Cat lifted her pen and pad ready to make notes.

But her eagerness made Stacey nervous. The teenager looked down to the floor and shook her head.

'You sure you don't know any of them?' Alex asked gently, a tone which rarely got an airing.

'No. Mary's never invited me to go with them. I don't know why not. I mean I was her friend when no one else would be. It's like I don't matter anymore. She's too interested in fitting in with them. You know she didn't even used to drink before she worked there? Now if you listen to her, it's like she's some sort of party animal. It's all just an act.' She looked across at Alex and then Cat. 'Is that what this is about? Has she done something stupid?'

Perhaps there was something in their expressions. The young girl's eyes widened and she grew even paler.

She put her hands to her face, covering her mouth, and started to shake her head.

'No... It can't be...'

Despite the detective's guarded response – Mary's body had yet to be formally identified – Stacey buried her head in her hands and began to cry.

Five

The detectives soon learned Stacey's tears hadn't been in vain, when, later that day, Pat Joseph positively identified the body as that of her daughter, Mary. Prioritising the investigation into the dead teenager's movements, Alex took the decision to interview the staff at Mary's place of work himself. He and Cat agreed to meet at 7:45 p.m. outside the McDonalds on the corner of the High Street

When Cat arrived, Alex was already there. He was leaning against a lamppost with his back to her, watching a group of lads retreat down the street, feeding their faces with burgers as they jostled and joked with one another. She noticed how the light fell across him, casting long shadows across the floor that made his muscular frame look even taller and broader than it already was. She drew close. The tap of the heels of her boots on the pavement must have caught his attention and he turned. She saw him smile in the amber glow of the street lamp.

They headed to the west of the town, where the nightclubs clustered together like prostitutes on a street corner, each one gaudier than the last, hoping to lure passing revellers in with their bright lights and happy hour offers.

'It's like a scene from Las Vegas,' Cat said, barely able to believe that this was the same place that looked like a derelict dump during daylight.

Alex let out a snort. 'Are we looking at the same thing?'

Cat turned to face him, and despite the fact that reflected in Alex's eyes was a whole carnival of dancing neon images, she said nothing.

It was still early as far as the nightclubs were concerned. Most of the clubbers wouldn't make an appearance until after midnight, preferring to take advantage of the cheaper priced local bars until closing time. Bars like The Exit, where Mary had been working all summer.

Cat and Alex turned into the road that The Exit was on and stopped. A couple of scantily clad teenage girls hurried past, appearing not to feel the cold as they swaggered confidently up to the bar before being swallowed up by the darkly lit interior. Two doormen guarded the entrance.

'Here we go. Laurel and Hardy have got the measure of us already,' Alex said, commenting on the hostile looks that the two doormen were giving them.

Both men were wearing black suits, paired with a white shirt and a black slim tie, an elegant ensemble that contrasted sharply with their shaven heads. The older of the two was a big, doughy looking guy; Cat guessed that what had once been brawn had long since turned to bulk and, judging by the tightness of his jacket, it was a downward trend. The second man was at least ten years his junior. Smaller all round, he was short and wiry and reminded Cat of a prize-winning bantamweight boxer; a friend of her brother from way back.

The two doormen watched every step of their approach, saying nothing, even when they were all within a few feet of each other.

'Good evening gentlemen. DI York,' he said, showing his badge. 'And this is DC McKenzie.'

They continued to look at Alex, their flat expressions unchanging.

'We're investigating the death of a teenager who was found near here on Tuesday. We think she may have gone missing at the weekend, possibly after a night out clubbing. We've been told that she used to work the bar here.'

The younger, more muscular of the two doormen unfolded his arms.

'Somebody's dead?' he said.

'A girl called Mary Joseph.'

'Don't ring any bells,' the doorman replied. 'But that don't mean anything, some of them are only here for a couple of weeks.' And then, as an afterthought, he added, 'What did she look like?'

Cat reached into her bag and pulled out a brown reinforced envelope. She tipped it up to reveal the four by five that had sat in pride of place on Mary's mother's sideboard. She handed it over. Both doormen stared at it, saying nothing. After a short while the older one shook his head.

'No. Sorry.'

Not giving up quite as easily, his partner walked over to the entrance and held the photo under the light. Eventually he too admitted defeat.

'Is this the only photo you've got?'

'At the moment, yes. She was a red head, more ginger than auburn,' Cat said, reaching up and tucking a strand of her own copper coloured hair behind her ear. 'Fair skinned. Young, just sixteen, five foot six and slender built.'

The young doorman took one last look before passing the picture back to Cat.

'So how did it happen?'

'Jim! Leave it out.' The older man said, visibly embarrassed at his partner's candour.

'That's what we're trying to find out,' Alex said over his shoulder, as he disappeared through the double doors.

From the foyer a short flight of stairs led down.

Inside, The Exit was a dimly lit cavern of a place, with beer-soaked carpets that stuck to your shoes and hand-written signs advertising *'Happy Hour'* that filled the grubby walls. A Happy Hour that perversely ran from six till eight every evening, offering the less discerning drinkers the chance to get twice as drunk for half the price, provided they didn't mind drinking the equivalent of branded meths.

Business was still quiet. The lights were low, as was the volume of the music. It was too low though, Cat noted, and the bass drowned everything out so that the vocals came over as nothing more than an irritating buzz, making the chart hit that was playing at the time barely recognisable.

'So, Mary was scraping a living together working here,' Alex said. 'Looking on the bright side, I suppose the only way is up.'

Cat looked around. It was certainly a no-frills type of gig. The aged red plastic leatherette seating was polka-dotted with cigarette burns through which the marshmallow foam filling burst through, reminding her of the kind of toadstools in fairy tales. Alex wandered off, disappearing behind a row of pillars to the right of a small dance floor, while Cat made straight for the bar at the back of the room. There was no one waiting to be served, which was fortunate, given there was no one serving.

Alex joined her.

'Nobody home?' he asked, leaning over the bar and looking around.

'Doesn't look like it,' Cat said, though a little prematurely, as at that moment a young woman slipped through a door carrying a crate of mixers. She set them down on the floor and came over to them.

'What'll it be?' she asked with a lazy drawl.

'We're here to see the boss,' Alex replied.

Either the request was typical or the barmaid just didn't care as she simply hooked a thumb towards the wall to the left of the bar. Cat looked over and for the first time noticed a door, its colour a match with the surrounding walls, making it almost invisible from a distance. A small sign stating: '*Management – Private*' was tacked on the wall next to the door.

Ignoring the demand for privacy, Alex knocked once and entered. The lights were dimmed and music played loudly from ceiling-mounted speakers. On top of a desk of fake mahogany a computer screen glowed bright in the room's relative darkness.

Facing away from them was a high-backed leather swivel chair. Alex cleared his throat loudly and the chair swung around, bringing them face to face with a small middle-aged man, who appeared to be a dark shade of orange. Cat couldn't quite decide whether his deep ochre tan had come from a bottle or a tanning bed. What she was sure of, was that Mother Nature hadn't had a hand in it.

The little man leaned forward in his seat and scowled. 'Who the fuck are you?'

'Police.' Alex casually flipped open his badge. 'And you are?'

'Paul Dorrigan,' he said. 'This just a courtesy call?'

'Are you the owner?' Alex asked.

'Yeah I'm the owner. What gives?'

'Mary Joseph. The name sound familiar?'

Cat scrutinised the bar owner's face but saw no flicker of recognition.

'Never heard of her.'

'You're not too familiar with your staff then?'

'So she works here.' He shrugged. 'Like I know any of them.'

'You don't know the names of the people who work for you?' Cat said. She didn't believe him. It was a small place; how difficult would it be to remember the names of a handful of staff?

'I don't do front of house.'

'Mary was only sixteen. If she was serving alcohol someone must have authorised her sales,' Alex said.

'I have a manager who does all that.'

'You wouldn't have got involved, or even known about it, if one of your staff was due to have worked but didn't show?'

'Like I said, I've got a manager for that sort of thing. She does the hiring and firing and deals with all the girls. We get through a lot of them, especially in the summer. They come, work a few weeks then fuck off somewhere else. They're not exactly renowned for their commitment.'

'What about problems? Are you aware of any tensions

recently between the staff or trouble with a punter or a jealous boyfriend?' Cat asked.

'Look, I just told you, I don't deal with the staff and I don't know this Mary whatsername. Any of them that work behind the bar will know more than me. Like I said–'

'What's the manager's name?' Alex asked, cutting him off.

'Charlie Winters.'

'Is she working tonight?'

'Supposed to be. I haven't seen her yet but she should be here by now.'

'We'll want to talk to her,' Alex said.

'Be my guest. One of the girls at the bar will point her out for you.' Dorrigan leaned back in his chair. 'What's she done then? Must be something serious to get you lot off your backsides.'

'Mary was found murdered. Not far from here in fact,' Cat said, trying hard to disguise her distaste for the man.

Dorrigan's eyes shot wide but the traces of a smile curled at the edges of his thin lips.

'No shit!'

'We'll need you to account for your whereabouts Saturday night through to Sunday,' Alex said, causing the bald-headed man to turn a darker shade of ochre.

'Hey, you can't seriously suspect me?'

'Purely routine.' Alex stared at him, devoid of emotion.

'Where was I? Christ, let me think.' Dorrigan drew a deep breath and exhaled.

He closed his eyes for a moment, before sitting upright and saying with some confidence, 'I closed up here and drove straight to Sheffield. I was there all of Sunday. I came back after lunch on Monday.'

'Can anyone corroborate your story?' Alex asked.

'You're shitting me?'

Alex simply waited, letting the intensity of his expression answer for him.

'Oh man, I can't believe you're serious.' Dorrigan sighed. 'One of the blokes on the door was with me when I locked up. It was the middle of the night by the time I got to my parents' place in Sheffield but I know they heard me arrive. You can call them.' He scribbled a number on the reverse of an advertising flyer.

Alex took it from him.

'We will.' He felt about in his breast pocket and pulled out a tatty business card. 'If you think of anything...'

'Yeah, yeah,' Dorrigan said as he dropped the dog-eared piece of card straight into an open drawer.

'What an arsehole!' Cat said as soon as they left the office, closing the door behind them.

'What?' Alex said, raising his voice to be heard above the loud music.

'Forget it,' she mouthed, realising the futility of a conversation so close to the dance-floor.

It was as though the place had woken up while they'd been in with Dorrigan. The lights were even lower, in contrast to the music, which had been ratcheted up to such a level that Cat could feel the thud of the bass reverberate through the floor and into her spine.

Alex gestured toward the bar and started to walk.

Despite the increased number of punters there was still only one girl serving, albeit a different one from before. Alex beckoned to the barmaid, who looked about the same age as Mary. She wore a lot of make-up and her figure-hugging clothes gave the appearance of someone much older, but she hadn't quite managed to shed the tell-tale signs of her youth. Up close Cat could see the spots the concealer had failed to cover. Not that it mattered. Her piercing blue eyes, baby-fine blonde hair and petite frame gave her a wide-eyed sort of innocence that more than made up for such minor imperfections.

Alex ordered a sparkling water for Cat and a pint of lager for himself.

The barmaid placed their drinks down.

'Nine-fifty, please.'

It was probably a good thing that Cat hadn't got as far as taking a drink. She would have choked at the extortionate price.

Alex handed over fifteen quid.

'Have one yourself.'

The barmaid gave him a thin smile to acknowledge the tip before dropping the change into a pint glass at the back of the bar.

'Expenses,' he said to Cat in response to her horrified expression.

'Well, if you were hoping to buy her attention it didn't work,' Cat said, as the girl walked away to serve another couple.

'It will. As soon as she's free I'll call her over.'

He picked up his pint and turned to stand with his back resting against the bar. The current track was something of a crowd pleaser and the dance floor was busy. Cat noticed him watching a couple of teenage girls nearby. Dressed in short skirts and skimpy tops, their gyrations drew attention to their slender legs and ample cleavages.

'This place doesn't seem that bad,' he shouted over his shoulder to her.

She rolled her eyes and turned back to watch the barmaid, busy serving at the far end of the bar. She waited until the teenager had taken the money and watched as she approached the tip jar, this time dropping in a crisp ten-pound note.

'Excuse me,' Cat called.

The barmaid smiled and walked over.

'I'd like to talk to you about Mary Joseph,' Cat said, just as Alex turned around.

The girl's piercing blue eyes shot wide.

'You're the police.' It was a statement not a question. 'I can't help you. I don't know anything.' She suddenly looked young and vulnerable.

'But you do know that Mary is dead?' Cat said.

'I've got people to serve.' The barmaid took off like a startled deer in the direction of a couple of lads who were approaching.

'They can wait,' Alex called out.

The barmaid stopped. Cat noticed her take a deep breath before covering the short distance back.

'Jim on the front door told me about Mary when you were talking with Mr Dorrigan.' She looked genuinely shaken. 'When did it happen? I mean... how?'

Cat was straining to hear what she was saying over the thumping backdrop of music.

'What's your name?' Cat asked.

'Emma.'

'Okay Emma, is there somewhere where we can talk?'

'I can't leave the bar.'

'There must be someone who could take over for a little while, a manager maybe?'

Emma cast a look over her shoulder to a closed door. Wearing a worried look she lifted up a hinged section of the bar.

'This way.'

She motioned to them to wait before disappearing into what Cat took to be the store room. Moments later she returned with an older woman who regarded them suspiciously while Emma ushered them through into a short corridor and out of the building. They exited by the back door into a storage area. Stacks of beer barrels and crates of empty bottles littered the small space.

'Were you and Mary friends?' Cat asked as soon as they were outside.

'Not really. I only knew her from here, and I've only been here since the start of the summer holidays.'

'But you got on with her okay?'

'Yes, sure, everyone did. She was really nice and you could have a laugh with her.'

'We've been told that sometimes a group of girls from here

used to go clubbing together. Did you ever go?'

'Sometimes.'

'With Mary?'

'Sometimes.'

Emma started to chew at a nail.

'How old are you, Emma?'

The barmaid stuck out her chin like a defiant child. 'Eighteen.'

'Mary was only sixteen, did you know that?' Cat asked.

'Course. That was why she wasn't allowed to serve behind the bar. She used to just clear tables and collect glasses.'

'Yet she went clubbing?'

Emma shrugged.

'When did you last see her?'

'Saturday night. We were both working.'

'Was this one of those times when you both went out afterwards?'

Emma shot a look behind her. She turned back and gave a nervous nod.

'But I don't remember anything. I wasn't very well.'

'Let's start with where you went,' Alex said.

'We went to Déjà vu but I went home early. I don't know how long the others stayed.'

Emma kept looking over to the door. On reflex Cat followed her gaze and was surprised to see the older woman from the bar there, watching. Tall and hard-faced, she was all tattoos and piercings.

'Emma, the bar's stacking up. How long are you going to be?' she asked, while holding Cat's stare.

'We'll be as quick as we can be,' Cat replied.

'And then we'll want a word with you,' Alex said.

After a short stand-off the woman spun around and disappeared into the unlit doorway.

'Was that your manager?' Cat asked.

Emma glanced back at the door. 'Yes. That's Charlie.'

'Did she go out with you on Saturday?'

An anxious look crossed the young barmaid's face.

'I don't really... I don't want her to think that I...'

'That's okay, we can ask her ourselves,' Alex said gently. 'Did anyone else go to the club with you?'

'No,' Emma said without any hesitation.

'Now I know you don't remember much but think back carefully. Did you see Mary talking to anyone? Anyone at all? Even if she just said hi to someone she knew, it would be helpful for us to know.'

'Honestly, I don't remember.' Emma sounded miserable now. 'We had some Sambuca shots before we left here. I don't normally drink. I was sick almost as soon as we got to the club. I left as soon as I could. I saw Charlie on my way out and told her that I was going. I don't remember seeing Mary.'

'Is it possible she may have already left?'

'I suppose so. I just assumed she was still there, but... I don't know, she could have done. Look, it wasn't my fault, I wasn't very well. I'd help if I could but...' She dashed away a tear from the side of her nose.

Cat looked at Alex but he just shook his head. Frustrated, she reached into her handbag and pulled out a small notepad and scribbled their contact details onto a page. She tore it out and handed it to Emma.

'If you think of anything, no matter how stupid or trivial, even if you're not sure please give me or DI York a call. I've put down both of our numbers.'

Emma sniffed and took the sheet, thrusting it in to the back pocket of her jeans. She gave them both a pitiful look and without another word she walked back inside, letting the door bang closed behind her.

Six

'If Dorrigan thinks that I buy that bullshit...' Alex said, loud enough for Cat to hear.

They were walking through the crowded bar, having just learned that Charlie had left mid-shift.

'You think her mother hasn't been taken ill?' Cat asked. Alex didn't even bother to turn around. She trotted to catch up with him. 'If you think it's not true then why don't we go and talk to her? We've got her address. We could go around there now and –'

'She's not that stupid. She'll have gone somewhere else. We'll go in the morning.'

'So what now?' Cat asked.

'We go home and start again tomorrow.'

'But I don't want to give up yet. There must be something we can do,' Cat said as they walked out into the fresh night air. 'Why don't we go to that club, where Mary went on Saturday, Déjà vu? Maybe someone saw something? It's got to be better than doing nothing, hasn't it?'

Maybe it was the hopeful tilt to her voice, or perhaps Alex was also feeling the need to do something; either way he looked at her and a smile sneaked out.

'Come on then, Polyanna. Let's go and see if we can salvage something from tonight.'

Three hours later, at nearly one in the morning, they were standing opposite the doorway of Déjà vu nursing polystyrene cups of coffee bought from the burger van that had already set up, ready to feed the junk-food cravings of the post-clubbing crowds. The steam rose thickly from the cups, clearly visible in the cloud-free night. Cat looked up, drawn by the thump of hard-core dance music that disturbed the quiet, escaping through the club's open doors. A group of youths staggered out.

'This is depressing,' she said. 'We must have spoken to a couple of hundred people and still nothing to show for it.'

Alex blew onto his coffee.

'I hadn't expected much but nothing?' she went on.

'That's good old-fashioned legwork for you,' Alex replied, stamping his feet on the ground. 'Anyway, it wasn't that bad. I thought I got a few flickers of recognition from the photo.'

'We haven't learnt anything new though have we?'

'No. But then I didn't expect to,' Alex said, as he looked at her, hugging her coffee cup in both hands. 'Come on, drink up. Time to call it a day.'

The following morning the sun seemed to have taken leave, allowing an opportunistic autumn to descend early on the South East of England. The sky had been grey and overcast since dawn and at last the threatened downpour arrived. Cat wiped the window clean of condensation and looked out through the rain at the people exiting their houses. Some, the more cautious souls, stuck their umbrellas up before they'd even left the house, others made a break from their front doors, running to their cars, hoping to escape unscathed. Yet, in every case, the rain won out and they all ended up wet and bedraggled, brushing the excess water from their clothes.

'Ready?' Alex asked.

Cat nodded. She zipped her jacket up and transferred her attention to the house opposite.

Although not geographically close to where Mary had lived, they were in another run-down street in a downtrodden district, only this time north of their patch. Charlie opened the door, looking a bit shabby herself. It took her a moment to recognise them. She tried to push the door closed but she wasn't nearly fast enough and before she could get her weight behind it Alex was already in the hallway, steamrollering her through to the tiny living room. Cat followed.

Just then a loud bang rang out through the house.

'The back door!' Cat said, rushing down the corridor.

By the time she entered the lounge Alex was standing, arms crossed, scowling at Charlie who was sitting on a sagging settee that looked as though it might have been salvaged from a skip at least a decade ago.

'A mate you say?' he said, before looking over at Cat, who was hovering in the door.

She shook her head. Alex turned back to Charlie.

'Then why'd they run?'

Charlie shrugged.

'Probably had to be somewhere in a hurry.'

'And this mate's name?' Alex asked.

Another shrug.

'Not sure they'd want me telling you.'

Alex leaned over and picked up a packet of paracetamol from the coffee table.

'Out drowning your sorrows last night, were you?'

Charlie curled her lip into a sneer.

'Your mum, on her deathbed. At least that's what we were told.'

'Yeah, well, she weren't as bad as they said.'

'So you thought you'd make the most of it and hit the clubs? Who did you go with, now that Mary isn't around?'

Charlie planted her hands either side of her on the settee and for a second it looked as though they might be in for a stand-up row, but she simply leaned forward to glower at Alex.

'How dare you accuse me like that! What right have you got to muscle your way in here anyway?'

'We can always continue this conversation down the nick if

41

you'd prefer?' Alex said without emotion.

Cat knew that Charlie's disappearing act the night before had irritated him, and although she thought the woman probably deserved a bit of a rough time, she didn't want to make their visit a bigger drama than it needed to be, so before she'd had time to consider keeping quiet for fear of saying something wrong, she'd already opened her mouth.

'Charlie, nobody's accusing you of anything and I'm sure we'd all prefer it if we can get some answers without any fuss. We just want to know what happened the night Mary went missing. The sooner you give us what we want, the sooner we leave and you can get back to bed.'

Cat looked across at Alex to see if he was annoyed with her for butting in but his stony features gave nothing away.

Charlie leaned her head against the back of the settee and closed her eyes.

'I don't know anything about Mary, about the night she died, or who did it.' She opened her eyes a fraction and looked over at Cat. 'Sorry.'

She didn't sound sorry.

'Now we know that's not true,' Cat said firmly. 'We know that you and Mary went to 'Déjà vu on Saturday night. How about starting with that?'

'Who told you that?'

Cat looked quickly at Alex who was showing no signs of saying anything anytime soon.

'It doesn't matter how we know,' she said. 'Let's get back to what happened that night.'

'I don't know anything, so end of.'

'Look, the more you act like this, the more it looks like you're hiding something.'

'You're just trying to catch me out. I know about your dirty tricks. I've got friends that have been framed by you lot. You have to get in your quota of arrests but you're not stitching me up.'

'Oh, for God's sake, just listen to yourself,' Cat snapped. 'We just want to find out what Mary was doing in the hours before she was killed. Unless you've got something to do with her death then you've got nothing to lose by talking to us. So let's start again. We know that you, Mary and Emma went out after you'd finished up on Saturday night–'

'Emma! I should've known she couldn't keep her trap shut. Well, she'll wish she never–'

'Ms Winter! Just answer the question before my colleague loses her patience and I get to haul your backside out of here and finish this conversation off at the station,' Alex said, with an air of someone who would enjoy manhandling her out into the street.

Cat took the cue.

'Too late. I'm already sick of waiting. Get your coat.'

Charlie buried her pale face in her hands. Her lank black-dyed hair – her roots badly in need of a touch up – hung limply.

'Hangover making itself felt?' Alex said.

Charlie shot him a venomous look.

Cat gave an exasperated sigh.

'Look, there's no need for any of this. Just talk to us and we'll get out of your way.'

For a moment Charlie sat motionless, looking at Alex through narrowed eyes – stalemate – but then she turned to Cat. 'What do you want to know?'

'Just talk us through what happened on Saturday.'

'Nothing happened. It was no different to any other night out.'

'Did you go out with Mary and Emma often?'

'Not really. They're not my cup of tea. They kind of just tagged along.'

'How many times?'

'I don't know, three or four.'

'Saturday then...'

43

'Like I said, it was nothing special. I was hardly with them. Emma was drunk before we even got there. We hadn't been in the club five minutes before she said she felt sick and went running into the bogs.'

'And Mary?'

'She hung around for a while, but then... I don't know. I can't remember.'

'Try harder,' Alex said.

'I'm telling you all I know, so don't talk to me like that. If I don't remember, I don't remember. You threatening me ain't going to change that.'

'So tell us what you do remember,' Cat said gently.

Charlie took a deep breath in and released it slowly, blowing it out through puffed-up cheeks. She shifted her gaze and stared at nothing in particular, giving the appearance of someone deep in thought. After a short while she began to talk.

'Soon after we got there I bumped into some friends I hadn't seen in ages. We just hung around by the bar, drinking and catching up, you know. Like I said, Emma was off being ill. Mary was hanging around nearby. I don't remember seeing her but she usually just blended into the background.'

'What about when Emma decided to leave? Did anyone wait with her for a taxi?' Cat asked.

'No. She was alright really. She looked a bit rough but who doesn't after spending half an hour with their head down the pan?' Charlie gave what must have been a rare smile.

'Where was Mary at this point?'

'I don't know. Emma came over and said she was off. I was with a guy who... well, it doesn't matter, it's just that I wasn't really paying much attention to anyone else. I can't remember whether Mary was there or not.'

Cat looked at the other woman coldly.

'Guilty conscious nagging you there?'

'Well I ain't no fucking nursemaid,' Charlie said. 'I was there to have a good time, not to babysit a couple of teenagers who were still wet behind the ears. I told them, if they wanted to hang around they could. I wasn't going to stop them. But if they got a better offer... well, they could do whatever they wanted, with whoever they wanted.'

There was something about the way that Charlie's tone changed, how she'd slowed down. Cat immediately seized upon it.

'You've remembered something. What is it?'

'I'm not sure. I think I do remember seeing Mary with some bloke. I dunno though, like I said I was with this good-looking guy.' She looked down to the floor, this time seeming embarrassed by her selfish confession.

'Did you recognise him?' Cat asked.

'Never seen him before.'

'Well what did he look like?' Cat tried to keep her excitement from reaching her voice.

'He was older than Mary, maybe in his thirties. He had dark hair, a bit dark skinned, you know, Italian or Greek or something like that.'

Cat took out her notepad and began to scribble furiously.

'Tall? Short? Fat? Thin?'

'Tall and thin. Oh, and he had an earring... no, two earrings.'

'You're going to have to come down to the station. We need a statement and a full description of this bloke,' Alex said.

'You're joking. I just told you everything I know.'

'I'm serious. Grab your shoes and coat.'

'Why can't I do it here?'

'We'll need you to work with a police artist.'

'I don't believe it! Are you sure there's nothing else I can help you with?' Charlie said in a tone that made the sweetness of her words turn to saccharine.

Alex said nothing.

Charlie raised herself from the stained and sagging sofa and walked lethargically to the door. Footsteps thumping heavily up the stairs were followed by the sound of a door being slammed, which sent sound waves reverberating through the ceiling.

'Ooh that's got to hurt,' Cat said.

Alex smiled.

'You're getting the hang of this interviewing lark,' he said as they waited. 'I liked the guilty conscience touch.'

'I don't know. I got the feeling that she wasn't being entirely honest.'

'Why's that?'

'Well, you know how with NLP they say that if your eyes look up to the right then–'

'NLP?'

'Neuro Linguistic Programming. You must have had some training. It's covered on the basic interrogation skills course. I found it really–'

Alex turned and looked her in the eye.

'I can't believe you go for all that bollocks. You should have left the lecture theatre behind when you decided to trade your flippers for a pair of steel toe-capped boots. What they forget to tell you on all these fancy pants courses is what really matters. This job is all about dealing with people and the only rule to remember is that where people are concerned, there are no rules.'

'You should tell that to the US Secret Service then; they've been using NLP for years,' Cat said. 'And getting it right,' she added, turning to look out of the window, not wanting to catch his eye a second time.

Seven

The weekend couldn't come soon enough. Cat had been thrilled when Alex asked her to cover the nightclubs with him, particularly as it had been her idea, and the overtime was always welcome, but a week of late nights took its toll. She had set her alarm to go off an hour later than usual and Saturday morning saw her wake feeling uncommonly refreshed.

She walked through the silent house, revelling in the quiet. No radio blaring in the background, no TV on in every room, because this weekend she was home alone. Mike was away playing golf with his mates. As she padded into the kitchen and flipped the switch on the kettle it occurred to her that most women would probably have been disappointed if their long-term boyfriend was away for yet another weekend.

She carried the breakfast tray into the living room, the smell of freshly brewed Colombian coffee percolating through the house. With her short cotton dressing gown pulled tightly around her she settled comfortably on the large leather settee and reached for the thick buttered toast. She chewed slowly. A clickety-clack of nails on wood caused her to smile and she took another bite of toast before tearing off a piece of the crust. She threw it towards the floor. The sixty-pound British bulldog's jaws snapped around it before even the smallest smear of butter could mar the polished wooden floor. Sensing the possibility of more to come, Harvey cocked his head in her direction, long laces of slobber dangling from his concertinaed muzzle.

'Oh here, you great lump.' Cat threw down half of a thick slice. 'Make the most of it. Tomorrow you're on a diet.'

She picked up a second slice of toast for herself and reached for the latest edition of the local newspaper, delivered the day before. She laid it open next to her. Her expression hardened. Mary's murder had made front page news. A photograph of the dead teenager and a sketch of the mystery older man accompanied a plea for anyone with information to contact the police. She flicked to page five, where the story continued with an account of the girl's short life and an interview with Mrs Joseph on the loss of her only daughter; by some miracle, the author had actually managed to inject some emotion into the piece. It was almost a tear-jerker.

'You're joking!' Cat threw her toast back down onto the plate, picked the paper up and reread the piece.

Mary's mother had obviously been told too much because now the whole world knew how Mary had been killed, potentially prejudicing the investigation.

Harvey looked up and whined, hinting at the toast that was growing cold. Cat gave him a look of exasperation but her appetite had abandoned her and after one more bite she let the remainder drop into the dog's slavering mouth.

She carried the tray back to the kitchen and set it down. She poured herself a coffee and leaned against the work surface, staring at the bare walls. The builders had been in for months, knocking the relatively small kitchen and separate dining room into a bright and spacious open-plan area fitted out with state-of-the-art appliances. All it needed now was a lick of paint but it had been easier to find excuses rather than time to complete the job. Sick of the bare plaster walls and dirty floorboards, Cat knew exactly how she was going to fill her weekend.

Dressed in old jeans and a faded t-shirt, she put on her favourite Foo Fighters' CD and cranked up the volume. She worked relentlessly through the day and by the time she was finished it was dark and she was hungry. She looked at the time and let out a groan: seven-thirty. She was supposed to have gone shopping and the local store closed at seven. Village life was great, until times like this, when she longed for a nearby twenty-four-hour supermarket. After a quick scan of the kitchen cupboards and fridge-freezer, the best she could muster was a small side-salad conjured up from a sorry-looking selection of soft and shrivelled salad vegetables and a ham and pineapple pizza – Mike's choice not hers. It had been a long time since she'd eaten meat and she had no intention of starting now.

She picked at the pizza surface, pulling off the small pink squares of ham and dropping them into Harvey's bowl. With the unwanted ingredient disposed of, she took her cobbled-together dinner into the living room and ate it, picking up the slices while skimming through the newspaper that she had earlier discarded. Grease marks began to bloom on the pages, while ink from the print left grey stains on her fingers. She wiped her hands with a sheet of kitchen towel, threw the paper back onto the magazine rack and reached for the TV remote. She smiled to herself: channel-hopping freedom, another benefit of having the house all to herself.

The next morning Cat woke to darkness. There was no fanfare from the blackbirds that tolerated her overgrown garden and no background hum of traffic from the nearby main road. Annoyed to have stirred so early but confident that she would soon drift back into a deep slumber, she patiently waited for sleep to return her to her dreams. But it wasn't to be. As she tossed and turned in her bed, so did the questions in her head. Half an hour later and still awake, she lay there with her thoughts running so fast they repeatedly thwarted any attempt she made to still her racing mind. No sooner had she driven out her musings on the murder than questions about Mike and their future together nagged away at her. His absences were becoming longer and more frequent and, although always one to enjoy his independence, now golf trips and stag weekends all seemed to merge into one.

But it was increasingly difficult to ignore the fact she almost preferred it when he was away. Eventually, with tiredness winning over, she began to doze and had almost slipped back into the silky black darkness of sleep when the radio alarm clock whirred into action. Gradually the newsreader crept into her semi-consciousness, snippets of the broadcast intermittently intruding into her dreams. She sat up, straining to hear what was being talked about. It was just inane chat about some celebrity's appeal to the world's paparazzi to stop hounding his unassuming girlfriend.

Then it hit her.

She leapt out of bed, nearly tripping over the dog in her eagerness to get down the stairs. She made straight for the living room and grabbed the paper she'd casually thrown down the previous night. With mounting excitement, she hurried to the hallway and picked up her phone. Alex's voicemail message played clearly into her ear and quickly her elated mood deflated. She left a message and, with nothing else to do, got ready for another day armed with a tin of paint and a brush.

Which was how she happened to be half way up a ladder when the doorbell rang.

'Alex!' she said, paintbrush still in hand.

'I got your message.'

'I didn't expect you to come over. A phone call would have done.'

'I was in the area. So, what've you got?' He stepped into the hall and began wiping his feet on the mat.

'Come through. Ignore the mess. I'm just in the middle of decorating.'

She ushered him into the kitchen and clicked the CD player off, silencing the Kings of Leon with a push of a button. She put the brush down on the upturned paint tin lid.

'I hope it's not a wasted trip. I feel a bit stupid calling you now. It was only an idea.'

'I'm here now. What is it?'

'Well, I'd been thinking about Mary's murder and this morning, lying in bed, I was listening to the radio and... Tell you what, wait here a sec, it's easier if I just show you.'

She slipped through the door into the hallway, returning a minute later. She handed Alex the copy of the Messenger.

'This is what I'm talking about.'

She pointed to a piece on the page that she'd circled in black marker pen and waited, watching his face intently.

'What is this?' he asked, staring at the picture.

It was a grainy copy of a photo of a group of teenagers, looking like they were trying too hard to give the impression of being the life and soul of the party.

'The paper has this regular feature. Every week they publish a photo of someone or a group of friends taken in a nightclub over the weekend. Anyone that's in the photograph gets free entry into the club the following week if they show the picture at the door.'

Alex looked just as confused.

'Notice the name of the club?' Cat said.

'It's the same one that Mary was last seen in.'

'Correct.'

'Is it always the same club?'

'From what I can tell,' she said. 'I had a look at a few back copies of the paper – I've been using them as dust sheets – and it was the same club in all of the ones I checked.'

Alex looked again at the photograph.

'I thought it's likely that more photos get taken than are printed,' Cat said. 'I know it's a long shot but maybe the photographer's got copies of photos taken the night that Mary was killed?' She looked hopefully at Alex. 'What do you think?'

He broke into a wide smile.

'It's bloody genius, that's what I think.'

Cat beamed back at him.

He reached into his inside pocket for his mobile.

'I know one of the journalists at the paper. I'll give her a ring. See if she can get hold of the photographer's details for me.'

Cat busied herself opening a new tin of paint as Alex made the call. He closed his phone and returned it to his pocket.

'Janey's going to see what she can do.'

'Well, that was easy.'

Just the name, Janey, conjured up an image in Cat's head of someone young and go-getting and keen to help.

'Even if she does produce the goods, that'll just be the start of it. If – and it's a bloody big if – if the previous weeks' photos have been kept they'll all need to be gone through. And Mary might not feature in any of them. I expect it'll be a bit of a slog.'

'But that's what the job is all about isn't it? Good old-fashioned legwork. At least, that's what you keep telling me.'

Alex gave her a quizzical look but his expression quickly softened.

'You've changed it around,' he said, looking around at the newly opened up area.

'Yeah, I always thought it was a bit dark and pokey before. It's so much brighter now.'

Standing in the half-decorated room, surrounded by paint pots, brushes and a rather old and unstable looking step-ladder, he gazed around at the walls which were striped with a single coat of paint. He looked back at Cat. Her auburn hair was loosely gathered up into a top-knot, although some had slipped out from the grips and now framed her paint-speckled face. Conscious of his attention she brushed a section of hair from her eyes, trying to tame it by tucking it behind an ear.

'So this is what you get up to in your spare time?'

He stooped to pick up a roller, the paint on which had already begun to dry.

'Hardly. I've just had enough of the bare plaster.'

Alex placed the roller back onto the paint tray.

'Are you doing this on your own?'

'Mike's away for the weekend.'

'Another stag weekend?'

'No, he's playing golf in Birmingham.'

'I take it he didn't much like the idea of you working late on Friday night then?'

Cat shot him a warning look.

'You thought you'd do something constructive,' he added, backtracking.

'Something like that.'

Alex once again surveyed the room.

'Very contemporary. I like it. Especially this striped, sort of patchy effect.'

'Ha-bloody-ha,' she said. 'It's still got another coat to go.'

Alex gave her a grin and picked the roller up again.

'Do you want a hand? I haven't got to be anywhere for a few hours. I could at least finish that wall for you.'

Cat looked at him for a sign that he was joking again. Suddenly the task no longer seemed the chore that it had been. She came within a hair's breadth of taking him up on his offer until her sense of propriety brought her back down to earth.

'No, I couldn't possibly ask. It's the weekend. You must have better things to do. And besides, I really don't mind painting and I've got the rest of the day to do it. Thanks though.'

Alex carefully placed the roller back, picked up the newspaper and followed Cat to the front door.

'You know where I am if you change your mind.'

She opened the door and stepped back to let him pass.

'Thanks, but I'll be fine. Enjoy the rest of your weekend, I'll see you tomorrow.'

Alex turned his head.

'I thought you were off until Wednesday.'

'I swapped, remember? I didn't want to miss anything.'

'Tomorrow then.'

He raised a hand in a brief goodbye as he started down the path. Half way to the pavement he stopped and turned back. 'You did good,' he said, saluting her with the folded newspaper.

Cat found it hard to concentrate on the decorating after Alex's visit. Her thoughts repeatedly strayed, wondering how he was getting on. At four o'clock she finally gave up. By six-thirty she'd managed to get to the shops before they'd closed, was freshly showered and looking forward to another night chilling in front of the TV. She was standing in front of the restocked fridge freezer, contemplating what to have for dinner when the doorbell rang. Cat frowned. For a split second she wondered whether it was Mike. He could have lost his key – again – but it was far too early.

She pulled the door open.

'Alex! Twice in one day. You'll have the neighbours talking,' she joked, causing him to look around uncomfortably. 'I was only kidding. Come in.'

Alex followed her into the house and through to the kitchen.

'Can I get you a drink?'

Bereft of make-up, dressed in a loose shirt and bleached jeans, she looked much younger than her twenty-eight years.

'Actually, that's what I came to ask you. Well, a drink and some food,' he said. 'I got a result from the photos. I thought it was only fair that you're the first to see them.'

Her eyes widened. 'Seriously? So soon. What have you found? Show me.'

Alex laughed.

'Well I'm glad I came around. I was going to leave it until tomorrow but then I remembered you were here on your own so I thought we could go out and grab a bite to eat and talk shop. I mean if you're okay with that. Mike's not back already is he?'

'No. He's not due back until late tonight. I'll leave him a note. He'll probably grab a curry with his mates on the way home anyway. I certainly wasn't expecting him back in time to eat. Give me two seconds,' she said before rushing out of the room.

By the time she returned with her coat and bag, the dog was writhing around on the floor, his legs in the air as Alex tickled his tummy.

'I can't believe he's grown into such a lump. I remember when Pete first got Harvey. He was so small,' Alex said.

'When was that though? It must have been at least six years ago?'

'A lifetime ago, eh?' he said, smiling up at her.

'Tell me about it.'

Cat couldn't believe just how her life had changed in such a short period of time since her brother's death. Sometimes it seemed just like yesterday, but it wasn't, it was almost five years ago; long enough for her to learn how to push the painful memories into the deep recesses of her mind.

She crossed to the door.

'Come on. I'm starving.'

Mickey's Bar was a spit and sawdust sort of place that did great pub grub. If you liked burger and chips, lasagne and chips, steak and kidney pie and chips, in fact anything with chips, then Mickey's was the place to go. Plus, it was close to the station, had a pool table, a quiz machine and plenty of seating. Manna from heaven for an off-duty copper after a day trudging around town looking for kids playing hooky or nicking shoplifters. More often than not, the one led to the other.

The bar was usually heaving, especially just after six when the shifts changed. But at seven o'clock on a Sunday night the place was comparatively quiet. Cat casually glanced around as they walked in and was relieved to see no one she knew. Alex pointed to an empty table tucked in the corner before heading to the bar. She took a seat and picked up the over-sized menu, but instead of looking at the laminated easy-to-wipe pages she found herself peering over it, watching Alex. She was still gazing in his direction when he picked up their drinks and turned to walk over to where she was sitting. Quickly she buried her head in the menu as he crossed the floor to their table, carrying a pint of bitter in one hand and a large glass of white wine in the other. He placed the drinks down and took off his overcoat, laying it over the back of a spare chair.

'Cheers! Here's to nailing the bastard.' Alex held out his pint.

'Cheers,' Cat said. 'Here's to nailing the bastard soon.'

Their glasses touched with a gentle chink.

Cat lifted her drink to her lips and sipped, savouring the cold, fresh taste as Alex took a sizeable swig of his pint.

'Must have been thirsty,' he said. 'What we need now is some food. Do you know what you want?'

'I'll have the veggie chilli but with rice instead of chips, no cheese and without the garlic bread.'

She handed the menu to Alex who put it straight down on the table in front of him. He stood up and reached into his coat pocket for his wallet.

'Aren't you going to look at it?' Cat asked.

'I don't need to. Mickey makes the best homemade cheeseburgers. Want to change your mind?'

Cat gave him a pointed look. He knew she didn't eat meat.

'I'll be right back,' he said.

Five minutes later he returned, carrying another round of drinks.

'Shit, Alex. Are you trying to get us drunk?'

'I thought I'd get some top-ups while I was there. It'll save me having to go when the food's here.'

He laid the fresh drinks down on the table.

'This looks like we're having a serious drinking session. How are you planning on getting home?'

'This is the first R and R I've had for weeks. And I can't remember the last time I managed to drag you out after work.' He looked at her for a response but she remained silent. 'So I'm going to make the most of it. We can share a cab home later. I'll get Mel to give me a lift in the morning.'

'Won't Mel be expecting you back earlier?'

'No. I called. She and the kids have already eaten. I told her I'd grab something here.'

For the first time Cat wondered what Mike would think of returning home to an empty house and a scribbled note stuck on the fridge door. It was the first time it had happened since they'd been together. Well, at least it would be a first for him. She'd come home to an empty house many a night. Suddenly a relaxing night out sounded very appealing.

'Okay, but I want to go easy on the drinks. I've still got work tomorrow morning and besides, there's the little matter of business to see to first. The photos?' she prompted.

'There wasn't just one photo of Mary, there were three.'

Cat felt her adrenalin level suddenly surge. She knew that this could be the turning point they'd been waiting for.

'Let me see,' she said, her fingers beckoning impatiently.

He reached into his coat pocket and pulled out an A5 brown envelope and passed it over. Cat immediately slipped the three photographs out of the envelope and started to study them. Seeing Mary full of life as she had once been, not as Cat had only ever known her, brought home what a tragedy it was. Although Cat had thought of her as a pretty teenager, she looked barely more than a child.

'How did you get them so quickly?' she asked.

'It was surprisingly easy. Janey spoke to one of the editorial team who contacted the guy who owns the club. It was as simple as that. He called me back within the hour. The photos that are printed in the paper are just shots from a cheap digital camera that he gives the bar staff at the start of each evening with the instruction to get as many pictures as possible of people enjoying themselves. The whole thing is designed to appeal to the club's posers, who would, as he pointed out countless times, do almost anything to get their picture in the local paper. Apparently it saves him paying for marketing material. All of the weekend's candid snaps are copied onto disc and used for promotions, adverts, the local paper's free entry competition, all that sort of stuff.'

'And these were taken by the bar staff the night Mary went missing?'

'Yes.'

'We were lucky he kept them.'

'He's got eighteen months' worth on disc. I just gave him the dates of the weekend that Mary disappeared. That narrowed it down to just over two hundred and fifty images. Although believe me, after the first fifty it's like looking at some maiden aunt's holiday snaps. But anyway, the rest is, as they say, history.'

'You should have called. I could have helped,' Cat said, still scrutinising the prints.

'You looked pretty busy to me, and I–'

'Have you noticed that the Greek guy with earrings that Charlie told us about doesn't appear in any of these photos?' she said, interrupting him mid-sentence. 'If Mary spent the evening with him surely he'd be in at least one of them, wouldn't he?'

'I did notice, yes. More importantly there were no photos of anyone fitting that description there that night.'

'Don't you think that's odd?'

'No. I expected it.'

Cat shot him a confused look.

'I don't understand.'

'What did you say when we were waiting to take Charlie in?' he asked.

She paused, the alcohol-induced haze in her brain dulling her memory.

'Oh crap. I said I thought she wasn't being entirely honest but I didn't think it was an out and out lie.'

'What am I always saying? Don't believe what anyone tells you until you've seen the proof for yourself.'

'But you believed her,' Cat challenged.

His eyebrows lifted, revealing a mischievous twinkle in his eyes.

'But you said...' Suddenly she remembered how Alex had remained silent on the subject. 'Seriously? You suspected all along that she was lying? But why would she lie?'

'Why indeed?'

Cat slipped the three photos of Mary back into their envelope.

'What do we do with these now?'

'Well, right now, nothing. But tomorrow morning you get to do some of that old-fashioned legwork.'

'Fine by me. What do you want me to do exactly?'

'You're going to show the photos to Emma, and Charlie, and Charlie's boss, whatever his name is, and old Mrs Joseph if it comes to it. In fact, you're going to show them to everyone remotely involved in the case until someone IDs the other people in these shots. I want to know who they are and what they had to do with Mary.'

'I'll get on to it straight after briefing.'

With her plans for the morning laid, Cat soon relaxed, and her infectious laugh could be heard throughout the bar. The alcohol worked its magic and with that mischievous twinkle still playing in his eyes, Alex recounted stories of bungled arrests and bodged investigations, some of which were clearly urban myths, others embarrassingly true. Cat had heard most of the stories before, although never from the horse's mouth, but that didn't matter; the intimacy in which they shared the laughs gave them a new life. After a while, Alex, having dominated the conversation with his story telling, tried to redress the balance and turned his attention to Cat.

'What made you want to join the force? You know, with your background and everything.'

'What do you mean, with a degree? It's not that uncommon.'

'But that's not exactly the case is it? I mean if you want to be black and white about it you could say, with a degree and a PhD and a fantastic research job in the Maldives studying plankton or whatever it was.'

'Actually, I hadn't quite got as far as finishing the PhD bit and whale sharks are a little bit bigger than plankton but I see what you're saying.'

'What made you change direction?'

Cat touched a finger to her glass, disturbing the veil of condensation on its surface. She watched as a thin rivulet ran down the side like a solitary tear.

'You know why.'

She could sense Alex looking at her.

'No, I don't,' he said, his voice low.

Cat felt her emotions surge as her memories erupted to the surface. She looked up at the ceiling and sighed before reaching for her glass.

'I remember the phone call. My aunt – my Mum's sister – was given the job of calling me. It was one o'clock in the morning over there, so as soon as I heard the phone, I knew there was something wrong.' She took a drink and returned the glass to the table. 'No one ever used to phone me. I mean apart from at agreed times.' She let her gaze drop. 'Anyway, she just blurted it out. Pete was dead. That was what she said. Just like that. She went on to say how he'd been in a hit and run and that he'd died at the scene. Oh, she tried to make it more palatable, if you know what I mean, like saying it was quick and there was nothing anyone could do. But all she did was conjure up an image of his mangled body.' She fell silent and Alex let her have a moment. After a little while she started talking again, this time trying but failing to sound upbeat. It sounded as though she was reading the shipping forecast on a fair-weather day. 'I booked myself on the next flight home. And then there was the funeral. Well, you know all about that, you were there. Afterwards, well it was like I was fourteen again, back in my old bedroom, Dad having a go at me for this and that. Pete had always been his golden boy.

'Anyway, there I was wondering how soon I could use my return ticket without it seeming improper, when all of a sudden I'd got a house and a dog to look after. I had responsibilities. I still can't believe Pete left me everything, including the bloody dog. We'd all just assumed it would all go to Mum and Dad. So anyway, that was that.'

Alex looked at her, his brows pinched together. 'What do you mean, that was that? You could have sold the house or rented it out. And I mean Harvey's a great dog but you could have found another home for him. You didn't have to give everything up. There must have been some other reason you stayed?'

Cat felt herself flush. She hated how Alex was so astute.

'I did think about renting the house out and going back but something Dad said to me made me change my mind. I can't remember his exact words,' she lied, rerunning every syllable in her head, 'but he said it was a shame I couldn't be more like my brother and do my bit for a society that had so far paid for me to have one long party.'

'What! And that didn't make you jump straight onto the next plane? I'd have been off like a shot if someone had said that to me.'

'That's because you're a contrary so-and-so.' Cat gave him a warm smile. 'Actually, I remember thinking he was probably right.'

'So, no regrets?'

'No.' She shook her head confidently. 'No regrets.'

Her father's lack of belief in her made her even more determined to prove him wrong. She was sure she could be every bit as good a detective as her brother had been, provided she worked hard and wanted it badly enough. She'd worried for a long time about whether the sudden career change had been a mistake but at last it was looking like her decision would be vindicated; already she felt she was making a difference to the investigation.

She picked up her almost empty glass and held it towards Alex for their third toast of the evening, suddenly feeling in the mood to celebrate.

It was the early hours of the morning when Cat looked out of the taxi window and saw the house loom into view. She said goodnight to Alex and climbed out of the cab. Maybe if she hadn't been drunk it would have dawned on her how long it was since she'd last had such a good night out, but she was, so it didn't.

Inside, she dropped her bag on the hallway floor, threw her coat over the banister and headed straight to the bedroom, trying but failing to creep noiselessly upstairs. The room was cloaked in darkness and she fumbled around at the foot of the bed as she slipped off her shoes and began to strip out of her clothes. The low light combined with too much Pinot Grigio made her clumsy and she lost her balance and fell onto the edge of the bed, still struggling to free her legs of the jeans that shackled her.

'You managed to find your way home then?' His voice, cold and controlled, cut through the darkness.

He'd obviously been lying awake waiting for her.

'Hi, did you have a nice weekend?' Cat mumbled in response, choosing not to rise to the bait.

Free at last she slipped on her nightshirt before disappearing into the en-suite bathroom, closing the door behind her. Less than five minutes later she emerged smelling of face cream and toothpaste and climbed into bed.

'Is that it?'

'What?' Cat said, already succumbing to her body's demand for sleep.

'Don't I get an explanation or an apology?'

'What for?'

'Your note never said anything about being back this late. I might have been worried.'

But were you? She wanted to ask.

Realising she wasn't going to get any sleep until she'd dealt with his questions she rolled onto her back, thankful that the light was off. At least she could keep her eyes closed.

'I didn't know how long I'd be out for. But I'm home now. Let's not fight.'

'And you've been in the pub all this time?'

'Yes.'

'Which one?'

'Mickey's.'

'Till this time of night?'

'Yes,' she said wearily. 'Look, I don't see why it's such a big deal. It's not like it happens all the time.'

'Exactly. It never happens. If I ask you to go out with me for the evening, it's always a no-go if you've got work the next day. And even when you haven't, you complain that you're too tired.'

'That's not true. Anyway, I didn't plan on staying out so late but you can rest easy in the knowledge that I'll regret it in the morning.'

The room fell quiet and Cat thought that perhaps Mike had said his piece and would now let her sleep. But she was not going to get off that lightly.

'Okay, tell me the last time the two of us went out?'

Cat groaned.

'Look, Mike, it's late and I'm tired. Please let's drop it. If you're determined to fight about this, you'll have to wait until the morning; I'm going to sleep. Goodnight.'

She took a firm grip of the quilt, rolled over and turned her back to her partner of three years.

Eight

After a night's rest that was more akin to being comatose than asleep, the shrill pitch of the bedside alarm seared through Cat's brain, abruptly catapulting her to consciousness. Her head was pounding and each beat of her heart brought with it a new pulse of pain. She leaned over and tried to focus, but her eyes remained stubbornly bleary. With half-opened lids, she reached out a hand and patted about on the bedside cabinet until her fingers felt the offending article. She slapped the off-button so forcibly that the clock slipped off the cupboard and onto the floor.

At least it did so silently.

She groaned and rolled over onto her back and pulled a pillow on to her face, savouring the cool cotton on her skin; some small relief for her throbbing forehead. Soon, with the silence restored, slumber sucked her down and she drifted back to sleep.

After what seemed like only minutes but was in reality nearly half an hour, she stirred. Feeling a little shaky she managed to rouse herself to sitting. She looked over to her bedside table and stared blankly at the empty space. Seconds passed before she realised that the clock that she expected to see was missing. She leaned forward, intent on scouring the floor, but the downward motion sent her head reeling.

'Oh God,' she moaned, leaning back. She heard Mike moving around the room. 'What time is it?'

'Nearly seven,' he said. It was little more than a grunt.

'Shit!' She threw the covers roughly to one side and clambered out of bed, sending yet another rush of blood to her head. 'Why didn't you wake me? I'm going to be late.'

She stumbled towards the bathroom and turned the shower

on full. Stripping off her short nightshirt, she reached a hand into the cubicle to test the temperature.

'Hey, don't have a go at me,' Mike yelled. 'You're the one that–'

She didn't hear the rest, choosing instead to step into the still icy spray, slamming the glass door behind her. Quickly the noise of the water drowned out all other sounds. The argument was over almost before it had begun.

The rest of the hour that followed went by in a blur. And although a little more sluggish than usual, Cat somehow managed to push her physical state to one side and was showered, dressed and had even found time for a quick breakfast of tea and toast before tackling the rush hour traffic. Relieved at having made it in on time, she was parking her car when her mobile started to ring. She reached into her bag and fumbled around until her hand grasped the phone's familiar form. Pulling it out she looked down and was surprised to see Alex's name on the Caller ID. With the phone propped between her ear and shoulder she continued to manoeuvre the car into position.

'Alex, hi, where are you?'

'Cat?'

'Yeah, hi Alex, what is it?'

'Sorry, I couldn't hear you. It's a bad line, hang on...'

The phone fell quiet at the other end, although Cat could hear some background noises that she struggled to place. Soon Alex was back.

'You still there?'

'Yep. What's up? Where are you?'

'Sorry, someone here needed to ask me something. Look Cat, I'm at the hospital. Cody is sick. They're just running some tests.'

Cat held her breath as Alex continued, 'I don't know when I'm going to be able to come in. I need to sit it out here until the results come back. Can you do what we agreed yesterday? Take the photos, show them around. See if you can come up with any names. I'm sorry, I've got to go.'

'Don't worry about anything. I'll sort things out here. We can catch up later.'

'I'll call you, just as soon as–'

'Just go,' she said forcibly. She was about to ring off but stopped herself. She put the phone back to her ear. 'Alex...?'

'Yeah?'

'Good luck.'

'Thanks.'

For a little while Cat remained with the phone pressed close to her ear, her breathing shallow and her heart beating fast, the dead line providing no comfort.

Monday morning banter filled the office. It bled out into the corridor as Cat opened the door and walked into the room. Her entrance caused a momentary lull. Everyone had turned to face her and then, just as suddenly, they turned away and resumed their conversations, killing time as they waited for the morning's briefing to start. It dawned on her that perhaps no one else knew Alex wouldn't be in.

'I see you made it in okay then. Late night was it?' Bob Bells said, sidling over to her.

Suddenly she felt very self-conscious; her tiredness translated into imagined dark circles, dull eyes and grey skin. Subconsciously her hand moved up to her face and she unhooked her hair from behind her ears, letting it fall across her face.

'Have you heard from Alex yet?' she asked.

She heard Bob sucking at his teeth.

'Don't tell me, he's running late. Got a bit of a thick head has he?' he said, confirming her suspicion that Bob knew where she and Alex had been the previous night. 'Well I can't hang around all day. I've got to be in court for ten.'

'Alex isn't late. His son's ill. He's in hospital. Alex called when I was parking the car. He left instructions that everyone is to continue with their existing duties,' she ad-libbed.

Bob's face clouded over.

'Why did he call you? I'm supposed to take over when he's not here. He should have called me.'

'I don't know Bob. You'll need to ask Alex that.'

Bob looked as though he was about to say something else but then he pulled his lips together in a hard line and shook his head.

'In that case you can team up with Quinn and Davis. They're reviewing the CCTV footage from Saturday night,' he said over his shoulder as he walked to the front of the room.

'Sorry, no can do,' she said to his retreating back, causing him to do an about turn.

'What?'

'I've already got something to be getting on with. Alex gave me instructions when he called earlier. I'll let you know how I get on,' she said, smiling sweetly at him, savouring the scowl that settled on his face.

The shop was quiet. Cat put it down to it being a Monday, though she couldn't imagine the designer clothes store was ever that busy. She took her time, strolling between the displays, her gaze sweeping the room until she spotted Emma tidying a display of lambswool sweaters that looked as soft as a kitten. Emma turned, a pleasant smile fixed on her lips; a well-practised warm welcome that evaporated the second she realised who it was.

'I'm glad to see that you are doing better for yourself now that you've given up pulling pints in that wreck of a bar,' Cat said as she approached.

'What do you want?' Emma hissed.

'What do you think? I need to talk to you.'

Cat joined her at the rack of clothes. She reached out and picked up a tailored silk shirt, feeling the fabric between her fingers.

'I never get the chance to wear anything this classy.' Glancing briefly at the price tag she let out a gasp. 'People don't really pay this much for a shirt, do they?'

'It's Dolce and Gabbana, a hundred per cent silk. How much did you think it would be?' Emma replied, taking the shirt off her and carefully returning it to the rail, making sure the hangers were perfectly aligned.

'No idea, obviously. For that price I hope they hand-spun the silk themselves.' Cat checked the price tag on another item and found it of a similar value.

Emma cast a nervous look over her shoulder, towards the rear of the shop.

'I can't talk now. Besides, I've already told you everything I know.'

'Well we've come across some new evidence that I was hoping you can help us with.'

'What, now? Can't it wait?'

'This won't take long. Is there somewhere we can go to talk for a few minutes?'

'No. I'm not allowed. I could lose my job.'

Emma twisted her fingers like an anxious child. Cat decided to cut her some slack.

'When's your next break?'

'I go for lunch at one.'

Before Cat could respond she became aware of someone approaching. She turned to see a statuesque blonde woman making her way over.

'It's Tara, my manager,' Emma whispered. 'Pretend to be thinking about buying the shirt.'

Cat watched the Amazonian Tara sashay over to them and marvelled at how she appeared to be oblivious to the fact she was wearing barely any clothes. Her entire five-foot eleven frame was inadequately covered by an almost sheer crimson midriff top, below which sat a tiny bottom-skimming black skirt. For a moment, even Cat felt intimidated by the expanse of toned abdominals, until she remembered why she was there.

'Is everything alright here?' Tara asked, almost without moving her lips, a haughty expression fixed on her face.

'I think we're okay, this lady was–'

'Just checking that Emma could make our lunch date,' Cat interrupted.

Emma looked anxiously across to Tara. 'I was just saying that I'm not off until one today.'

Tara tilted her head back and looked down her nose at Cat; now that she knew that she wasn't a customer she didn't need to disguise her contempt.

'Perhaps you could come back at lunchtime then, so that Emma can get back to work.'

And with that she slinked away, back to her vantage point at the back of the store.

'One o'clock then. I'll be waiting for you at the door,' Cat said, before leaving Emma looking less than happy.

At twelve fifty-five she returned, weighed down with half a dozen bags. She dropped them to the floor and leaned against the glass, settling in for the wait. At five past one she was about to go in and look for Emma when the teenager came rushing out.

'I don't get long and I need to get something to eat.'

'Okay, where would you like to go?'

'Wherever,' Emma said in a petulant tone.

Wherever turned out to be a small sandwich bar tucked away at the far end of the shopping centre. A run of tan vinyl cushioned stools sat against a tall counter at the front of the shop that overlooked a busy walkway. The rest of the store was filled with booths upholstered in the same brown leatherette between which were sandwiched white glossy melamine tables, much more suitable for a private lunchtime conversation.

Cat pushed a twenty-pound note into Emma's hand.

'Get whatever you want. I'll have a cappuccino if they do it, filter coffee if they don't. I'll get us a seat at the back, over there,' she said, gesturing to an empty booth at the rear of the shop.

Cat dropped her shopping on the seat by the wall and slid along the bench to sit next to it. Within a few minutes Emma approached carrying a laden tray. She set it down heavily, causing Cat's cappuccino to slop over the lip of the large mug. She flopped onto the bench opposite Cat and lifted a can of coke and plate of sandwiches off the flooded tray, leaving Cat to deal with the pool of froth and coffee that puddled around her cup.

'Are you allowed to do that when you're on duty?' Emma asked as she clicked open her can.

'What? Drink coffee?'

'No. I meant the shopping,' she said, gesturing towards the pile of bags.

'I have a lunch break too, only I have to take it when I can fit it in. I thought I'd make the most of it while I was here.'

For the following five minutes, despite Cat's attempts to engage her, Emma showed no interested in anything other than what was on the table in front of her and it wasn't until the sandwich was finished that she spoke.

'How did you know where to find me anyway?'

'It's not difficult, not when you're in legitimate employment.'

Not difficult, but definitely not straightforward. It had taken Cat two hours of back-to-back phone calls to track Emma down after she had learned that the teenager had quit her bar job.

'So what do you want?' Emma asked.

'We've managed to get hold of some photos that were taken on the night that Mary went missing.'

Cat pulled an envelope from her bag and slid the three prints from it. She passed the first one across. It showed Mary standing some distance away from a group of girls. Without even glancing at it Emma laid it face down on the table.

'I don't know if I can.'

'These are only photos from the nightclub. There's nothing to be worried about.'

Emma reached down and picked the photograph up. She took a long look at it.

'Oh God, I'd sort of forgotten what she looked like. That's bad isn't it?'

'No. That's normal.'

She continued staring at it for some time, before shaking her head.

'I'm sorry. I don't know what you want me to say.'

'Well, do you recognise any of the other people in the photo?'

Once again Emma bent her head to look closely at the picture in her hands. She took her time and appeared to be looking from face to face. It was a good shot and the faces of the girls were clear.

'No, I don't know any of them. They seem a bit familiar but I've probably just seen them around.'

'Okay. How about this one?' Cat passed her the second picture.

It showed Mary with a different set of people – three girls and two guys. Mary was face on to the camera and had an almost full drink in her hand. She was leaning in the direction of a man with greasy shoulder-length hair and a face that sneered at the camera in a contrived James Dean pose. There was less than a foot between them.

'Do you recognise this guy?' Cat asked, pointing to the James Dean wannabe.

'Yeah. His name's Terry.'

Cat felt her heart do a little dance. 'You know him?'

Emma shook her head vigorously.

'No. I steer clear of people like him.'

'Why? What do you mean, people like him?'

'He's a bit of a druggy and I... well, I don't do drugs. Like I told you before, I don't really drink. I only got the job in the bar while I was waiting for something better.'

'Do you know his surname?'

Emma took another drink of coke.

'No.'

'How do you know him?'

'He's one of Charlie's mates. To be honest I gave all of her friends like that a wide berth.' She looked up from the photo to Cat. 'Do you think he had anything to do with Mary's death?'

'Do you think that's a possibility?'

Emma shrugged.

'How am I supposed to know? That's your job isn't it?'

With a possible name to go on Cat could barely contain her excitement and as soon as she got back to the office, she put a call through to an old friend in the Drug Squad, or rather an old friend of her brother.

'Mona, it's Cat McKenzie.'

'Hi Cat. It's been a long time. How you doing?'

'Yeah, I'm alright. You okay?'

'Sure, same old, same old, you know?'

'Yeah.'

'Hey I heard about you making the grade. Welcome to the jungle.'

'Huh?' Cat said.

'You made detective, didn't you?'

'Oh, I see. Yeah, sorry – I haven't heard anyone call it that before.'

'So, what can I do for you?'

Cat explained her predicament – a photo, the name, and a yet unsolved murder.

'Ping the photo over and leave it with me. I'll see what I can do.'

'Mona, you're a godsend. Thanks.'

'Don't worry about it. I'll have a trawl and call you later.'

Later turned out to be pretty damn soon and Cat got a call back within the hour.

'Terence Phillips,' Mona said sounding confident. 'He's got form as long as your arm.' She gave Cat a quick rundown of the long list of crimes that lay at Mr Phillips' door, or those they knew about at least.

'But he can't be much older than twenty.'

'He's nineteen.'

'I really should know better than to be surprised.'

'I guess you want those contact details?'

Cat picked up her pen. 'Fire away.'

Mona gave her two addresses and it was as she was writing down the second that a frown descended on Cat's brow.

'Did I hear that right – did you say sixty-three Marine Terrace?'

'Yeah, that's right. Do you know it?'

'I might do. I don't suppose you've got details of anyone else living there?'

'A half-sister. She posted bail for him last time. Charlene Winter.'

Bloody Charlie!

After exchanging goodbyes and promises to keep in touch, Cat hung up, grabbed her bag and her car keys, and then stopped dead in her tracks.

She couldn't go after Terry on her own and she still had no idea of when Alex was going to be back. She looked around. Spencer was at his desk, head down, tapping away at his keyboard, concentration making a tense mask of his face. Her gaze continued to scan the room. Everyone else was out. Everyone apart from Bob, who was by the kettle topping up his mug with the thick black gloop that passed as coffee in the detective ranks.

'Shit,' Cat said under her breath. It was going to have to be Bob. She couldn't do it with Spencer; he was as inexperienced as she was. She waited for Bob to sit down before moseying over to his desk.

'Bob...'

'What?' he asked without bothering to look up from his newspaper – a national tabloid opened at the sports pages.

She took a deep breath. There was no easy way of doing this.

'Bob, I need some help.'

He looked up, a gleeful expression on his face.

'Do you now. Well, I'm pretty busy... research you know,' he said, tapping the paper with a finger.

'Yes, I can see that.' Keep smiling she told herself through gritted teeth. 'But this could be a bit of a big deal. I think I might have found Mary's murderer. I need someone to help me bring him in.'

That got his attention.

'Are you serious?' he said, jumping upright in his seat.

'I think it's a guy called Terry Philips, he–'

Bob stood up and grabbed his coat.

'What are you waiting for? Come on, you can fill me in on the way there.'

'You're sure this is him?' Bob asked, as Cat started the car's engine and pulled away. He was waving the sheet of paper that Cat had used to scribble the name and address on.

'Yep. Terry Phillips. He's got form as long as your arm,' she said, remembering Mona's choice of words. 'And not just for drug dealing; GBH, robbery with violence, disturbing the peace, you name it, he's done it. He's been in and out of institutions all of his life.'

Twenty minutes later Cat slowed the car down to a crawl as they passed Terry's house. It was just after two and the road was quiet. Cat pulled the car into the kerb a little further along. She killed the engine and was just turning to ask Bob how they were going to approach it when he slipped off his seat belt and started to climb out of the door.

'Bob, wait...'

'Come on, let's get the little scrote,' he said without a backwards look.

Cat rushed to follow him as he ran across the road towards the house. He announced his arrival with a succession of heavy-handed thumps on the timber-framed door. Cat didn't say anything but she couldn't help thinking a seasoned recidivist like Terry would have been on the receiving end of a police visit enough times to know this was no social call. It didn't surprise her then that five minutes of intermittent banging brought no response. Not even an indiscreet curtain twitch. Bob turned away from the door. He appeared about to say something when his expression changed. A sly smile crept across his lizard-like lips.

'Stay here and watch the door,' he said, before running back down the pathway. He climbed into her Ford. She could see him through the car's open door speaking into the police radio. Shortly afterwards he emerged and walked over to an old Vauxhall hatchback that was parked in a resident's bay on the opposite side of the road. The car had been heavily customised with a testosterone-inspired body kit, large bore exhaust, all topped off with a Ferrari red paint job. Cat looked on speechless as Bob put his weight against the bonnet and began rocking the car, causing the alarm to go off, the horn honking like an over-enthusiastic sea lion.

Astonished by his audacity but seeing what he was trying to achieve, Cat waited patiently by the front door. As a result, she was in no position to do anything other than watch when Terry sprinted from the alleyway at the side of the house, a baseball bat held rigid in his hand.

He stopped a few metres away from Bob.

'Step away from the car, old man.'

'Terry, Police! Put the bat down. We just want to talk to you,' Cat called out, but Terry didn't so much as acknowledge her presence.

Bob was still rocking on the bonnet of the car.

'I said get off my fucking car!' Terry lifted the baseball bat to head height and took a step forward.

Bob stared at him, deadpan.

'Make me.'

Suddenly Terry charged. Cat sprinted after him but by the time she had reached the gate at the end of the house's narrow front path Terry was already at the car, about to take his first swing. But she needn't have worried. Despite packing a pillow-sized paunch, Bob had surprisingly good reflexes. He quickly swung his feet around, catching his would-be attacker full force in the gut. Terry pitched backwards. He dropped the bat, which clattered on the floor at his feet. Bent double and clutching his stomach, he staggered a few steps forwards and set his hands onto the car bonnet for support.

Terry's obvious physical distress appeared to have no effect on Bob, however. He ignored the tirade of abuse that was thrown his way as he read Terry his rights in a flat monotone. It would have given anyone listening the distinct impression that the jaded detective had said it more times than he cared to remember.

Back at the station Terry was taken straight to the custody suite. The custody sergeant was otherwise engaged so Bob made his excuses – probably overdue a caffeine fix – and left Cat to supervise their suspect. Bored after a ten-minute wait, she took out her mobile and checked it for messages. There had been no missed calls and no emails other than the usual trickle of unwanted junk that her spam filter had failed to pick up. She was just returning her phone to her bag, having barely turned her back on the young delinquent for less than a minute, when she heard the strike of a match. She turned around to find Terry slouching against the wall of the detention room with a straw-thin roll-up to his lips, despite the 'No Smoking' signs that were clearly visible.

'You can't smoke in here. Put it out.'

Ignoring her, he took another drag, drawing it deep into his lungs, before leaning his head back to exhale a plume of blue smoke towards the ceiling.

Cat took a step towards him.

'I said put it out.'

Again, he lifted the roll-up back to his lips, took one long drag and then flicked the half-smoked stub at the floor where it lay smouldering. But his arrogance was a mistake. In contrast to the impression of indifference he was obviously keen to convey, Cat noticed the slight tremor of his hand as he lifted the cigarette to his lips, and how he held the smoke in his lungs longer than normal. She knew he was nervous. And for a repeat offender such as Terry, well-seasoned in the criminal prosecution system, that could only indicate one thing – guilt. But for a chancer like Terry it was anyone's guess exactly what he was guilty of, though Cat thought she had a pretty good idea.

And it wasn't long before she had the chance to air her theory. Within the hour she was sitting opposite Terry, across a scratched and scarred interview table. After waiting for everyone to settle in their seats, Cat leaned over to the CD recorder and inserted a new disc. Following brief by-the-book introductions the interview began.

'Terry, this is a bit of a change in direction for you isn't it? These are some serious charges,' Bob said, sounding somehow amused by the turn of events.

Terry stayed silent. Sitting with his head bent he stared at the empty table, motionless, except for his right hand, the fingers of which moved as though he was flicking a spent match between his fingers with well-practised dexterity. The detectives let the silence mount. Terry knew the drill. He'd been in and out of institutions and youth detention centres for more than half of his young life, graduating to low-security prison within ten weeks of his eighteenth birthday for dealing in class 'C' drugs. Even though this would be his first murder charge, Cat knew he wasn't going to give anything away without a little cunning on their part.

'Terry, come on, talk to us,' she said, gently. 'Given the amount of evidence we've got that implicates you in Mary's murder you've got some explaining to do.'

'That's bullshit,' he said, spitting the words out. 'I don't even know this Mary you keep going on about.'

Cat had expected as much and in response she reached for the blue document folder resting on the table in front of her. Opening it, she selected the top sheet, a large colour photograph, and slid it across the desk towards Terry.

'The suspect is being shown a photograph of the murder victim, Mary Joseph,' Cat said in a clear voice.

Terry couldn't resist letting his eyes roam towards the glossy print in front of him. It was a blow up of a snap taken at a Christmas party the previous year, courtesy of Mary's friend Stacey. It showed the dead girl happily posing with some of her school friends, smiling into the camera.

Terry pushed the glossy print away with one finger.

'Never seen her before. Can I go now?'

Cat leaned over and took back the picture, returning it to the document wallet. She selected a second print and they repeated the exercise. She pushed the picture across the table until it rested under Terry's gaze.

'Maybe this one will jog your memory. You and Mary on the night she was murdered.'

This time Terry barely looked at it, obviously recognising its contents. He quickly turned his head away.

'That proves nothing. I just happened to be standing next to her at the bar. If this is all you've got on me then—'

'This is just one of a number of photos,' Cat said, as she once again reached for the folder. 'Do you want to see the rest?'

Cat kept her fingers crossed, hoping that he wouldn't take her up on her offer. She wasn't lying; they did have more photos, only none of them showed Mary and Terry in the same frame.

'It still means nothing. Okay, I was in the club with her. That don't mean I left with her, because I didn't. And if I didn't leave with her you can't prove nothing.'

He stared defiantly at Cat.

'Do you know who she did leave with?' Bob asked.

Terry tipped his head to one side and stared at Bob through half-closed lids. He said nothing. Bob glowered back at him in response.

'Who did you leave with?' Cat asked.

'No one. I left on my own.'

'What time?'

He curled his lip into an ugly sneer.

'Don't remember.'

The questions went on and on, and Terry answered each as curtly as he could. According to Terry that night was about as uneventful as they get; a quiet night out, where he met no one in particular and did nothing much. Cat thought back to the souped-up Vauxhall and wondered whether he'd been drink-driving, before remembering his history of drug abuse. Throughout the interview he remained consistent. Admit nothing, deny everything and give nothing new away.

Bob leaned back in his chair, took a deep breath and exhaled noisily. Cat recognised the signs; Bob was about to go for the jugular. If it had been Alex, Cat knew it would have been time for her to blend into the background and before she'd even thought about it she had pushed her chair back slightly, distancing herself from the table. But before Bob had a chance to move in, she had second thoughts. She pulled her chair back up to the table, leaned forward and turned the photo of Terry and Mary to face her. Ignoring the sounds of Bob shuffling in his seat, she tapped the photo.

'There's one thing about all of this that puzzles me Terry,' she said. 'I mean, it's obvious you were with Mary the night she was murdered. Apart from the fact she was at the club with your sister, we know from the photos you were hanging around with her. But what I don't get is *why* you were with her. I mean, a girl like Mary. She wasn't a bad looker, but she was hardly a stunner. If I was being cruel, I might say she was a bit plain, and well, a bit young-looking for you.'

Terry shifted in his seat.

'I told you I wasn't with her.'

'That's not what it looks like. I mean there's you...' she pointed to the picture of the two of them, 'and there's Mary. Like I said, I'm just a bit surprised. I would have thought you'd have gone for someone a bit tastier. Or do you have a thing for red heads?'

'I told you, I didn't have anything for her. I don't go for ginger nuts. They're not my type!'

'What is your type?'

'Blonde, big tits, no brains,' he bragged. 'Which ain't too difficult given most women ain't got a brain anyway.' He guffawed theatrically for effect whilst keeping Cat locked in his sights.

She let him have his little laugh but her face remained deadpan.

'And yet we've got the pictures and you don't exactly look like you're trying to get rid of her.'

He shrugged.

'So what happened on Saturday night? I don't see Charlie in any of these pictures.'

'She was with some bloke.'

'Meaning Mary was at a loose end. I bet you thought your luck was in? I notice in the pictures that it was always Mary that was paying at the bar and I suppose you didn't run out of cigarettes that night?' Cat said, hazarding a guess at describing a scene she could only imagine. But she knew his type.

A slight smirk played on Terry's lips.

Cat continued, 'So there she was, abandoned by her mates and lavishing attention on you in the form of free drinks and ciggies, so it would only be right to return the generosity. Is that what happened – you offered her a lift home? God, if she was grateful for your attention before, what would she be like once you got her in the car? Willing to go all the way? Wasn't that what you were you expecting? Was that when you couldn't hold back any more? Isn't that what happened? And then once you'd got her on your own...'

There it was! A fleeting upward glance.

Despite Alex's cynicism, Cat knew that being able to interpret body language was a skill second to none in their line of work. Even people well practised in deception and misdirection could be let down by their accomplice – their physical being – which could unleash a whole range of reactions from a quick sideways glance to a split-second intake of breath, all of which are capable of betraying the subconscious as clearly as a pointed finger. And to her credit, Cat was adept at reading most of them.

She knew that the upward flick of his eyes was an involuntary reaction that indicated memory recall and guessed that, however brief, her words had Terry replaying scenes dragged up from somewhere within.

She also knew that within the blink of an eye that fleeting memory would have sent a shot of adrenalin to course through his veins, causing his pupils to dilate. He would feel his heart quicken and his stomach flip. She knew that he would sense the danger that his reactions were putting him in and there...

He reacted just as she would have expected. He slumped forward and buried his head in his arms, where he stayed, hunched over the table top.

But he wasn't quick enough. Cat knew as sure as night follows day that they had found Mary's killer.

But it wasn't just Cat who was fired with a renewed sense of determination. The close call had strengthened Terry's resolve and he responded to the questions that followed with a poker face and a response of no comment. It wasn't long before he refused to answer any more of their questions without legal representation. Three hours into the interrogation it was time for a break.

'Did you see it?' Cat turned to Bob as soon as they left the room. 'His reaction when I talked about the lift home? It's him. I'm sure it is,' she said, unable to disguise her excitement.

'It's not enough,' Bob said flatly. 'We're going to need a damn sight more if we've any chance of making this stick. You should have let me take over. I'd have put the fucking fear of God into the little shit.'

'Hardly,' she said. 'He's had years of practice in blocking out tough men like you. I think we just need to keep a gentle pressure on, lull him into a false sense of security.'

'I don't agree. They all cave in the end.'

'So what now?' she asked, determined not to let him annoy her.

'You tell me. If I'd have had my way—'

'Bob,' she said forcibly, 'I said what *now*, not what then.'

Bob glared at her with his washed-out grey eyes. She knew it was killing him to have to work so closely with her but she also knew how badly he'd want to make the charge.

'Let him sweat it while you get a search warrant. Focus on the car first. If you're right then that's where it happened.'

Nine

Over the course of the day the intermittent showers had multiplied, mutating into a deluge the equivalent of Niagara. Or at least so it seemed to Cat as she ran from her front door to Alex's waiting car.

'How shit is this weather?' she said as she took down her hood, running her fingers through her hair. She turned the heater up to maximum.

'What's happened?' she asked as the car pulled away at speed.

Alex had been so brief when he phoned, she knew nothing more than the body of a woman had been found.

'Some guy coming from the train station in Riverdale spotted what he thought was a woman collapsed. He tried to resuscitate her but it was too late. He called an ambulance and they called it in.'

Cat began to rummage in her bag.

'Signs of foul play then, I take it.'

'I guess we'll find out when... What the hell have you got there?' Alex asked. He was staring at the cellophane-bound package that Cat was busy unwrapping.

'It's a sandwich. I haven't had any dinner yet.' Alex shook his head. Cat added, 'I bet you wish you'd thought of it. Do you want half?'

But Alex didn't reply.

Cat took the opportunity to steal a glance at him as she started on her sandwich. Dark circles like bruises underlined his eyes and his brow was corrugated with deep furrows.

The rain continued to hammer down and yet Alex drove with his foot hard on the accelerator and threw the speeding car so tight into the turns that Cat was forced to hold on to the handle above her door to keep from sliding about in her seat. Thankfully, by the time they reached Riverdale, with its busy roads and plethora of parked cars, the rain had eased and Alex dropped his speed to one that didn't feel quite as life-threatening. It was only then that Cat judged it safe to talk.

'How's Cody?' she asked cautiously.

But Alex appeared not to hear.

Cat noticed the sign for the train station but they continued past until they reached a small parade of shops where Alex brought the car to a stop. A screen had already been erected at the entrance of the alley, blocking the scene from prying eyes. They climbed out of the car, pulled the hoods up on their regulation issue black Gore-Tex jackets and crossed the road to where two shadowy figures stood, shoulders hunched to guard against the rain.

Spencer and a young guy in uniform stopped chatting on seeing them approach. The pair looked fresh out of school.

Alex looked up and down the road.

'Any sign of Bob?'

'Not yet, boss,' Spencer said.

Cat thought about saying something sarcastic about Bob's late arrival, hoping to make light of the situation, but thought better of it.

'Anything to report so far?' Alex asked.

'Looks like we've got an ID and address for the dead woman.'

Cat looked at him wide-eyed.

'That was quick,' she said.

'Make a note of it,' Alex told her. 'You'll be going there later.'

Spencer took a few steps over to a square plastic bin that sat at the entrance to the screened section. He lifted the lid and retrieved a sealed evidence bag. 'It was in her shoulder bag,' he explained, passing it to Cat. 'There's still thirty quid's worth of notes in it and some loose change.'

Cat turned the item over in her hands. It was a woman's purse, unfolded so as to expose its interior. Clearly visible, through a transparent plastic window, was a current rail pass complete with photograph, name and address. As she looked at it the details started to blur, distorted by the rain that landed on the plastic.

'Not a robbery-motivated attack then, unless... maybe the guy who found her interrupted them?'

Alex said nothing. Cat took out her pad and started to take down the details. Out of the corner of her eye she noticed him start to slip into a white protective jumpsuit. She hurriedly handed the purse back to Spencer and followed suit. They donned the regulation booties, waited for the uniformed officer to log their attendance and then stepped around the screen onto the crime scene.

Cat gave herself a moment to take it all in.

The dead woman lay sprawled across the floor like a pile of hastily fly-tipped rubbish. In her early to mid-thirties, her legs were twisted, bent beneath her, her face turned skywards. Two figures in white hooded jumpsuits squatted over the body. Cat approached and peered over their shoulders. Under the harsh light of the portable rigs the woman's skin looked waxier and paler than usually seen on the recently dead.

Having grown aware of the detectives' presence behind them, the two men working the scene turned around.

'Andy,' Cat said, breaking into a smile on seeing a familiar face looking back at her. 'It's been a long time.'

The man raised a hand, shading his eyes from the harsh light.

'It's Cat,' she said, realising that it would be hard to recognise her in the hooded plastic outfit.

'Cat? Hi. How are you?'

'I'm good thanks. How are you and Amy?'

'I'm alright. I don't know about Amy. We split up. Didn't she tell you?'

'I haven't spoken to Amy for ages. I keep meaning to ring but it never gets any less busy.'

Suddenly Cat became aware of Alex standing beside her.

'I'm sorry. Andy Wallis, this is DI York.'

The two men nodded to each other.

'Alex.'

'Andy.'

'Oh, you know one another,' Cat said.

'Small world,' Alex said.

He stepped closer to the dead woman and went to squat down.

'Be careful,' Andy said. 'There are bits of broken glass all over the place. One of the streetlights has been smashed.'

Alex stood and looked up but the top of the street lamp was beyond the reach of the arc lights.

'That might explain why the attacker chose here,' he said.

He turned back and bent over the body. Cat did likewise.

'Her eyes, they haven't started to cloud yet,' she said.

Even though she knew first-hand the timeline of post-mortem changes in rats, where very soon the low oxygen levels in the eyes have a visible effect, she couldn't claim to have the same knowledge in the case of humans. Her biology lab classes hadn't let her go that far.

'She hasn't been dead long, that's why,' Andy said. 'Based on the temperature reading that I took when we got here I'd say we're looking at an attack sometime within the last hour, hour and a half tops. I'll be able to give you a more accurate estimate when I've finished my examination.'

Alex pointed a finger to the angry red ring that marred the smooth skin of the victim's neck.

'This mark; could it have been done by a wire?'

'I would say that was almost definitely the case,' Andy replied. 'Something thin and strong. Done properly she would have been overpowered pretty quickly.'

Cat stood up and shivered, enough for Andy to notice.

'Look, it's cold out here. You could wait in your car. I'll come and find you when we're done.'

Alex was still looking at the body. He straightened up and nodded. Thrusting his hands in his coat pocket he started back towards the street, where a small crowd was already gathered. He pulled his car keys out and held them out to Cat.

'Take these and wait for me in the car. I want a word with Bob.' He gestured in the direction of a blue SUV that had just pulled up.

'I'm alright, I'll come with you. It's not that cold.'

He pushed the keys into her hand.

'Just wait in the car.'

He turned and walked towards Bob who was making his way towards them.

Muttering under her breath, Cat climbed into the BMW. From the window she watched the two men exchange a few words before disappearing behind the cordon. According to the red digital display of the car's clock, eight minutes passed before Alex climbed in the driver's seat. Cat had an overwhelming impulse to behave as childishly as she felt she had been treated and was staring sullenly out of the passenger window. But then Bob climbed into the back seat and Alex dealt her a game changer.

'Bob's going to take over the case from here. I wanted to come and check things out before handing it over, but from now until I'm back Bob's in charge.'

'What?' Cat asked, confused. 'Why? What's happening? Where are you going?' Even she could hear the hint of panic that lifted her words a clear octave higher.

'It doesn't matter. I'll be back as soon as I can. You'll have to wait for your friend in Bob's car, I've got to leave now.'

'What friend?' Bob asked, as they walked to his car.

Once again, the rain started to fall.

'Andy, the pathologist.' Cat said. 'He said he'll come over and update us as soon as he's finished.

Bob turned on the ignition and fiddled with the heating controls.

'What's going on with Alex?' she asked.

'It's not for me to say. If the boss wanted you to know, he'd have told you himself.'

'Oh,' Cat said. She should have known. 'Well, when's he coming back?'

'I don't know.'

The meaning of his words suddenly sank in. Alex had instructed Bob to take over the case.

Cat's expression grew solemn.

'Is it serious?'

Bob gave a short unsmiling nod. Cat looked past him, out of the window in the direction of latest crime scene.

'Do you think it's the same guy?' she asked.

'That killed Mary?'

'Yeah.'

'Well, if I was a betting man...'

'What does this do to our case against Terry?'

'Well it doesn't look good does it? Face it kid, you called it wrong.'

Ten

Cat pushed the bell. On hearing the chimes through the door, she took a step back. A heavy fog had descended on the night. Its wet touch lay on her skin like a cold flannel. She cupped her hands over her mouth and let out a long, slow breath in an attempt to bring the life back to her frozen fingers.

'I hate this bit,' she said in a voice barely more than a whisper.

Bob continued to stare, unblinking, at the door.

But even before the faint white plume of her breath from those few uttered words had started to fade, the sound of approaching footsteps could be heard ringing out in the hallway beyond. Cat steeled herself as the catch turned and the door opened, revealing a slim figure dressed in jeans and a sweater. An overhead porch lamp cast a feeble buttery wash of light onto his head, which was crowned with a mass of blonde curls.

'Yes?' he asked, yawning. Maybe he thought they were a couple of election candidates walking the campaign trail, or worse, salespeople trying to sell him something he neither wanted nor needed. In hindsight he'd have wished he was right.

'Mr Daniels?' Cat asked.

'Yes,' he said.

He looked beyond the two of them. *Waiting for his wife to come home?* Cat wondered.

'Mr Daniels, I'm DC McKenzie and this is DS Bells. Could we come in please?'

He looked at Cat; a frown puckered his brow that even the poor half-light couldn't disguise.

'What is it?' he asked, not moving from the threshold.

'It's in connection with a Mrs Megan Daniels. Is she your

wife?'

'Megan?' he said. He looked from Cat to Bob. 'What's happened?'

'Mr Daniels, I think it would be better if we could discuss this inside,' Cat said, taking a step forward.

And without any further challenge Craig Daniels let the two of them into his home and sat in stunned silence as they told him what little they knew.

The following morning, over a breakfast of tea and porridge, the TV talked to itself whilst Cat sat staring at nothing. She was thinking about the recently widowed Mr Daniels' reaction: his pale face and trembling hands when she'd passed him a cup of strong coffee doused with a generous swig of brandy.

A noise at the door, not so much a knock as a loud bang, roused her from her thoughts. She set the spoon down into the bowl and went to answer it.

'I'll get it,' she shouted as she passed the bottom of the stairs.

By the time she got to the door Bob was almost at his car.

'You're early,' she called out after him. He turned around. 'We said eight. I'm still having breakfast.' She held up a still steaming mug.

'Get in. We can grab something on the way.'

Twenty minutes later they were sitting at a melamine-topped table in a greasy spoon on the parade of shops just down from the station. Cat listened with half an ear as the waitress relayed their order to a harried-looking man bent over a sizzling grill. Seated next to the window, she let her gaze wander over the road towards where Megan Daniels had been found the previous night. But there was nothing to see now and it barely warranted a second look.

She turned back to Bob.

'Okay, so what's the drill for today?' she asked.

She'd come to know Alex well enough to know exactly how he would have approached things. With Bob, it was anyone's guess.

'Well obviously we start with the husband. That's why we're here.'

'I thought we were here to take him to get a positive ID of the body.'

'What do you think I am, a bloody taxi service? Nah, we'll leave that to someone from uniform to do later. No, I want to see what he's got to say for himself.'

'You think he had something to do with it? He was devastated last night and it seemed like genuine shock to me. I know I'm no expert–'

As soon as it was out of her mouth Cat knew it was the wrong thing to say.

'Let me guess,' Bob interrupted. 'Your ladybird guide to detecting says the fact that he's a shirt and jeans man with a nice haircut means he's innocent?'

Cat was about to protest but managed to stop just in time. She was getting used to the put-downs. Thankfully, the waitress arrived with their order, giving Bob something to focus on other than Cat's shortcomings.

'One mug of coffee and an all-day breakfast,' the amply proportioned woman said, laying a full plate in front of Bob. 'And scrambled eggs on toast and a pot of tea.' She placed Cat's healthier option down.

'Hungry?' Bob asked.

Cat looked down at her overflowing forkful.

'I haven't had anything to eat for over twelve hours, too bloody right I'm hungry.' She looked over to his plate and winced as he dredged salt over a breakfast already slathered in ketchup. 'You're not going to do your blood pressure any good. There's a ton of salt in ketchup, you don't need to add more.'

As Bob chewed, he held up the bottle to read the label. He

quickly returned it to the tarnished chrome holder.

'So how come you didn't eat last night?' he asked.

'It was too late to start cooking by the time I got in.'

'You didn't eat anything?'

'I had a beer and a handful of nuts while watching reruns on Sky. I don't know what it is but I can't go straight to bed when I get in late. I always need a bit of time to switch off, even if it's only half an hour.'

'And that's what you call the healthy option?'

'Touché.'

'Didn't your other half leave you anything to sling in the microwave when you got in?'

'Are you kidding?' Cat gave a humourless laugh. 'Mike doesn't do domestic. He had takeout pizza as I wasn't there to cook.' She laid her knife and fork down on the empty plate. 'Going back to my original question, do you really think the husband had something to do with it?'

'Clearly, you don't.'

Cat thought carefully for a minute. Bob may rib her for her lack of experience but she had always trusted her own judgement. It had rarely let her down.

'No I don't.'

'Why's that then?'

She'd hoped he wouldn't ask. Women's intuition was never going to win her any brownie points.

'I don't know. It's just a feeling. The way he handled the news I suppose.'

'We'll see,' Bob said.

Clearly, he thought differently.

Craig Daniels opened the door and looked at the two detectives. Cat noticed the strain was already beginning to show. The lines etched across his face and pink-rimmed puffy eyes had aged him overnight. He stood in the doorway like a man filled with an immeasurable tiredness.

'Morning Mr Daniels,' Bob said briskly. He stepped into the porch, forcing the other man backwards.

After opting for an amply proportioned leather settee that was perfectly positioned between two lamp tables, Cat looked around the room for the second time in twelve hours. The neutral but safe décor could have looked bland and characterless were it not for the abundance of houseplants and framed photographs of the couple smiling and laughing that gave the space a warm and lived-in feel. She looked from the photographs to their host who was hovering uneasily by the lounge door, looking like a ghost of the man in the photographs.

'Please, sit down Mr Daniels,' Bob said.

Craig Daniels perched on the edge of the seat of a large armchair.

'I realise it's difficult to talk about what has happened so soon,' Bob continued, 'but if we're to make any progress on catching your wife's killer we need to move quickly.'

Flat eyes looked back at him. 'I understand.'

'Did your wife always take the same route home from the station?'

Craig Daniels blinked, the question appearing to physically take him aback, but he quickly composed himself.

'As far as I know, yes.'

'It's just that the road where she was found isn't exactly on the way here from the station,' Bob said.

A frown appeared on the other man's face.

'I don't understand. I thought you said she was found in the station car park.'

'Not in the car park. It was on a pathway just across the road.'

'Oh,' Craig Daniels sounded confused. 'I don't see why she would have been there.'

'Did she always take the train?' Cat asked.

'Yes... well, mostly. Occasionally in the school holidays she would drive to work when the traffic was a bit lighter and it was easier to park but normally she took the train.' The skin at the corners of his eyes creased as he regarded them suspiciously. 'Why all these questions about her journey home from work?'

'I should have thought that was obvious,' Bob said. 'Given that she was on a footpath that leads in the opposite direction to here, we need to understand why she was there.'

'But she wasn't coming from work. She went out for something to eat with her cousin last night.'

Bob and Cat looked at each other. A flash of irritation crossed Bob's face.

'Now you tell us,' he said. 'Why the hell didn't you mention this last night?'

'I didn't realise you didn't know.'

Now Cat could see why the supposedly devoted husband hadn't exhibited any signs of worry at his wife's late return; he hadn't been expecting her home until late. But then it was Cat's turn to look confused. Her gaze slipped to the floor as she tried to make sense of what he'd said. Slowly she started to shake her head.

'That can't be right. What time was she supposed to be meeting her cousin?' she asked.

'Ten to seven. She was going to take the usual train home and meet her cousin, Caroline, at the station.'

'But your wife was attacked not much later than that. There wouldn't have been time for her to have been out for something to eat.'

'But I thought...' Craig Daniels suddenly looked young and vulnerable, like a lost little boy. 'But you didn't come here till much later.'

Cat waited a beat for Bob to reply but when he didn't, she took it upon herself to.

'You're right. I'm sorry; we should have said, Megan was–'

'Meeting a cousin, you say?' Bob jumped in, suddenly animated. 'That might explain why she was found where she was. Where were they supposed to be going?'

'I don't know. I don't even know if they'd agreed on anywhere. I got the impression they were just going to wander into town.'

'Has her cousin been in touch? Presumably she'll have wondered why Megan didn't show,' Cat said.

Craig Daniels shook his head.

'No.'

'That's odd.'

A feeling of dread stole through Cat. What if there was another victim out there yet to be found?

'We'll want to talk to her. We need a name and address,' Bob said.

'Caroline something. I'm sorry, I can't remember her married name. It'll be with Megan's things, along with her address. I'll go and dig it out for you.' Craig rose from his seat.

Bob raised a hand, palm out.

'That's okay. We don't need it right this minute. Please sit back down.'

Craig slumped back into his seat.

'As it looks like your wife got off the train the same time as usual, we have to accept it's possible whoever killed her knew her routine. They could have even been sitting waiting for her. Now Mr Daniels, this is very important; think about it before you answer. Do you have any idea who might have done this? Has anybody had a disagreement or a falling out with your wife?'

Cat could see the anguish cross the other man's face.

'No, no one,' Craig Daniels said, shaking his head. 'Everyone who knew Megan loved her.'

'Could she have had a run in with any of the people she worked with?' Bob went on.

Craig ran his fingers through his unwashed hair, leaving it

ruffled and unkempt.

'I don't see how; most of the time she worked on her own. She designed shop window displays. How many enemies is she going to make doing that for Christ sakes?'

'Maybe your wife mentioned something that didn't seem important at the time? I don't know, someone showed more than a passing interest in her or in what she was working on. Nothing obvious, just something that jarred,' Cat said.

'Well, she never mentioned anything like that but she might not have done.' Cat could see that he was starting to choke up. 'I've been in Canada for almost two months. We've barely spoken. I was working all hours. I only... We've only been able to speak once a week.'

'What do you do Mr Daniels?' Bob asked.

'I'm a shipping lawyer.'

'Do you work away much?'

'It depends. I have recently. I've been involved in closing an important deal.'

Cat watched as Bob's eyes lit up.

'Could your wife have been involved with someone while you were away?' he suggested with all of the subtlety of a bulldozer.

The colour drained from the other man's face.

Alex had better sort out whatever it was that was keeping him from the case, Cat thought. Bob was a bloody liability.

Craig Daniels jumped up out of his seat.

'What the hell are you suggesting? You come here under some pretence of wanting to help and then start accusing Megan of what, of being unfaithful? How dare you!'

Bob leaned forward in his seat, hands on his knees; too aggressive a stance in Cat's opinion.

'Mr Daniels sit down,' Bob instructed.

'How dare you!' he repeated. He bunched his fists and a florid bloom had appeared around his shirt collar and was quickly spreading upwards.

'Please sit down, Mr Daniels,' Cat urged in a calm voice. 'We're not suggesting anything of the sort but we have to ask the question. Sometimes couples go through a bad patch and that can include being involved with other people and sometimes, when that comes to an end, the jilted party can become vengeful.'

He retook his seat.

'Well that doesn't apply to us,' he said, flashing Bob an angry look. 'We haven't got any problems now and we never have had, we are...' he stopped, as though suddenly slapped. He inhaled deeply. 'We were very happy.' His face was still flushed red. It looked like he was fighting a fever. 'I loved Megan more than I can describe. And she loved me just as much. I know she did.'

At last he couldn't contain his sorrow any longer and for a while there was little they could do other than wait.

At her own suggestion – made quickly to avoid having it thrust upon her – Cat volunteered to make drinks, giving Craig Daniels time to calm down. She returned to the lounge with a tray loaded with tea and biscuits, only to find Bob alone, studying a framed photograph that he'd picked up from a shelf. She set the tray down on a low coffee table.

'Where is he?'

'Bathroom,' Bob said, without looking up.

Just then Craig Daniels walked back in.

Cat noticed the still wet curls that framed his face. He sat and reached for a drink.

'Can I ask a question?' he asked, nestling the mug between his hands.

'Of course,' Cat said, and instinctively she knew what was coming.

'You seem convinced that it was someone she knew. Why? I mean... how do you know it wasn't just some nutter who stopped the first person they came across?'

'We don't know for sure but–' Cat started.

'Eighty per cent of murders are committed by someone

known to the victim,' Bob said. His watery grey eyes fixed on Craig as though defying him to argue with the facts.

'And if your wife knew her assailant then it's likely that you do too,' Cat added. 'That's why you need to tell us if you can think of anyone it might have been or anything that has happened recently, no matter how trivial, which could somehow be related.'

Craig Daniels looked at her.

'But I really don't know of anything. We're not the sort to fall out with people.'

'Did Megan have much of a social life to keep herself occupied when you were away?' Cat asked.

'Not really. She'd have the occasional night out. I know she was out with some girlfriends last week but she spent most of her spare time on her hobby. She was into genealogy, you know... researching her family tree.'

'How did she do her research? Was it mainly on the internet?' Cat asked.

'The internet, libraries, public record archives, distant relatives. If the information was out there then she'd find it. She loved digging around trying to find out little titbits about people's past. It fascinated her. I always joked she'd have made a great detective.'

Cat bit back the desire to make some comment as to the stakes being a little higher.

'Had she got far?' she asked.

'Yes. She'd been doing it for years. Just when I thought she'd found out as much as there was to find, she'd come up with something else. There were always relatives popping up from one line of enquiry or another. Like this cousin of hers, the one she was meeting last night. She'd been living in Cyprus for years. Megan was really looking forward to seeing her and finding out more about the husband's side of the family.'

'What if there was someone who didn't want her digging into

their history?' Bob asked.

'She wouldn't have pushed herself on anyone. To be honest it was usually the other way around. Megan wasn't precious about her research. She always offered to let anyone have what she'd got so far. It's one of those things that everyone says they've always wanted to do but have never got around to.'

'Are you aware of any link with anyone called Joseph?' Cat asked, reminding herself of the likely possibility that they were dealing with a double murder.

'First name or surname?'

'Sorry, surname.'

'It doesn't ring any bells. The main family lines that Megan was interested in were Williams and Barker. But that's not to say there wasn't someone of that name that married into the family.'

'I think what DC McKenzie meant to ask was, do you know a young girl, name of Mary Joseph?'

Craig Daniels screwed his face up, and then shook his head. 'No.'

Bob gave him a dead-eyed look. Just when Cat was about to say something Bob leaned forward a fraction.

'Are you sure?'

The other man returned Bob's steady stare.

'Positive. I don't know anyone of that name. Has she got something to do with Megan's death? Is there something you're not telling me?'

'It may be nothing. It's just that her name has come up in another investigation,' Cat said.

Bob rose to his feet.

'We'll need to take a look at Mrs Daniels' things.'

'Of course. Her clothes and personal thing are in our bedroom, but she also has, sorry had, a study upstairs as well.'

'We'll start with the bedroom and then move on to the study,' Bob said.

After they had found nothing of any significance in the

couple's bedroom, Craig Daniels led them to the landing where a second smaller flight of stairs spurred off at an angle. At the top was a closed but unlocked door. He turned the handle and pushed it open, revealing a small attic room that had been converted into a study devoted to Megan's hobby.

'She used to keep a diary of sorts. I would imagine that'll have the details of who she's seen recently, including her cousin Caroline. It should be around here somewhere.' He started to pick over the items on the desk. 'I haven't got a clue where anything is. I hardly ever come up here.'

Cat had followed him across the threshold. Lost for words, she looked about the room, trying to take it all in.

Lit by a large dormer window, the room was dominated by three tall bookcases that groaned under the weight of an assortment of texts, files and photograph albums. On the room's longest wall, a four-foot square family tree filled the space. Handwritten in a beautifully neat script, it was framed with a collage of family photographs.

'This looks like a work of art.' Cat said, stepping in close to get a better look.

At first sight the branching lines gave it the appearance of a dysfunctional tube map, lines merging and dividing, but on closer inspection the links were shorter and more numerous. Cat followed the lines and slowly the 'map' took on a greater significance, revealing the hierarchy that was six generations of the dead woman's heredity.

Cat let her gaze drop to the desk, to a large bound photograph album. She reached down and slowly peeled the pages open to reveal an eclectic mix of families frozen in time. Curled-edged sepia prints of men in suits and smart hats with elegantly gowned ladies at their side, a hand resting gently on the crook of their partner's arm, contrasted sharply with brightly coloured snapshots of the seventies. The flares and skinny-rib tops in tartan and stripes looked outlandish and comedic against their earlier counterparts.

'Are these all Megan's family?' Cat asked.

'Yes. Each photo should say on the back who it is and where and when it was taken.'

Cat selected a photograph and slipped it out of the plastic window. She turned it over.

'What's this?' she asked, pointing to an alphanumeric sequence written against the name of the photograph's subject.

'It's an indexed reference number. Megan kept a small database on her computer. She cross-referenced everything.'

Craig returned to his hunt for the diary, riffling through the desk drawers.

While they waited Cat looked through a box file that lay open on the desk, stopping every so often to look up some detail on the family tree.

'Got it,' Craig said.

In his hand was a red, A5 leather-bound book. He offered it to Cat.

She opened the pad and thumbed through to the entry for the previous day; a glossy snapshot marked the page. She slipped the photo out and took a closer look. 'Somebody's birthday party... eighth birthday, judging by the number of candles on the cake.'

She turned the picture over.

'Caroline Williams, twenty years ago. The cousin?'

'Yes. Though she's not called that now.' He peered over her shoulder and read from the final entry. 'Berry – that's it. She's Caroline Berry now.'

Cat slipped the photo back in between the same pages.

'I'll take that, if you don't mind.' Bob reached over and snatched the book from her. 'Write the man out a receipt,' he said, pocketing the diary. 'We'll send someone round to fetch the rest of the stuff in here. It'll all need going through.'

'Take whatever you need. I just hope it's some use.'

'I'm sorry we've had to intrude on you like this,' Cat said, as they left the room. 'But as I said before we need to learn as much as we can about your wife, as fast as we can, so that we have the best possible chance of catching whoever did this.'

'And you really think it was someone she knew?'

'Over eighty per cent Mr Daniels,' Bob repeated.

Craig Daniels gave a tired nod and with shoulders sagging he trudged heavily down the stairs, looking like a man burdened with the heavy weight of sadness.

Eleven

The office was unusually quiet on their return. The lack of chatter and sea of straight faces made Cat wonder if she wasn't the only one fighting a feeling of failure with this second murder. She slumped into her seat, shoved her handbag on the floor by her feet, and set down a bag containing a still warm pastry. She pushed it away, repulsed by the grease-stained paper, regretting having been tempted by Bob's suggestion to stop off at a bakery on their way back.

Instead, she turned to a mug of steaming coffee to stem the rumbling of her stomach, switched her computer on and started on the notes of the interview with Craig Daniels. It was an absorbing task and the afternoon passed easily. She logged and filed the freshly printed sheets into a neatly labelled folder, signed her name and took it over to Bob's desk, to await his signature. She dropped it down next to a paper bag containing Bob's uneaten lunch, the greasy contents of which had left an oily slick on the pale wood veneer.

She returned to her desk, wondering whether Bob's absence was significant. He'd never knowingly missed a meal, but with Alex away, things were surely going to be different.

She sat down and looked over to her in-tray. The file on Mary Joseph lay on top; she'd put it there after she'd finished typing up her notes from the interview with Terry the previous day. Suddenly the memory of her excitement, the thrill of playing a key role in securing a cast-iron conviction, came rushing back.

How everything had changed in such a short space of time.

She reached for the folder and flicked through. The findings from the forensic search of Terry's car were still pending. One of those loose ends that Alex would want tying up, regardless of recent events. But Bob had been clear; no one was to do anything without his say so.

'Spencer, have you seen Bob?' she called over to the youngster, who had his head buried in paperwork.

He looked over to Bob's desk as though having to confirm for himself the scruffy detective's absence.

'No.'

He went back to whatever it was he was reading.

'Well do you have any idea where he might be?' she asked.

'Probably trying to find out the latest on Alex.'

She could feel her heart thump out a warning.

'What about Alex?'

Spencer opened his mouth to speak but stopped. He stood up and covered the short distance to her desk.

'You can't tell anyone you know this. I only know because Debbie in HR told me.' He took a sly look about him and a cold feeling started to crawl down Cat's spine. 'It's his son. He's got meningitis.'

Cat's mouth fell open. 'Cody? Shit. Is he bad?'

'He's in intensive care. Apparently, they don't know if he's going to make it.'

'Oh my God.' Cat felt her stomach tighten. 'But Alex was at the scene with us last night. He didn't say anything. Why was he there if his son was so ill?'

Spencer gave a shrug and shook his head before returning to his desk.

'Oh,' Cat said weakly.

She couldn't begin to imagine how Alex must be feeling. She'd been upset enough at Pete's death, but the loss of a big brother couldn't possibly be compared to a son, especially one so young.

The motion of the tear as it splashed on the printed page beneath took her by surprise. She wiped a hand discreetly across her cheek and looked around her to check that no one had noticed. Her gaze settled once more on the file for Mary Joseph.

She needed to keep busy. She reached for the phone and put it to her ear. Thinking she could hear Bob, she paused. She looked around but Bob was still nowhere to be seen. Her hand hovered over the phone's keypad.

If Bob wasn't around what was she supposed to do?

'Oh, this is ridiculous,' she muttered before making the call.

The young man in a white lab coat checked Cat's ID.

'You were quick,' he said. There had been little traffic between the station and the forensic labs. 'I'll just fetch it. I got it out straight after you called.'

He left Cat waiting and slipped out of the room, returning moments later with a small carton the size of a shoebox. He set it down on the counter in front of her.

'Look on the bright side, we found virtually nothing in the car. Someone had given it a bloody good clean.' He slid a form and a pen across the counter. 'Just need a signature.'

'I was told there were still some test results outstanding. Any idea when they'll be done?' Cat said, as she scrawled illegibly in the required box.

'Shouldn't be too long. I can give you a ring when they're in if you like?'

'That'd be helpful, thanks.'

The lab assistant filed the signed release in a tall cabinet. He sent the green metal drawer clanging back into place. They said their goodbyes and Cat was halfway out of the door when she turned back.

'Excuse me!' she called.

The lab assistant stopped at the door and looked back at her.

'What did you mean, look on the bright side?'

'It was only an observation. It's just that we found no trace of any fluids, like blood or semen and the only prints we found were his. There was no evidence that anyone else has ever been in that car.'

'How's that good?'

'The car has been completely cleaned, and I mean soaped down, inside and out. Recently and pretty thoroughly too. It's one of the cleanest cars I've ever seen. Pretty unusual for a small-time drug dealer; even keen car enthusiasts don't tend to be as meticulous.'

Cat remembered all too clearly what a pit Terry's house had been. Oh, and the smell. She wrinkled her nose at the memory of the stench, a mixture of unwashed dishes, dirty clothes and sweaty flesh.

'A clean car, huh?'

'A *very* clean car.'

She held up the box that she'd traipsed all the way there for. 'I don't suppose there's much of interest in here then?'

The lab assistant gave a twitch of his eyebrows.

'You'll be surprised.'

Cat gave him a puzzled look, before putting the box back under her arm and making her exit. And like a good girl on the advent of Christmas she waited until she was back in the office before sliding a finger under the seal and lifting the lid open.

Inside was a small collection of labelled plastic bags and bottles, each one marked with an evidence reference number. She lifted them out and examined them one at a time. Most was rubbish: a crumpled cigarette packet and the odd sweet wrapper. She returned those to the box. Of more interest, in a clear plastic evidence bag, was what looked like a bar of chocolate partly sheathed in a homemade aluminium foil wrapper. The label showed that it had yet to be identified, pending chemical analysis. She peered at an open end. On closer inspection she could see that it was more fibrous and crumblier than chocolate. Picking up the packet, she approached Spencer.

'Spence, take a look at this.'

He took the bag from her and turned it over, pressing it gently between his fingers.

'Black, probably from Pakistan.' He handed the bag back to her.

'That's what I thought... that it was dope I mean. I hadn't got a clue what type. How can you tell?'

'Years of practice,' Spencer said, tapping his nose. 'Where'd you get it from?'

'It was in Terry Phillip's car. His prints are all over it.'

'What a muppet.'

Cat let slip a small smile, not at Spencer's choice of words but rather at their good fortune. A dope charge would mean more time for Terry in custody, which meant more time to consider the case against him.

An hour later and Cat was standing in front of the murder board for Mary. It was six-thirty and she was alone in the office. Or rather, she had been.

'What are you doing still here?' Bob Bells said as he walked through the door, a cup of vending machine coffee in his hand.

He sounded suspicious.

Cat was considering her answer when he started to cough and choke.

'For God's sake! It's the twenty-first century, we can put a man on the moon but we can't get a machine that can turn out a decent cup of instant coffee.' Grimacing he set the cup down roughly on the table and thrust a finger in his mouth trying to prise out bits of gritty un-dissolved coffee caught between his teeth.

He picked the vending machine cup up and walked over to join her at the murder board.

'What are you up to?' he said, looking from Cat to the murder board.

She turned towards the tired-looking detective. The skin around his teeth and jaw rippled and ballooned as his tongue

107

squirmed around the inside of his mouth, chasing down the last of the coffee granules. She turned back to the board to stop her distaste from showing.

'Nothing,' she said.

Out of the corner of her eye she could see him scowl at her.

'Bullshit. Everyone else has packed up for the day yet you're still here. Why?'

Why did he have to be so confrontational?

She sighed.

'I don't know...' She looked back at the board. 'I was just trying to figure out how Terry fits in to all of this. We found some hash in his car.'

'I heard.'

Cat shot him a look.

'Custody Sarge told me on the way through. I also heard that they've found a load more in a lock-up that he rents. But that don't make him no killer.'

Cat flinched at his choice of vernacular which sounded like some poor imitation of an American gumshoe. Maybe that explained the ruffled, dirty mackintosh he had taken to wearing.

'I know that but...'

'Cat,' he said, in an overly affected patronising tone. 'Terry Phillips was tucked up in bed, courtesy of the taxpayer when Megan Daniels was killed. He couldn't have done it. I said it before and I don't mind saying it again: you got it wrong.'

She looked at him but a suitable rejoinder eluded her. She broke off her stare and walked over to her desk, reaching down its side to retrieve a black fabric case.

'What are you doing now?' he asked.

'I'm taking my laptop home. I've got some notes to finish off.'

'Tonight?'

'Yes. Is there a problem with that?'

Without waiting for him to reply Cat unlatched the device from its docking station and slipped it into the bag.

'Doesn't your husband mind you working at night?' Bob said.

'Mike's not my husband and anyway he's away with some friends.'

'On a Tuesday?'

'That's what I said.'

'Anywhere nice?'

'Las Vegas. It's a stag do.'

She realised she'd said too much the second the words left her mouth.

'Get in my son!'

'Bob, just think about who you're saying that to. We may not be married but we do live together.'

'You were the one that said he's not your husband. You can't have it both ways.'

Cat bit her tongue. She was tired. It had been a long day. There had been many an occasion when she had felt sorry for Mrs Bob Bells but none more so than now.

Grabbing her handbag and the computer case, she slung them over her shoulder and made her way to the door.

'See you tomorrow, bright and early,' Bob called out after her.

The sound of her heels growing quieter on the tiled floor was her only reply.

The next morning Cat arrived at the office to find her desk hidden behind a barricade of reinforced cardboard storage crates. There were at least twenty, maybe even thirty boxes. She divested herself of her coat and bag, dragged a couple of the large containers aside to clear enough space to get to her chair and sat down. She looked around for any note to explain the wall of cardboard, but apart from her own files her desk was empty.

She stood up again and, choosing a box at random, lifted the lid. Immediately she recognised the contents as having come from Megan Daniels' study. She was about to go looking for Bob, intending to ask what the hell he wanted her to do with them all, when his voice rang out from behind her.

'This is a bloody health and safety hazard.' Cat watched him navigate his way through the maze of boxes with an over-filled mug of tea in one hand and a round of buttered toast in the other. 'Should keep you busy for a while though,' he said as he passed.

Cat cast him a sideways glance, unsurprised to see a sly smile on his face.

'What am I supposed to do with it all?' she asked.

Bob paused and laid down his mug on top of one of the boxes. He took a large bite of toast before balancing what remained of the slice on the rim of the cup. Without wiping the melted butter from his fingers, he took a handful of papers from the open box and began flicking through them, a trail of greasy prints marking his progress.

'What you're going to do is read through this lot and see if you can find anything that might lead us to someone who wanted the woman dead. Especially any links to Ginger.'

'You mean Mary.'

'That's what I said.' He pushed the papers towards her chest. She took them from him.

'And you want me to do all of it? On my own?'

'You're always saying how you like to be busy.'

'What's Spencer doing? Can't he help?'

'Don't you worry your pretty little head about what anyone else is doing.' He picked up his tea and toast. 'Chop-chop. The sooner you start, the sooner you'll be finished.'

Speechless, Cat watched Bob amble over to his desk, where he took another bite of his breakfast whilst unfolding a rumpled copy of the Daily Mail that he'd extracted from his raincoat pocket. She knew then that he'd never intended to bring her into the investigation, regardless of what Alex may have told him to do.

The unjustness of it rankled. Seething, she roughly shunted

the boxes around. All the while an internal commentary raced through her head as she envisaged a whole range of dark and delicious ways to get back at Bob. Soon, though, she became engrossed in the contents of the boxes and her anger abated. As intimate as it was interesting, Cat found herself gaining a great insight into the dead woman that she could never have got from simply talking to her husband.

Every so often she would pause and think about Craig Daniels and of her growing realisation that the victims of murder weren't only those who had died, but also those who were left behind. Death of a loved one transformed the weak, the old, the strong and the young into one and the same. No one escaped the relentless strain that their emotions subjected them to. After one such moment of sentimental reflection, Cat happened to glance around at the boxes that remained untouched. Her back gave a sudden twinge, the tension in her muscles making itself felt. She stood up and rolled her shoulders, then stretched and twisted from side to side. It was while rolling her neck, grimacing at the crunching and clicking noises it made, that she spotted Bob at Alex's desk. He had the phone pressed to his ear. Just at that moment he noticed her looking and beckoned for her to join him. She felt a small glimmer of hope. He lowered the phone and covered the mouthpiece.

'Have you seen the post-mortem report on Megan Daniels?'

'No, I–'

But Bob raised a finger, stopping her mid-sentence. He wedged the phone between his ear and his shoulder.

'When did you say you sent it?' He began to root through Alex's in-tray, sending unopened letters and junk mail toppling. 'Hang on. This might be it.' He pulled out an oversized manila envelope and tore it open. After upending the package into his hand, he tilted his head and read the cover sheet. 'Yep, got it. Thanks. Bye.'

Bob put the phone down and switched his attention to Cat.

'You can go now. I got what I was after.'

'You're sure there's nothing you want any help with?'

Bob looked surprised and for a split-second Cat thought she had misjudged him.

'You've finished going through the boxes?'

'No, but I thought...'

'Now that's where you're going wrong. You don't think, you just do. Do as I tell you.'

Cat could feel her face flush as her anger flooded through her like lava through a volcano. Only there was nowhere for her frustration to vent, not without getting herself into trouble.

'You still here?' Bob said.

Too angry to go back to her desk, Cat decided to take a break. Ten minutes later, with her blood pressure restored to a healthy level, she was back at her desk with a large mug of coffee and a packet of sandwiches, which she set about wrestling out of their plastic moulded wrapper. Exhaling noisily, she lifted the lid on her eighth box and carried on where she'd left off. Two boxes later, it was nearly the end of the shift when Bob sidled up to her, a smug smile fixed on his scrawny lips.

He threw a package onto her desk. Cat recognised the thick envelope from its ripped-open end. She looked back at Bob.

'Post-mortem report for Megan Daniels. Read it and weep. Strangled with a thin wire or cord. Guess the same perp did for her as did for Ginger. This lets that little scrote Terry Philips off the hook, given he was banged up when the Daniels woman was killed. Looks like I was right after all.'

She clenched her jaw; it was the only way she was going to stop herself saying something she might regret. Bob appeared not to notice. He was looking over the columns of boxes that surrounded Cat's desk like a cardboard fort constructed by an eight-year-old.

'How are you getting on?'

'These are done,' she said, pointing to a row to the left of her desk. It accounted for about a third of the boxes. 'That just leaves these.' She gestured despondently to the rest.

Bob gingerly lifted up a vending pack in which a half-eaten cheese and pickle sandwich lay curling at the edges. He moved it to one side before picking up a handful of papers from a pile that Cat had carefully sorted.

'No, no, no...' She reached across and quickly grabbed them from him. 'Don't mix those up. I'm trying to put the important stuff in chronological order. Whoever packed this must have just stuffed it in. It's all over the place.'

'Probably knew how much you like a puzzle,' Bob said with a malicious grin. 'Well, keep at it, only another twenty to go,' he said, walking away. Cat watched him pick his coat up and head for the door.

She gave herself a mental shake, brushing off the anger before it could settle, and kneeled down, ready to start on the next box. Legwork, as Alex had told her so many times, was the backbone of detective work. Cat didn't know about backbone, but it was certainly backbreaking. She sat back on her heels and stretched her arms wide. Her hand connected with something solid.

'Hey, watch out.'

She turned.

'Sorry Spence. I wasn't expecting you to be there. Are you alright?'

'I'm fine,' he said. 'I just wondered if you wanted a hand.'

'Are you serious?'

'Yeah, well, I've finished what I had to do.'

'But it's the end of the shift. You could just go home.'

'Look, do you want some help or not?'

Six hours on and they had cleared the contents of all twenty-seven boxes. Twenty-eight if you included the pizza box in which only a few crumbs remained of a large cheese and mushroom thin crust. They had run out of coffee hours ago. But what they didn't know of the lives and loves of Megan's far-reaching family wasn't worth knowing.

'Are we done?' Spencer asked, rolling his shoulders.

'I think so. Thanks. I don't know what I'd have done without you.'

Cat pushed her fingers through her hair. She didn't need a mirror to know that there were dark circles under her eyes, serving to underline her tiredness.

Spencer stretched his arms wide, flexing his back, while he walked to his desk.

'At least we got two potential lines of enquiry, excluding the cousin of course,' Cat said, putting the lid onto the last box, her desk finally free of papers. 'I expect Bob's already interviewed her.'

'Two? Who else is there apart from that other Mrs Daniels?' Spencer asked, referring to an entry in Megan's diary, which showed a coffee date with someone of the same name.

'There's the haemophilia clinic. Megan had an appointment there recently.'

Spencer screwed his nose up.

'What is that anyway?'

'What – haemophilia?'

'Yeah.'

'It's like a blood disorder, where the body doesn't make enough clotting agent. In the past sufferers would bleed to death if they had a deep enough cut. But there are drugs to help manage it these days.'

'She didn't have a lot of luck, did she?'

'I don't think she had it. If I've understood her family tree correctly, she was just a carrier.'

'So does it matter then? What are you going to ask them at the clinic?'

'I know it's a bit of a long shot but I thought if she went regularly, then... well, I don't know – maybe someone there took a shine to her.'

'Like a stalker?' Spencer said as he slipped his coat on.

'I don't know. To be honest I'm just clutching at straws.'

'You never know,' Spencer said. 'I remember reading about a serial killer who chose his victims by where they sat in the hospital waiting room relative to him when he went for dialysis. We could go and see them tomorrow.'

'We?'

'I'll come with you,' he volunteered. 'You shouldn't go on your own.'

Cat paused for a minute and thought about it. It was a ridiculous suggestion… but then Bob was being such an arse.

Twelve

Philip Wilson, the Clinical Director of the Haemophilia Treatment Centre, stood and reached across his desk to shake their hands. A tall, willowy man, he moved with a grace that portrayed an air of respectability and confidence that befitted his seniority.

Cat and Spencer sat across from him and explained the reason for their visit. The director adopted a thoughtful expression as he listened; occasionally he would raise an index finger, stopping their account to clarify a detail. When they'd finished, he turned to his computer and set about interrogating the Unit's various data bases for any reference to Megan Daniels.

While she waited, Cat looked around the sparsely furnished, windowless room. She hated hospitals. Hated hospital rooms, soulless voids with walls impregnated with the smell of antiseptic cleaners, which only emphasised the presence of sickness, death and disease.

She thought about Alex; wondered whether Cody was any better. Hoped he was, so Alex would return to work soon, and immediately felt selfish for it.

'Cat,' Spencer said sharply.

She looked at him, aware she'd zoned out of the conversation.

'Yes?' she said, hoping he'd have the sense to repeat the question.

'The date?'

Cat looked at him blankly. She felt a hit of panic – which date? The grey-haired man opposite was watching her with a benign smile. She knew she'd have to take a punt.

'The twenty-ninth,' she said, quoting the day of the

appointment that had been recorded in Megan Daniels' diary.

The director looked down to his small notepad. He looked back up at Cat, peering over his half-moon spectacles, pen poised.

'I believe that was the date Mrs Daniels had down as having an appointment here – an appointment that we have no record of. What I was asking for was the date that Mrs Daniels was attacked.'

'Oh, that was just three days ago, the seventh,' she said.

Mr Wilson noted the second date in his pad before returning the cap to his Mont Blanc fountain pen.

'Okay. Well, as our data bases have drawn a blank, I can confidently say that we have not recently treated this woman in any capacity but I will ask the staff if they know the name. I'll also get someone to check the archives, just in case. Do you have a number you can be contacted on?'

Cat handed the director a business card, which he carefully placed on the blotter that rested next to his computer. He stood up, lifting his chair to prevent it scraping noisily across the floor.

'If that's everything?'

'Yes, thank you,' Cat said. 'We appreciate you sparing the time.'

She couldn't help but wonder what exactly they had accomplished.

The director glanced at his watch.

'The hospital will do whatever it can to help but now, if you will excuse me, I've got a clinic that was due to start five minutes ago.' He picked up a binder full of papers and guided the two detectives out into the corridor.

'Christ, I made a balls-up of that,' Cat said, as they made their way out of the hospital. 'He must think we're fresh out of kindergarten.'

'It wasn't that bad,' Spencer said, unconvincingly.

She just shook her head and sighed.

To Cat's relief, no one commented on her and Spencer's late arrival at the office, probably because the only person who would have cared wasn't there. Her stomach danced a little jig on seeing Bob's unoccupied chair. She knew she was going to have to face a ton of grief when he found out about their off-piste visit to the haemophilia unit but better later, or never, she reasoned.

She turned and stared at her own desk and the mountain of boxes surrounding it. Her heart sank. She'd forgotten about the boxes. And to make matters worse someone had moved them, shunting them back in front of her desk to make it easier for everyone else to get around the office.

Fed up with working in the equivalent of a Syrian shanty town, she dropped her bag and coat on the floor where she stood and started to heft the boxes over to the wall nearest her desk. One by one she humped the crates into five neat stacks, until only one remained on her desk, obscuring her computer, in-tray and – even more sacrilegious – her coffee mug. She reached for the box and, bracing herself, knowing how heavy it was likely to be, she yanked it towards her. The noise of files and pens and God knows what else clattering onto the floor filled her with dread. She froze. Setting the box down, she blew her cheeks out and peered over the edge of her desk. The box had clipped the corner of her in-tray, sending it and its contents tumbling. There was paperwork everywhere.

She closed her eyes and counted to ten before rounding her desk where she began the arduous task of gathering up the scattered items. Her heart sank even further when she spotted the evidence box from Terry's car that she'd picked up from the lab the day before. It was lying on its side, its lid some distance away. She'd left it by her in-tray, not quite ready to give up on it and log it into the evidence store. She started to throw the plastic evidence bags back into the box. Suddenly a feeling of cold dread stole over her. One of the bags appeared to be empty. Taking care not to move her feet, for fear of treading on anything or kicking whatever it was under the desk, she held the bag up and read the label. It was supposed to contain a small decorative bead – a plastic simulated pearl with a small hole through its centre.

As she read, Cat noticed that the bag was still sealed. She held it up to the light and squinted and there, tucked in a corner, was a single bead, just as the label described. Cursing herself for jumping to conclusions she threw the bag with the bead back into the evidence box and replaced the lid.

With her desk finally cleared and order restored, Cat reached for her computer's on-button. She opened her notepad to her record of the meeting with the director of the haemophilia unit, ready to start her write-up, when she paused. What was Bob going to make of it when she showed it to him? Plus, there was her trip to the forensics lab. At what point was she going to mention she'd made two unscheduled trips in two days?

She looked at the evidence box from Terry's car. Protocol dictated that she make Bob aware she'd got it, but he'd all but dismissed Terry as a suspect. He'd probably just tell her to return it, minus the dope.

Before he did, she just wanted to be sure...

She tipped the contents of the box on to her desk and, more slowly than before, took a close look at each item. She picked up the packet containing the tiny bead. The label informed her that the bead had been found under the front passenger seat, wedged in the adjustment mechanism. She turned it over in her hand. It didn't appear to have suffered any damage. A frown clouded her brow. Seized with an idea, she slipped the packet into her pocket and stopped by Spencer's desk to ask yet another favour.

Cat entered the interview room. Terry was already sitting at the table. To her frustration he looked no less tired or stressed than the last time she had last seen him. In fact, he looked like he'd had an extremely recuperative night's sleep. She pressed the door closed behind her.

'Hey, what's this? Where's the other guy?'

'If you mean DS Bells he's tied up on other business. I'll be conducting your interview today,' she told him as she took a new disc out of its case and slotted it into the recorder.

'I want to talk to the organ grinder not the monkey. I'm saying nothing till the boss can be bothered to come and talk to me himself.' Terry slouched down in his seat, stretched his legs, crossing them at the ankles, and clasped his hands behind his head.

The door opened and Spencer walked in, carrying three cups of vending machine coffee. He set them down on the table. He slid one of the plastic cups across to Terry as Cat pulled a single cigarette and box of matches from her pocket. Terry may have been motionless but his eyes followed her every move. She held the cigarette towards him, tantalisingly close. His snatched for it, but Cat was faster. She whipped it out of his reach.

'Whoa, not just yet, you don't. You can't smoke in here but if you stay and talk, then we'll arrange to take you back to your custody cell via the courtyard and you get to enjoy this. Act like a child and you can go straight back into the lockup.'

A look of longing crossed Terry's face.

'Ask away but don't expect anything different today.'

Cat switched the recorder on. After the usual formalities she began.

'You'll be pleased to hear that forensics have given your car a thorough going over.'

Terry's trademark sneer sprung on his lips.

'They hadn't better have damaged anything. I'll fucking sue if they have.'

'You should be thanking us,' Cat said. 'Your car has never been so clean. At least not since you last wiped it down. When exactly was that?' But without waiting for him to answer she continued, 'Based on the evidence, it looks like it was soon after the night that Mary disappeared.'

'You've found nothing,' he said, with an arrogant tilt to his chin.

'Not quite true.' Cat smiled. 'Now Terry, would I be right in saying that running a Hoover around isn't your forte? It would be easy after all to miss something small. A piece of jewellery, for example?'

'I don't know what you're talking about.'

If what Cat was saying was worrying him he was doing a good job of concealing it. She thought it may solicit a bigger response if she adopted a more direct approach.

'Let me spell it out for you. When searching your car, aside from the class 'C' drugs, we found something that puts Mary slap bang in it on the night of her murder.'

'Bullshit. If you found something it means nothing. I could have had plenty of girls in the back of the car besides Mary.'

Cat was sure that if he could have swaggered as he spoke, he would have. But confidence comes before a fall and she seized the opportunity to give him a helping push.

'*Besides* Mary? You're admitting that you did in fact have Mary in the car at some point? For the record Mr Phillips clearly stated that he may have had other women in his car *besides* Mary.'

'You're twisting my words.'

'Your words Terry, not mine.'

'I meant it didn't have to be Mary. It could have been someone else.'

'Okay Terry, give us a list of other women that you have had in your car who could have dropped a piece of jewellery and we'll go and talk to them.'

'What sort of jewellery?'

'The sort that Mary was wearing. Does that help?'

'Very fucking funny.' He locked eyes with Cat, his lip curled into a nasty snarl. 'You're a lying bitch. You've got nothing on me.'

'That's where you're wrong. So why don't you start talking.'

'I'll talk alright.'

Cat resisted the urge to smile.

'Good,' she said.

'No comment – that talking enough for you?'

She let out a sigh and started to gather the cups up from the table.

'So why haven't you charged me? Eh? If you've got all this evidence. You're gonna have to let me go soon.'

Cat formally ended the interview and she and Spencer left the room.

'Oi, bitch, what about that fag you promised...' Terry called after them.

'God, he's a cool customer,' she whispered as they walked away, seriously doubting their ability to break him.

Back in the office they returned to what they should have been doing. Sick of the sight of paperwork, Cat was contemplating when would be a respectable time to head home, when she heard a bang as the office door slammed into the wall. She looked up. Bob had just come in and was heading her way. He planted both hands down on her desk and leaned towards her, his livid face inches from hers. She pulled her head back, away from the sour stench of stale coffee and cigarettes. Bob moved his head forward, closing the gap even further.

'What's this I've heard about you interviewing a suspect?'

Cat wheeled her chair a few inches from her desk.

'I came across some evidence which I thought might get a response from Terry and... well, you weren't here, so I–'

'Evidence?'

Cat started to rummage around in the evidence box for the small polythene packet that had first given her the idea.

Bob didn't look happy.

'Here,' she said, handing him the small package.

But Bob didn't bother to look at it. He was too busy glaring at her.

'Have you forgotten our earlier conversation?' Cat looked at him blankly. 'I already told you, the game has moved on with the Daniels woman's death. Your man didn't do it. Not unless he's bloody Houdini.'

'You're right.' Cat said. Bob eased back and regarded her suspiciously. 'I don't think Terry did kill Mrs Daniels. I was planning on arresting him for the murder of Mary Joseph.'

Bob pushed himself away from her desk angrily.

'Well then you're more stupid than I thought,' he said more loudly than was warranted, and Cat was sure the rest of the office would now be looking at them. He stuck a finger out and pointed towards the door. 'Go down to custody and tell them to let Mr Philips go. Now!'

He started to walk away, but then stopped and looked at the plastic bag still in his hand. He turned back and flung it at Cat. It landed at her feet.

Her cheeks were burning. Not just at Bob's comments but at the fact she knew she was being watched by the others, most of whom would have enjoyed seeing her get torn off a strip. And so she smiled. Only a small curve of the lips but it was enough to give the impression that she didn't care; a small achievement perhaps, but worth doing nonetheless.

Cat threw the bead back into the evidence box. It had seemed such an inspired discovery but as she sat there, she wondered how she could have got it so wrong.

If Terry was responsible for Mary's death, then who the hell had killed Megan? She opened her notepad and scanned the notes she had made from her review of Megan's belongings. Essentially it had come down to three simple questions:

1. Caroline Berry: if Megan didn't meet her cousin as planned why didn't her cousin call Megan's home to see where she was?

2. The haemophilia clinic: was Megan's recent appointment there relevant?

3. The coffee date with Mrs Daniels the day before she died: who is she?
   Did Megan say anything to her when they met?

She tapped the final line with her pencil. Nowhere in all of the boxes of paperwork did she find a number or address for Mrs Daniels. She thought back to Craig Daniels. One quick call was all it would take.

Her hand was halfway to the phone when Spencer walked past.

'Hey, Spence,' she said.

He stopped and turned around.

'What?'

'Are you planning on leaving soon?' She kept her voice low but above whispering level to avoid any unwanted attention.

'Whatever it is, I don't want to know.' He started to walk away.

Cat hated using her girly, whiny voice but sometimes she was left with no alternative.

'Spence, please...' She gave a smile like a four-year-old begging for just one more ride on the carousel.

Spencer hesitated. 'What is it?' he asked over his shoulder.

'It's only that I was thinking of following up on the other lead we got from Megan Daniels' diary.'

'Lead?'

'Okay, that might be over-egging it a bit. I meant that other Mrs Daniels, the one Megan had coffee with the day before she died. I was thinking of calling Craig Daniels to see if he'd got a number for her. If I go, will you come with me?'

He slipped his hands into his trouser pockets. Cat took his lack of reply as a positive sign.

'It won't take long. Somebody needs to check these things out.'

'Maybe they already are.'

'I don't see how; nobody knows about them. Bob didn't give me a chance to tell him.' Cat looked over at Bob's empty desk. 'Where is Bob anyway?'

'I don't know. I heard him bitching about some problems with the house-to-house enquiries; not enough uniforms or something. He might have gone to sort that out.'

Cat gave a little snort.

'He's probably out there doing the house-to-house himself. I mean why wouldn't he, when he's got a team of trained professionals who could get involved?'

Spencer shifted about uncomfortably.

'Sorry Spence. I don't mean to sound off at you. He just pisses me off. The way he does stuff... nobody knows anything because he hasn't held a single team briefing since he's been in charge. All I want is to do something useful so we can make some progress, so when Alex gets back–'

'And get more of what Bob dished out to you earlier?' Spencer interrupted. 'No thank you.'

Cat knew it had been a long shot. Spencer was so much more one of the boys than she'd ever be.

'It's okay. It was only a thought. God, I wish Alex was here.' She was sure he would have encouraged her to take the initiative and follow things up on her own; provided she gave him a heads-up, of course.

'But he isn't and Bob is,' Spencer said.

'Don't I know it? Look, don't worry about it. I'll go on my own. I wouldn't want to get you into trouble.'

Spencer looked at his watch. It was already gone five.

'It's just that I'm supposed to be…'

He looked at his watch again and tutted and sighed like a used car salesman being pressured for a bigger discount.

'Alright, I'll do it. I'll come with you. But only if we can be quick about it.'

'Spence you're a star. Tell you what, we'll go in our own cars, so you can go straight home. Let me give Craig Daniels a quick call to get this woman's address and phone number then we'll go. Okay?'

They set off across the car park at a brisk pace. Cat focussed on keeping her head held high, walking tall, not wanting to look as guilty as she felt. Spencer on the other hand looked about furtively.

'We need to get over to the other side of town,' she explained. 'Mrs Daniels lives on Bradbury Road.'

'What is she then? Some relative?' Spencer asked.

'It seems not. It's just a coincidence that they had the same name. Craig Daniels said that Megan had helped the old woman with some funeral arrangements. Apparently, she's something to do with the church.'

'Why are we bothering then?'

'I assume that was a rhetorical question, given she was one of the last people who saw Megan before she died,' she said, trying not to make him sound stupid. She really didn't want to have to go on her own.

In contrast to most of Cat's recent house calls, the outside of 117 Bradbury Road was immaculate. The same could be said of Mrs Daniels. A petite and well-spoken lady, she was perfectly attired in a black cashmere jersey and grey woollen skirt. Despite no obvious physical similarity, when the front door opened Cat was immediately reminded of her mother. It was only when the old lady leaned forward and greeted her, gently clasping Cat's hand between her own elegant manicured fingers that Cat understood why. The same exotically spiced, woody notes of her mother's choice of perfume caught in the back of her throat, the feminine fragrance escaping on the warm, central-heated air.

With the introductions complete and good-quality English breakfast tea poured into her best bone china cups, the elderly Mrs Daniels turned her attention to the two detectives. She spoke with a soft voice that still retained a hint of the local dialect. Although very eloquent and clearly very much still with it, she responded to their questions with some timidity.

'I couldn't believe it when I heard the terrible news. It really shook me up. It's a wicked world that we live in where somebody so kind and considerate can be struck down like that.'

Cat nodded sympathetically.

'Of course, I'm very keen to help but I'm not sure I know anything.' Mrs Daniels gave them both an intense look with grey watery eyes.

'It looks like you were one of the last people to have seen Megan before she died. There's a chance something she said to you is significant.'

'Was I really? Oh.' The old lady's face grew a shade paler.

'Why don't you tell us how you and Megan knew each other?' Cat suggested, hoping the question would serve as a gentle warm-up.

Mrs Daniels eased back in her seat.

'I only met her recently. You see I do a lot of work at the local church. I help with the flower arrangements and organise the odd coffee morning, that sort of thing. Well, a couple of months ago a friend of mine sadly passed away. He was one of our parishioners; a regular church-goer. A real old-fashioned gentleman. When I heard he wasn't going to be given a proper funeral I was beside myself. It just wasn't right. I contacted his daughter and told her what I thought of that idea. In the end she –
'

'I'm sorry Mrs Daniels,' Cat said, interrupting. 'Are you talking about Megan? Only I thought her father had died some time ago?'

The old lady's wrinkled features smoothed a little.

'No, the daughter's name is Caroline. But oh yes, I see. I should have explained. The gentleman who died was Megan's uncle, Howard Williams. You're right about Megan's father. In fact, both of her parents died in the same car accident when she was little more than a girl. I didn't know them but I remember hearing about it at the time. A terrible tragedy.'

'The woman that you spoke to, that was Megan's cousin, Caroline Berry?' Cat asked.

'Yes, that's right. Actually, it was her husband I talked to. Apparently, Caroline was too ill to travel and wasn't up to making the funeral arrangements.' She gave a sad shake of her head. 'I know the woman couldn't help being unwell but you can't let that get in the way of organising a decent Christian burial, can you? I must admit I was quite taken aback. Mr Williams had spoken of his daughter so fondly in recent months. I thought she would have found some way to sort it all out. In the end, I saw no alternative but to do it myself. It's such a shame, such bad timing.'

'And Megan?' Cat prompted.

'What a thoughtful girl.' Once again, the powdery features of the old woman folded with the semblance of a smile. 'She really was a Godsend. I don't know what I would have done without her. I was determined to make sure that Howard's funeral was properly attended but you see I only knew him from his involvement in the church. And then somebody...' She paused and momentarily closed her eyes. 'No, I'm sorry, it's gone. Anyway, whoever it was, they told me that Megan would know who to invite because she knew all of the family. You know about her interest in her family tree?'

Cat nodded.

Mrs Daniels continued, 'I hadn't realised, but it turns out that when Megan's parents died, Howard and his wife, she was alive then God bless her, took Megan in. Howard even gave her away at her wedding. Did you know that?' Cat shook her head and was about to make a comment but Mrs Daniels pressed on. 'No, I didn't either. Howard was so modest about his own benevolence.'

A faraway look settled on her face and she sat saying nothing for a few seconds. She gave a little shake of her head. 'Well as it turned out, Megan was able to give me details of Howard's relatives as well as some of his old business contacts. It was so nice that everybody had the chance to say goodbye to him. You should have seen the beautiful things that they wrote on the condolence cards that came with the wreaths. Megan and I went through them all after the funeral.' The old lady sighed. 'We really did give him a wonderful send off.'

'I'm sure you did. And I imagine the family are very grateful.' Cat waited a beat before bringing the conversation back to the reason for their call. 'So the other day, when Megan called, was it just for a chat or was there a reason for her visit?'

'Oh, that was just for a chat. It was lovely to see her in... well, better circumstances. We hadn't seen each other since the funeral. We said then that it would be nice to stay in touch. I was over the moon when she called last week. She told me she'd arranged to meet Caroline and wondered if I still had the condolence cards I just told you about.'

Thirteen

Cat lay in bed contemplating an early morning run after another fitful night's sleep, unable to settle with the case playing heavily on her mind. After five minutes of thinking about it, she dismissed the idea, knowing her heart wasn't in it, and settled for a light breakfast and an early start in the office.

To say the sight of Alex sitting at his desk, a cup of coffee steaming at his elbow, took her aback was an understatement. Cat literally recoiled on walking through the door. She hadn't expected to see him there. Not yet, not so soon. He looked as though he'd never been away. Only, that wasn't strictly true. He was scowling at her and he had hardly ever done that before.

'Alex,' she said cautiously. 'You're back.'

'Clearly,' he said in a voice that could cut crystal.

If Cat was unsure before, she was in no doubt now: he was mad at her. She looked over at Bob's desk. Unsmiling, Bob was watching her. His pursed lips twitched and Cat imagined how hard it must have been for him to refrain from making his usual malignant comments. Maybe he had nothing more to say. From the look on Alex's face, Bob had already taken the opportunity to bad-mouth her.

But Cat was determined not to rise to the bait. She continued on to her desk and set her bag down before removing her coat. She knew she was going to have to give Alex an account of everything she had been doing but she was smart enough to know that eight o'clock on the first morning of his return wasn't perhaps the best time.

But Cat wasn't the one calling the shots.

Within the hour Cat found herself sitting facing Alex across a table in one of the private meeting rooms, recounting the details behind Terry's arrest, the visit to the haemophilia centre and her meeting with the elderly Mrs Daniels.

'It all sounds like good stuff Cat,' Alex said

Cat smiled, until she saw his mouth begin to form the shape of the next word. 'But...' She let her gaze drop to the floor. She knew what was coming, 'at what point did you decide to blatantly ignore the instruction of a senior officer?'

He didn't have to shout. They both knew she was in the wrong. But then suddenly something snapped. She wasn't going to let Bob the Bullshitter's crap stick to her this time.

'Hang on a minute,' she said. 'I know I should have gone about it differently but if Bob had tried to listen to me once, just once, then I would have gone back to him and tried to talk to him. But he didn't. He didn't try to involve anyone in the case. Instead he disappeared off, no doubt doing the initial enquiries into Megan's murder on his own. He didn't tell any of us what he was doing. And he left me here to go through all the crap that we got from her house. If Spencer hadn't offered to help, I'd still be doing it now. And he never even asked me what I'd found. So okay, I took it on myself to look into a few things. But Alex, Bob wasn't going to bother.' She paused for breath and looked at Alex for any indication that her protestations were having an effect.

'Have you finished?' he asked, his left eyebrow cocked.

'Yes... Well, no. Actually, I thought you'd understand. You're always saying how important it is to be open-minded. Why aren't you having a go at Bob? Just because he's too blinkered to see how maybe there could be two murderers doesn't mean that...'

She stopped, aware of the heat in her face and of Alex's blank expression. She blinked but kept looking at him.

'Now have you finished?'

Alex's features had remained impassive the whole time and Cat still had no idea what he was thinking or whether her impassioned plea had made any difference.

She nodded and pressed her lips tight together.

'There's no room here for mavericks. You're part of a team, whether you like it or not. You should have tried to talk to Bob. The fact that you just assumed he wouldn't listen and didn't bother isn't acceptable. Do you realise that if it wasn't for the custody sergeant checking we could have breached Terry's rights? You can't hold people indefinitely you know.'

Cat nodded.

Alex sat looking at her and she wondered if there was more to come but he emitted a loud sigh and stood up.

'Well, I think I've said enough.'

'What now?'

'I want you to focus on Megan Daniels' murder. Go back to your desk and carry on working on whatever it was Bob told you to do last.'

'But Alex–' Cat was about to repeat her comment about Bob's lack of instruction but he quickly held up an index finger, silencing any further protest.

Feeling raw, after what she felt was an unfair dressing down, she spent the morning rereading and revising her notes, making sure, irrespective of what Alex thought of her judgement, he would have no cause to criticise her efforts when it came to her commitment, or the quality of her paperwork. It came as a complete surprise then, when he later breezed into the office.

'Grab your coat, we're off out,' he said as he passed her desk.

'What? Where to?'

For some reason Cat looked about her, as though someone else was going to supply the answers.

Alex grabbed his car keys off his desk.

'To talk to Mrs Caroline Berry. She's expecting us within the next hour.'

Cat gave him a puzzled look.

'But I thought–'

She was going to say how she thought Bob would have already

been to see her but she didn't want to reopen that can of worms.

'I'm just surprised you want me to come with you,' she ad-libbed quickly.

'I can take someone else if you prefer?'

She didn't need asking twice. Inside she was doing cartwheels. On the surface she kept a straight face. She knew she wasn't out of the woods just yet.

The journey to Mrs Berry's home took Cat and Alex into the stockbroker belt and soon they swapped the city's congested streets for leafy lanes and a landscape of green pastures and ancient woodland.

They navigated through a string of towns and villages until they reached an area known as Roswell Park, an affluent suburb that had found favour with London's elite since the early 1900s. Everything about the place shouted money: smart cars on long driveways, landscaped gardens with perfectly manicured lawns, and houses designed to comfortably accommodate a family of five with space for live-in help. It was a different world from the one they had left behind.

Cat waited until the traffic had thinned before asking the question that had been on her lips all morning.

'How's Cody?'

She continued to look straight ahead at the passing scenery.

The silence stretched for a moment before Alex replied, 'Stable.' His voice cracked a little.

Cat let go of her breath.

'You must be so relieved.'

'It's still early days.'

'But he's out of intensive care?' Cat turned in her seat to look at him.

'Not just yet. Purely precautionary though, so they say.'

She wanted to ask him why he wasn't still sitting it out at the hospital. Why he wasn't waiting by his only son's bedside.

She took another look at his haggard features. A muscle bulged on his jawline; she could see him clenching his teeth. She turned back and watched the road ahead.

A few miles passed and neither of them said anything. Eventually Alex broke the silence.

'So, tell me again, what do we know about this woman?'

With Alex driving, Cat was free to read from her notes.

'Caroline Berry, nee Caroline Williams. Thirty-four years old. She returned to the UK earlier this year following her father's death. She lives with her husband, Steve, and four-year-old son, Jake. They'd been living in Cyprus, where her husband was posted with the army. They'd been there for...' she consulted her notes, 'actually, I don't have that detail. We know from the old lady I talked to that Megan had been very close to her cousin. After Megan's parents died her uncle and aunt, Mr and Mrs Williams, took her in, so she actually lived with Caroline until she went to university. In Megan's diary, marking the page of the day she died, there was a clipping from the local paper's obituary column reporting the death of Howard Williams earlier this year and a family photo of Caroline's eighth birthday. Megan's husband told us Megan had arranged to meet Caroline in the station car park after work. The CCTV shows Megan got off the train at the station as planned but we have no idea what happened after that. I don't know whether someone's already spoken to Caroline Berry to find out why she didn't meet Megan as arranged, or whether she has any idea what Megan was doing in the alley where the assault happened.'

Alex turned onto the Roswell Park estate, slowing the car as they approached a gated entrance.

'Okay. What else? What about possible motives?'

'Howard Williams, Caroline's father, was a very wealthy man.'

'Lucky old Caroline.'

'And lucky old Megan,' she added. 'Well, she would have been, if she'd have lived to enjoy her inheritance. She got a sizeable legacy. We're still waiting for it to be confirmed, but we think it'll go to her husband now.'

'Interesting.'

Alex slowed the car down and stopped opposite the security lodge that guarded the main entrance. As the electric window whirred down, he reached into his jacket pocket for his warrant card and badge, which he held up for the security guard to scrutinise.

'The Laurels, Willow Lane for Mrs Berry.'

Without any challenge the guard flicked a switch and the gate began to slide smoothly open.

'Straight ahead and then first left. The Laurels is the sixth house down, just on the brow of the hill.'

'Thanks,' Alex said but instead of pulling away he leaned out of the window. 'Have you worked here long?'

The guard stepped out of his shelter and walked over to the car. He crouched down.

'A couple of years.'

'Do you know the residents well?'

'Some of them. You get those, mainly the older retired residents, who'll stop and chat. Others barely say hello.'

'What about Mr and Mrs Berry? Are they the type to stop and say hello?'

'They're pleasant enough, I suppose.'

'Only pleasant enough?'

The guard shrugged.

'They haven't been here long. They only moved in after Mr Williams, Mrs Berry's father, died earlier this year. Now he was a friendly guy. He'd always stop and pass the time of day, especially since he retired.'

'Okay, well thanks for your time... Gary,' he said, reading the name off the badge pinned to the security guard's shirt. He started to pull the car away.

'Is it anything serious?' the guard called out.

Alex pressed his foot to the brake and leaned out of the open window.

'What?'

'The reason for your visit: is there something I should know?'

Alex smiled.

'Just routine enquiries.'

He slipped the car into gear and started up the wide tree-lined road, the dappled sunlight making it look like a scene straight out of an American movie.

Alex drove slowly in anticipation of their destination being close. But he hadn't taken account of the houses' extensive grounds. Each mansion-like home sat cocooned in a vacuum of privacy-giving gardens that comfortably distanced it from its nearest neighbour. As a result, it was over a mile before the grounds of the sixth house loomed into view. Alex slowed and stopped by a sign that confirmed that they had finally found 'The Laurels'. Normally he would have parked the car on the road and walked to the house but this wasn't an ordinary house and after the shortest of pauses he put the car into gear and started the long climb up the drive. Cherry trees and laurels marked the boundary to the left and a lawn of bowling-green quality stretched away to their right. The garden rose to a gentle hill at the top of which was a picture-perfect house of a Queen Anne design. Its enormous proportions towered above the surrounding shrubbery. Alex parked the car in front of a triple-bay garage and led the way to the huge double-width front door, theatrically framed by a large decorative portico.

He nodded to the old-fashioned bell-pull.

'Fancy or what?' he said, before pulling down on it hard.

They waited in silence. Soon Cat heard the latch being turned. It would have been quite in keeping if a maid had greeted them, complete with black and white uniform and starched hat, or perhaps an elderly butler, some faithful retainer of the family. Instead it was a thirty-something woman in a casual but expensive-looking outfit who opened the door. Cat took in the heavy make-up and styled hair and concluded that she had either gone to a lot of trouble for their visit or this was a woman with far too much time on her hands.

'You must be the detectives who called.'

'Mrs Berry?' Alex said.

'Oh, call me Caroline,' she said, presenting a hand, her perfectly polished nails shining like freshly poured plastic. 'Come in, come in...' she said after the introductions were complete.

She swept through the cavernous marble-floored hallway and into a tastefully decorated sitting room where she introduced her husband who was standing awkwardly by the fireplace.

'Please take a seat,' she said, offering Alex a chair that looked old and expensive. Cat took in the rest of the furniture, an eclectic mix of antique and modern pieces, all of which oozed quality.

She held back a smile as she watched Alex shift his fourteen stone uneasily on the delicately proportioned piece. She, on the other hand, was ushered to a substantial but equally expensive-looking armchair. She perched on the seat's edge. Any further back and her feet would have been left hanging, barely able to touch the floor. The psychological impact was tangible. She felt like Alice through the looking glass after taking the shrinking potion marked 'drink me'; small and insignificant. She couldn't help but wonder whether the choice of seating had been deliberate. In contrast to their discomfort, Caroline Berry appeared relaxed, settled on a pretty but worn chaise-longue upholstered in red velvet that had faded to the colour of raspberry milkshake. Steve Berry remained standing, centre stage in front of the large marble fireplace, retaining a dominant position. With his pinched features, short cropped hair, jeans and a combat jumper, he looked about as unlikely a candidate for Lord of the Manor as you could get. He observed them through narrowed eyes that fixed his expression into a permanent scowl. Caroline on the other hand was chatty from the outset.

'I still can't believe it. It was such a shock when you called. To think that someone I know, I mean *family*, has been murdered.'

Cat didn't miss the husband's reaction; he flinched at his wife's choice of words but kept his mouth shut.

'Did you know Megan well?' Cat asked, choosing to give the impression they knew nothing about the family background.

'Not really. I hadn't seen her for years. But all the same it's still a shock.' Caroline sounded defensive.

'Of course,' Cat said.

'We understand you were due to meet the afternoon it happened,' Alex said.

Caroline seemed to tense in her seat and cast a glance in the direction of her husband. Cat followed her gaze and saw Steve Berry's pinched scowl intensify. A deep V formed between his brows.

'I was supposed to but I didn't,' she said quickly.

'Why was that?' Alex asked.

'I had a terrible migraine that afternoon. I thought it might pass if I took some tablets and went to bed. And it did. Only I overslept. It was only when Megan phoned, to see where I was, that I woke up – that was just after I was supposed to meet her. Well, I was beside myself. I told her I'd throw some clothes on and drive straight over but she was so understanding, she wouldn't hear of it. We agreed to reschedule when I was feeling better. I felt terrible for letting her down. And now that I know what happened...' She put the back of her hand to her mouth and stifled a sob.

'When she phoned did she say where she was?' Alex asked.

Caroline gave him a puzzled look.

'At the station. That's where I was supposed to meet her.'

'And she told you she was still there, did she?'

'Well, no. I mean, I just assumed.'

Cat made a note of her answer.

Alex continued, 'Did Megan say what she was going to do next?'

'She was just going to go home.'

'And she actually said that?'

'I think so, yes.' Caroline let her eyes roam around the room, a soft frown formed on her forehead. She looked back over to Alex. 'Maybe she didn't. Perhaps it's just what I thought she would do. Sorry, I'm not being much help, am I?'

'That's okay, you're doing your best,' Alex said. 'Now I want you to think very carefully about this next question.' Wide-eyed, Caroline nodded. Alex continued, 'When Megan was on the phone did you hear anything that, with hindsight, given what happened straight afterwards, might be important? Maybe you heard someone in the background, someone trying to talk to her while she was on the phone to you? Perhaps someone asked her the time or what time the next train goes. That type of thing.'

Caroline screwed up her face. Fine lines fanned around her eyes adding at least five years to her appearance.

She shook her head.

'No. I don't remember anything like that.'

Suddenly she opened her mouth, as if to say something, but stopped herself.

'What is it?' Alex said.

'I'm sure it's nothing. It's just that I remember hearing footsteps. I thought Megan had started to walk home while she was on the phone to me but now I'm not so sure. I suppose it could have been someone walking over to her.'

Alex let it go. He looked at Cat, who took the prompt. She leaned forward in her seat and turned to Caroline Berry.

'Mrs Berry, do you know or have you heard of a girl called Mary Joseph?'

Cat heard Steve Berry shift about at his spot by the fire.

'No. I'm sorry. I've never heard of her,' Caroline replied.

Cat looked over to her husband who was staring intently at the carpet.

'What about you, Mr Berry? Does the name mean anything to you?'

He looked up, catching Cat's eye.

'No.'

'Who is she?' Caroline asked.

'It doesn't matter. It's just one of our lines of enquiry,' Cat said.

'Is that everything?' Steve Berry asked, taking a step towards the door.

'Yes, I think so,' Alex said. 'Thank you both for your time.'

He rose from his seat and walked over to the fireplace, to where Steve Berry had been standing. On the mantelpiece was a gilt-framed photograph of a young boy, a formal portrait, old-fashioned and stuffy-looking.

'Good-looking lad,' Alex said.

Steve Berry turned back and smiled. He picked the picture up.

'That's Jake, my son.'

'How old?'

'Just turned four.'

'I bet he's a bit of a handful.' Alex said. 'My boy's five and he...' he stopped and gave a tight-lipped smile. 'Well, he was certainly full of energy at that age.'

'Tell me about it,' Steve Berry said. 'You need eyes in the back of your head sometimes.'

'Especially with his condition,' Caroline added. 'He's got haemophilia. Even with medication he has to be so careful.'

Steve Berry returned the frame to its position on the mantle.

'He's gone swimming with a friend this morning. There's not too much harm that can come to him surrounded by water. Or at least you hope there isn't.'

'Do either of you suffer from it? It's hereditary isn't it?' Cat asked.

140

'No, thank God. All those needles. I can't even stand to watch Jake have his daily injections.' Caroline gave an overdramatic shiver to which her husband rolled his eyes.

He caught Cat watching and momentarily looked embarrassed.

'I'll show you out,' he said, leading them to the front door.

Cat hung back to chat to Caroline.

'You must have been really looking forward to meeting up with your cousin.'

'Yes. Megan helped with the arrangements for my father's funeral. She insisted on meeting up to give me the condolence cards.'

Steve Berry turned and shot his wife an irritated look. 'You should have just left it.' He was still scowling as he explained, 'There was no point. Caroline had been out of touch with her family for so long she wouldn't have a clue who the cards were from.'

He leaned forward and opened the door for his departing guests.

Cat stayed where she was and looked at Caroline, who looked uncomfortable at her husband's candour.

'My father and I had a bit of a falling out,' she said. 'I left home and moved to Cyprus with Steve when he was posted there. It was all a very long time ago.'

'How long?' Cat asked.

'Oh, I don't know, fifteen years ago.'

'Fourteen,' her husband corrected.

Cat turned to Steve Berry. 'Larnaca?'

'That's right.'

'My father served over there briefly in the seventies,' she said.

'Glad to be back?' Alex asked.

'Couldn't be happier, could we darling?' Steve Berry said, turning to his wife. His lips twitched into a semblance of a smile, though his eyes looked flat and expressionless.

'And what do you do now?' Alex asked.

'I've got a little workshop; keep myself busy doing up old classics.'

'Is that just a hobby or...?'

The ex-army man thrust his hands into his pockets and gave Alex a serious look.

'No. I intend on selling them when they're finished. There's a tidy profit to be had in the classic car business.'

'If you know what you're doing,' Caroline said.

Her husband shot her a glance but said nothing.

'Well, that was interesting,' Alex said, as he turned the car around. He was about to begin the descent down to the road when he spotted a car making its way up the drive. He waited for it to pass. Cat looked across at the silver Mercedes and noticed a young boy staring at her through the glass, his blonde tousled hair still damp.

'That'll be the son, back from his swim,' Cat said.

Alex shot a look into the rear-view mirror.

'Nice looking kid.'

'Hope for his sake they work it out,' Cat said.

'Huh?'

'They're obviously going through a rough patch. Her husband couldn't say two words to her without them sounding like an insult.'

'It wasn't that bad.'

Cat pressed her lips together. It wasn't worth arguing over.

Alex put the car into gear. 'Did you say you checked out the old man's will?'

'No. I just heard Bob talking about it. He thinks Megan's inheritance gives her husband a pretty strong motive.'

'He's right.'

She looked at him, surprised.

'You think Megan was killed for money?'

'It wouldn't be the first time.'

The set of Cat's mouth, sulky like a child, showed her displeasure at the idea.

'If it was him, why choose that night?' she said. 'He was expecting her to be out with her cousin. And why the alley? That was pretty high risk.'

'It's the opposite direction to their home. He might have been psychologically distancing himself from the crime.'

She screwed her nose up, showing him exactly what she thought of that theory.

'What about CCTV at the train station? What checks have been done?' Alex asked.

'I don't know. You'd need to ask Bob that.'

Shortly she added, 'Personally I don't think we should just focus on the husband. There must be other people it could have been.'

'I agree. Why do you think I've got Bob following up on that ex-boyfriend thing?'

'What ex-boyfriend thing?' she asked, unable to keep the edge out of her voice.

Alex gave her a sidelong look.

'Seriously?'

'This is the first I've heard about any ex-boyfriend.'

Alex sighed. 'So there really was no briefing?'

Cat fixed him with a stare that could freeze mercury.

'Okay, I'll deal with it,' he said.

'So, what's the ex-boyfriend thing?' she asked.

'Megan had an ex-boyfriend to stay on one of the nights her husband was away.'

Cat whistled.

'So much for the doting couple? What's the ex's take on what's happened?'

'No one's spoken to him yet. Bob's gone to talk to him today.'

'How do we know he stayed?'

'A neighbour mentioned she'd seen a bloke leave the house

early one morning. Bob spoke to Megan's husband about it. He said he knew the ex was coming over for dinner. Megan had told him.'

'And Craig Daniels wasn't upset to learn that he'd actually stayed over?'

'Didn't seem to be. He said they broke up years ago. They're just good friends now. It seems the ex is going through a tough time with his marriage and needed someone to talk to. He said Megan regularly let him bunk down in the spare room when he and his missus had a falling out.'

'Wow.'

'Wow indeed. Jealous husband or jilted lover – take your pick. I'm not sure which one I'd put my money on first. Though given the position with the will, I'd say it's not looking all that good for the husband right now.'

Fourteen

At the point at which the moon and the sun were about to change shifts, the figure of a man cut across the horizon against the backdrop of a mist-clothed lake. He walked briskly with his face buried in his scarf to fend off the damp air that was gnawing at his bones.

He let the energetic cocker spaniel off the lead and stood watching as it bounded around, exhilarated by the fresh morning air. Seconds later it shot towards the water. He whistled and shouted but the dog didn't spare him a backward look. Realising the futility of his calls the man gave up and started after it. His breath billowed from his mouth like a plume of cigarette smoke as he cursed the wretched thing, imagining his wife's complaints at the muddy paw prints through the house. But such trivial concerns vanished the second he spotted the woman, lying motionless, with eyes that stared blankly at the breaking dawn.

'And he didn't recognise her?' Cat asked Alex as they sped towards the lake. He'd picked her up on the way, in response to yet another call about a dead woman found in suspicious circumstances.

'He says she seemed familiar but it was still dark and she'd got a hat on.'

'You said on the phone it must have only just happened.'

'He tried to do CPR but it was too late. He said she still felt quite warm.'

'And no ID?'

'No. But there is a dog.'

Cat looked at him sharply.

'A dog?'

'They found a dog next to the body.'

'Alive?'

'Very much so. With a name tag and contact number. The dog's owner is on his way over. Someone's supposed to be keeping an eye open for him.'

'Let's just hope that the dog hasn't run away from somewhere else,' Cat said.

She didn't venture any more questions but as she stared out of the window, the scenery passing by in a blur, she considered the implications of this latest development. A third woman found dead in as many weeks. If they didn't get a result soon...

'I guess it's pretty clear I was wrong about Terry. I was so sure he'd killed Mary but this has got to be the work of some sort of serial killer, hasn't it?'

'We don't know what we're dealing with yet. This one may bear no resemblance to Megan's murder. And if it does, then look on the bright side; this could be the break we've been waiting for.'

Cat wondered how many times in her career she would hear that said. Knowing he was right didn't really help and an uneasy tension formed deep in the pit of her stomach.

By the time they arrived at the crime scene the early morning mist had cleared to a fine haze of vapour. It bathed the lake in a washed-out grey, making it look eerily flat and monochrome.

Climbing out of the car Cat reached for the zip on her jacket, pulling it up to her chin to keep the bone-chilling damp air out.

'Come on, let's see what we've got,' Alex said, walking briskly towards the taped-off area which was already abuzz with activity.

Cat spotted Andy, the pathologist, deep in conversation with Tony, the photographer. Both men appeared oblivious to the body of the dead woman at their feet.

'Andy,' Alex said striding over confidently. 'Anything so far?'

'I've only just got started. It's going to take some time to get all the forensics on this one.'

Alex looked around.

'Bit of an odd choice for an opportunist attack. It's so exposed.'

Andy nodded.

'I know. It's very strange. Especially when you look around, there are so many better places.' He pointed to a low stone footbridge. 'See that bridge? There's a path just behind it that leads through the woods. I would have thought somewhere like that would have been better for an ambush.'

'Maybe whoever did it isn't familiar with the different routes through?' Alex said.

'Maybe the dead woman didn't come that way,' Cat suggested.

'The car park's that way,' Andy replied.

Cat wasn't to be put off. 'Maybe she walked from home?'

Alex crouched down to get a closer look at the body. 'Or maybe she knew her killer and they took the first opportunity they got.' He glanced up at Andy. 'Initial thoughts on the cause of death?'

'It's easier if I show you.'

Andy bent over the body, gently turned the woman's head and lightly brushed her hair to one side. Even from her vantage point, peering over Alex's shoulder, Cat could see the lines that spanned the victim's neck.

'Recognise these?' Andy said.

'Strangulation marks from a thin ligature,' Cat replied before Alex had chance.

'I'm no expert but these look pretty similar to the others,' Alex said.

Andy stood up and took a step away. 'Can't say for sure yet but it certainly looks like more of the same.'

Alex remained stooped over the body, looking intently at the marks for a minute longer before straightening up. He dusted imaginary dirt off his knees, nodded briefly to Andy and started to walk towards the Incident Support Unit – a shabby-looking Mercedes Sprinter equipped with a plentiful supply of hot coffee, bottled water and digestive biscuits. Once they reached the ISU Alex stuck his head through the door.

'Any coffee going?' Cat heard him ask.

She continued past, heading towards the dog that was tethered by its lead to the tow bar at the rear of the van. The retriever greeted her enthusiastically; bouncing up, its tail wagging excitedly. Its coat was matted and muddied from its frolics at the lakeside but otherwise it seemed in good health.

Alex joined her, though he kept his distance from the dog. Minutes later a uniformed officer hopped out of the van with two steaming mugs. But the constable never got any further, for suddenly the dog lunged forward. Barking frantically, it strained in the direction of a battered old white Combi van that was approaching.

The vehicle cut across the grass and came to a stop next to the cordon tape. Cat muttered soothing words but the dog howled and strained against its shackles. The lead slipped over the tow bar. Cat reached for it but missed and the dog bounded towards the van as the driver climbed out; a short, thick-set man in blue coveralls peppered with spots and smears of different coloured paint. He paused and looked towards the barking dog.

'That'll be the dog's owner then. Go over and get him,' Alex said.

Cat set off at a hurried jog. She watched the dog jump up and smother the man's face with slobbery kisses.

'Get down!' the man shouted, gently pushing the dog to the floor and patting its flanks. 'Sorry if he's been any trouble,' he said to Cat as she approached.

The dog, sitting now, looked up adoringly at the man. Its tail swept the floor with the regularity of a metronome.

'I keep meaning to change the details on his collar,' he went on. 'It should really be the wife's number, not mine. She's the one who walks him.'

Cat gave him a weak smile and gestured with a hand towards the ISU.

'If you could come this way, please sir, and if you could keep a tight hold on the dog, I'd appreciate it.'

'Some paperwork or some such is there?' the man asked as they walked.

'Something like that,' Cat said.

She was relieved when they reached the van and Alex stepped forward to greet the man.

'You must be the dog's owner. I'm DI York.'

'Don Francis.'

The two men shook hands.

'You were at work when you got the call?' Alex asked.

'Yes. I came straight over. I was saying to your colleague; the collar should really have my wife's number on it. She's probably at home going out of her mind with worry.'

'Mr Francis–' Alex said, but the other man was in full flow.

'He's normally really good off the lead. In fact, I don't think he's ever run off before. Sometimes he bolts after a squirrel or a bird but he always comes back, eventually.'

'Mr Francis, do I take it your wife was walking the dog here this morning?' Alex asked.

'Yes. Jane brings him every morning.' The door on the pathologist's van slammed shut and the sound rang out loudly in the quiet morning air. Don Francis looked across and spotted the jump-suited scientist. 'Hey, what's going on here anyway?'

'Mr Francis, can you give me a brief description of your wife? Perhaps you can tell me what she was wearing this morning?' Alex asked.

Slowly Don Francis' face fell slack.

'She... She was wearing a grey woollen coat and black trousers. They were tucked into her wellingtons. She didn't want to get them muddy. She had to go to work you see.' His voice was barely a whisper.

Cat noticed Alex tip his chin down just a fraction. He took a breath before looking the other man straight in the eye.

'Mr Francis, there's no easy way for me to tell you this. I'm sorry but we believe your wife has been the victim of a violent attack.'

Cat marvelled at how articulate he sounded and yet he never made the words sound routine or glib.

Alex continued, 'The body of a woman was found–'

Don Francis was shaking his head.

'There must be some sort of mistake.'

'Obviously we will need you to confirm her identity but based on your description of your wife, it looks like–'

'No!' Don Francis snapped. He scowled at them. 'Let me see her, this woman. Where is she? I'll be able to tell you straight away that you're wrong.' He looked about him with a feverish expression. His gaze settled on where the Scene of Crime team were still working. He took a step towards the cordoned-off area.

Cat reached for his arm and gently restrained him.

'Mr Francis...'

He looked back at her. His chin began to tremble and Cat knew that despite his protests, reality was slowly hitting home.

'How can this be?' he said, sounding broken. 'First Megan and now Jane. Who is doing this?'

Fifteen

With her phone pressed to her ear, Cat smiled at Alex as he approached. She held out an index finger and he perched on the edge of her desk and waited.

She replaced the handset and looked up at him.

'An oversight. He simply forgot to put her on the list.'

After the revelation from Don Francis that Megan Daniels and his wife had met at university and had been friends ever since, Alex's first question was why this latest victim hadn't been included on the list of Megan's friends that Craig Daniels had provided them with.

'Now that he's been reminded of it,' Cat said, 'he thinks the appointment in Megan's diary for the haemophilia unit was probably a lunch date with Jane Francis. That was where she worked.'

'And he remembers this now?'

'The man's been in shock since Megan died. He won't have given what was in her diary a second thought.'

'Obviously,' Alex said. 'So how did he sound?'

'Like I'd expect him to after hearing about another woman's death. Shocked, upset, confused. To be honest I'm not sure how much of it sank in.'

'Did he know Jane Francis well?'

'I don't think so. He described her as one of Megan's friends. He said the last time he saw her was a couple of years ago, when he picked Megan up after a night on the town with Jane and some of her other Uni friends.'

Alex rubbed his chin but said nothing.

'It sounded like the truth to me,' Cat said, still feeling that

Craig Daniels needed someone on his side. 'The other thing that might interest you is it wasn't just Megan and Jane who bunked together at Uni. Caroline was there at the same time. At least she was until she dropped out and ran off to Cyprus. And wait for it … so was the ex-boyfriend who Megan invited to dinner last week.'

Cat saw Alex's eyes widen slightly.

'So how is Bob getting on with getting that statement from the ex-boyfriend?' she asked, trying not to sound too bitchy.

Alex looked over his shoulder at the scruffy detective. Bob was on the phone, lounging back in his chair, having what looked like a relaxed conversation. He turned back to Cat.

'You focus on what you've got to do. Leave me to worry about the rest.'

Sitting on a grey plastic chair, one of twenty that filled the daisy-yellow waiting room, Cat exhaled loudly, drawing the attention of the couple that sat across from her. She returned their gaze with a polite but bored smile. With Bob still trying to trace the elusive ex, Cat had been tasked with talking to colleagues of Jane Francis at the hospital where she had worked. Despite having phoned ahead to set up the meeting she had been ushered into the waiting room along with everyone else. She hated being kept waiting almost as much as she hated hospitals.

She looked at her watch again, the fifth time in as many minutes. Rising from her seat she strolled over to a corner table and looked over the small selection of tatty and torn magazines but returned to her seat empty handed. She repositioned herself in the chair. The hard plastic was wreaking havoc with her back. The couple sitting opposite her had barely said two sentences to each other since arriving. The woman played nervously with her wedding band, while her husband casually thumbed through an old issue of Gardeners' Weekly, its dog-eared front cover threatening to come adrift from the single staple that anchored it to the body of the magazine. To their left was a young woman with a toddler, a boy with short fair hair and a cheeky grin. He was playing with a toy truck, running it up and down the floor in front of his mother's feet. The woman looked over to Cat and smiled. She casually brushed a hand across her son's hair before switching her attention to a magazine that lay open on her lap.

There was no one else to watch.

Finally frustrated enough to do something about it, Cat stood up and was about to take her indignation to the reception desk when a young woman in a smart navy pencil skirt and cream shirt approached. She immediately apologised for the wait – they were short-staffed – and led Cat through into a small meeting room, pointing out a flask of hot tea and one of coffee for Cat's enjoyment before leaving her to await the first of her interviewees.

One by one, three doctors, six nursing staff, two orderlies and a receptionist came and shared their shock and sadness at their colleague's death. Jane had been well liked and equally well respected but she had also been a private person and as a result the interviews contained little of any interest. Cat resigned herself to the fact that the sessions were going to be a waste of time. And then she met Staff Nurse Maggie Ball.

Maggie smiled as she gripped Cat's hand in a firm handshake but there was sadness in those wide, almond-shaped eyes. She and Jane had been friends as well as colleagues. She spoke highly of the dead woman, echoing the sentiments of other colleagues. Cat reached the end of her questions and was winding up the interview when Maggie fixed her with a piercing stare.

'What's being done to stop this monster?' she asked.

Cat blinked, taken aback by the woman's directness.

'I'm sorry?'

'First Megan and now Jane.

'You knew Megan?'

Cat felt a flicker of excitement.

'Well enough to say hello. She used to accompany her uncle to his appointments, plus I'd see her occasionally when she dropped by to see Jane. They'd been friends for years. In fact, I saw her not long before she died. She came to pick Jane up; they were going out for lunch.'

Craig Daniels had been right, Cat noted.

'Small world,' she said.

The nurse nodded.

'It certainly is in this business. Haemophilia is hereditary. In fact, only last week Howard Williams' grandson was in for a check-up. I remember Jane being a bit nervous about it. She said she used to be friends with the kid's mother but hadn't seen her for years. I think she'd been living overseas or something. Jane wasn't sure whether the woman would have heard about Megan's murder. She didn't want to be the one to break the news. Can't say as I blame her.'

Cat leaned forward in her seat.

'And how did it go? Did Jane end up having to break the news?' she asked.

'No. She needn't have worried. The kid's mother didn't come in the end, someone else brought him.'

'Can you remember what day that was?'

The nurse frowned. 'No. I'd have to check. Jane was talking to me about it Monday or Tuesday last week. All I know is that the appointment was for some time later in the week.'

'Any idea who brought the kid in? Was it his father?'

'I've no idea, sorry.'

'Could you find out for me?' Cat asked. She wasn't sure why, but she wanted to know.

'Leave it with me.'

It was just after midday by the time the interviews had finished and Cat emerged to find the grey drizzle of the morning had been blown away to reveal a crisp, bright autumn day. She'd

154

grabbed a pre-packed sandwich from a vending machine in the hospital foyer on her way to the car. Now comfortable in her personal haven, she ripped open the plastic packaging and was halfway through the egg salad sandwich when her phone rang. Immediately recognising the ring tone as Alex's mobile, she ditched the sandwich and took the call through the car's Bluetooth system.

'Any news?' he asked.

'I've only just finished the interviews. I got the usual character stuff: she was a hard worker, smart, friendly, blah blah blah. I did learn one thing, though I'm not sure whether it's important or not. The nurse said Howard Williams' grandson had an appointment there last week. She was obviously talking about Jake Berry. She said Jane was eager to see his mother who she hadn't seen in years – remember, Jane and Caroline Berry were at Uni together – but that Jane was nervous about seeing her, given what had happened to Megan. She didn't want to be the one to break the news.'

'Small world,' Alex said.

'That's what I said.'

'So what happened?'

'Nothing. Turns out someone else brought the boy.'

'That'll be Steve Berry won't it?'

'I did say I wasn't sure if it was something or nothing. Just thought I'd mention it.'

'Was there anything else?' Alex asked. He sounded less than impressed to Cat's critical ear.

'While I was on site, I thought I'd check if there are any records of Mary Joseph ever having been a patient.'

'And?' Now he sounded interested.

'Nothing. There's a slim chance she might have attended years ago before they computerised their records; the old stuff is archived. They're going to let me know. For now, it looks like we're still missing a link between Mary and the other two.'

'There might not be a link,' Alex said. 'The three of them could know their murderer independently. You never know, Jane and Megan's friendship could just be a coincidence.'

Alex was always telling her there were no such things as coincidences in a murder enquiry. She was about to say as much when his voice rang through the speakers once more.

'As you're over that side of town, go and call in on Mrs Joseph,' he said. 'Ask her whether there's a family history of haemophilia. Maybe Mary used to accompany a family member to the Clinic? You can also see if Megan or Jane's names mean anything to her while you're at it.'

Cat let out a groan, not realising that the microphone above the driver's seat was sensitive to the slightest sounds.

'What's the matter?' Alex asked.

'Nothing. It's just... well, you know how hard it was to get anything out of her the last time we spoke to her.'

Her comment was met with silence.

'I'll come in as soon as I've finished,' she said.

'Right. I'll see you later.'

'Wait... How about you, did you get anything?'

Alex had spent the morning attending Jane Francis' post-mortem and although nobody was expecting any surprises Cat didn't want to be the last to know.

'It was pretty much as expected. The marks on her neck were consistent with being strangled with a thin electrical cable or coated garden wire. It was the same backward force and–'

'Hang on, are you sure about the wire?' Cat interrupted.

'That's what they said.'

'But the wire – don't you remember at Mary's post-mortem the professor said her injuries were consistent with a much thinner wire, more like nylon fishing line, which is nothing like coated gardening wire or electrical cable. And I thought the PM report for Megan said that she'd been killed with the same MO as Mary. I know it's only a minor point but...'

Alex was silent.

Cat ran over in her mind the words of the pathologist as he carved up the remains of Mary's body. She was sure she was right.

'And you're positive the report for Megan said *thin* wire?' Alex asked.

'No,' Cat said, frantically trying to remember what Bob had said about the PM report.

'No, it wasn't thin wire?'

Although Cat couldn't see his face, she could imagine the frown that would be puckering Alex's brow.

'I'm not sure. I don't know.' She faltered. 'I didn't read the PM report for Megan. I'm only going on what Bob told me. I'm sure he said that the PM results let Terry off the hook given that the two women had been killed with the same MO. I just assumed that...'

Silence filled the airspace.

'Maybe the choice of wire isn't important?' she said, cringing. She knew it was a stupid thing to say.

'Don't be ridiculous. A well-publicised murder followed shortly by another, with a similar but not exactly the same MO. What do you think?'

'A copy-cat?' Cat said. 'Are you serious?'

'Given how much press coverage Mary's murder got it's possible that it could have given someone ideas,' he said. 'And it's certainly muddied the waters. We could have been fucking around with the wrong bloody suspects all this time. I don't believe it.' Alex sounded like he'd just been told all overtime was cancelled. 'Forget about seeing Mary's mother. Get yourself back here. Shit! This could change everything.'

Alex disconnected the call.

'Shit indeed,' Cat said to herself as she thought of Terry, who they'd sent on his cocky little way.

Sixteen

A feeling of cold dread stole through Cat as she made the journey back to the station. She thought of the copy of the PM report for Megan still unread, on her desk and guilt churned her stomach like a wave, sending the breath crashing right out of her chest. She knew she wasn't entirely to blame. Bob should have picked up the difference between the two cases as well – after all, he'd read both post-mortem reports – but knowing that didn't appease her conscience any.

Alex called again fifteen minutes later.

'Change of plan,' he said. 'Get yourself over to Craig Daniels. See if he's got any idea where this missing ex-boyfriend of Megan's could be.'

She could tell from the strained pitch that he was angry, but it was also clear who he was angry with, and it wasn't her. Bob clearly hadn't located the missing man.

Standing outside Craig Daniels' home, Cat put on a warm smile and waited. He opened the door looking gaunt and tired and physically blanched at the sight of her. Cat felt the smile dissolve on her lips.

'I'm sorry to bother you again Mr Daniels. I wonder if I could come in. I have more questions I'm afraid.'

Craig Daniels nodded and walked back into the house, leaving the door open for her to follow. If he was interested in the reason for her visit, he didn't show it. Even once Cat was inside the house, seated on an oversized three-seater at his invitation, he remained distant and remote.

'Have you ever lost anyone close?' he asked.

'No. No, I haven't,' she lied.

Unsettled by the question she moved forward onto the edge of her seat. She reminded herself that she needed to focus on the reason for her visit but before she could speak, he started to talk.

'There's no let-up you know. No escaping the memories. Everything you see, hear, touch, or smell, it all makes you hunger for what you've lost.' For a moment Cat thought he might cry but then he appeared to compose himself. 'But the hardest thing,' he said, with an obvious wobble in his voice, 'is that even though remembering hurts so much, you so desperately don't want to forget. All you really want to do is wrap yourself up in memories, terrified that if you don't, they'll just disappear and be gone forever.'

He fell quiet for a moment and Cat saw a depth of sadness in him she had rarely seen before. He wasn't falling to pieces in the conventional way. He didn't appear to be struggling to look after himself. His hair was combed, his face freshly shaved and his clothes neatly ironed. But he seemed to be in a place that was so very far away, his eyes occasionally looking into the distance, to an imaginary horizon as he retreated within his own thoughts.

'Mr Daniels, I'm really very sorry to have to intrude on your grief like this but I need to ask you some more questions about Megan's ex-boyfriend, the one who was here last week.'

He seemed to snap out of his stupor and turned his attention back to her.

'Of course,' he said. 'What do you need to know?'

Wherever in his head he had been, he was back now.

'We're having trouble finding Mr Stewart.'

'Oh.' He sounded surprised, though not shocked. 'What about his wife, doesn't she know?'

'She says she has no idea where he is. It seems they had a big fight. He'd already left the marital home a week before he came round to see Megan.'

'What about work? He's a self-employed kitchen fitter. He subcontracts for some of the big companies. He wouldn't just walk out on a job.'

'He was between contracts.'

'Well I don't know then. He's always been a bit unreliable. I'm not surprised Shelley kicked him out. He seems to spend all of his time drinking and playing computer games. He never really matured beyond his university days. It might have been alright to do that then but he's got a kid now.'

Cat was well aware of the missing man's flaws, having read the notes from the interview with Shelley, his wife, who had finally grown sick of turning a blind eye to his lax ways and affinity for the bottle. She had kicked him out of the family home with an ultimatum to shape up or ship out and hadn't seen him since.

'How do you think Megan would have been with him? Was she sympathetic?'

'God no. She was always telling him to grow up. She still tried to be a good friend, supportive and all that, but she was definitely from the school of tough love. She'd told him before to go and get help but he never listened.' A look of alarm slowly crept across his face.

'Are you alright Mr Daniels?' Cat said, having to stop herself from laying a reassuring hand on his arm.

He turned to her, wide-eyed.

'You think he did it? That's why you're asking all these questions.'

'I'm not saying anything of the sort. We just need to speak to Mr Stewart. He's one of the last people to have seen Megan alive. He may have information that could help us.'

Craig looked at her unblinking. She could see him thinking through what she'd said.

'But what if Megan went too far? What if he just flipped? That could be why he's disappeared. He might have killed himself out of remorse. Oh my God, I bet that's what happened. I just said it, didn't I, the bloke was unreliable and selfish and probably drunk.'

Cat set her hands out in front of her and slowly lowered them; a move intended to quieten the agitated man.

'Calm down. Although we have to consider all of the possibilities, I don't think what you're suggesting is very likely. If he'd flipped, chances are he'd have done something that night, not wait a week.'

Craig Daniels regarded her warily but after a short spell he nodded.

'I suppose.'

'And you can't think of anywhere else Mr Stewart might be or how to contact him?'

'No.'

'If you do think of anything, you've got my details.' Cat rose from her seat.

'Of course.'

Back in her car, Cat put the keys in the ignition but instead of starting the engine she sat, deep in thought, pondering the significance of the ex-boyfriend's disappearance. She was still sitting motionless when a knock on the glass next to her head caused her to jump. She looked out to see Craig Daniels. He gave a small wave.

She reached for the window switch.

He crouched down and spoke through the gap. 'I'm sorry. I meant to ask you; all of Megan's research on her family tree, it meant so much to her, and... well, I haven't got any use for it. I wondered whether Caroline Berry would be interested. You've met her, what do you think?'

Cat thought about the question, and thought about what it was Steve Berry had said.

'I really don't know,' she replied. 'Personally, I think it's a really nice idea. Why don't you call and ask her?'

'I was going to and then I thought it might be too upsetting for her, so I sort of put it off.'

'Upsetting?'

'Well, you know. She's had so much bad luck recently; with her father's death and then Megan. And even though Jane wasn't family, the two were friends. I wasn't sure if the family tree stuff would just be too much.' He paused. A sad smile twitched at the corner of his mouth. 'I remember how excited Megan had been when she'd heard Caroline was coming back. And Howard... he was over the moon at the prospect of seeing his grandson for the first time.' The line of his mouth tightened. 'It's all a bloody mess isn't it?' he said before starting back to the house.

Cat reached for the ignition but paused.

She climbed out of the car. 'Mr Daniels. Mr Daniels...'

Craig Daniels stopped and waited for her at the front door.

'I'm sorry but something you just said about Howard Williams,' Cat said on reaching him, 'about him being over the moon meeting his grandson, but he died before Caroline returned to the UK, didn't he?'

'That's right.' He must have seen the confusion in Cat's face because he added, 'I was talking about how much he had been looking forward to seeing them before he died. It's just a shame that it happened when it did.'

'Caroline was due to visit the UK before her father died?'

'Not visit. Live. Caroline was leaving her husband and coming back to live. Megan told me that they were planning on staying with Howard at the big house, at least for the foreseeable future.'

'She was leaving her husband?' Cat repeated. 'Are you sure about that, because she's still with him now?'

'That's what Megan told me.'

'How did she know?'

'She and Caroline had been in touch for years, mainly by email. Perhaps Caroline felt differently about striking out on her own after her father had died?'

Cat returned to her car and sat with the engine still cold as she chewed over the new information. She drummed her fingers absentmindedly on the steering wheel while she considered what to do next; her recent telling-off from Alex still fresh in her mind.

Reaching for her bag she pulled out her mobile. The speed dial key routed her through to his voicemail. She rang off and tried a different number but got the same result. This time she left a message.

'Alex. It's Cat. Just updating you on my visit to Mr Daniels. Sorry, but he's got no idea where Anthony Stewart is. While I was there he was talking about... well, all sorts of stuff. He mentioned that Megan and Caroline had kept in touch over the years, and then he mentioned Jane.' She paused, wondering how best to set out her intentions. 'Well anyway, it made me realise that Caroline might not know about Jane's murder. And the two women were friends, once. Given that I'm not far...'

Again, she paused. What was the point of explaining her train of thought; if Alex wasn't there, he couldn't exactly give his go ahead for what she wanted to do.

A beep rang through the earpiece. She'd run out of recording space.

'Shit,' she said chewing on her lip.

The silence in the car was depressing. She missed having Alex there to bounce ideas off. It occurred to her that perhaps she needed Alex's input a little too much sometimes. She'd love to be able to give him something for a change.

She threw the mobile onto the passenger seat and started the engine.

On hitting the roundabout that would take her back into town, instead of going straight over she continued round, past the exit that she should have taken, and rejoined the main road to head back in the direction she had just come from.

Gary the security guard was still in his little booth, keeping watch over the well-to-do residents of the Roswell Park estate. Cat stopped the car and wound down the window.

'Mr and Mrs Berry, The Laurels.'

Instead of hitting the button to lift the barrier as he had done with Alex, Gary reached over and picked up a sheet of paper from a nearby shelf.

'Name?' he asked.

'DC McKenzie.'

Cat watched as he consulted a list of names handwritten on the sheet.

'Sorry, you're not on the list. I'll have to give them a call.'

'Hey, wait,' Cat said, leaning further out of the car window. 'What list? I'm here as part of a police investigation. I wouldn't expect to be on any list. Look,' she said, showing him her badge. 'I was here last week with Detective Inspector York.'

Gary bent down and gave Cat a second look.

'Oh, I'm sorry. I didn't recognise you. You can go straight up. I take it you know where it is?'

'Yes, thank you.'

Cat brushed off her initial irritation with the man. He was only doing his job. 'Anyway, what's with the list?' she called over to him.

'Viewings. They've put the place on the market. I've got a list of people who are coming to see it.'

'Ah, okay.' Cat tried to sound casual, concealing the tingle of excitement that his news had stirred in her.

Five minutes later her car pulled up noisily on the gravel drive.

She heard the doorbell peal through the house as she tugged the bell. Too busy worrying about what Alex might think about her impromptu and unauthorised visit, Cat hadn't stopped to consider that the Berrys may not be at home. Until now. But before she had the chance to decide what she would do if they weren't in, the white panelled front door swung open.

Caroline Berry stood in the hallway. Her smile faded when she saw who it was.

'Good afternoon Mrs Berry,' Cat said. 'I'm sorry to bother you but something has come up that I thought you should know about.'

Caroline crossed her arms.

'Oh really?'

'Perhaps I could come in?'

Caroline looked over Cat's shoulder towards her car.

'Are you on your own today?'

'Yes. Detective Inspector York is attending to other business.'

'That's what they all say, isn't it?' Caroline said with little hint of humour.

'This shouldn't take long.'

'I suppose you'd better come through then. I was in the middle of making a coffee.'

Cat followed Caroline into a large country kitchen. She stopped by the door and stood watching while Caroline walked to the central island and picked up a jar of instant coffee. Steam poured out of the spout of a kettle on the counter behind her.

'I've just come from seeing Craig Daniels,' Cat said.

Caroline spooned the coffee into a mug. She didn't look up.

'Megan's husband,' Cat added.

Caroline looked at her. 'Oh, yes, of course.'

'We were talking about Jane Francis and I thought–'

Caroline paused with the kettle in hand.

'Jane who?'

'Jane Francis?'

Caroline poured the boiled water over the coffee granules.

'No, I'm sorry,' she said over her shoulder.

'An old friend of yours from university.'

Caroline twitched her lips and furrowed her brow. Suddenly her expression lifted.

'Oh, *that* Jane. I didn't recognise her married name.' Caroline reached into the fridge and pulled out an open milk carton. She added a splash to her mug. 'God, I haven't seen her in years. How is she?'

Cat broke the news. All the while Caroline stood blinking with a hand pressed to her chest.

'I thought you might already know. The story's been all over the news,' Cat said.

Caroline turned and looked at her, wide-eyed.

'You mean... she was the nurse that was found murdered on Monday?'

'That's right. She worked at the haemophilia unit. In fact, she was the nurse who saw your son at his appointment last week.'

Caroline shook her head and hugged her mug to her chest. She appeared to be deep in her own thoughts. 'Do you think their deaths are related – Jane and Megan?' she asked.

'We don't know yet. It's possible.'

Cat thought of Alex. She wondered what his reading of the post-mortem reports had revealed.

'Possible or probable?' Caroline asked.

'We're doing our best to find out.' Seized with an idea, Cat asked, 'Did you know someone called Anthony Stewart at university?'

Caroline's eyes flashed wide.

'Is he dead too?'

'No, no,' Cat said quickly. 'At least we don't think he is. We just want to talk to him. I wondered if you'd heard from him recently.'

'No. I can't even remember the last time I heard his name.'

Cat looked around the room. Its palatial dimensions made the space feel cold and clinical.

'It must be strange coming back here after all these years.'

'You have no idea.'

'I hear you're selling up.'

Caroline sighed.

'I miss the sun. We're moving to Spain or maybe even Florida.'

'So were you only coming back here for your father's sake?' Cat said.

Caroline froze, her coffee cup half way to her lips.

'I'm sorry?'

'I heard you were coming back here to live with your father.' Cat saw the alarm in the other woman's eyes. 'Don't worry,' she added quickly, 'I won't say anything to your husband if that's what you're worried about.'

Caroline rose from her seat and crossed to the sink. She tipped away the still steaming coffee and slammed the mug down on the drainer and stood with her back to Cat.

'I'm sorry. I didn't mean to upset you,' Cat said. 'I realise you must be reeling from all of the shocks you've had recently. It can be very traumatic to be involved in a murder investigation.' Caroline was still facing away from her. 'You know, if there's anything you're worried about, or want to talk about, you can always call me.'

'There's nothing to talk about,' Caroline said, her voice as cold as the marble counter her hands were resting on. 'I'd like you to go now please,' she said, addressing the kitchen window.

Cat could see that she'd misjudged her audience enormously. She picked up her bag and coat and walked to the kitchen door.

'If you change your mind and would like somebody to talk to, you know where I am.'

Cat was both relieved and nervous to see Alex at his desk on her return to the office. She took a deep breath and walked over.

'Have you got a minute?' she asked.

He spun in his chair to face her.

'Sure. What's up?'

'I thought I should update you on what came out of this afternoon's visits.'

'Okay,' he said, swivelling his chair back around to pick up his empty mug. He held it out towards her. 'I'm about due a break. Why don't you grab a couple of coffees? I'll just finish what I'm doing here and then I'm all yours.'

Five minutes later she returned to Alex's desk, two mugs of

hot coffee in hand.

'Sorry I missed your call earlier,' Alex said, as she sat down. 'I had to pick Mel's sister up from the airport.'

Cat looked at him. She hadn't expected any sort of explanation.

'The sister who lives in Ireland?'

'Yes. She's over for the week. Bit of company for Mel.'

Cat gave him a small smile. 'Good idea.'

Alex simply nodded and looked down into his coffee before clearing his throat.

'You were going to fill me in on how you got on. So, what've you found?'

Cat recounted her conversation with Craig Daniels. Like her, Alex was surprised to learn of Caroline's plans prior to her father's demise.

'I know. I was kicking myself driving away from there,' she said. 'The old woman, Mrs Daniels, said as much and I missed it. So I went to see Mrs Berry. I thought someone should tell her about Jane Francis; I mean, the two women were friends once. I'm glad I did. She didn't know. Anyway, while I was there, I mentioned that I knew about her plan to leave her husband. Suffice to say, she was not happy about it.'

Alex winced. 'You just *happened* to mention it?'

'I know, don't,' she said, still unable to believe how she'd got it so wrong.

'So, what happened?'

'I don't know. I was just trying to empathise with her, wanted her to feel that I appreciated how difficult a time she's having. But immediately the barriers went up. Do you think she could be a victim of domestic abuse?'

'I think you're over-analysing it. The woman's in a new house, virtually a new country and suddenly there are detectives popping by for coffee to talk about dead friends and relatives. And you wonder why she seems a bit on edge?'

'When you put it like that...' She took a drink of her coffee.

'I don't suppose you asked Mrs Berry whether she knew the whereabouts of Anthony Stewart?'

'Funnily enough, I did.'

'No dice?'

'No. I take it Bob's had no luck either?'

'No.'

Cat gave a nod. 'Oh. So anyway, how did you get on? Did you get to the bottom of post-mortem findings – were the injuries the same on all three women?'

Alex's face grew even longer.

'From my reading of the PM reports I'd say Mary's was different. But what do I know? I'm waiting for a call back from Professor Jarrett.'

They drank the rest of their coffee in silence.

Cat picked up their empty mugs and was about to walk away when she stopped.

'One more thing – the Berrys have put the house on the market.'

Alex's eyebrows shot up.

'Really?'

'Yep. Heading back overseas. Somewhere hot.'

'McKenzie. A Mr Steve Berry for you,' Bob Bells shouted across the office. He held his phone out towards her, a hand clasped over the mouthpiece.

She looked back at Alex who nodded.

'Take it. We're done for now.'

By the time Cat had finished the call, Alex was busy, chatting animatedly on his phone. She watched him scribble frantically in a spiral-bound reporter's pad. A few minutes later he hung up and she wandered over. She plonked herself down in the chair at the side of his desk. Alex looked at her with an enquiring eyebrow.

'Thought I'd better warn you,' she said. 'The call earlier, Steve

Berry – Caroline must have told him about my visit.'

'And?'

'He wants to know what we intend to do to protect his wife.'

'From what?'

'From whoever's running around killing all of her university year.'

'What's he on about? What the hell did you say to her?'

Cat thought back to the conversation.

'It was nothing really. Caroline asked me if Megan and Jane's deaths were connected and I said they might be. What was I supposed to do, lie?'

'Anything else?'

'No.' She paused, then added, 'Well, you know I mentioned that we were looking for Anthony Stewart. Thinking about it, she did ask if he was also dead. Obviously, I said, not as far as we know...'

Suddenly Cat could see how it might have looked to Caroline Berry.

Deep furrows across Alex's brow underlined his unease.

'So now they're worried she could be next?' he asked.

'Yes. He said he wants police protection for Caroline until whoever's doing this is caught.'

'That's impossible.'

'I told him we can't provide round the clock protection for everyone who happened to know the victims. I made the point we don't know for sure there's even a link between the two murders.'

'How did he react?'

'Not well. He said if anything happened to her, the blame would sit firmly at our door.'

'Interesting.'

'Is it?'

'I think so. If you're a man intent on killing your wife what better time to do it than when the whole world is looking for some crazed serial killer.'

'You think he might stage a copy-cat killing?' Cat asked.

Alex leaned back in his seat. His frown hardened.

'No. I think he might have already staged two copy-cat killings and is about to go for the hat-trick.'

Seventeen

At six a.m. the alarm stirred Cat from her slumbers. She quickly silenced it and crept through to the bathroom where she threw on her tracksuit before stealing out of the house, leaving Mike behind, still sound asleep.

It was a well-rehearsed routine. Most mornings, come rain or shine, she managed to haul herself out of bed an hour earlier than she otherwise needed to and put some miles under her belt. Not from any desire to be a perfect size ten, although she'd be the first to admit that was a welcome bonus, but because it helped to keep her stress levels low and her concentration strong. Occasionally, on a particularly cold or wet morning, her good intentions would lapse and she would indulge in an extra hour cosseted within the folds of her warm bed. But not today. Not with three open murder enquiries torturing her thoughts. Rather than lie awake in bed, allowing her mind to tease her with ideas of what might have been, she found tranquillity in the solitude of the still dark, deserted streets, where, to the rhythmic sound of her breath, she let her mind run free.

She thought back to her conversation with Alex the day before. His idea seemed so outlandish. It would take some balls, not to mention planning, but Mary's murder had been all over the media. Even the details of how she'd been attacked were public knowledge, courtesy of Mrs Joseph's heart-rending story in the local rag. *How many bottles of gin that had paid for?*

Alex's theory also provided an answer to one of the questions that continued to elude them – why had Jane Francis died? Unfortunately for Mary, wasters like Terry didn't need a motive. He was a convicted crook and drug dealer; an all-round bad guy with a short fuse and a violent temper. And the motives for Megan's murder were plentiful – she could have been killed for the cash, or jealousy, or love, or lust... but Jane?

Could Alex be right? Were the two women simply collateral damage – red herrings designed to draw the scent away from the real target?

Full of frustration and desperate to achieve something from her labours, Cat forced all thoughts of the case out of her mind and pushed herself over the last hundred metres with a lung-bursting, arm-pumping, flat-out sprint until she reached the postbox at the end of the road. She quickly stopped the timer on her watch. Letting her legs slow to a walk she allowed herself a small smile – twenty-one seconds better than her previous personal best; a success of sorts at least.

Back home the water jetted out of the shower head, hot and strong, its temperature in stark contrast to that of her body, which had been subject to the lung chilling, frost-filled air during her five-mile stint.

She froze, sure she had heard something.

The radio alarm was off by the time she had returned to the house and with Mike having already left for work the house should have been quiet.

Quickly, she turned off the shower.

There it was again.

She flew out of the cubicle, grabbed a towel from the heated rail as she passed and raced around the bed, miraculously managing to reach the bedside cabinet and grab the phone whilst it was still ringing.

'Hello?' she said, putting it to her ear in the hope she wasn't too late.

'Detective York?' a heavily accented, gravelly voice asked.

'No, this is Detective Constable McKenzie. Can I help you?'

There was a delay of a few seconds before the caller's voice came through again.

'This is Detective Glafcos Theophanus of the Cyprus Police. Detective York called to speak to me yesterday.'

Did he? He hadn't mentioned it.

'I'm sorry. He's not on this number. If you've got a pen, I can give you his mobile.'

'Please, this is the fourth number I have tried. Detective York is not in his office or answering his mobile phone. The woman I spoke to at his home gave me this number.'

It was unheard of for Alex's wife to give out someone else's number. Cat felt a horrible hollow feeling in the pit of her stomach as it occurred to her that perhaps Cody had taken a turn for the worse.

'Well I should be seeing DI York later so if you'd like to give me a message, I'll make sure he gets it,' she said, walking over to her wardrobe where she pulled out a black dress and held it up to her front.

She looked in the mirror and pulled a face.

'Thank you. Please tell him that we hold no information on the suspect. He was not in any trouble with the police when he was here.'

'Suspect?'

'Mr Steven Berry.'

'Oh,' she said.

'Please tell Detective York I hope he has more success with his enquiries of the British Army.'

Despite the thick accent the words were enunciated with a linguistic skill that shamed Cat, who had never progressed beyond a sub-standard school-girl French.

'Thank you, I will.'

'There is one more thing. I have information that may be of interest I think, but there is problems.' Cat ignored the minor mistake. He continued, 'We have an open murder. How do you call it...?'

Cat threw the dress onto the bed and sat down next to it.

'An unsolved case?'

'Yes. A woman, found in the mountains three months ago. She had been dead for some time.'

'And was she known to the suspect?'

'We do not know. We have no identity for her.'

'And you suspect it's somehow linked?' Cat wondered when he was going to get to the point.

'I do not have any such suspicions, no. Detective York just asked me for information on any possible murders in the last ten years.'

Cat's hopes took a dive. Still covered only with a towel, she walked over to the window and looked out over a quiet close. The day was an ominous grey but at least it wasn't raining. She was starting to get cold and a glance at the clock on the bedside table told her that she would soon be running late.

'Well, if you want to send the details over, we'll bear it in mind.'

Eighteen

The vibrations spread upwards from the floor to her feet and then eventually to her seat, causing everything around her to rattle and shake as the plane gained momentum. Cat leaned forward and peered out of the Plexiglas window. The orange sodium street lights receded from view and soon they looked no bigger than a string of fairy lights hung with geometric accuracy over a patchwork of Surrey countryside.

The twenty-four hours that followed the call from the Greek detective had passed by in a blur. Cat turned her head to look at Alex in the next seat, busy fastening his seatbelt. He looked up and smiled.

'Apparently it's twenty-one degrees and cloud-free over there. A bit different to twelve degrees and peeing it down.'

Cat nodded but said nothing.

'What's up?'

'Nothing.'

'Something's obviously bothering you. You look like you've got the weight of the world on your shoulders.'

'It's just... well, I'm not sure why we needed to go to Cyprus now. Couldn't this have waited? I mean with Cody only just coming out of intensive care. Surely Mel's going to want to be at the hospital all the time. Who's going to be there for Sarah? This will have hit her hard too. I remember you saying how close the two of them are. It's at times like these a little girl needs her dad.'

She felt him go rigid in his seat; looking down she noticed his hand grip the arm rest. Her stomach lurched in anticipation of the backlash but instead he resumed fussing with the fastening on his seatbelt.

'Alex?'

'Mel's got her sister there to help now.'

...The sister who it turned out had dished out Cat's mobile number to the Greek detective.

'Wouldn't it make you feel better if you were there too?'

'Everything's fine. Please just leave it.'

Cat opened her mouth to say something more but she caught the firm set of his jaw and decided against it.

Nothing more was said during the trouble-free take-off and as soon as the illuminated sign went out Alex unclipped the belt from his lap. He stood up and retrieved his briefcase from the overhead locker.

'We've not got long in Cyprus, which means doing as much prep as we can.' He pulled an A4 notepad and pen out of his bag and set them down on the small fold-down tray in front of him. 'Between now and when we land, I want to go over what we know, where the gaps are, and give some thought as to possible motive.'

'Are you including Mary's murder in this?' Cat said, dropping her voice, conscious of the proximity of other passengers.

'We can keep Mary in mind but I don't want it to distract us, given that it's possible we have two killers.'

'Okay. Well, in that case, what jumps out at me is how Howard Williams' death seems to have featured in so many of the conversations I've had recently: Megan helped organise his funeral, Jane went to it, and Caroline cried off. I think that's odd in itself. I mean even if she was ill, why didn't her husband put in an appearance? Or, God forbid, he could have organised it and saved putting on Mrs Daniels and Megan.'

Alex looked at her with a face that looked like someone had put sour milk on his cereal.

'Can you really see Berry going out of his way to organise the funeral of someone who he thought had cut them off years ago?'

'Good point. I can imagine Berry digging his heels in over

something like that.' Cat thought for a moment before asking, 'Do you still think it's possible he's planning on killing Caroline and making it look like it's some serial killer from her student days?'

'I don't know. It sounds a bit thin when you say it like that. Especially when you take into account the fact that she hasn't been in touch with her friends since she left the country.'

'That's not strictly true. We know she stayed in touch with Megan,' Cat reminded him.

'Yes, but what about Jane?' Alex said. 'She was a friend from way back. Steve might never have even met her.'

'But he might have,' Cat said. 'Steve and Caroline started dating when she was at Uni. He could have met Jane then.' Cat's eyes widened. 'What if Megan and Jane knew something that made them a threat?'

'Like what?'

'Like if they knew that Howard had changed his will making Caroline his beneficiary again?'

'How would that make them a threat?'

'If Steve killed Caroline, they'd have known he had a motive.'

'We'd find that out, with or without them. And anyway, despite what everyone might have thought, Caroline was never disinherited.'

'Oh. Well I don't know then.'

Cat leaned her head back against the headrest. She let her head roll to the side to look at Alex.

'We don't know whether Megan would have recognised Steve, do we?'

'No, we don't. What are you thinking?'

'I'm not sure...' She shook her head. 'Forget about it, it's a stupid idea.'

'Come on. We're just wasting time.' Alex opened his pad to a fresh page. 'Let's start with Steve Berry. After all, he's the reason we're here.'

Together they ran through what they knew about the ex-army man and his wife. The gaps in their knowledge gave life to a long list of questions and by the time the cabin crew started to wheel out industrial-looking stainless-steel trolleys, carrying trays of in-flight meals, they were fresh out of ideas.

Alex stowed his briefcase in the locker and returned to his seat.

'I'm looking forward to this,' Cat said, unlatching the fold-down tray from the back of the seat in front.

'You like airline food?'

'Yeah. Don't you?'

'It's all right but I'm not sure I'd go as far as to say I'm looking forward to it.'

'It reminds me of being on holiday.' After a moment's pause she said, 'You know, I haven't been on a plane since I came back from the Maldives.'

'But that was what, four, five years ago?'

'Uh-huh. Mike uses all of his leave on golf trips and holidays with his mates. I've lost count of how many stag-dos he's been on in the last couple of years. I don't mind really. I've been busy doing the house up.'

'Hardly the same though is it?'

Just then the food trolley pulled alongside the row of seats in front of theirs, saving Cat from having to continue what was likely to have been an uncomfortable conversation.

Given that neither of them had eaten that morning, the chat stopped while they greedily devoured the contents of an assortment of different sized plastic moulded tubs, which, after peeling off the steamed-up cellophane covers, for Cat turned out to be a half-decent, albeit miniature vegetable frittata, accompanied by a bread roll, a tiny tub of strawberry jam and a carton of orange juice.

Shortly afterwards the stewardess returned with the coffee pot. Cat passed her the small plastic cup off her breakfast tray. While she waited, she caught the eye of a fellow passenger; tall and dark, he reminded her of her brother.

She looked back at Alex. 'You know, my Mum and Dad have still got that photo of you and Pete out on display. The one from California. You two are on some beach, wearing wet-suits and holding surfboards, trying to look cool.'

Alex broke into a grin.

'You're joking, that was like over fifteen years ago. It was just after we left police college. We must have been, I don't know, nineteen or twenty. I can't believe they've not thrown it in the loft... or the bin.'

'No. It's still there.' She reached for her filled cup and waited for Alex to take his.

'Well, I suppose, given the circumstances,' Alex said.

'There were always loads of pictures of Pete around the place. Mum and Dad were very proud of him. Although you're right, there are probably more since he died.' She blew gently onto the surface of the hot black coffee, causing ripples to skim across the surface. 'What does Mel think about you disappearing to Cyprus for three days so soon?'

'She's fine. Like I said, she's got her sister with her.'

'But still...'

'She's fine,' he repeated, stressing it in such a way that he may as well have said *mind your own business.* But Cat never was one to shy away from those awkward questions.

'And how about you, Alex?' she asked, shifting slightly in her seat to turn to face him more directly. 'How are you doing?'

He looked down into his cup and took a drink. Cat saw him recoil as the hot liquid burned his lips.

'Cody's on the mend now, that's all that matters.'

There was something about his choice of words that left her feeling that there was a lot more being left unsaid.

'Of course, but I can imagine it must have been a nightmare, not knowing whether–'

'Look Cat,' Alex interjected. 'I appreciate your concern, I do, but I really don't want to talk about it.'

'Okay, I'll shut up.' Cat opened her book, but instead of looking down she twisted her head and looked at Alex. 'I bet you would have talked to Peter about it.'

'Pete and I were friends for a long time. He would have known not to ask. Now read your book.'

They spoke very little over the course of the following half hour. As the flight attendants hurriedly cleared up the breakfast trays, Cat read while Alex flicked through a magazine he'd picked up at the airport. After a while Cat felt him move in his seat and sensed him looking at her. She lowered her book.

'What?' she asked.

'What about you? Was Mike okay about the trip?'

Cat slid her bookmark onto the page that she was reading and pressed the pages closed. She leaned her head back on to the headrest and her mouth took a sad downward turn.

'Not really. But you know how it is with him.' She gave a tired smile. 'He's such an asshole,' she said in a mock American accent, making Alex laugh. 'I thought things were getting better between us but it must have either been my imagination or a temporary blip, because things seem to be going from bad to worse.'

'He's not still going on about the job, is he?'

'Sometimes,' Cat said. 'It's hard to give specific examples. It's more to do with his attitude. It's taken as read that he can go out with his mates on a whim, or that he can bring half a dozen beered-up blokes back to the house when the football's on and that I'll stick a couple of pizzas in the oven and make myself scarce. But as soon as I want something then I'm being unreasonable.'

'Sounds okay to me,' Alex said lightly, but on seeing Cat's face he held up both hands in defence. 'Only joking.'

'The thing is Alex, I can't remember a time when it was any better. And I've tried. I really have. I thought if I could remember what it used to be like then maybe I could figure out what's going wrong or at least when it changed. But I can't. He's always been the same. And you know what? I've always put up with it. Why is that?'

'You're the clever one. If you don't know then I'm not sure I will, but as you've asked, I reckon you should think back to why you first got together.'

'How will that help?'

'Well, people get together for various reasons. Sometimes it's lust. Sometimes they've got something in common, you know, like a shared interest. But a lot of the time it's just convenience. One by one your mates start to become couples and then you meet someone you get on okay with and before you know it you've coupled up because it's easier to go with someone than to stay on your own. Weeks turn into months, months into years. Provided they don't make any major fuck-ups, like beat you up or have a string of affairs, then it's easy to settle for companionship. Unless, of course, one day something happens which makes you wonder what the hell you ever saw in them, when really there wasn't much there in the first place. It's just that you've never looked.'

Cat was stunned. She hadn't expected any response from Alex, let alone one as astute or sensitive as the one he furnished her with.

'But I'm not saying that applies to you and Mike,' he quickly added.

'No Alex, I think you're absolutely right.' A puzzled look crossed Cat's face. 'But if what you're saying is true, then why has this suddenly become an issue if I've put up with it for years?'

'If he hasn't changed, then you must have. Something or someone has come into your line of sight and taken the blinkers off. You just haven't figured out who or what and whether it's enough to make you jump ship... not yet anyway.'

Cat could feel herself blush. She felt naked and exposed by his assessment and she didn't like it.

'Listen to you, Sigmund Freud. You'll be telling me next that it all stems from some childhood experience that I can't even remember. Just remind me never to lie on a couch around you,' she said, making a good show of laughing it off.

They passed the rest of the flight in idle conversation and it wasn't until they had buckled up for the descent that Cat allowed herself a brief moment of contemplation.

She thought about what Alex had said and tried to identify the catalyst that he'd referred to. Eventually the mechanical sound of the wheels being lowered and the whine of the engines during the reverse thrust interrupted her musing. Putting all thoughts of her private life to one side, she forced herself to focus on what lay ahead over the following forty-eight hours.

She would have time enough on the return flight to consider what waited for her at home.

Nineteen

A haze hung over the tarmac as the air shimmered from the heat; a heat that intensified with every step Cat took down the mobile air-stairs. In rich contrast to the frost-filled mornings and rain-soaked days back home, the sun beat down a glorious seven hours a day across the Cypriot landscape. Cat turned her face up towards the sun, revelling in its touch. She inhaled deeply and, as the dry, warm air filled her lungs, felt something close to contentment for the first time in weeks.

She felt the light touch of his hand on her back.

'Come on, there isn't time to stand around. We've got a tight schedule, remember?' Alex pushed gently in the direction of the shuttle bus that was waiting to ferry them to the arrivals gate.

They entered the cool air-conditioned confines of the terminal building and looked around. A huge giant of a man with warm olive skin and a thick thatch of short black hair stood holding aloft a card bearing Alex's name. After introducing himself as Detective Glafcos Theophanus he ushered them to a dust-covered people carrier conspicuously parked in a no park zone.

They quickly left the built-up port city of Larnaca and travelled along smooth, wide roads through a largely barren landscape. Even though it was late in the year the terrain was a dry scrub after a typically hot summer.

Soon the appearance of villages on the east of the island marked their return to civilisation. Turning off the main highway, the car wound its way through a series of small residential roads, the houses growing more luxurious with every passing mile.

'Here we are,' Glafcos said, pulling onto the driveway of a single-storey white building. Its crisp, clean lines provided a perfect backdrop to the bright pinks and purples of geranium, bougainvillea and hibiscus that filled the borders and climbed skyward either side of the door.

Alex stepped out of the car.

'Are you serious?'

Glafcos walked ahead and unlocked the heavy white oak door. Cat followed behind. She placed her overnight bag on the floor in the hallway and turned to admire their accommodation.

'This is beautiful.'

Characteristically Mediterranean, the simple combination of cool white walls and terracotta floor tiles could have been plucked straight from the pages of any lifestyle magazine.

'I am glad you like it,' Glafcos said.

He continued through the open-plan lounge-diner to a set of French doors at the rear of the room. Cat followed and waited as he twisted a key in the lock and swung the doors open to reveal a large terrace, on which a table and chairs were positioned to maximise the view of the shimmering blue pool.

'Alex,' she called. 'Come and look at this.'

Alex stepped out onto the terrace to join them and whistled in admiration.

'This is unreal. I'd better warn you, if you ever have to come to stay with us under a reciprocal arrangement, you'll be bitterly disappointed. The best we could manage would be some flea-ridden police house, complete with leaky shower and concrete yard.' He looked around at the well-tended gardens, beyond which he could see the golden sands of the beach that stretched temptingly into the sea. 'What is this place?'

'It is my own. It is let it out for holiday rentals,' Glafcos replied. 'The season has passed and there are no bookings now until next spring.' He stepped back through the French doors. 'Come, let me show you around.'

After a quick tour, Cat and Alex changed into clothes more suitable for the warm weather and they and Glafcos returned to Larnaca, to the British Army base. Within the hour they were in the company of Captain William Benton-Jones, the first on their list to be interviewed.

A secretary opened the door and made introductions. Benton-Jones was sitting at a solid-looking, leather-embossed desk, its age and classic design at odds with the black plastic of the computer that rested on its polished surface. In full uniform, with short back and sides and a clipped moustache, he looked every inch the English officer. An image that was made whole the second he spoke.

'I trust you will join me in a cup of tea?' he said, in a perfectly preserved plummy English accent.

They crossed the floor of the office. Heavy oak pieces had been used to make different parts of the massive room functionally distinct. Captain Benton-Jones showed his guests to one corner where four high-backed armchairs surrounded a low table on which an ornate silver teapot and china tea service had been set out. Cat settled into the chair nearest to an open veranda overlooking an immaculately manicured, verdant lawn. She twisted in her seat and looked around the room. Just beyond the desk, floor-to-ceiling bookcases ran the length of the wall. Modern texts sat shoulder-to-shoulder with weighty dust-covered tomes. In the opposite corner to where they were sitting a colossal conference table dominated the space. A large world map and white-board as big as a king-size sheet conjured up images of tense boardroom battles where countless military strategies had been won and lost.

Benton-Jones offered to play mother and poured the drinks. No gritty tasteless vending machine offerings here. Both Cat and Alex chose Earl Grey, which they took with lemon, rather than milk, in deference to the heat. But if they had assumed from the lavish surroundings and gracious hospitality that the captain was one to indulge in sociable chit-chat they were soon proved wrong. The second their drinks were poured, he began.

'Detective Inspector York, I understand from your telephone call that you are making enquiries about a soldier who once served here?'

'Yes sir. That is correct. As I explained yesterday, we are trying to obtain information on a Mr Steven Berry.'

'I'm not sure what information you are looking for but I have looked into what we know of this man and there is nothing that stands out. From his record Berry was a good soldier, he trained hard and kept his nose clean. If he ever got into trouble it never reached my ears.'

'We were hoping to be able to speak to someone who knew Berry quite well. Someone who can tell us what sort of person he is.'

Benton-Jones nodded.

'I have arranged for one my sergeants, Jack Moore, to be available to talk to you. He led Berry's squad at the time he was here. My secretary will escort you to where he is waiting.'

And with that the uniformed officer drank his tea in record time and waited courteously for his guests to do likewise.

Cat was first into the third-floor conference room in which Jack Moore was already waiting. Standing, looking out of the room's only window, he turned as they entered. Just as the room had none of the opulence of the private office that they had just left, the contrast between the man and his superior officer was equally marked. Moore was short, stocky and had an American-styled crew cut. An array of tattoos littered his arms, disappearing up beyond the limits of his short-sleeve shirt. As they entered, he stood to attention and saluted.

Alex waved a dismissive hand.

'No need to salute, this is a civilian investigation. Please sit down. We'd just like to ask you a couple of questions about one of your ex-subordinates.'

The sergeant sat facing the door. Alex sat directly opposite him, flanked on either side by Cat and Glafcos.

'I'm not sure how much you know about the reason for our being here, but I just have a few simple background questions to ask about an ex-soldier, Steven Berry.'

'Yes sir.'

'You knew Mr Berry?'

'Yes sir. He was under my command.'

'For how many years?'

The officer paused before replying.

'Around twelve years, sir.'

'You must have known him pretty well,' Alex said.

'Yes sir.'

'And how did you find him as a subordinate?'

'He was a very good soldier, sir.'

'I'm sorry, but what does that mean?'

'He did as he was told.'

'He followed orders.'

'Yes sir.'

'How about initiative? Did he have any?'

'Yes sir, but only when it was called for.'

'So, the model employee?'

'Yes sir.'

'And did he enjoy his job?'

'From what I could tell.'

'So, no complaints?'

'Not from me.'

The army officer remained bolt upright throughout the entire exchange and appeared to offer his answers freely enough, but from the watchful look of his eyes and his clipped answers Cat suspected the man harboured an inner suspicion and she quickly grew to question the value of the interview. She jumped in at the first opportunity and hoped to be able to elicit more useful information by steering the discussion in a different direction.

'What was Berry like as a person?'

The uniformed man looked genuinely confused by the question.

'You know, off-duty, socially,' Cat elaborated.

'I did not associate with him in a social sense.'

'Not at all? Not even at Christmas?'

'No, ma'am.'

'Who did he socialise with?'

'Others of his rank or similar ranks.'

'Would you happen to know any of his friends?'

'I'm not sure that I would ma'am.'

'Okay...' Cat was surprised but she wasn't deterred. 'Are there any specific bars or pubs where people who live on the barracks tend to go to?'

'There are two pubs. One is part of the social club at the barracks. The other is the Irish, which is just down the road. On the weekends a lot of the lads go into the tourist areas where things are a bit livelier.'

'What about Berry, did he go to one bar more than another?'

'I couldn't say with any certainty.'

'I'm not interested in certainty. In your opinion, did he visit one bar more than the other?' Cat pressed.

Suddenly aware of the hard tone that had crept into her voice she paused and took the opportunity to give Sergeant Moore a polite smile. He stared back at her unblinking.

Cat sensed that he had been asked a direct question that he knew the answer to but for whatever reason didn't want to say. After a moment's deliberation he had made a decision.

'The Irish Bar,' he said grudgingly.

'Thank you,' Cat said, relieved at having got a straight answer.

'Was he a regular there?' Alex asked.

'I'm sorry sir, I can't say for sure. He did go there a lot.'

'Wouldn't that make him a regular?'

'I suppose so, yes, sir.'

'Did you ever suspect him of having a drink problem?'

'No sir. I never had any cause to suspect that at all.'

Alex pressed on, 'How was Mr Berry's relationship with his wife?'

Cat watched the sergeant's face closely. But the army man gave nothing away. He continued to look impassively at the wall opposite.

'He never discussed his marital situation with me.'

'Did he socialise much with his wife?'

'I don't know sir.'

'Well, did you ever see him out with her?'

'No sir, I can't say that I did.'

'Is that normal? I mean don't wives go out in the evenings with their husbands?'

'Some do, some don't.'

'Did you actually know Mrs Berry?'

'I had met her on a couple of occasions at formal events, but that was all.'

He stopped and looked at each of his questioners in turn.

Alex cleared his throat.

'Were you surprised when you learned that Mr Berry was returning to the UK?'

Cat noticed the uniformed man grow even more rigid.

'At first, until I found out the circumstances,' he replied.

Alex frowned.

'What... that his father-in-law had died and his wife wanted to return to her childhood home or that he was stinking rich and didn't need to work anymore?'

Cat cringed, fearful that Alex had pushed him too far.

Moore stared at the wall behind Alex's shoulder but he was too well trained to ignore such a direct request.

'The former, sir.'

Alex nodded.

'I think that's all of our questions,' Alex said. 'Unless of course my colleagues have got anything they would like to ask?'

'Yes. I've got a question,' Cat said making eye contact with the uniformed officer. 'Sergeant Moore, how did Mr Berry use his holiday entitlement?'

'I'm sorry, I don't understand?'

'How did he book his holidays? Did he used to book a year in advance in two-week blocks, or did he take it when he needed it, in dribs and drabs?'

'I can't say I remember.'

'Well could you find out? I'd like to see exactly what leave he took in the twelve months before he left, and when he first booked it.'

If Sergeant Moore thought the request unusual, he didn't show it.

'Of course, ma'am.'

'Actually, I'd like details of all of the leave he took, including any parental or compassionate leave he might have taken.'

'Special leave is very tightly regulated.'

'Presumably the fact his son had such a serious condition would have made him at least eligible to be considered for special leave?' Cat challenged.

'I don't know anything about his son's condition,' Moore said.

'You didn't know he suffers from haemophilia?'

Moore looked totally thrown.

'I'm sorry but I don't know what that is. Is it some sort of VD?'

Cat stared at the man, trying to figure out whether he was trying it on, or whether he really didn't know. Going on instinct, she thought it was the latter.

'No sergeant, it isn't a venereal disease, although I think the correct term these days is sexually transmitted disease. Haemophilia is a genetic blood disorder.' Cat watched the uniformed man's eyes widened momentarily before he resumed his static composure. 'And you're sure you didn't know that Steve Berry's son had haemophilia?'

'No ma'am, I did not.'

'I take it then that he never took time off to take his son to hospital or to the doctors, nothing like that?'

'Not as far as I know. Though of course he could have used his leave. Provided he booked it in accordance with procedure I would have no cause to enquire as to the reason.'

'Okay, thank you. That's everything from me,' Cat said.

'Detective Theophanus?' Alex said, turning towards Glafcos.

'Yes, I have one question.' Moore looked at him and waited. 'Sergeant, in the years that you have worked here are you aware of anyone going missing or leaving unexpectedly?'

'Do you mean AWOL, because that would be classified?'

'No, I don't mean absent without leave, I mean gone away at a moment's notice. Maybe you have heard a tale of a wife having deserted her husband for someone else, leaving everything behind, or perhaps of a daughter who has run off with some undesirable?'

Moore chewed on his lip and narrowed his eyes. After a short pause he shook his head.

'I can't think of anyone off the top of my head. There's bound to be someone. Army life, especially on tour, doesn't suit everyone. Occasionally I get to hear of wives who've jacked it all in and gone back home.'

'But surely in those cases they keep in touch with their friends here, the other wives, at least for a while, don't they? I'm talking about situations where no one hears from them ever again.'

'In which case then, no. I don't know anything like that. Usually break-ups are messy affairs. There's a lot of mud-slinging goes on, in public as well as in private.' More than a hint of bitterness had entered his voice, which made Cat wonder whether he was speaking from experience. 'To be honest, I wish more would just disappear overnight. It would make my life a damn sight easier.' He added as an afterthought, 'I'm normally the one that has to convince the broken man that life, and by that, I mean work, must go on.'

Twenty

The Irish Pub was a typical 'Brits abroad' affair, with chalkboards propped either side of the doorway, tempting passers-by with the promise of cheap bitter and genuine Irish stout.

Trading the bright sunlight for the pub's dark atmosphere, Cat felt as though she was stepping into some sort of a surreal film-noir set. Despite the fact that it was only three-thirty in the afternoon, it was already busy and patronised solely by men, most of whom stood at the bar, pints in hand, chatting.

The Britishness was even more in evidence on the inside. Jars of pickled eggs and baskets of crisps in flavours such as smoky bacon and prawn cocktail lined the shelves on the back wall and beer towels hung, festooned around clip-frames that contained photographs of punters in various stages of sobriety, enjoying the local hospitality.

The hard clack of resin rang out from somewhere at the back of the room where it turned a corner. Alex set off in the direction of the noise. Cat followed him, though noticing Glafcos stop at the bar, she only ventured far enough to be able to see around the corner.

A pool tournament appeared to be in full swing; eight men at two tables. Over-table lamps highlighted motes of dust hanging in the air, intermingled with e-cigarette vapour. Alex turned and signalled to Cat to wait. She stayed where she was and watched as he approached the players – off-duty soldiers, she guessed. They responded to the interruption with interest. After the briefest of exchanges Alex approached the bar, bringing one of the men with him.

'Detectives Theophanus and McKenzie,' Alex said, gesturing

to Glafcos and Cat in turn.

'Martin Briggs. Good to meet you.' The surprisingly young-looking squaddie set down his pint glass and pulled up a stool. 'So, you want to talk to me about my old pal Steve. What's he been up to then?' he asked in a soft Geordie accent. Dressed in jeans and a t-shirt he looked comfortably at ease.

'Just routine enquiries,' Alex said. 'You and Steve were good mates, were you?'

'Used to be. Well I thought we were. We certainly went back a long way. But you know I've not had so much as a lousy text since he left. Not even after I'd sent him one. I left a message for him when I was over there visiting family, but I heard nothing back. And there I was thinking he'd jump at the chance to get out of the house for a while. But I suppose a life of luxury isn't too bad a trade-off for having to live with the miserable witch.' He grinned and reached for his pint.

'Are you talking about Caroline, his wife?' Cat asked, the surprise clear in her voice.

'Yeah.' Slowly his smile started to fade. 'Say, this isn't about her is it?'

'Would that surprise you?' Alex asked. 'Was he violent with his wife? Smack her around a bit, did he?'

The other man's eyes widened.

'Oh no, nothing like that.'

He set his pint back onto the bar.

'But he threatened to, is that it?'

'No, honestly, he isn't like that. He's not a violent sort of bloke.'

'He was a soldier,' Alex said.

The army man shot him an indignant look.

'Just because you're a soldier doesn't mean you settle everything with your fists.'

'I'm sorry. I'm just trying to understand what he was like. You sound very sure that he wouldn't do anything to hurt his wife but

195

in the privacy of their own home people can say and do all sorts of things that otherwise seem out of character.'

'Yeah, maybe, but not Steve. He might have said things – you know, bitched about her and stuff – but it was obvious he was just letting off steam. Doesn't everyone when they're going through a bad patch? And anyway, when he got fed up he just gave her a wide berth. He'd come in here, shoot some pool. He was here that often I'd be surprised if they were under the same roof long enough to fight.'

'You said Steve said some stuff, letting off a bit of steam,' Cat said. 'What sort of things did he say?'

'I don't know, just general moaning. To be honest, if she was my wife I'd have said a lot worse. His missus's a miserable bag. She hated living here. She never used to come out with Steve, thank God, and from what Steve said, she was just as glad to get him out of the house. She just wanted to stay at home nursing that little boy of theirs. The kid's got something wrong with him; poor little beggar had to have injections every day.' He reached for his glass and took a drink this time. 'So, what's he done?'

He looked from face to face. Suddenly his eyes lit up. 'He's made off with her money, is that it? It's got to be something like that to have you lot traipsing around asking questions.'

'Do you think that's what it comes down to, the reason they're together – the money?' Alex said.

Martin shrugged.

'Can't see what else it would be.'

'What about his son? Even if he had nothing else to stay for surely it was worth trying to make it work for his son's sake?'

'S'pose.'

Just then the landlord approached. A six-foot-six giant of a man, almost as wide as he was tall. Obviously, a martyr to his trade, he sported an enormous beer belly. He gestured to Martin's glass; only an inch of the straw-coloured pilsner remained.

'Go ahead, if you want. I'll stand you another,' Alex said.

Martin knocked back the last finger of drink and handed over the empty glass.

'Fond of his cars isn't he, your old mate?' Alex said.

'I don't know, is he?'

'I figured he must be, given he's set himself up in the classic car business.'

'Well he didn't have time for anything like that when he was here. Or the money.'

'From what you're saying, Steve Berry was just your average Joe,' Alex said.

'That's right.'

The landlord placed a freshly pulled pint on the counter.

'If things were so bad why did he stay with his wife?' Cat asked.

'For an easy life I suppose.'

'But you just described her as an old witch and said how he spent most of his time here to avoid her.'

Martin looked down; he twisted his mouth.

'Well, that wasn't the only reason he came in here.'

'Was he seeing someone else?' Alex asked as he handed the barman money for the beer.

Martin nodded. Cat felt a little buzz.

'There was a woman who used to work here, one of the barmaids. You remember Jenny, don't you Frank?' he said, addressing the landlord. 'The one who Steve Berry was, you know...'

'Aye, nice lass,' the landlord said in a broad Irish brogue.

'She was a damn sight friendlier than the old trout. And she knew how to have a laugh.'

'Does she still work here?' Alex asked.

'No,' the landlord, said. 'She buggered off after Steve stopped coming.'

'What reason did she give?'

'Said she was going travelling. I was gutted. She was as reliable as clock-work, seven days a week, week in, week out. The only holiday she had was when her Ma died and she had to go back for the funeral. And the punters loved her. She stayed 'til I got someone else for her shifts but she was gone within a couple of weeks. I suppose I should have been grateful she stayed as long as she did; bar staff usually only stay a couple of months.'

'Did she give a forwarding address?' Cat asked.

'Yeah. Just for posting stuff on. But there was never any need to contact her after she went. I paid her up to the last day.'

The three detectives exchanged a volley of glances.

'What was her surname?' Glafcos asked.

A look of concentration descended on Martin's face up as he tried to remember.

'Black. Jenny Black,' Frank said quickly. 'I remember 'cos it rhymes with Penny Black, you know the oldest postage stamp.'

Martin gave him a surprised look.

'What?' Frank said. 'I used to have a stamp collection when I was a kid. It's the sort of thing kids do.'

'You surprise me,' Martin said. 'I can't imagine your fat fingers fondling dainty little–'

'What about that forwarding address, any chance you've still got that? Alex asked, ignoring the banter that was developing between the two men.

The barman looked doubtful.

'I'll go take a look but I'll not promise anything.'

Frank padded off and disappeared through a door at the back of the bar. Shortly they heard his heavy footsteps thump above their heads. Five minutes later he reappeared, shaking his head.

'Sorry,' he said.

'Okay. Thanks for looking.'

The landlord started back towards the busy bar, where half-a-dozen or so men looked expectantly at him, their empty pint glasses doing all the talking.

'Hang on,' Cat called out. 'Just one more thing.'

Frank turned.

'Do you have a photo?' Cat asked him. 'Of Jenny, I mean.'

Frank let his gaze roam around the room, framed photographs in abundance.

'Well, there's sure to be one or two of her amongst this lot.'

He glanced back to his customers, drawn by the rising level of the men's murmurs.

'Tell you what. I'll take a look tonight after we've shut. I'll choose a couple o' good ones and send them over to you. How does that sound?'

'The address is on the card,' Glafcos said, passing over a typed business card.

Frank pocketed it and walked away, leaving the detectives to quiz Martin until their questions ran dry. To show their appreciation, Alex pushed a couple of notes into the squaddie's hand.

As they left the cool darkness of the bar Cat was surprised to find the glaring light of the afternoon had given way to the thin smokiness of twilight.

They began a slow stroll back to the car. Cat turned to say something to Glafcos when she realised he was no longer beside her.

She turned and looked behind her.

'Glafcos, are you alright?' she called to the Greek detective. He'd stopped walking and was standing a short distance away, a look of intense concentration on his face.

He walked over to join them.

'Yes. I am fine.' But then he shook his head. 'The conversations today, they have reminded me of something but my memory, it is too foggy.'

Cat and Alex looked at him.

'This condition, this heemapheelyak, I have heard of it before. The woman found in the mountains...'

'She had haemophilia?' Alex asked.

Glafcos shook his head but without conviction.

'I do not say that. I do not know. Only that there was something in the pathology report. I will need to check. I will also make some enquiries into this Jenny Black.'

'How long will that take?' Alex asked.

'Maybe tomorrow, maybe longer. I will make a call now and then we go straight to the villa. I will wait while you, how do you say it, freshen up for dinner?'

'Dinner?' Cat said.

'Of course, you are my guests. You will eat at my house tonight.'

'This is very good of you Glafcos. We really do appreciate all the effort you are going to.'

'It is no trouble. But it is interesting also. We can carry on with our discussions but where it is more relaxing.'

Glafcos' home was only a short walk from the villa where Alex and Cat were staying and as they approached, they could see it was every inch as impressive, only considerably larger. The difference was more marked once they entered the house. The whole interior design had been so cleverly executed. The open layout and tall, whitewashed walls breathed light and space into the rooms. Striking pieces of original art adorned the walls and large vases, bursting with fresh tropical flowers smelling of orange blossom, made it feel warm and homely. Cat looked about her, trying to take it all in as they were ushered through a wide set of glass doors into the lush gardens. Well stocked meticulously tended, subtle lighting gave a sophisticated and romantic atmosphere. Cat stood at the threshold and just stared in awe.

Glafcos led them through to a wide patio that overlooked the pool. Sofia, his wife, was relaxing on a wicker settee, its plump cushions ideal for lazy evenings under the stars. Sofia rose and set down her glass of white wine on a low coffee table, next to three clean glasses and a bottle of Chablis that was chilling in an ice bucket. She greeted them with a light touch of her cheek to theirs, both sides. An intoxicating blend of tropical scents and citrus notes lingered on her skin.

Sofia was a very beautiful woman and obviously the creative inspiration behind their stylish home. Her white linen tunic and trousers emphasised her olive skin and glossy, ebony hair, and formed a perfect foil to a striking pendant necklace made up of deep blue lapis and bright turquoise. Despite the few streaks of silver that ran through her dark hair, she wore her fifty-plus years well.

Cat felt overwhelmingly under-dressed in a navy linen skirt and loose tailored shirt. She was just grateful she'd remembered to pack the jade necklace and earrings that complemented the leaf motif of her shirt and highlighted the green of her eyes.

Sofia left her guests with full glasses and disappeared into the house to continue with the dinner preparations. Glafcos took the opportunity to show them around the extensive garden while they quizzed him about life on the island and his experiences in the job.

'It sounds idyllic,' Cat said, as they returned to the terrace, already seduced by the thought of hot days and warm evenings.

'It is not like your English cities. I cannot complain. We have such low crime rates because we are quick to act and the penalties are severe. And our crime prevention agencies co-operate well across the island so criminals rarely leave without capture. This is what makes this case so frustrating. How can someone be murdered and yet no one to have even noticed her missing? If it hadn't been for the chance finding by the forestry workers accidentally uncovering the remains, she may never have been found.'

'Could she have been an illegal immigrant, maybe from the Turkish side?' Cat asked.

'We thought that initially but DNA analysis ruled that out. This woman is not of Greek or Turkish descent. I have always thought a tourist but we checked with the airports and boat operators and there is no one unaccounted for that remotely matches.'

Over dinner the case took a back seat and the conversation meandered around more agreeable topics whilst they feasted on a traditional Greek Cypriot meze. They ate alfresco, sitting on the terrace, illuminated by the stars, the candles on the table and the dappled glow from the pool's lighting. The conversation flowed freely, as did the food and wine and it was only after the dessert plates had been taken away that they allowed their thoughts to turn back to the circumstances that had brought them together. By the time Sofia returned from the kitchen with freshly brewed coffee the three of them were in the midst of dissecting the day's findings, digesting the facts along with their dinner.

'So here we have a man who, one day, was a good soldier and one of the lads, trapped in a loveless marriage who was openly making up for it by indulging elsewhere. The next day, his father-in-law ups and dies, so off he trots to play the doting husband and father, friendless and jobless. It's almost as though the old Steve Berry died the same time the old man did,' Alex said.

'Well, I've been thinking it through and can't help but puzzle about this woman, Jenny,' Cat said. 'I wonder whether she really did leave lonely and rejected, set to travel the world on her own, or whether she headed straight back to England. Maybe she settled somewhere not a million miles from an exclusive estate called Roswell Park, where she has regular visits from an old pal, someone she used to know in Cyprus. What do you think?'

'That's where Steve Berry lives,' Alex explained to their hosts. 'So that's why you wanted the photo'?'

Cat nodded.

'You think that she went to be with her lover?' Glafcos said.

'Well that could be one reason why Berry, who's now a very rich man, chooses to spends his days tucked away in that garage of his,' Cat said.

'With any luck Spencer or Bob may have something to tell us when we get back. I got them doing some surveillance on the garage while we're away,' Alex said.

Sofia took a sip of her wine. As she gently placed her glass down on the table in front of her, she looked at Cat and Alex, a puzzled expression on her face.

'So, in England a man cannot leave his wife and have the money?' she asked.

'He can leave, yes, but they would have to share the money,' Cat said. 'The law isn't clear-cut and he may not even get half. It depends on what the couple and their solicitors agree to.'

'But you say that the wife, her father was rich?'

'Yes, very.'

'So why would this man stay with a wife that he hates, when he can have half of a lot of money and be with a woman he loves? A half of a lot is still a lot, isn't it?'

They all fell silent. It seemed that Sofia's simplistic view had them stuck for words.

After a while Cat's expression brightened.

'Maybe there was a pre-nup?

'Maybe it was for the sake of his son?' Alex suggested, for the second time.

Cat stole a glance in his direction, but he had turned away from her and was staring out at the pool, which cast an eerie glow against the dark garden. She wondered whether the emotional strain of his son's illness was finally getting to him. Sofia, oblivious to recent events, waved his statement away with the flick of her hand.

'Nonsense,' she said, 'these things can be worked out. It is not the end of the world to divorce... No?'

'It might have seemed that way to Berry if he found out that his wife was going to leave him and return to the UK, back in the summer before her father died,' Alex said. 'Especially if there was no pre-nup. Caroline could have paid for the best solicitors to make sure Berry got very little.'

Cat began to roll her red wine around the bowl of the glass.

'Alex, your idea that Berry might be planning on killing Caroline, hoping to make it look like the work of a serial killer... well, what if you're right? But what if it's even more sinister? What if Berry killed Howard Williams and now intends to kill his wife and inherit the lot?'

Cat waited for a barrage of challenges but everyone remained quiet and thoughtful.

'What if Berry travelled to the UK and somehow orchestrated Howard Williams' death?' she said. 'Isn't it possible that Megan and Jane saw him when he was there but didn't recognise him at that time? That could explain why he didn't want to be seen at his father-in-law's funeral. And all the time they were around they'd pose a risk, wouldn't they?'

'So that's why you asked about his holiday entitlement earlier today,' Alex said.

'Yeah,' Cat said. 'I've been thinking all along that this all started with Howard's death but just couldn't make it fit. But if you think of his death being in the middle of a series of events it makes much more sense. I think it was Caroline threatening to leave Berry and return home to her father that was the catalyst.'

Theories abounded for the rest of the evening, until just after midnight when they agreed to call it a day. Cat and Alex started the short stroll back to the villa, retracing their steps from earlier, the stars lighting their path. It was a cloudless night and the air was cool but Cat was in a thoughtful mood, content to walk slowly, her jacket keeping the chill at bay.

'We seem to have it so wrong in our country don't you think?' she said.

'In what way?' Alex asked.

'Everything seems so much better here. The pace of life, the weather...'

'Well, the weather is the weather. You can't do much about

that. And, to be honest, a lot of everything else to do with the lifestyle stems from the weather. Take tonight, sitting out by the pool, the stuffed vine leaves, the wonderful salads, the tropical gardens, that's just part and parcel of a Mediterranean life. Well, a middle-class Mediterranean life. I'm sure every household in Cyprus isn't the same. On the other hand, they have to go to work when the weather is this good all year and I doubt if they sit out every night, talking and drinking like we did tonight. And besides, they don't get to have snow-ball fights in winter and drought is a given, not just something that happens once in a while.'

'I suppose.'

'You know, happiness is more about where you are in your head, not where you happen to be in the world.'

'You *are* very philosophical today,' Cat said as she waited for him to open the door to their villa.

'Perhaps you're pining for your old life?' he said. 'I've always thought you were mad to give up those blue seas and deserted beaches for crowded streets and grimy estates. You only get one shot at life, you know.' He stepped inside and turned on a light, Cat followed. 'Anyway, enough chat. The car is picking us up in...' He squinted to see his watch in the poor light, 'exactly seven hours.'

Cat groaned and said goodnight before retreating to her room, too tired to give any serious thought to what Alex had said. Besides, she wasn't sure she even wanted to consider it. He might just be right.

She woke at six, feeling sluggish and thick-headed, thanks to too little sleep and too much wine. She opened the French doors on what promised to be another beautiful sunny day. After an invigorating shower and a freshly squeezed orange juice she was ready to face the world.

'Don't take too long,' she called out to Alex as he emerged from his room en route to the shared bathroom. 'Breakfast is ready.'

'I'll be quick. Why don't you open the French doors? We should make the most of the sunshine and have breakfast on the patio.'

'Already have. Coffee and croissants are waiting.'

Minutes later Alex, already dressed in bark-coloured lightweight trousers and a short-sleeve shirt, emerged from the bathroom, a cloud of steam trailing behind him. He joined Cat on the terrace, where she had already made a start on the food.

'I can't believe Sofia has gone to so much trouble,' he said, taking a seat at the table.

'I know. This coffee is fantastic, nice and strong.'

'You seem in good spirits,' he said, between mouthfuls of his first pastry.

'Must be the sunshine,' she said, smiling.

Forty minutes later they left the house. Glafcos greeted them from the passenger seat of a waiting jeep. As they travelled, he played the part of tour guide, teaching them about Cyprus' still divided and controversial history. Their journey took them inland. Leaving behind the flat coastal roads they climbed up into rocky mountain terrain where Glafcos' commentary turned into an impromptu geography lesson.

'The Troodos mountains are the backbone of Southern Cyprus. They cover almost a quarter of the island's surface area. The landscape varies a lot; some parts in the west are dense forest, yet in some of the eastern resorts it is harsh with few trees. In summer everyone comes for the walking. The forestry department is opening up many old paths and tracks between the highest villages and monasteries. They draw maps for nature trails. It was while clearing one of the old paths they found the bones.' Glafcos looked out of the window momentarily before instructing the driver, 'Stop anywhere here.' Turning back to his passengers he explained, 'We must travel on foot from here.'

The car had pulled into a small lay-by that was carved into the side of the steep hillside. The three of them set off down a small dust track that left the road, leaving their driver waiting with the car. Glafcos walked quickly and confidently and Cat noticed he didn't even pause when faced with a fork in the path.

'You know the way to this place without a map?'

'I used a map at first. I have come back here many times. So now I remember.'

After a twenty-minute hike, Glafcos halted them by raising a hand. Cat was grateful for the break. The temperature was almost twenty-five degrees, despite being in the shade, and Glafcos had set a vigorous pace. She stooped down to retrieve a water bottle from her bag and after slaking her thirst she walked over to where the two men were standing. Glafcos waited for her to draw level.

'This rock here is where they found the first bones.' He gestured towards a large boulder that rested next to the expansive trunk of an ancient Cedar tree. 'The body had been buried in a shallow grave a little further up.' He pointed twenty or so metres up the slope to their right. 'It is thought that heavy rainfall had exposed part of the body and scavengers pulled the lower limbs away. Either the animals or later rains carried the bones down the hill until they were caught by the rocks and the tree here. We did eventually manage to retrieve the whole skeleton. There were differing degrees of decomposition. The body parts that remained buried were much better preserved. The bones that had been exposed showed some signs of weathering and some animal damage though they were still largely intact.'

'You said there was evidence of a blow to the head,' Cat said, remembering an earlier conversation.

'That is correct. There was a crack at the back of the skull that was later determined to be the most likely cause of death.'

'And nothing else was found on the site? No fragments of clothing or anything that could help to identify her?' Cat asked.

'A few scraps were found, but we have nothing to match them to. Like the bones.'

Cat and Alex started to walk around the site, scanning the ground and surrounding greenery. Cat moved systematically up the hill away from the boulder, scouring the floor at her feet. Occasionally she would stoop to dust away earth from the tinder-dry forest floor, desperately hoping to alight upon some previously overlooked clue. She looked over to Alex and noticed him doing the same.

An hour later Glafcos approached her.

'I think we are done. There is nothing more here.'

The car took them straight to the Police Headquarters. Despite the fact that the heat had gone out of the day, Glafcos' office was still stiflingly hot, the room's air conditioning unit having lain idle during his absence. Cat and Alex both nursed a glass of cold water while Glafcos riffled through his in-tray.

'Tsk. Nothing.' He swivelled in his seat and jabbed a fat finger at the computer's power button.

'Tonight, you must go to Kamaris. It is the best place and not too far from the house,' he said while typing in his password. 'They serve very good fish and good meze. You will enjoy.'

'I'm sure we will,' Alex replied.

'Would you like me to book it for you? It is very popular.'

The computer sprang into life and Glafcos opened up his email system and began to run his eye down the long line of messages.

'Glafcos you need to get going, don't you? Didn't you say that you had to be out of the house by six?' Cat looked at her watch. 'It's four-thirty already.'

Her words seemed to send Glafcos into a frenzy of panic. He continued to scan through his emails.

'I'm sure it will be here somewhere. I told them to let me know. It must be here.'

'What are you looking for?' Alex asked.

'The responses from the doctors... Wait, here, this must be it.'

He fell silent, his eyes flicked across the screen as his finger manipulated the mouse to scroll down the page.

'I was right. The dead woman, she was, how you say carrying the haemophilia.' His eyes continued to skim the screen. 'With the barmaid we have no luck. It will take more time to trace this woman.'

He swiped at the power button, not bothering with the logout routines.

'Once again, please accept my apologies – but the tickets, they have been booked for a long time.'

'Don't worry about it Glafcos. Have a wonderful time at the theatre. We'll see you tomorrow.'

Glafcos glanced down at his watch.

'I am sorry. I must go. Please, enjoy the rest of your stay,' he said before rushing from his office.

Kamaris turned out to be a traditional Greek tavern, and, as Glafcos had warned, a very popular one. Most tables were already occupied when they arrived. They were fully booked, the maître d' explained apologetically.

'We should have listened to Glafcos and got him to book it earlier.' Alex said to Cat before turning back to the smart-suited young Cypriot. 'I am sorry we will not be able to sample your wonderful meze. It has been highly recommended to us by our friends, Glafcos and Sofia Theophanus. They told us a trip to Cyprus without a visit to Kamaris was a wasted trip.'

The other man's expression lifted.

'Ahh! Friends of Glafcos and Sofia. You are staying with them, yes?'

'Yes, until tomorrow. This is our last night.'

The maître d' looked back across the busy restaurant.

'One moment. I will see what I can do.'

After a short wait, they were ushered to a small, beautifully laid table. It was a little cramped, tucked in a corner of a moonlit terrace overlooking the garden, but it was better than the alternative – neither of them had thought to ask Glafcos for suggestions of alternative places to eat.

They kept the conversation clear of murder, sticking to topics more suitable for the dinner table and, while waiting for their food to arrive, they broke from their chat to listen to the musician that serenaded them with his violin. They clapped gently in appreciation and he moved on to another table.

Cat looked around.

'I can't remember the last time I've been to such a classy restaurant.'

She touched a finger gently to the floral centrepiece.

'Don't you and Mike go out much then?'

She gave a wry smile. 'Try never.' Alex raised an eyebrow, causing her to elaborate. 'He says it's my fault: that I never want to go out. That's not true. I just don't want to go out when all that's on offer is a beery night in the pub with him and his mates.'

Alex gave her a puzzled look and reached for his lager. He took a drink and returned the glass to the table before asking, 'Why do you stay with him? It's not like you're desperate or anything.' Cat shot him a look. 'Come on, you're not, are you? You're an attractive, intelligent woman. You could have your pick of men.'

She looked down and tucked a stray strand of hair behind her ear.

'Seriously,' he said. 'Life's too short. You deserve better.'

This time it was Cat's turn to reach for her glass, biding for time. After a sip of wine, she looked back at Alex.

'Do you and Mel go out much then?'

He cast his eyes down and fiddled with the edge of his napkin.

'We've got kids. Everything changes when you've got kids.' He mustered a smile.

'Better make the most of tonight then. It sounds like it could be a long time before either of us gets to do it again.'

Alex held up his glass. 'I'll drink to that.'

Twenty-One

A grey and miserable London awaited their return, adding to Cat's already dampened spirits.

'I wish we had more to show for our trip,' she said, staring out of the window at the rain bouncing off the road.

Alex shrugged.

'That's just the way it goes sometimes. Besides, it was useful thinking time.'

'Mmm.' Cat sounded dubious. Their return journey had been marred by the news that Steve Berry had been present and correct on the base at the time of Howard Williams' death. In fact, there was no evidence that he had travelled to the UK at any time during the preceding twelve months.

'He could have still had something to do with Howard's death. They could have done it together,' Cat said.

'Who?'

'Steve Berry. He could have done it, if Jenny helped.'

Alex gave her a look.

'Let it go. It doesn't work.'

She didn't speak again until they were approaching the station, where her car was parked. 'Can you drop me by the back door rather than the car park? I want to grab a couple of things from the office before I head home.'

Alex parked next to the covered entrance. He quickly hopped out and passed Cat her overnight bag from the boot. She took the luggage and moved to the door where she swiped her pass over the electronic reader.

'Well I guess I'll see you Monday then?' she said, pulling the door open

'Monday.' He nodded. 'Have a good weekend.'

The kettle had barely clicked off when Cat poured the still-bubbling water over the instant coffee granules that lay at the bottom of the mug. She paused and cocked her head. She was sure she'd heard something in the corridor outside. Listening harder now, she could clearly make out the sound of footsteps.

The office door swung open.

'Alex! What are you doing sneaking in? I wondered who the hell it was. Did you forget something?'

'Make me one while you're at it.'

He hung his wet coat over the back of his chair.

Cat grabbed another mug.

'Here,' she said, walking over to his desk with the two mugs of coffee. She put them both down before delving into her bag for the biscuits she'd picked up in the airport's duty-free shop.

'I would have thought you'd have wanted to go straight home,' she said as Alex grappled with the packet.

'Mel's sister's still here. I expect they'll be out shopping somewhere.'

'In this rain?'

'What about you? Won't Mike be expecting you?'

'I didn't tell him what time my flight was and he didn't ask.' She reached for a biscuit. 'Changing the subject, while we were away something came in that I think might be of interest. Do you remember I mentioned a nurse at the haemophilia unit saying how Jane had been relieved yet disappointed because Caroline didn't take Jake to his appointment?'

'What of it?'

'I asked her if she could find out who did take him, whether it was a man or a woman and what they looked like. Well, one of the nurses on duty that day has emailed me. She says she saw the woman who brought Jake in.'

Alex helped himself to another biscuit.

Moving to her desk Cat picked up a sheet of paper. 'Blonde,

thirty-something, heavily made up,' she read. 'I mentioned the appointment to Caroline when I saw her last week. She didn't say anything about who took Jake. I just assumed it was Steve Berry. Maybe Caroline did too?'

'You think Jenny Black might have taken the kid?'

'Could be.'

Slowly Alex nodded, a thoughtful look on his face.

'Is it worth bringing Steve Berry in for a chat?' she asked.

'Not yet.'

'Why not? We've got a missing barmaid and a body in the mountains, both of which we only became aware of because of checking up on him.'

'It's all circumstantial. And besides, the barmaid isn't missing. We just don't know where she is. It's not the same thing.'

'Well, whatever. Don't you think we should do what we can to find Jenny Black? If she is living around here it's possible that they're still an item.'

Alex said nothing. Most people might have got the message and given up, but not Cat.

'So we're going to just do nothing?' She let out a loud sigh, just in case he hadn't already picked up on her frustration.

'Look, I agree we've got to do something. I'm just not sure what exactly.'

'Why don't we just go and talk to him then? We can mention the findings in Cyprus. Push the link between him and the murder victims and see how he reacts.'

'I can tell you exactly how he'll react,' he said, but Cat knew an open door when she saw one.

By the time they arrived at the house it was late afternoon. The clouds had parted and the sun broke free, bringing with it welcome warmth to the cool autumn air. But after five minutes of Alex's pounding at the door they turned around and started to walk back to the car. Cat never could explain what caused her to slip through the wrought iron gate and peer around the back of the house. Maybe she heard something. But it was lucky she did, given it was then she caught sight of Caroline Berry at the bottom of the garden, in a large Victorian greenhouse.

She beckoned to Alex but just then his phone rang. He checked the caller display.

'It's Mel. I'd better take it. You carry on. I'll join you in a minute.'

Cat set off down the path.

'Mrs Berry! Mrs Berry, sorry to bother you,' she called as she made her way towards the glass structure.

But Caroline Berry obviously hadn't heard and continued to work at a long bench, with her back turned towards the detective. Cat knocked on the wooden frame; Caroline turned and gave a startled cry. She clasped a hand to her chest, dropping the pair of pruning shears she'd been holding.

'What the hell are you doing sneaking up on me like that?'

'Mrs Berry, I'm sorry. I didn't mean to startle you. I did call out several times.'

Caroline bent over and picked up the shears with manicured hands. Her nails were painted a vivid shade of pink, a match to the fuchsia velour tracksuit she was wearing. Bereft of make-up and with her highlighted hair tied tightly into a pony tail she looked tired.

'Well, what do you want?'

'Is your husband in?'

'No. I'll tell him you called. If that's everything, I'd like to get on.'

'Do you know when he's likely to be back?'

But the other woman didn't reply. Instead she was looking back up the path.

'Good afternoon Mrs Berry,' Alex said, coming to stand at Cat's side.

Just then the woman's expression brightened and any sign of tension on her face dissolved. She was still looking up towards the house.

The two detectives turned to see Steve Berry making his way down the lawn, dressed in a pair of blue overalls that were covered in oil and paint splashes.

Strolling slowly, he called out, 'I take it you're here because you have news?'

'There has been a development yes,' Alex said. 'We've come across some additional information in relation to the murders of Megan Daniels and Jane Francis. The body of a woman has been discovered in Cyprus. Another murder victim.'

Steve Berry waited, looking at Alex with a blank expression.

He continued, 'That victim also happened to be a haemophilia carrier.'

'So?' Steve Berry shrugged.

'Haemophilia appears to be a common thread across all of these murders,' Alex said.

'Bit tenuous isn't it? Had either of those two women, Megan and whatever her name was, ever been to Cyprus?'

'No. But you had.'

The ex-army man screwed his face up.

'What? Who was this woman anyway? How do you know she had anything to do with these other cases?'

'We can't say at this stage,' Cat replied honestly, choosing her words carefully.

'Perhaps you can guess who it is? How many other haemophilia carriers did you know while you were out there?' Alex asked.

'We didn't know any,' Steve Berry said.

'You never met any when you visited the hospital with your son?'

'Life on the barracks was centred on the base. We used the medical facilities on the base and our friends were all British forces who lived on the base. Have any of those gone missing? I don't think so.'

'Did either of you know a woman by the name of Jenny Black?' Alex asked.

Caroline's knuckles went white as she tightened the grip on the pruning shears. Was that because she was remembering her husband's historic dalliance or was it a more recent memory, Cat wondered.

Neither husband or wife replied.

'Mr Berry?' Alex pushed.

Steve Berry took a breath.

'Yeah, I remember her,' he said. 'She was a barmaid in a pub I used to go to. What about her?'

'Do you know where she is now?'

'No idea.'

'When was the last time you saw her?'

'Probably the last time I went to the pub before we left.'

'And you've not been in touch with her since?'

'No I have not. What is this about? I don't see how—'

'Did you know her, Mrs Berry?' Alex asked, leaving Steve Berry open-mouthed.

'No,' Caroline said, before clearing her throat. 'No, I don't think I ever met the woman.' Her still white knuckles begged to differ.

'What has some barmaid from Cyprus got to do with anything?' Steve Berry asked. 'I've already told you, I didn't know anyone else there that had haemophilia or who was a carrier. And nor did my wife.' He looked at Caroline. 'Did you?'

'No.'

'So, if that's everything?' Steve Berry said.

'It seems that Ms Black has disappeared,' Alex said, stretching the truth a little. 'She was last seen around the time that you left so I thought I'd mention it.'

He looked from Steve to Caroline. Both remained quiet, stretching the silence to beyond comfortable.

Alex thrust his hands into his pockets and jerked his head

towards the gate, indicating to Cat it was time to leave. But instead she turned back to Caroline.

'Actually, there is one other small matter. Mrs Berry, the last time I was here I broke the news about your friend, Jane Francis.'

Caroline stared at her, saying nothing.

Cat continued, 'I told you that Jane was on duty at the haemophilia unit the day that Jake had his last appointment.'

Still tight-lipped, the other woman nodded.

Cat turned to her husband.

'I take it, Mr Berry, you took your son?'

Steve Berry looked confused.

'To his last appointment?'

'Yes,' Cat said.

'No. I was at a car auction and couldn't get back in time.' He looked at his wife. 'You took him.'

She gave a curt shake of her head.

'I wasn't well. Don't you remember?'

Cat and Alex exchanged glances.

'Oh, I remember now,' Steve Berry said. 'Another one of your migraines.'

'Then who did take your son?' Alex asked.

'A friend. One of the mums from Jake's playschool,' Caroline said, with a defiant tilt to her chin that brought a pucker to Cat's brow.

But Alex seemed satisfied.

'I think that's everything. Thank you for your co-operation. We can see ourselves out.'

He gave the couple a curt nod and started up the path, back to the gate. Cat walked alongside him. They had almost reached the house when they heard Steve Berry calling for them to wait.

'Pretend you haven't heard him,' Alex muttered through half-closed lips.

They kept walking.

A gentle jog brought Berry close enough for them not to be

able to ignore him any longer. Clearly within hearing distance he repeated his call. Alex stopped and turned.

'Mr Berry,' he said, sounding exasperated. 'Was there something else?'

'Perhaps we could talk around the front?'

'Nice motor,' Alex observed, gesturing towards a gleaming dark blue Jaguar E-Type coupé that was parked on the drive.

'Gorgeous, isn't it? Got it at a real knock down price. Needed a complete overhaul.'

'Well you've done a great job.'

Momentarily Steve Berry's face lit up. Cars were evidently his passion.

'Thanks. I just picked up another real gem in Germany. It needs a bit of TLC, but it'll be fantastic by the time I finish with it.'

'You went all the way over to Germany just to look at a car?' Cat said.

'No. I was there for a classic car show. Got chatting to one of the traders, he was–'

Alex cut him off. 'Mr Berry, I'm sure you didn't follow us out here just to talk about cars. We've other places we need to be.'

'Of course. You know I feel really bad about what has happened,' he said, appearing very earnest. 'This whole experience is, well, to be honest it's very unsettling, especially for my wife.'

He glanced over his shoulder, as though expecting her to suddenly appear.

'Murder is an upsetting business,' Alex said drily.

'Yes, I realise that, I just meant... Look, the reason I wanted to talk to you, it's about the barmaid in Cyprus. Well, I used to be a bit of a regular in the bar where Jenny worked. In fact, I'd usually call in for a drink on my way home most days, play a few shots of pool, catch up with my mates.'

Alex remained stony faced.

'Anyway, Jenny was usually there. She was pretty easy to get on with. Pretty easy on the eye, as a matter of fact. You could say we sort of hit it off.'

'Hit it off?' Alex said.

'We had something going for a while. But it was all over by the time I left.'

Steve Berry glanced anxiously from Alex to Cat.

'Look, I had no idea she was missing. She was certainly still working there when I left. I know because I spent most of the time trying to avoid her.'

'Why?' Cat asked.

'Because it was over and I was afraid she'd tell Caroline about us. Look, you can't say any of this to my wife. At one stage Caroline and I weren't getting on very well. Things are different now but even so I'm not sure that she would appreciate having it all raked up.' He lowered his voice. 'It was fizzling out well before Caroline's father died. I made a decision to cut my losses with Jenny and make a fresh start with my wife. I came back here and I've not seen her since.'

'That's the problem,' Alex said. 'Nobody has.'

An anxious look crossed the ex-soldier's face.

Twenty-Two

Alex smoothly reversed his BMW into one of the parking spaces and turned off the ignition.

'Got time for a quick drink?'

Cat looked at him suspiciously.

'Am I missing something? You've been away for three days. In fact, given the early check-in time on Thursday morning, I'm guessing you won't have seen Mel and Sarah since Wednesday night, which makes it closer to four days. Shouldn't you go home?'

'They're not at home.' Cat gave him a sharp look. 'Apparently Sarah's struggling at school. They think she's not concentrating with Cody still being in hospital. Mel thought it might help if she took her to her Sarah's grandparents for a few days. Mel's sister's gone with her. Bit of a family get together. I'll only be going back to an empty house.'

Some family get together, with an absent father, Cat thought.

'How long have they gone for?' she asked.

'I don't know. Not long.'

Cat studied his face. She was still sensing that there was something he wasn't telling her.

She checked her watch.

'Come on then – but it'll have to be a quick one. I've probably got an hour before Mike starts to wonder who's going to cook his dinner.'

'Well, here we are again.' Cat motioned her glass towards Alex.

Alex touched his glass to hers.

'Here's to making some sense of it all.'

'I'll drink to that.' She took a sip of her spritzer. 'You know, I was really hopeful when Glafcos called but all that's happened is that we've added another unsolved murder to our list. That's not what was supposed to happen.'

'Plus, we've lost even more time,' Alex said.

'I take it Steve Berry is out of the running now, if he was in Germany at that car show, like he says?' Cat said.

After a moment's contemplation Alex shrugged.

'It needs confirming but it sounds like he's got an alibi, at least for the Monday when Jane was attacked.'

Cat thought back to their earlier conversation.

'Could he have flown out at a different time?'

'Like I said, it'll need confirming – something for you to do on Monday.'

They both fell silent. Cat played with the drink in front of her, drawing patterns in the beads of condensation that formed on the cold glass. After she had wiped clean most of the once frosted surface, she lifted it to her lips and took a small sip.

'I guess we're back at square one then,' she said, her usual optimism having abandoned her.

'It looks that way.' Even Alex sounded unusually down. He looked into his almost empty pint glass before draining it dry.

Cat passed on the offer of a second drink and left Alex heading for the bar for a refill.

Alex paid the barmaid and, without waiting for the creamy head to settle on the newly pulled pint of bitter, made his way over to a space-age looking quiz machine, where a solitary figure stood, pumping in coins.

He stood just behind the man's right shoulder and watched the first question appear on the screen.

'B, The Sudan,' he said, just as the guy smacked a button that corresponded to the fourth option, D.

A large black cross appeared across the screen.

'Should've gone for B,' Alex said, gesturing at the screen with his pint.

The guy paused and looked over his shoulder. His scowl melted.

'Hey, Alex, mate, how are you?'

He gave a wide grin as he pumped Alex's hand.

'Give me a minute and I'll be right with you. Just got to beat this damn machine.'

'Dan, you should know better. No one ever wins at these things. It's just a con.'

'Yeah, I know, but it beats standing at the bar like a sad bastard Billy-no-mates,' he said, before turning back and hitting the continue button.

After an embarrassingly short stint the game was over. Alex's friend grabbed his pint from off the top of the machine and followed Alex to the bar, where they both settled on a couple of stools.

'How's it going mate? The job still giving you murder?'

'Yep, how about you? Still enjoying a life of vice?'

'Sure am, beats working for a living.'

The old friends both laughed at their long-standing joke.

For a while they passed the time catching up on each other's news and swapping stories of mutual friends. As they finished their third pint Alex checked his watch.

'How about we go somewhere else? We could get another couple of rounds in before it's time to call it a day.'

Despite having already had three pints on an empty stomach Alex felt none the worse for wear, courtesy of a misspent youth and too many years in the rugby club, where drinking games and heavy nights out had been obligatory.

'Sure. There's no one waiting at home for me, so I'm easy.'

'You still not hooked up with anyone since the divorce?'

'Nah. Won't you be expected home though?'

'No, Mel's sister's over. They've gone to the in-laws' for the weekend. I've got a free pass.'

'Well it'd be a shame to waste it,' Dan said, already putting his jacket on.

They made their way through the town centre, which was virtually deserted, apart from the occasional group of friends – mostly drunk – ambling between pubs. Alex and Dan looked like they belonged. After walking aimlessly for five minutes they settled on a not too trendy lounge bar. It was a big place that combined alcohol, loud music and an American-diner inspired menu. An hour later, with their appetite satisfied by a couple of burgers, Dan drank the last of his pint.

'Up for another?' he asked.

Alex passed him his empty glass.

'Be rude not to.'

'We should check out the action on the dance floor once we've got the drinks.'

'I'm up for it as long as I don't have to dance.' Alex wasn't nearly drunk enough to subject himself to what he always considered to be the ultimate humiliation, having been born with two left feet.

'I was only suggesting we go for a gander, you know, a bit of talent spotting.' Alex gave Dan a warning look. 'Don't worry,' Dan said, 'I know you're not interested. I'm not talking about pulling or anything like that. I just thought it'd be good for a laugh.'

Minutes later, perched on a couple of bar stools overlooking the crowded dance floor, they watched the clubbers bob up and down, dancing to a seventies' revival disco mix.

Alex didn't recognise him at first. The dance floor was crowded and the flashing lights made it difficult to make out people's faces but once he knew he was there Alex found it hard not to stare. It was obvious the guy was trying to impress his choice of dance partner, moving in close, and then even closer as the music slowed to a hip-crunching grind and the dancing got more and more 'dirty'. Alex considered his options, unsure of whether he wanted to be seen or not. He made up his mind and turned away from the action on the dance floor and leaned towards Dan, beckoning with his hand to draw close.

'What's up?' Dan shouted into his ear.

'You okay if we go back where we were earlier? At least we could talk there.'

Dan picked up his pint. He led the way, skirting the dance floor, to where a short set of steps would take them back to the quieter seating area. But just as Alex turned to leave, he felt a sharp jab to his right shoulder. He spun around.

'Yeah? Oh, hi,' he said, feigning surprise. 'Mike, isn't it?' He fixed a thin sliver of a smile on his lips.

Alex looked at Mike's scowl-ridden face with its designer stubble and chiselled jaw-line and the slick well-groomed hair. He always thought Cat would have gone for more of a man's man.

'Are you checking up on me?' Mike said, having to shout to be heard above the thudding beat of the music.

'What did you say?' Alex said, wondering if he'd misheard.

'I said fuck off and mind your own business!' Mike hollered, just as the track changed and the volume dropped.

'Look, I don't know what your problem is but I think you need to calm down and think about what you're saying,' Alex said. He could see that the guy was reeling drunk.

'That's rich coming from you. You sniff around her like she's some bitch in heat. It's not enough that you're with her all day, every fucking day. 'Cos of course what you do is so fucking important, you can't possibly do it in normal hours, like everyone else.' He was on a roll now. 'Then some dead nobody turns up a million miles away and you just have to go and check it out. Couldn't go on your own though, could you?'

Alex had heard enough.

'You need to sort your issues out with Cat on your own. Don't drag me into it.'

He turned his back on Mike and started to walk away but evidently Mike wasn't finished with him and he laid a restraining hand on Alex's arm, pulling him back round to face him.

Alex had to suppress a laugh when he saw Mike squaring up to him. Drunk *and* posturing. But Mike wasn't letting up. At first Alex couldn't make out much of what Mike was saying. Music from the nearby speakers drowned out his garbled accusations, but then during a momentary lull in the current track Alex heard enough.

More than enough, in fact.

Alex would have let most things pass but when he heard those slurred words accusing him of using his son's illness to foster enough sympathy from Cat that might one day get her into bed with him, he snapped. He formed a fist and with as much force as he could muster, he put every ounce of his energy into an upper-cut that hit Mike square in the solar plexus, wiping the sneer off the bastard's face.

Without saying a word Alex walked away looking calm and relaxed. He found Dan waiting patiently by the door. They were outside before anyone had even spotted the ill-looking guy retching and heaving for breath at the side of the dance floor.

As they walked down the high street toward the taxi rank Dan slowed to light a cigarette, stopping to cup his hands around a match to shelter it from the chilling wind that had whipped up.

His cigarette lit, he turned to Alex.

'Friend of yours?'

Alex cast a look back in the direction of the bar, an angry brooding expression across his face.

'No friend of mine.'

Twenty-Three

The previous day's grey had cleared to reveal bright sunshine and blue skies, which would ordinarily have had Cat thinking fondly of the summer past. But not today; today she had other things on her mind.

The office was dark and deserted when she arrived. Waiting for the kettle to boil, she peered into a large Tupperware tub and picked out a chocolate digestive from the half-full container. She was just about to take her first bite when she heard something behind her. With the biscuit still poised before her open lips she looked over her shoulder and physically started on spotting Alex at his desk, watching her. One corner of his mouth tugged upwards into a smile.

'Caught you,' he said.

The tired tone of his voice didn't accord with the playfulness of his words.

Cat looked at him, puzzled for a moment, before looking down at the biscuit in her hand. She switched her attention back to Alex and noticed his dishevelled state. He was unshaven and his hair looked like it would have benefited from having a comb pulled through it.

She turned her back on him and poured the hot water into her mug. She clenched her jaw and took a deep breath.

'What are you doing here?' she asked, her voice sounding hard and flat.

'Mel thought it would be a good idea for her and Sarah to spend the day with her Nana and Grandad. I thought I might as well come in and do something useful.'

'In the dark?' Cat asked, remembering the lack of light when she'd first walked in. She looked over at his desk and spotted a packet of ibuprofen.

'What about you? It's the weekend. I'd have thought you'd have had better things to do,' he said.

'Funnily enough Mike wasn't in the mood to play happy families after your stupid stunt last night. Instead he's out enjoying the weather, playing golf with his mates. So since I've got nothing better to do, through no fault of my own I might add, I thought I'd come in and finish off some paperwork. But if I'd known you were here, I wouldn't have bothered.'

Alex groaned.

'Cat, look I'm sorry, but–'

Cat's face flushed livid with colour.

'Alex, you might be my boss and an old friend of my brother's and I know you've been through a lot recently, and as much as I admire you, if you ever do anything like that again so help me God...'

Although she took care to keep her voice low, trying to maintain control, her tone still managed to portray the menace that her words held.

'But it wasn't like that–'

Cat held an index finger up in front of her and shook her head; a move she'd seen Alex use enough times. Her tightly pursed lips made it clear she was in no mood to chat. Her eyes though, wide and solemn-looking, reflected her hurt.

'Okay, I get the message,' he said.

She turned her back on him and got back to fixing herself that coffee.

Cat spent the morning working on the paperwork from Megan Daniels' attic. Most of it wasn't needed and could be returned but Cat first needed to make a full inventory of the documents they were keeping. As a result, she didn't have cause to speak to Alex all morning and he left her to her own devices until just before lunchtime.

'What did he say?' he asked, approaching her desk.

She looked up at him.

'What?'

'Mike. What did he say happened? Because whatever it was, he was lying.'

'He said you punched him. Are you saying you didn't?'

'No, I did, but I meant did he–'

He didn't get the chance to finish his sentence.

'He wasn't lying then? You punched him?' She leaned back in her seat and regarded him with piercing eyes. 'I don't know where you think you get off Alex, really I don't. I don't know whether you were playing big brother or jealous colleague but whatever it was...'

Alex recoiled.

He stared at her for a moment and she glared back until he turned and made his way back to his desk where he slumped in his chair. She watched him reach for his mobile phone and begin toying with it. Her breath caught in her chest as the audacity of her challenge hit home. She felt a momentary pang of guilt; until she remembered the heated accusations she'd been subject to on Mike's return the night before.

She took a deep breath and looked at the boxes and files that surrounded her desk. She added her signature to the inventory and attached it to the box at the top to be returned to Craig Daniels. That left just one box remaining, which she picked up and carried to the evidence cupboard. It slid neatly in next to the box of items that had been found in Terry's car.

Cat was about to return to her desk, but paused. Seeing the box reminded her of Bob's bitchy behaviour and the fact that they'd let Terry walk.

She reached in and removed the box and set it on the nearest table. She lifted the lid and peered in.

There wasn't much to look at. Picking up the small packet that housed the plastic pearl-like bead she remembered how excited, how exhilarated she'd felt when she'd first got her hands on it.

Her thoughts turned to Mary.

Her murder was still at odds with everything else that had happened. She strolled over to the murder board. Her fingers absent-mindedly played with the bead through the plastic packet. Standing in front of the photographs of Mary on the night she died, Cat tried to see her as she would have appeared that night. It was a very different Mary to the one that Cat remembered from the mortuary slab. Despite what she'd said to Terry that time, there was a hint of an attractive girl underneath all that make-up and although she was wearing a short skirt and tight top, like every other teenage girl captured in the photographs, at least, unlike many of them, she had the figure for it.

Cat took a step closer. She peered intently at the photos, scouring every detail. Suddenly her heart quickened. She reached up and removed one of the photos from the board. Back at her desk she set it down under the desk lamp and took an even closer look.

'Alex!' she called to him, her earlier anger forgotten in a flash.

'What?' he asked, sounding unusually cautious.

'Come here. There's something I want you to see.'

Cat sounded excited. Alex quickly covered the short distance to her desk.

'What is it?'

He looked down at the photograph. She was pointing to something.

'Look, here. When I saw this before I thought it was just part of the pattern of her top, but I don't think it is. I think it's a necklace.'

'So?'

Cat held up the small packet.

'This is the bead that was found in Terry's car.'

She handed him the evidence bag. He took a closer look,

before leaning in and looking again at the photo.

'Well, I'll be damned!'

'When you look at it, you can see how it could have happened,' Cat said to Spencer as he reached into the small Marks and Spencer's bag that she had just handed him.

'Emma, the girl who used to work at the Exit with Mary, helped me pick it out. She's got one virtually the same; apparently Mary had copied her.'

'And Mary was definitely wearing it the night she went missing?' Spencer asked, gingerly fingering the necklace as though fearful it might break.

Cat nodded.

'Emma confirmed it. And anyway, you can see it in the photos.'

Spencer slipped the necklace back into the bag.

'You did well to spot it. It'll be fucking amazing if it turns out to be the murder weapon.'

As they talked Bob turned up, like the proverbial bad penny.

'Let's have a look,' he said, snatching the bag from Spencer's grip.

Cat watched as the scruffy detective tipped its contents into his palm. The nylon strings entwined with one another, causing the beads to settle into a small pile like a puddle of pearls.

Cat reached over and took them off him, shaking the necklace gently to restore its proper form.

'And the pathologist has confirmed it, has he, that the marks on her neck are consistent with a backward force on a necklace like this?' he asked.

She gave him a smug smile. 'Of course.'

After first getting the idea, Cat had shot straight to the shopping centre. Thankfully Emma worked Sundays, and although the magnificent Tara hadn't been happy about it, she had acquiesced and let Emma accompany Cat to buy a replica necklace. Even more importantly, while she'd been picking up the evidence, Alex had called in a few favours, arranging for Cat to drop in on Professor Jarrett on her way back to the office.

'The professor said that during a struggle the beads could have moved to the side,' she said. 'That would have left more of the bare nylon exposed at the front, by the windpipe. Provided there was enough backward pressure it would have been enough to asphyxiate. And we know that Terry was pulling hard because he managed to snap the necklace, which is how we came to find one of the beads in the car.'

'The beads *could have* moved to the side. Could've my arse,' Bob argued. 'And if the necklace broke then it would have taken the pressure off her throat wouldn't it?'

Just then Alex entered the office.

'We've got a result!' he shouted, loud enough for everyone to hear, his fist punching the air

The office broke out into applause.

Cat turned to look at Bob, wanting to savour the moment, but he was already walking away. Going to lick his wounds, she hoped.

Alex came over and perched on the side of her desk.

'We got a full confession. His defence is pushing for accidental death but with his rap sheet I dare say they'll settle for a plea of manslaughter.'

Cat felt her stomach flip.

'What did he say happened?'

'Terry says he was giving Mary a lift home. Fancying his chances, he decided to pull over in a quiet country lane. He says up until this point she'd been going along with him, until, who knows, maybe she changed her mind when she realised quite how far he expected her to go. Don't forget she was barely sixteen and nothing like the wild-child she was making out to be. By this stage he was committed, plus he'd been indulging in a bit of crack cocaine that night and you know what a nasty bastard that can turn some people into. Anyway, he says she tried to get away and he tried to stop her. He grabbed the first thing he could get hold of, which happened to be her necklace. According to him he didn't realise he was pulling so hard until it broke in his hands.'

'Yeah right,' Spencer said.

'Well, that'll be for a jury to decide. All we've got to do is make sure we deliver on our end of it. That means I want notes written up ASAP.'

'I've more or less finished them. Just need to do a final read through,' Cat said.

'It was a great spot, well done,' Alex said as he eased onto his feet.

'Thanks.'

But instead of walking away, Alex turned and squatted next to her seat. Face to face, he lowered his voice.

'Next time, try and put a bit more effort into getting someone to share your conviction. This could have all been done and dusted by now.'

Cat stared open-mouthed at him.

'What?'

'I was just saying, trust your instincts more. You backed the right horse. If you hadn't given up so easily you might have noticed the necklace sooner, that's all.'

She was tempted to let it go, but hell, that wasn't deserved.

'I can't believe you just said that,' she hissed. 'When I wanted to arrest him, I was told in no uncertain terms by Bob that we had fuck all and that I was an idiot. And you sided with him. I don't think you can lay it all on me.'

Alex stared at her for a brief moment. 'Let's not spoil it. We've just got a fantastic result. We should both be happy.'

Cat went to speak, but changed her mind.

'Besides, we've got unfinished business,' he said as he straightened up. 'There's the little matter of two unsolved

232

murders. Now that we know they're not related to Mary's death we should finally be able to make some progress.'

Twenty-Four

'Do you think we'll get to see the holiday snaps?' Bob said under his breath to Spencer but loud enough for Cat to hear. They were waiting for Alex to start the team briefing.

Alex took them through what they had learned about Steve Berry and the elusive Jenny Black, from his and Cat's trip to Cyprus and their subsequent conversations with Mr and Mrs Berry. When he finished Bob was the first to speak.

'Are you saying this barmaid who Berry was shagging had nothing in her medical records to indicate that she had anything to do with haemophilia?'

'That's the latest from Cyprus,' Alex said. 'I've been told there's still a possibility she was a carrier. If anyone in her family had suffered from haemophilia in living memory then it's likely she would have been tested and the outcome recorded in her medical records but if she came from a long line of girls it could well go undetected.'

'Let me get this straight,' Bob said, doing nothing to hide the sneer of disbelief on his face. 'She might be a carrier or she might not. Which means she might be the pile of bones they found or she might not.'

'Yes,' Alex said. 'That's why the Cypriot police are trying to get hold of her dental records.'

Alex looked from Bob to the faces of the remaining half a dozen detectives in the room.

'So, that's everything from the Cyprus trip. Not quite as productive as we'd hoped,' he admitted. 'How about you lot? I don't see much new information on the board. Bob?'

He looked at the older detective, who he'd asked to oversee the team's activities in his absence. Bob's gaunt face paled and he met Alex with a blank expression.

'No news.'

'You're kidding me? What about Anthony Stewart? Don't tell me we're no closer to finding out where the fucker is?'

Bob shifted his gaze to the floor.

Alex glowered and the scruffy detective seemed to unravel and grow even more dishevelled.

'What can I say? We still haven't found the guy. I don't know what more we can do. There's been no sign of him. No activity on his bank account or credit card. He's made no contact with his wife or the contractor who he gets most of his work from. It's like he's dropped off the face of the planet.'

'It's not good enough,' Alex said, raising his voice. 'He's got to be somewhere. Dead or alive I want him found. Go and talk to his wife again, and his friends, and his work contacts. Go over everything you know about him. You must have missed something.'

Bob's pursed lips twitched. Alex stared at him until eventually he added, 'Yes, sir.'

Alex turned to Cat.

'Cat, I want you to look into Steve Berry's movements the morning Jane Francis was attacked.'

'Will do guv.'

'I thought you said he was in Germany,' Bob said. There was still some fight in him yet.

'What I said was that he told us he was in Germany. Now I want to know if he was telling the truth.'

Cat held back on the temptation to smile. It was good to see Bob get the sharp end of Alex's tongue for a change.

It was close on four o'clock and Cat was still working on tracing Steve Berry's movements when Alex's voice erupted from across the office.

'Are you winding me up?'

She looked over. He was yelling into his mobile. He ran a hand through his tousled black hair, making it look even more ruffled and unkempt than usual.

She watched him terminate the call and shove the phone in his pocket. He walked over to Spencer and set a hand on the young rookie's desk. He leaned forward and started to say something. Cat could see that he was in full rant mode but he was doing a good job of keeping his voice low. Low enough that she couldn't hear a thing being said. Spencer was nodding keenly.

Suddenly Alex turned and strode out of the room. Spencer rose from his seat and slipped on his coat.

Cat was desperate to know what was going on. Just as Spencer walked past her desk, she put out a hand.

'Spence, what's happening?' she asked quietly.

He took a cursory look around before replying.

'Bob's in deep shit.'

'Why? What's he done?'

'Alex called him to find out what he's up to and it turns out he's been doing an accurate reconstruction of Anthony Stewart's last known movements. Too accurate, if you know what I mean.'

'I have no idea what you're talking about.'

'He's done a tour of all of the pubs that Stewart is known to have frequented.'

'Isn't that what Alex asked him to do?'

Spencer looked around again and leaned in closer.

'He's only gone and got himself pissed,' he whispered. 'Absolutely rat arsed. I've been told to go and fetch him.'

Twenty minutes later Spencer hurried past on his way back to his desk. He shrugged off his coat and took his seat, before reaching over and unlocking his computer.

Cat swivelled her chair around. Bob was just outside the office door. She wasn't sure but it looked like he might have been swaying a little. He caught her looking and gave a sly smile. Cocky as ever.

She looked away as Alex appeared. From the corner of her eye she watched as he held out a guiding hand and ushered Bob into one of the private, sound-proofed meeting rooms.

'Spoilsport,' she said under her breath.

She returned to her work. She had made good progress so far. Suffice to say, Steve Berry had been less than happy to hear from her again so soon, but despite his angry protests he had eventually given her everything she needed. Furnished with his flight information and details of the hotel he had supposedly stayed at, it was just a case of ringing around and getting confirmation that he had been where he said he was. So far it looked like his account of his movements stacked up.

Cat was on the phone to the car parking company, who operated the meet and greet service that Berry claimed to have used, when Alex returned to the office. He was on his own. While scribbling down the details of the car pick-up time, Cat swivelled in her seat and scanned the corridor. There was no sign of Bob.

By the time she'd finished the call Alex was not alone. The HR manager was with him at his desk. They conversed in low voices, their heads bowed. Alex was frowning, though he didn't look quite as angry as before.

Cat was typing up her notes when she heard him approach. She gave an anxious smile, worried he might have brought his bad mood with him.

'How are you getting on?' he asked.

He sounded weary.

'Okay, I think.' She reached for her notepad and started to read. 'It looks like Berry was telling the truth about having gone to a car show in Germany. He said he flew out early Monday morning – the day Jane was killed – and returned late Tuesday afternoon. I've spoken to the airline and to the hotel where he stayed the night before his flight. Both confirmed his version of events. I–'

'What time was his flight out on Monday?' Alex interrupted.

Cat peered at her notes.

'Ten am.'

'That's not an alibi. He could have easily driven back, killed Jane and got back in time for his flight.' He gave her a cold look.

She held his gaze.

'I hadn't finished. I was going to add that he used a meet and greet parking service which required him to give his car keys in at the reception when he checked in on Sunday night. At some point that evening his car was taken to a secure compound until he called from the terminal on his return. I checked the details with the hotel. The following morning Berry had breakfast booked in the hotel. He also paid for tickets for the transfer bus to the terminal where he checked in on time. Given that he didn't have his car keys he couldn't have driven to meet Jane Francis the next morning, killed her and got back before breakfast. And I think even Berry wouldn't have the balls to ask a taxi driver to keep a car on the meter while he nipped into the woods.'

Alex's previous calm started to slip away.

'Shit!' he said. 'Okay, find out exactly what time they took his car. Could it have been the following day? He could have taken a spare set of keys. I use those services and with some of them you don't have to give your keys in on arrival, you might need to go back to the car for something.' He was scowling now. 'I want positive confirmation from the hotel that the car was removed from the hotel grounds the night before his flight. And while you're at it get a picture of him and show it to the staff until you find someone who is prepared to swear that they saw him at breakfast. Better still, that they served him. And I want it done today.'

Cat nodded.

'No problem.'

In contrast to the confidence of her words, a worried look had settled on her face.

'Well, what are you waiting for?'

'Where do I get a photo of him from?'

'For Christ-sakes Cat, use your initiative.'

Cat focused her attention on the first of her tasks, which turned out to be easy enough. Steve Berry's car had been picked up by the meet and greet operator at twenty-past eight on the Sunday night.

She tapped her pen on her desk while she thought it through.

'If he did go back and kill Jane Francis the following morning, he did it in someone else's car,' she said to herself. 'An accomplice?'

She scratched out the details of the timing on a fresh sheet of paper. It was possible, she decided. In fact, if that was the case, he'd come up with a pretty convincing alibi.

Then she remembered the breakfast. There was no way he could have got to Jane in time to kill her and make it back to the hotel to have breakfast when he said he did. Not unless he'd got a helicopter stashed away somewhere.

'Better get hold of that photo then,' she muttered to herself.

She threw her pencil down and rose from her desk.

'Spencer,' she said, sidling up to him.

'Yeah.' He was still tapping away at the computer keyboard.

'Alex said something about a surveillance exercise on Steve Berry while we were away. Were you part of it?'

'I did a few stints at the garage. Never saw anything though. Berry turned up in the morning and left about five. Apart from yesterday – he left around half-twelve but he only went as far as the caff down the road. He was back in the garage half an hour later. Just writing it up now.' He looked up at her. 'Why?'

'Did you just see his car or did you actually see him in the workshop?'

'Most of the time, just the car. One day he had the garage doors open for a while. He was washing a nifty-looking sports car.'

'Does this place have another exit?'

'There's a fire-door around the back.'

'Could he have used that to slip out? Maybe used a different car?'

Spencer appeared to think about it before screwing up his nose.

'Nah, I'd have noticed.'

Cat knew he was probably right. She also knew, if it had been when Bob was there, his habit of burying his head in the sports pages at every opportunity made him, in her opinion at least, something of an unreliable witness.

'I don't suppose you happened to take any surveillance shots, did you?'

A glimmer of hope hung in the air. Just for a second.

'Of what?' he said. 'A closed garage door?'

She sighed.

'Thought it was too good to be true.' Spencer gave her a puzzled look. In return she gave a hopeful smile. 'Don't suppose you fancy a trip out do you? There's a pint in it if you do.'

'That's his car there,' Spencer said, pointing to a dark blue E-type Jaguar.

They were in Spencer's car, staring out of the windscreen at Steve Berry's lock-up. Cat was hoping they'd be able to get a photograph of him as he left.

'Okay, pull in over there, behind that van. That way, when he comes out of the garage and walks towards his car, you should be able to get a good shot of him face-on.'

'I will? What are you going to be doing?'

'I'll be behind that pile of scrap by the entrance. I'm going to try to get some of him while he's locking up.' She reached for the door handle. 'Try to keep out of sight.' She caught Spencer rolling his eyes. 'Sorry. I know you know that.'

She trotted lightly over to the garage and took up her position behind a collection of body parts that looked as though they were part of some giant car jigsaw puzzle. She was close to the garage's front wall, only fifteen metres from the door.

As soon as she was settled in position, she became aware of a loud ruckus. She flinched at the sound of metal hitting metal with a violence that made her uneasy. In between the banging and crashing Steve Berry's voice could be heard hurling abuse. Cat couldn't hear anyone reply. She was about to go running in, when a sense of self-preservation turned her feet to lead. She suddenly felt very exposed. Images of a wrench-wielding madman flashed through her mind. A prickle of fear quickened her pulse. Spurred on by a sudden release of adrenalin she abandoned her vantage point and ran hurriedly back to the car.

Spencer put his camera down and looked at her as she slipped into the passenger seat. She slid down low and peered out through the window at the garage's entrance, her breath coming out in quick bursts.

'What's up?'

'He's in there, going ballistic. I don't want to be in striking distance when he comes out. I don't know what—'

Just at that moment the garage door swung open and Steve Berry stomped out with hunched shoulders and clenched fists. He slammed the door angrily behind him, not bothering to lock it. Within seconds he'd pulled away, his accelerated exit stirring up a cloud of dust across the forecourt, leaving Cat and Spencer open-mouthed and empty-handed.

'So what sort of thing was he saying?' Spencer asked as the two of them walked over to the unlocked garage door.

'I couldn't really hear properly. I think I heard him say bitch, or fucking bitch a few times.'

Cat reached a tentative hand towards the door.

'What are you doing?' Spencer asked in a hushed whisper.

'Someone needs to make sure there's no one hurt in there.'

Spencer put out a restraining hand on her arm.

'I'll do it. It might be dangerous.'

Cat shot him a look and Spencer quickly let go.

Slowly she pushed at the sturdy door. It opened quietly. When there was enough space, she put her ear to the gap and listened. Spencer leaned in close next to her.

They looked at each other. Cat pushed the door open a little wider. She peered in.

The room was in darkness.

She felt around on the wall by the door until she found the light switch. She took a deep breath, steeled herself and flicked it on.

'Wow,' Spencer said from somewhere over her shoulder.

The room was strewn with tools and chrome and painted body parts. Pages torn from a car maintenance manual covered the floor like confetti.

'Looks like someone's had a bit of tantrum,' Cat said.

Spencer bent down and picked up one of the separated pages.

'It's for an Aston Martin. That's what he was busy polishing the other day. Gorgeous car. It looked like a silver bullet. James Bond used to have one. I think that was in silver as well. I thought about going and talking to him, you know, like pretending to be a punter or something, just so I could have a go at sitting in it. But then I thought of what Alex would do if he found out.'

Cat looked around the garage, at the classic cars in their various states of repair. 'Well it's not here now.'

The tyres crunched noisily over the gravel as the car made its way up the drive.

'The boss made good time,' Spencer said, pulling his car in behind Alex's black BMW.

Cat noticed the driver door swing open. She hurried to unclip her seatbelt, watching as Alex emerged. By the time she'd climbed out he was almost at the front door. He waited for them under the covered portico.

'Ready?' he said, before reaching up and yanking on the bell-pull.

They didn't have long to wait before Cat found out she'd been right to guess Steve Berry would return home. The ex-army man opened the door with the sound of the bell still pealing through the house's cavernous interior. He looked at the detectives and scowled.

'What now?'

'Is Mrs Berry at home?' Alex asked.

'No. And I don't know when she'll be back.'

He made to close the door.

'Mind if we come in?' Alex said. His foot was already over the threshold. 'Mr Berry, don't walk away. I want to talk to you,' he called to the figure retreating down the hallway.

By the time they got to the lounge Steve Berry was already slumped in a tall-backed leather armchair that faced the pristine gardens. Alex crossed the room and stood in front of him, causing him to look up.

'Where is your wife Mr Berry?' Alex asked.

'Out. I don't know exactly.'

'Why did you smash up your workshop?'

Berry stiffened.

'Got some anger issues have you?' Alex went on. 'What else have you taken it out on?'

When Berry didn't reply Alex walked over to the fireplace. He leaned a hand against the hearth and looked down at the clean grate. Decorative lanterns with large church candles filled the space.

'I tell you what I think,' he said. 'I think your wife is frightened of you. And I think she has reason to be.' Steve Berry looked over to Alex. He continued, 'It must be terrifying living with a man who you believe is responsible for the deaths of at least two other women.'

Berry's face contorted with anger.

'You can't keep accusing me like this. What evidence have you got? Hey? Tell me that?' he ranted. 'You can't, can you? That's because you've got nothing. Because there is nothing! For Christsakes, I wasn't even in the country when that nurse was killed.'

Alex locked eyes with Berry.

'So you say.'

For a moment there was a stand-off. Both men stood staring, saying nothing.

Berry shook his head and slumped back, his face drawn and pale. He closed his eyes.

'Do you have any idea where your wife is, Mr Berry?' Cat asked.

Out of the corner of her eye Cat saw Alex pick up the photograph of the couple's young son. The only photograph in the room, she noted. Berry was also watching him and didn't appear to have heard her question.

'I can imagine how you must be feeling,' Alex said. 'I would be devastated if my wife left and took my children with her.'

Alex gently returned the framed picture.

Steve Berry shot out of his seat.

'She's taken Jake? No. She wouldn't.' He rushed into the hallway.

'Spencer, stop him,' Alex barked.

Cat and Alex exchanged glances. Moments later, Spencer ushered in Steve Berry, who was talking animatedly on his mobile.

He ended the call and threw the phone on a table before dropping back into the chair. He let out a long breath.

'He's still at the childminder's.'

Cat could see the colour returning to his face.

Now it was Alex's turn to look troubled.

'Mr Berry. Where is your wife?'

Steve Berry looked at each of the three detectives in turn, as though appreciating the significance of their presence for the first time.

'She's been finding things quite stressful, with everything that's happened. We thought it'd be a good idea for her to get away for a few days.'

'You said you didn't know where she was,' Alex said.

'I said I don't know *exactly* and I don't. Not the exact location. Not yet, I mean. She was going to see what she could get last minute. Said she'll call me when she's settled.'

He gave them a tense smile. Alex fixed him with a flat stare.

'When did she go?' Cat asked.

'I'm not sure. She was here to say goodbye to Jake when I left with him for the childminder's this morning. I went straight from there to the garage.'

'And she didn't pop by on her way out to say goodbye?' Cat asked.

Steve Berry ran a hand around the neck of his sweater.

'Maybe it was this afternoon. I was at the dentist. I suppose she might have called while I was out.'

Cat gave a slow nod, the sort that says 'bullshit'.

'Look, does it matter?' Berry was sounding anxious now.

'Did you have a row?' she asked.

'No.'

'Are you sure?'

'I told you, I haven't spoken to her since I left with Jake this morning.'

'Mr Berry, why would your wife leave without taking your son?' Alex asked.

'She didn't want to upset his routine.'

Alex looked at him like he would a prostitute who said she did it for the company.

'What about your actions at your garage earlier today? You were overheard. It sounded like you were furious with your wife. So angry that you–'

Steve Berry was shaking his head.

'No. You don't understand. That wasn't about my wife. I was angry at a car. I was trying to do something and... well, I couldn't. I just lost my temper.'

Cat gave him an incredulous look.

'You were calling a car 'a bitch'?'

'Sounds ridiculous when you say it like that.'

'Mind if we take a look around?' Alex said as he scanned the room.

Berry looked at him with a flicker of interest, before shrugging.

'Be my guest.'

Alex directed Spencer to cover the garage and outbuildings while he and Cat took the house. The three of them returned to the lounge a short while later. Cat was the last to enter. Alex looked at her expectantly. She shook her head.

Steve Berry was still in the tall-backed chair. He took a swig of beer from a bottle he was holding. He looked pretty relaxed, given the circumstances. Cat looked back at Alex who reached into the back pocket of his trousers and pulled out a small, burgundy-bound book.

'Recognise this, Mr Berry?'

Berry squinted at it. 'I don't think I...'

Alex stepped closer and Cat noticed the embossed gold emblem on the cover.

'A passport?' the ex-army man said.

'That's right. It's your wife's passport.'

Berry shrugged.

'So, she's not gone abroad.'

'Then why has she taken all of her summer clothes?' Alex said. 'In fact, why has she taken all of her clothes? The wardrobes and drawers don't contain a single item of women's clothing – even underwear. I'd say it looks like your wife's planning on being away a lot longer than a week.'

Alex pocketed the passport.

'It wasn't that long ago you were demanding police protection for your wife. You were convinced she was going to be the next victim. I notice you don't seem to be overly worried about her sudden departure.'

Berry turned and looked at Alex.

'Are you suggesting I killed her now? Seriously? You have me down as some sort of serial killer? This must be a joke.'

'Spencer, read him his rights. Mr Berry, get your shoes on. You're coming with us.' Alex ushered Cat to the door, out of earshot of the others. 'Get onto social services,' he said. 'We'll need someone to take care of the kid.'

Back at the station Alex hung his jacket on a hook by the door and was about to head to the custody suite when Cat stopped him.

'Can I have a quick word?'

He looked surprised but said, 'Sure. What's up?'

'I hope I'm not speaking out of turn, but I just wondered, should we really be interviewing Berry until we're sure he could have killed Jane Francis? At the moment it looks increasingly likely that he couldn't have. Without that all we've got is the fact that it looks like his wife has done a bunk.'

'Or he's done her in.'

'But where's the evidence? Where's the body?'

Alex rubbed a hand over his face. He was looking tired.

'What if we go back to your theory: that Jenny Black is somehow in on it?' he said. 'She could have picked him up from the hotel and taken him to the park, waited while he tracked Jane down and then drove him back to the hotel.'

'Even if Jenny is still on the scene and was prepared to do that for him the timing's tight. I'm not sure it's possible. He definitely couldn't have made it back in time for breakfast.'

Alex looked at her sharply.

'You didn't tell me you've confirmed that he ate breakfast there?'

'I haven't, not yet. But forget that for a minute; what I'm really not sure about is his motive. Why would he want to kill Caroline? Like Sofia said, he could have just got divorced.'

'Greed can do terrible things to a person.' He paused, and after a moment added, 'But then so can love. Maybe he'd planned all along to divorce Caroline but what if she did something to raise the stakes, like threaten to take his son away from him? You saw how he reacted when he thought she'd taken the kid.'

'Yes, but that still doesn't explain why Megan and Jane were killed.'

'Caroline was their friend. What if she'd told them what she was planning on doing? And he knew that. If he killed her, they'd be ready to point the finger. If he was determined to get rid of her, he'd have to get rid of them first.'

'That's what I said.'

Alex frowned.

'Did you? Well, maybe you were right. Okay, let's push on and get something a bit more solid to go on.'

He clapped his hands.

'Spence, I've got a job for you.' Spencer looked up. 'I want you to ring around hotels, letting companies and estate agents and see if you can find anyone who has had any dealings with Caroline Berry. If she really has left her husband then she's going to need somewhere to stay. Focus on a ten... no, make that twenty-mile radius of the Roswell Estate. I'm guessing she won't want to be too far from her son. And while you're at it, see if the name Jenny Black brings any results.'

'Sure, boss.'

Alex turned to Cat and handed her a slip of paper. She glanced at the scribbled name and number.

'Details for the Berrys' family solicitors. Can you chase? I'm still waiting to hear whether there was any pre-nup in place. Oh, and don't forget the Heathrow hotel. Get a copy of his mugshot. See if we can get anyone to confirm he was at breakfast that morning.'

She nodded, though the pout of her lips made her disappointment obvious.

'What's the problem?' he asked.

'Nothing. It's just that I was hoping to do the interview with you.' She looked over to Bob's empty desk. 'Who are you taking in with you?'

Alex rolled his eyes.

'Come on then.'

'Let me just get my pad,' she said, running back for her bag.

On entering the interview room, they found Berry sitting bolt upright in the chair with a poker-straight back, his chin jutting out proudly. Flanked on his left by a duty solicitor, he looked ahead, registering no emotion. Cat ran through the standard introductions, before settling back in her seat. Berry looked at her.

'Found her yet?'

Cat opened her mouth to reply but Alex beat her to it.

'Hardly likely, given that we have no information on where she might have gone.'

'I told you I don't know,' Berry said.

'What about her car?' Cat said. 'It would help if we had a description of the car she was driving.'

Berry looked at his solicitor.

'Do I answer that?'

The lawyer looked at him blandly.

'It sounds like a reasonable request to me.'

Berry looked down at the table and mumbled his response.

'It's an Aston Martin DB5 in silver birch on a 1965 plate.'

'Is that the car that you kept in your lockup?' Cat asked, remembering Spencer's gushing account of some silver dream machine.

'That's right.'

Cat looked across at Berry and noticed his clenched fists and white knuckles.

Alex whistled.

'Very nice. Should be easy enough to track down.'

'If she hasn't sold it.'

'Why would she do that?' Alex asked sharply.

Too sharply, Cat thought as she noticed Berry suddenly press his lips together.

He gave a languid shrug.

'Is she the registered owner?' Alex asked.

'No. All of the cars are in my name.'

'Well she won't be able to sell it then, will she? What's the reg number? We'll get an alert out?'

Berry recited the registration number of the car and leaned back in his chair. He put his fingers to his eyes and pinched the bridge of his nose.

They remained in that small box of an interview room for almost two and a half hours. The warm air grew stagnant as the time ticked by. Cat could feel a headache coming on. Berry answered in monosyllables. He stuck to his story, the same story, no matter how many times he was challenged.

No, he didn't know where Caroline was.

No, he hadn't killed her.

No, he didn't kill Megan.

No, he didn't kill Jane.

Without Caroline they had no one to confirm, or deny, his version of events. The case against him was dissolving before their very eyes.

Cat left the interview exhausted. She rubbed her hands over her face, inadvertently smearing her make-up, making the dark circles around her eyes even worse. Now she looked as tired as she felt. What she needed was a bit of fresh air.

A cold wind blew through the corridor, slipping in through the fire door propped open with a heavy red fire extinguisher – probably by one of the station's dwindling number of smokers, ironically. Ordinarily Cat would have returned the extinguisher, but not today. Instead she took advantage of someone else's lax habits, thankful she was saved from having to walk the long way around.

Outside, she took a deep breath. The air smelled fresh and inviting despite the chill. She strolled slowly down the path. Running parallel to the red brick building, it led to a small, cultivated plot filled with English roses and surrounded by a low lavender hedge. In summer the air would have been full of their heady aroma but on that cold autumn afternoon the roses were little more than twigs and the lavender spires mere spindles, grey and fragrance-free. It was the garden of remembrance. Plaques dedicated to lost colleagues served to remind those that worked there of the dangers of the job and of their own vulnerability.

Cat sat on one of the four wooden benches that faced the small patch. On its back was a brass plate dulled by the years that had passed since the inscription was first etched. She reached for the corner of her cardigan and, forming it into a wad, started to rub. After a short while the sun prised its way through a mass of curvy cauliflower clouds high in the sky. Its watery rays glinted off the buffed plaque. She paused and became aware of approaching footsteps. She looked up just as Alex rounded the corner. He joined her on the bench.

'How did you know I was here?' she asked.

'I thought you'd gone to the loo but after fifteen minutes I figured I'd better come looking.'

'Sorry. I didn't realise I'd been gone that long.'

'That's alright. As long as you're okay?'

'Yeah I'm fine. I just needed some peace and quiet.'

'And a little divine intervention?'

'Huh?'

Alex gestured to the name plate on the back of the bench.

Peter McKenzie

Lived in valour so as not to die in vain

Cat rolled her eyes and smacked him playfully on the arm.

'No, you idiot. It's just I can't think straight when there's so much noise.'

'That's because you spent too many years mollycoddled as a student.'

It was the sort of thing her father would have said to her.

'Maybe,' she said.

'Has it helped?'

'No. Not really.' She paused for a moment. 'Families are funny things, don't you think?'

Alex raised both eyebrows but said nothing.

'You know, when Pete died I remember my Dad saying that no parent should ever have to bury a child. If the parental bond is so strong then how can a parent walk out on their child?'

'I don't know,' he said, his voice barely a whisper.

'Yet we're supposed to believe that Caroline Berry, who by all accounts is devoted to her son, is prepared to leave Jake with Steve. It doesn't make sense.'

'Nothing is making much sense at the moment,' Alex said, taking to his feet. 'Come on. I'll make us a couple of strong black coffees. I need something to perk me up. We can have another shot at Berry later. In the meantime, we keep running with our enquiries. If Caroline really has gone into hiding, now that we've got their bank details, we should be able to get a trace from any withdrawals she makes.'

Cat started after him.

'I'll get on to that solicitor again. They promised to get back to me but I haven't heard anything. If Caroline has left him, I would have thought she'll get onto her solicitors pretty quickly. She'll want Berry out of the house as fast as possible, won't she?'

'She might have a long wait if there's no pre-nup and he's determined to stay, especially as she's walked out on the kid.'

The following morning Cat entered the office and slung her bag on her chair. First stop: the kettle. Spencer held out his mug with a hopeful expression as she passed. His phone started to ring.

He was still on the phone when she handed him his mug, filled with a fresh brew. He smiled and gave her an upturned thumb.

Back at her desk she sipped at the steaming coffee and picked up a scribbled telephone message. While she'd been out, the long-awaited call from the Williams' family solicitor had come in and yet again she'd not been in to take it.

It made her trip to the Heathrow hotel feel even more of a waste of time. She gave a tired sigh. Her four-thirty start was making itself felt. She'd had to get to the hotel for five-thirty to make it in time for the start of the breakfast service of which she didn't partake, having no appetite at that hour in the morning. Going through the motions, she'd asked the staff if they remembered seeing Steve Berry on the date in question, but no one could. Nor had she expected them to: it was a breakfast buffet, one of those help-yourself arrangements.

Cat looked down at the note still gripped between her fingers. She reached for the phone when Spencer jumped up out of his seat.

'I think I've got something,' he shouted, sounding excited.

He hurried over towards Alex's desk.

Cat replaced the handset.

She noticed Alex's level expression and knew he was reserving judgement; it could be something, or nothing. She leaned forward in her seat, straining to hear.

'I just got a call from a classic car dealer in response to the alert that went out for the Aston Martin,' Spencer said. 'He gave me a description of a woman that matched Caroline Berry who took in a 1965 DB5 yesterday afternoon. She gave him some sob story about her husband dying suddenly. She told him that her husband had recently been declared bankrupt which brought on his heart attack and the only thing she had left was the car.'

'And?' Alex asked.

'He made her an offer that she accepted.'

'Even though she wasn't the registered keeper on the log book and didn't have a death certificate?' Alex said.

'Apparently she completed the V5 as executor of the will. He said it all looked in order. She even showed him a medical certificate for the death, a marriage certificate and a will. He said she was very convincing. Though I bet he didn't try too hard to see through the cracks. I did a bit of digging on the internet to find out what the going rate is for a car like that and he only paid a fraction of what the car's really worth.'

'How the hell did she get hold of a medical certificate?' Cat asked.

'They're easy enough to forge,' Alex said.

'The woman wanted it settled in cash,' Spencer said, 'but the garage owner was insistent that he wouldn't pay more than ten thou' in notes. He said they never go over the money laundering threshold.'

Alex rolled his eyes.

'Thank heaven for small mercies.'

'So how did he pay the rest?' Cat asked.

'Bank transfer,' Spencer said.

'Which means you've got her bank details,' she said.

Spencer shook his head but his eyes gleamed with excitement and Cat could see he was struggling to maintain the suspense.

'Well, get back onto the garage and get them, pronto,' Alex

snapped. 'When you've done that, contact the bank and get an address for her.'

'I haven't told you the best bit yet,' Spencer said, not letting Alex's curt tone deflate his enthusiasm. 'She said the cash would cover the funeral but the rest of it was needed to settle one of her husband's debts. Well, that's the reason she gave for wanting the money transferred into someone else's account.'

He paused and Alex gave him a pointed look.

'And...?'

'She wanted it paid into an account in the name of Jenny Black.'

'What?' Alex and Cat said in unison.

Alex shook his head.

'What the hell is going on?'

Twenty-Five

'No comment. That's all he says. I'll give him no fucking comment,' Alex said as he spun his chair out from under his desk and slumped into it.

He'd just come from another session with Steve Berry.

'Locating Jenny Black is our number one priority. We get her and we get a chance to break him.' Everyone was nodding. 'Spencer, any luck with the bank?'

'The account is registered to the same address as when Jenny Black set it up over fifteen years ago. She obviously didn't change it when she moved out.'

'This is ridiculous. If it was Caroline who took the car in, why is she giving Jenny's account details? And if it was Jenny, how the hell did she get her hands on the car and the log book?' Alex said.

Everyone looked equally confused.

Cat turned to Spencer.

'What about the garage owner? I thought you said he gave a description of a woman that matched Caroline Berry.'

'He did. Average height, in her thirties, with blonde mid-length hair, nicely styled. She was wearing smart clothes and had manicured nails. He said she looked like a woman with expensive tastes. We were looking for Caroline Berry, and it sounded like Caroline Berry. Can you blame me?'

Alex groaned.

'I wouldn't be surprised if Jenny is similar looking to Caroline. People tend to gravitate towards a certain type. We need to get our hands on a photo of Jenny Black,' he said.

'I thought Glafcos was going to send one over once he'd got it from that Irish bar,' Cat said. 'Do you want me to call him?'

'No. I'll call him myself. If it does turn out to be her, Berry's going to have one hell of a shitstorm coming his way.' And for the first time in a long time, Alex cracked a smile. 'Finally, things are looking up.'

For the next couple of hours, the office hummed with activity; the phones were busy, keyboards rattled, and conversations crisscrossed around the room.

Alex glanced up from the computer screen as Cat approached. 'No pre-nup,' she said. 'The solicitors confirmed that they represented both Howard Williams and Caroline before and after she was married. Mr Williams' will was straightforward – apart from the sizeable inheritance he left to Megan, the rest of his estate was to go to Caroline, unless her death preceded his, in which case it was to go into a trust fund for his grandson until his eighteenth birthday. Caroline had also made a will, leaving half to her husband and the other half to be put into trust for her son, again until his eighteenth birthday.'

'Hmm, without a pre-nup Berry would have probably done alright out of a divorce settlement. Well at least we know,' Alex said. 'Hang on a minute...' He stood up from his chair. 'Bob!' he called, just as the old hand was slipping into his creased and ill-fitting jacket.

Bob looked over.

'Boss?'

Alex made an obvious move to look at his watch.

'I did say I'd got to go early,' Bob said. 'I'm helping Nathan move his stuff this afternoon, remember? The girlfriend's finally seen sense and sent him packing. Unfortunately, that means we're going to have to put up with him at home again. I don't know why the lad can't find somewhere on his own. I had to in my day. But his mother won't hear of it.'

'Yes, you did say. Sorry, I'd forgotten,' Alex said. 'Hope the move goes okay.'

Bob gave a nod and went straight out.

By the time Alex looked back at Cat she was staring into space, nursing a frown.

'What's up with you?' he asked.

She turned to him and smiled.

'Nothing. I was just thinking.' But a hint of a frown crept back across her brow. 'This might sound stupid but something Bob just said has given me an idea. What if Jenny Black has gone back home?'

'That would be a really inspired comment, if we knew where home was.'

'I meant home as in where she grew up,' Cat said. Her idea was gathering weight and she could feel her excitement mount. 'I was trying to think where she might have gone, given she's been out of the country for so long. She could be holed up in a hotel or renting somewhere but given she's using a bank account which lists her address as the house where she grew up, well, Bob just said it, didn't he? Kids gravitate home when they're in a fix or need somewhere to stay.'

Her eyes lit up.

'Do you remember what the barman in that Irish bar told us? About Jenny returning home for her mother's funeral? What if she inherited the house and never sold it? She could have used a management company or agent, or whatever you call them, for the day-to-day arrangements. The rental income could have been building up for years and the house will have been steadily increasing in value. A pretty valuable asset for someone used to making a living as a barmaid.'

'And even more valuable for someone looking for a place to hide out,' Alex said.

Cat smiled.

'Exactly what I was thinking.'

Cat put the phone down and swivelled her chair around to face

Alex's desk.

'That was Alphabet Lettings,' she called over to him. 'They've confirmed they're the managing agents for a house let on behalf of a Ms Jennifer Black. They've been paying the rental income directly into an account in the same name.'

'Is the house still being let out?' he asked.

'No. But that's only been the case for a week. Before that they'd had the same tenants in for the last couple of years. About a month ago Jenny wrote to them and said she wanted to end the arrangement. She told them to serve notice on the current tenants.'

Cat watched Alex as the information sunk in.

'Only a month ago?'

She nodded.

'The date on the letter was the day after Megan's murder,' she said.

'So where has she been in the meantime?'

'Maybe Berry put her up somewhere. Does it matter? We've got a pretty good idea where she is now.'

'Grab your coat.'

In the hour it took to reach Jenny Black's childhood home, Cat and Alex had grown tired of speculating. They still had no idea what role the woman had played in the murders, if any, and the possibility that they might be wasting precious time on a wild goose chase had been mentioned more than once. As a result, they spent the latter part of the journey in silence.

Alex brought the car to a stop a short distance from the house, an unassuming nineteen-thirties' semi-detached that didn't look too badly in need of repair. A small patch of grass that bridged the gap between the house and the pavement was a little overgrown and a handful of weeds sprouted through the poorly tarmacked drive but on the whole the place looked well-maintained.

Cat shifted in her seat.

'I wonder what the arrangement with the agents was for dealing with problems,' she said. 'You know, like if there was a leaky boiler or a fence got blown down. Doesn't the cost of that type of thing normally get paid for by the landlord? If that's the case, they must have up-to-date contact details for her.'

Alex kept his eyes on the house. 'Not necessarily. She could have given them money on account. She'd only have to call them every so often to check things were okay. But it's a good point, something to ask the agents. Come on. Let's take a look around,' he said, climbing out of the car.

Cat walked up to the garage that adjoined the house on its left-hand side. The paintwork on the wooden doors was blistered and patches of bare wood peeped through. With little protection from the wet weather the doors had bowed slightly and no longer closed properly. Cat peered through the gap.

'It's empty,' she called to Alex.

Alex opened the outer door of the storm porch and stepped inside, reappearing moments later.

'Nothing in there and from what I could tell there's no post on the floor inside either. Somebody must be coming in regularly otherwise there'd be a pile of free papers and junk mail.'

He closed the porch door.

'You wait here. I'll be back in a minute.'

He headed off down the street and disappeared down an alleyway, which Cat assumed would give access to the back of the house. Soon enough he reappeared, jogging down the road, to join her by the front door. He walked straight past and re-entered the porch where he reached for the doorbell. Cat heard the chimes ring out through the glazed front door.

'I don't know why I'm bothering. She's obviously not here,' he said. 'Or if she is then she's lying low. I managed to get right around the back and could see through to the front. It doesn't look like anyone's living here.' He took his finger away from the doorbell.

'Maybe the neighbours will know?'

Five minutes later they were standing outside their fourth house. Having had no luck at the first three it was a relief to hear the sound of a lock turning. Cat waited, a neutral expression on her face. The door opened slowly to reveal a man, late sixties or early seventies, dressed smartly in grey slacks and yellow sweater. His initial smile melted from his face.

'Oh, I'm sorry; I thought you were someone else.' He peered at them quizzically. 'Can I help you?'

Alex opened his wallet to reveal his ID.

'The police?' He sounded alarmed.

'There's nothing to worry about sir,' Cat said. 'I wonder if you can spare a few minutes?'

'I suppose, but I haven't got much time. I'm expecting a friend. He's picking me up for a game of golf. Our tee-time's already booked, we can't change it,' he said. He looked at them, concern clear on his face. 'I won't have to miss it will I?'

'Don't worry about that sir,' Alex said. 'This really shouldn't take very long.'

Cat looked up at the clear blue sky.

'Nice day for a game of golf.'

The pensioner appeared to relax a little.

'Oh, I dare say it won't hurt Ted if he has to wait a few minutes.'

The old man seemed to be on the verge of inviting the two detectives in, but as he took a step back into his hallway he stalled.

'Can I take another look at that badge?'

'Of course,' Alex replied, pulling out his ID again. This time he gave the man a chance to properly scrutinise it.

'You're not local?'

'That's right sir. I didn't mean to mislead you. I should have explained. We suspect that someone wanted for crimes in our area may have settled around here.'

He took a second, closer look at the ID. And then let his eyes roam over the two detectives. He stepped back to let the pair of them in.

'Sorry about that but you can't be too careful. Come through. Would you like a drink?'

'You did the right thing to check. And no thank you, we won't keep you any longer than we need to,' Alex said. 'We have a lot of houses to cover. We simply want to know whether you have noticed any new people in the neighbourhood.'

Their host took a seat by the window, perhaps so that he could see his friend arriving.

'Neighbourhoods aren't what they used to be in my day,' he said. 'You used to know everyone in your street. And I mean the whole family; their mother and father, aunts and uncles. These days no one settles anywhere for very long.'

'Have there been any moves recently?' Alex asked.

'Well, there's been a change two doors down, that was last weekend. Mandy and Jim, lovely couple, were living there. Never had any trouble with them. In fact, I can remember a time when I was laid low with a nasty flu bug.'

Cat recognised the signs. If they let him, he would be taking them on a trip down memory lane for as long as they'd listen. Not wanting to chance it, she jumped in. 'I take it they've moved?'

'Yes. Not that they wanted to, mind you. They were more than happy there. But they got their marching orders. One month's notice, that's all they were entitled to. Shocking isn't it? Mandy was quite teary when we said goodbye. That seems to be the way it is these days. Nothing's forever is it?'

Cat gave him a sympathetic smile.

'What's happening with the house, do you know?' Alex asked.

'Well, that's a funny thing in its own right. Me and my wife, she passed away a few years ago now, well, we were friends with Rose and George. They'd lived in that house all their married life, almost as long as me and Mavis had been here. They're both dead now of course. Anyway, they had a little girl, Jennifer.' He gave a disapproving shake of his head. 'She led them a merry dance when she was growing up, I can tell you. And you know, after she'd left home, she hardly ever came back to see them, even after George died and Rose fell ill. She was overseas somewhere... I can't remember where. I'd all but forgotten her, so imagine my surprise when I saw her coming out of the house only yesterday. She may be all grown up but I'd have recognised her anywhere. I think she was just as surprised to see me. I bet she thought I'd be dead too by now.'

'At least we know where she's hiding out,' Cat said, as they made their way back to the car.

'Not necessarily. He may have caught her on a fleeting visit,' Alex said. Cat shot him an annoyed look. 'I was simply stating a possibility. You're right though, the most obvious explanation is that she's staying here.'

'Now what?' she asked.

'We wait for her to come back.'

Cat groaned.

'Can't we do something more useful? Let's go to the letting agents? It's only ten minutes away and we can get details of the arrangement she had with them. They may even have a mobile number for her. If we had that we'd have no trouble tracking her down.'

Cat knew that with the advances made in mobile telephone technology it was possible to trace the location of a phone just from its proximity to the transmitter sites.

'I don't suppose it could hurt; we're here now. What's the address?'

Cat rummaged through her handbag and retrieved her notepad. She pulled the biro out from the pad's spiral binding and flicked through its creased pages until she found what she was looking for.

'Alphabet Lettings. Eleven, The Maltings.'

Alex input the details into the satnav and soon they were

being guided through a maze of traffic-laden roads.

'Why's it so busy?' Alex grumbled as they circled the one-way system for the third time.

'Maybe it's market day? You know what it's like at home – the town gets gridlocked.'

'Shit. This is useless. I'm going to have to go back around. Keep looking for a space.'

He turned onto the ring road, back to where they started. Cat continued to scour the narrow side streets for somewhere to park.

'Wait! Over there,' she said, pointing to the sign of a supermarket. 'They'll have parking.'

Alex followed the signs down a short access road around a corner to a large Sainsbury's and its ample car park.

'Well spotted,' he said, pulling the car into the first space he came across.

They climbed out. Alex locked the car and started to walk away, back in the direction of the town.

'Alex,' Cat called, 'Ticket!' She pointed to a prominent sign advising shoppers of the need for a valid parking ticket.

He looked back across the car roof at her.

'But it's a supermarket.'

He rolled his eyes and started to scan the car park for the nearest meter. He thrust his hand into his trouser pocket and pulled out a selection of coins.

'Back in a sec.'

Cat leaned against the side of the car. The sound of gears crunching nearby caused her to look over as a small red hatchback lurched out of its parking space and made a messy three-point turn towards the exit. A trolley rolled aimlessly into the middle of the traffic lane nearby, a bag full of shopping still in it.

'Hey!' Cat shouted at the retreating car. She started after it, waving.

She cut through a row of parked cars and was so busy trying to attract the attention of the red hatchback she didn't see the car coming from her left until it was almost too late. Mercifully, the driver stopped just in time.

At such close quarters the horn sounded impossibly loud. Cat looked into the car at the driver who was glowering at her from behind the wheel. Her heart pounding, she mouthed 'sorry' and held up her hands apologetically. She stepped back and let the car pass before setting off again, careful this time not to leap in front of any moving vehicles.

The red Peugeot was still waiting in line to leave. Cat thought she saw the woman driver spot her in the mirror, so she waved and started to jog over. The woman hastily turned away from her.

Cat's stomach flipped.

She moved quickly now, running alongside the queuing cars. Just then the car at the front pulled away. Still watching the red Peugeot, Cat was suddenly cloaked in a white cloud of exhaust fumes. She heard the screams of an engine being revved too hard followed by the sound of metal on metal as the gears grated and suddenly the car in front of her hurled towards her. With only seconds to spare she threw herself sideways. Landing heavily, the air exploded from her as she rolled away from the approaching rear bumper. The car stopped. Slowly Cat raised herself to her knees and took a moment to catch her breath. She was winded and bruised, but overall, she'd had a lucky escape. Her heart was banging out a military tattoo in her chest as she struggled to her feet. She stumbled out into the road, getting there just in time to see the red car disappear around the corner.

'Are you alright dear?'

Cat turned back. An elderly lady had approached and was peering at her; her wrinkled, tissue-paper skin creased with concern. Cat realised she was the driver of the car that had nearly mown her down.

'I'm so sorry but I didn't see you there. You see, the car in front of me started to reverse...'

Car horns started to blare behind them. Cat saw the old

woman's car, its hazard lights blinking, blocking the exit.

'I had to do something. It would have hit me. It just started to reverse,' the elderly lady repeated.

The honking grew more persistent.

'Look, I'm fine,' Cat said. 'Just get back in your car. You're blocking the exit.'

'If you're sure you're okay?'

But Cat was already walking away, back to the unmarked car and to a waiting Alex.

'Where the hell have you been? I've...'

He stopped on seeing her dishevelled appearance and flushed face.

'What happened to you?'

'I think I've just seen Jenny Black.' Her voice wobbled as she spoke, caused by a combination of anger and the adrenalin that was coursing through her body.

'But how...? You don't know what she looks like.'

'Some woman has just gone screaming out of here after seeing me. I didn't see much of her but she was blonde and not too dissimilar to Caroline. I remembered what Spence said about the description the garage owner gave.'

'How would she know you?' Alex challenged. 'She's never even met you. Couldn't she have just been a shit driver?'

'She left her trolley rolling in the middle of the road with shopping still in it.'

'Okay, that does sound dodgy. But it's too late now; she's long gone.'

Cat looked back towards the car park's exit.

'Who says? She doesn't know we've got her address.' She opened the passenger door and looked at Alex across the roof of the car. 'I bet she's gone back to the house.'

They both jumped into the car. Alex drove while Cat put out an alert for the red Peugeot.

'No number plate?' he asked, after she had finished calling it in.

She gave him a withering look.

'Tell you what, get on the blower to Bob and ask him whether those photos have come through from Cyprus yet. They should've sent them by now.'

Turning into the road which they had visited for the first time less than an hour ago, Alex slowed the car to a crawl and continued along until number fifty-three came into view. Still some hundred metres before the house Alex pulled the car into the kerb and turned off the engine.

'That's the car...' Cat pointed towards a red Peugeot parked on the road in front of the house.

'Well, I take it back,' Alex said. 'I honestly thought this was going to be a total waste of time.'

Cat was too busy calling in the car's number plate to reply.

Unfastening his seat belt, Alex turned to her.

'You take the back and I'll take the front,' he said, clipping his radio to his belt.

'With respect, that doesn't make sense,' Cat said. 'If Jenny did somehow recognise me, then she knows I'm in the area. We've got to assume she doesn't know that you are. Wouldn't it be better for me to go to the front door, give a little shout through the letter box, the usual 'yoohoo', and if she tries to make a run for it out the back you can be there ready to grab her.'

'I'm not sure,' Alex said. 'I think it'd be better if I go to the front and you cover the back.'

'Don't you mean it would make you feel better?'

Cat tensed, waiting for the backlash, but Alex said nothing. She sensed he was torn.

'Look Alex, based on her reaction in the car park, she's going to make a run for it. I'd rather you be by the back door to stop her.'

Alex looked over to the house.

'Alright. Give me enough time to get in position, say two

minutes, before you go over. But if she doesn't make a run for it, you let me in and we deal with her together.'

'Of course. It's not like I'm doing this to be some sort of hero.' Alex shot her a look. 'Honestly Alex, I'm not Peter.'

'Look, I said we'll do it your way.'

As he slipped out of the car, Cat saw him shaking his head.

After waiting ninety seconds Cat walked purposefully up the pathway. On reaching the front door she gave a casual look about her, anxious to see if her approach had been noticed. She kept close to the front of the house so as not to be visible from any of the upstairs windows and moved sideways to the large bay window. She peered through from the side but the light reflecting off the glass made it impossible to see in. She cupped her hands around her eyes and tried again. This time she could just about make out the shapes of a couple of chairs through the privacy-giving net curtains. Two chairs and maybe a coffee table, but that was all. She walked back to the door and stepped inside the glass porch. She looked at her watch. The two minutes were up.

She took a deep breath to steady her nerves.

'Here goes,' she said out loud and pushed a finger firmly on the doorbell.

While Cat was busy psyching herself up, Alex jogged along the alley that skirted the backs of the houses. A wheeled bin with a large white number fifty-three affixed helpfully guided him to the right house. He slipped the latch and opened the gate just a couple of inches, enough to take in the garden beyond. Although a little overgrown, it looked to have been recently tended and the thirty-foot stretch of lawn bordered either side by shrubs and flowers offered little in the way of cover.

Conscious that Cat would soon be knocking at the front door, he knew he needed to move quickly. He slipped through the gate and, keeping low, ran to a grubby white plastic table and chair set some twenty feet away. He squatted behind the table and scanned the windows for signs of movement. Seeing nothing, and aware that time was ticking by, Alex broke cover and sprinted the short distance to the rear wall of the house. He pressed himself against the rough red brick, next to the glazed back door.

Just then his phone let out a quiet chime.

Cat heard the nerve-jangling trill ring of the bell ricochet around the house. She waited before pressing it a second time; waited and listened. The obscure glass that had been used in the door, intended to let light in but keep prying eyes out, made it impossible to make out anything other than shadows in the hallway beyond. Soon she heard what sounded like an approaching tread, heels on a wooden floor. Her eyes scanned the darkness of the hallway beyond as she attempted to follow the muffled footfall. Squinting, she thought she could make out someone bending down at the foot of the stairs, they straightened up and disappeared back into the darkness. She raised a finger to the bell and pushed it again. The figure returned, this time drawing closer to the door. As the latch snapped back Cat jumped and realised shamefully that she had been holding her breath.

What had happened to all the training that had supposedly taught her to take control over both herself and the situation?

She took a deep breath as the door swung slowly open.

Alex glanced down. The phone had signalled an incoming message from Bob. Still alert to any movement coming from the back door, he moved his fingers deftly over the screen and opened the text.

Photo from Cyprus, the message said.

Alex, used to Bob's brevity, scrolled down and looked at the attached image.

He blew out his cheeks with a heavy breath.

'If you want something doing right...'

His fingers moved rapidly as he fired off a quick reply.

Cat steeled herself for a full-on assault but, when the moment for action arrived, nothing happened. The door swung open and Cat found herself blinking, doubting her eyes, at the figure standing in the shadowy hallway in front of her.

'Mrs Berry?' she said, still questioning what she knew she could see.

'I thought it might be you. Come in,' Caroline Berry said flatly as she stepped away from the door, giving Cat access into the house.

Still transfixed at the sight of the woman she'd given up for dead, Cat twisted sideways and pushed the door closed, carefully slipping it onto the latch. She noted the overnight bag and small suitcase at the foot of the stairs as she followed Caroline into the open plan lounge.

'What do you want?' Caroline asked as she unzipped a large tote bag that lay on the dining table.

Cat quickly took in the room. It was spotlessly tidy, apart from the bag on the table and a few bits and pieces, including a set of car keys with a Peugeot key fob that rested on top of a paperback; a train ticket jutted out of its pages.

Alex waited, still poised in position by the back door. Just as the doorbell rang, he heard his phone chime with the arrival of another text. Ignoring it, he readied himself to jump into action.

Nothing.

He waited some more.

As the seconds ticked by he couldn't stand the inertia any

longer and decided to risk a look through the window. Keeping wide of the glass back door he edged along and straightened up until he could see into the kitchen and the lounge beyond. Although the room was poorly lit he could clearly make out the outlines of two women.

'Shit,' he said under his breath.

He could see a woman standing by the dining table. She had her back to him and although he couldn't see her face it was obvious from the way she was moving that she was talking. She appeared to be searching through a bag that rested on the table in front of her. He realised she wasn't looking in the bag but was actually packing it. Or rather she was pushing something forcibly into it. He transferred his attention across the room to the doorway where Cat was standing. Now she was talking. He watched as she moved her hands, gesturing as she spoke. He looked back at the woman just as she snatched something off the table, a small purse perhaps? Whatever it was she flung it on top of the bag, whilst talking animatedly to Cat.

The phone chimed a second time, a reminder of the unread text.

'If she's texted me, I'll...'

Reaching into his pocket he pulled out his phone but the text was a reply from Bob.

'What are you doing here?' Cat asked, ignoring Caroline's question.

'What does it look like?'

'If you're hiding from your husband, if he's threatened you in any way, you don't need to worry, he's in custody.'

For the first time the other woman registered a look of shock. 'What for?'

'Suspected murder. To be honest I'm surprised to find you here. We thought... well, your disappearance had us all worried.'

Caroline looked at her, a weak smile on her face. She gave a small shake of the head and began to pack the contents of the table into the open bag.

'So how come you're here – I mean in Jenny Black's house?'

'It was the only place I could think of he didn't know about.'

'Steve?' Cat asked.

'Of course.'

'And Jenny? Is she staying here too?'

Caroline gave her a sharp look.

'She's dead. He killed her, like the others.'

The bag packing grew more frantic.

'I don't understand. He can't have done,' Cat said. 'A neighbour said he saw Jenny only yesterday.'

'Oh, I see.' Caroline stopped in her tracks. 'That changes everything.' She sighed and for the first time looked tired. 'Would you like a drink? I think I need one.'

'No thanks.'

'Not even a glass of water?'

'Okay, a glass of water will be fine, thank you,' Cat said, just to appease.

Caroline walked into the small kitchen.

Alex ducked as the woman turned. Crouching down, he heard the sound of a tap running just moments before water gurgled in the drain at his feet. Taking the opportunity, he looked down at his phone.

No mistake. Have been back to the Greek to confirm, Bob's latest message read.

Alex frowned. He opened up the original text from Bob and returned it, with the message '*Glafcos is sure this is a photo of Jenny Black?*'

He hit send.

He didn't have long to wait; within the minute he got a reply he had not expected.

Caroline turned the tap on and let it run while she clattered around in a cupboard before pulling out two tall glass tumblers. She bent down and reached into the under-counter refrigerator and pulled out what looked like a half-empty bottle of white wine, a cork stuck crudely out of its neck. She yanked out the stopper and hurriedly poured herself a drink, sloppily spilling the chilled liquid over the work surface.

Cat walked over to the table while she waited. She pushed a Clarins' make-up bag to one side, revealing the title of the paperback.

'The Da Vinci Code. I wouldn't have had you down as a fan of action-packed thrillers,' she said.

'That's because you don't know anything about me,' Caroline replied with a vehemence that took Cat by surprise.

Caroline put the second glass under the running tap. She turned just as Cat picked up the paperback, revealing the small burgundy book that lay hidden underneath. Caroline banged the glass down and rushed over. She hurriedly threw the passport and the rest of the items on the table into the bag before grabbing the book from Cat's fingers. She shoved it into the bag with such a force she almost tore the front cover clean off before rushing back to the kitchen.

Cat watched as Caroline picked up the nearly full tumbler and discarded the water into the sink before refilling the glass from the still running tap.

'Where did you get that passport from?' she asked.

'The passport office, where do you think?' Caroline said over her shoulder.

'But we found your passport at the house.'

Cat felt the hairs on the back of her neck begin to bristle.

Caroline was approaching, holding out the glass of water in

one hand. A tea towel hung stiffly from the other hand.

'It's you. You're Jenny,' Cat said, the words faltering on her lips, barely bringing herself to believe it. Suddenly it all made sense. 'You killed them. To stop them from seeing you for the imposter you are.'

In an instance Cat saw the glass quickly move up towards her face. It stopped inches away, just as the hot water hit, momentarily blinding her, her senses confused by its heat. The other woman grabbed her bag and barged roughly past into the hallway

'Stop! There's no point in running. It's too late,' Cat shouted after her.

Her demand fell on deaf ears. Cat made to follow but a sharp pain shot down her side. Her legs felt suddenly weak.

A chill crept through her. She looked down to where a dark stain was spreading quickly through her shirt. A second later she heard the click of the latch.

Alex slowly stretched to full height. His knees creaked and clicked as he eased out of his cramped position. Momentarily paralysed by pins and needles as the circulation returned to his legs, he watched events unfold remotely through the kitchen window, witnessing something that caused him to regret every single decision he had taken that afternoon.

He ran around to the front of the house and arrived just in time to see the Peugeot accelerate away. After finding the front door locked, he rapidly weighed up his options. Experience had taught him not to even bother to try to smash through the sealed double-glazed unit. Forced to watch helplessly, the image of Cat stumbling towards the table was imprinted on his mind. He'd known straight away that something bad had happened. He needed to push the growing sensation of panic to one side and think straight. Turning on his heels he started back towards the rear of the house, shouting instructions into the radio as he ran - an ambulance for Cat and a pursuit vehicle for the Peugeot. At the back door he wasted no time. Picking up a garden chair he launched it at the glazed door, causing the single pane of glass to shatter.

Cat was on the floor in the living room, slumped against the side of one of the settees. Alex rushed to her side; the fear constricted his chest so tightly he felt physically sick. She was holding a tea towel pressed against her side, but already it was soiled a dark crimson colour, too small and thin to stem the flow of blood.

'The bitch went and stabbed me. It was Caroline. I mean Jenny. Jenny is Caroline.'

'I know,' he said. 'I just got the photo from Glafcos.'

'She and Berry must have been in it together. They had to get rid of Megan and Jane. They'd have known instantly she wasn't Caroline,' Cat said in between short gasps. It hurt to breathe too deeply.

'An ambulance is on its way,' Alex said, climbing to his feet. He stepped over her and headed back to the kitchen. 'You need something better than that to stop the bleeding.'

He roughly pulled open cupboard doors and drawers until he came upon a pile of clean towels. He grabbed a handful.

'Glafcos will be happy,' Cat said, wincing as Alex tended her wound.

'What? Why?'

'The body in the hills... It's going to be Caroline, isn't it?'

'I don't think anyone's going to be happy that it's ended like this,' he said. 'Shit, Cat, you should have waited for me. I was mad to let you come in alone.'

Cat let out a disparaging snort, shortly followed by a sharp intake of breath. She grimaced.

'Ooh, that hurt.' She shot Alex a thin smile. 'What are you still doing here? Go after her. I'll be fine.'

Alex looked up towards the window as the sound of sirens grew louder.

'Here, keep this pressed down,' he said, lifting her hands to rest on top of the towel. 'I'll go and flag them down.'

As the paramedics worked, Alex kept his distance. Pacing back and forth like an expectant father. He stopped in his tracks when he noticed the telephone nestled in the open pages of a directory.

He put the phone to one side and picked up the thick book, looking for anything that might help him: local tourist information, leisure centre adverts, and there it was... public transport details, including train enquiries. Grabbing the phone, he jabbed a finger on the redial button. The phone clicked into action. As he waited, he stopped pacing and watched the paramedics lift Cat onto a trolley. A pre-recorded message came through the earpiece.

The paramedics started to wheel Cat out of the room.

Alex put a hand out.

'Wait. Is it okay if I ask her a couple of questions before you go?'

'Only if you're quick.'

'Cat, the last number that Jenny dialled was for rail enquiries.'

'Mmm. There was a train ticket...' she said in a thin, wavering voice.

'Where it was for?'

She closed her eyes. The morphine that she'd been given to manage the pain was beginning to take effect.

Alex reached over and held her hand.

'Do you have any idea where she's going?'

'Sorry mate, we need to get going,' one of the paramedics said. They started to push the gurney through the lounge door. Cat's hand slipped out of his grip.

'A passport and a book,' she murmured. '...Da Vinci C...' Her words trailed away as they pushed her out of the front door.

Alex heard what she said but it didn't make any sense.

'Wait. Cat... I don't understand. Wait, just a second...'

'Look mate, we know you think it's important to talk to her but we have to get her to hospital. You'll have to talk to her later, when she's been taken care of.'

Alex looked at her face, pain-free and relaxed.

The image shocked him to the core. It reminded him so much of recent events with his son. He felt wretched. How could he have let Cat go in alone? Stunned by the powerful emotions it had stirred up in him, Alex stood watching as the ambulance doors closed. Fighting an overwhelming feeling of hopelessness, he pushed all thoughts of dark days to the back of his mind and ran to his car, determined that someone was going to pay.

Twenty-Six

The motorway was busy and despite travelling under the immunity of blue lights Alex was making slow progress. He had found Jenny's car abandoned at the local railway station. In her haste she had evidently become sloppy and had made no attempt at a discreet getaway. The ticket clerk was eager to help and quickly recognised her picture from the photograph on Alex's phone. Not only could the clerk remember serving Jenny but he could also remember where she was headed.

'London. And she paid cash. She had a purse stuffed full of notes. I've never seen so much. Well... I mean not in real life. I have in the movies, of course but... Has she robbed a bank?'

'What time did the train leave?' Alex asked.

The clerk looked up to the large clock that was on the wall behind him.

'Ten minutes ago.'

'When's it due to arrive?'

'It takes forty minutes provided there aren't any delays further down the line. I can–'

But Alex was already running to his car, hoping that luck and a flashing blue light was enough to give him a fighting chance to get there in time.

He called the office. Bob answered. Despite his shortcomings Alex knew he could trust Bob to do what was needed.

'First off, get someone on to the airports and talking to the transport police. Send Jenny's picture over. There's a chance she may be wearing a hat or scarf but from what I could tell she looks much the same as the photo, no dyed hair or anything like that. I want particular attention to be paid to routes to Italy.'

'Whereabouts in Italy?'

'I don't know. Cat said something about Da Vinci. And he was Italian, so...'

'That's a bit loose, isn't it?'

'I know,' Alex said, 'but it's the only thing we've got to go on for now.'

'Okay.'

'And Bob, once you've done all that, get your car and meet me at the station. With any luck I'll have her in custody by the time you get there.'

Alex wasted no time when he arrived at the London station; abandoning his car in a parking bay reserved for British Transport Police he set off at a run through the busy concourse, searching for a guard or anyone that could point him in the right direction. Finally, he spotted a porter and in between gasping breaths managed to convey what he was after.

The porter pointed towards a set of the barriers to the far right of where they stood.

'Platform six or eight. It depends on....'

But Alex didn't wait to hear the why's and where's; the clock was ticking but there was still a chance, albeit a slim one, that he might be in time to catch up with Jenny.

His optimism didn't last long. An empty train sat at the end of a deserted platform. Two armed-transport police officers stood waiting. Alex slowed his run to a walk and made his way over to them.

After standing down the two armed-officers, Alex was considering his options when his phone started to ring. It was Bob.

'Hey boss, I've just arrived. I'm by the shops and heading towards the platforms. Where are you?'

'Stay where you are. I'll come and find you.'

'Don's liaising with Heathrow,' Bob explained to Alex once they'd met up. 'He called me just before I got here. They've seen nothing so far, although they have confirmed that there are no reservations for today in the name of Berry or Black. Spence is dealing with Gatwick. Again, nothing booked in either name. I've also put the ports on alert and sent the picture over.'

'Thanks,' Alex said.

'Any more news on Cat?' Bob asked.

Alex's stomach lurched at the mention of her name. He'd heard nothing from the hospital.

'No, but I wouldn't expect to. I'm sure she'll be alright. She's young and fit and healthy,' he said, sounding a lot more upbeat than he felt.

'Yeah, sure. Bad luck though. So what now?'

'I don't know. What about Stansted? A couple of budget airlines fly from there to Italy.'

'Already done. Photo sent the same time as the others.' Bob paused. 'You sure you just want the focus on Italy?'

'Christ Bob, I don't know. I've got nothing else to go on. As they were wheeling Cat to the ambulance, I was pushing her for ideas. She was on her own with Jenny. I could see the two were talking. I figured she might have some clue as to where Jenny was planning on going. But she didn't know anything. The only thing she said was that there was a train ticket, a book and something to do with Da Vinci. That was all. Well the first part was right – she definitely got the train here, the guy in the ticket office confirmed that. The book reference I'm not so sure about and Da Vinci could mean anything. I figured maybe Italy, Da Vinci's birthplace? But I'm not sure.'

'Could it have been Code?' Bob asked.

'Why would she bother talking to me in code? It's not as though she would have wanted to keep it a secret from the ambulance crew.'

Bob let out a snort.

'I don't mean was she talking in code. I meant could she have said *The Da Vinci Code?* As in the book.'

How could he have been so stupid? There had even been a film made of it.

'Oh God,' he groaned. 'That makes more sense,' Alex said, recalling Jenny stuffing a book into her bag. 'Have you read it? Do you know where it's set?'

'Now you're asking. I read it on holiday a couple of years back but I can't remember much about it. There are a few places mentioned, mainly in France. I think some bits are set in London and the end is somewhere in Scotland, somewhere really remote. I can't really remember any particular place names, apart from Paris. The opening chapters are set in the Louvre.'

'I'm an idiot,' Alex said, looking at the signs posted around the concourse. 'The Eurostar goes direct to Paris. Come on.'

They set off, running, in the direction of the signs.

'I should have realised,' Alex said. 'Cat told me Jenny had a train ticket with her and yet Jenny still had to get a ticket to here from her local station. The ticket she already had must be for travelling out of London.'

As they ran it felt as though the whole world was conspiring against them. They darted around the day-trippers and tourists who ambled their way around the station and dodged the commuters that forged their way through the crowds, determined to get home. But in spite of all of the obstacles the blue and yellow banner that hung above the Eurostar barrier soon loomed ahead. An announcement rang out in French. Alex's heart skipped a beat and he was suddenly seized by a fear that they were running out of time. Turning a deaf ear to the indignant cries of queue jumping from the people who had been patiently waiting their turn, he ran straight up to the check-in where he came to an undignified stop, his new leather shoes sending him sliding over the polished marble floor and into the desk. He only narrowly avoided careering into the impeccably-groomed woman who was directing passengers to the appropriate check-in. A look of hostility crossed her face but that soon dissolved once her eyes had locked on to the badge that Alex was holding out.

'When's the next train to Paris?' he asked urgently, his breath coming out in short bursts. 'And please don't say I've just missed it,' he said, hoping to God that he wasn't too late.

She answered quickly.

'It leaves in eight minutes from platform three.'

'I need you to call the Transport Police,' Alex said. 'I think a woman wanted for murder is on one of your trains.'

He hoped he was right.

For a fraction of a second the check-in clerk looked at him with wide eyes but then she picked up the phone and spoke calmly, relaying his request.

She put the phone down just as Alex pulled his mobile out of his pocket. He opened Bob's earlier text.

'This is the woman. I think she's heading to Paris.'

The clerk took his phone and studied the photograph of Jenny Black.'

'Is this a good resemblance?'

'Not too bad. You'd recognise her from that.'

'Then no, I haven't seen her. One of my colleagues may have dealt with her. I could–'

Before she could say anything more, two armed police officers jogged up to the desk. Alex recognised them as the same two that had been waiting on the platform when he'd first arrived. They introduced themselves as Joe and Tobe. Both looked like they meant business.

'...and I realise that she may not even have come through passport control yet,' Alex said, 'but my guess is that she would have headed straight here after getting off her train.'

'And you think she's armed?' Tobe said, referring to the brief that had been circulated by Bob earlier.

'I don't know,' Alex said. 'She used a kitchen knife on my partner but it's also possible she's managed to get her hands on an army issue handgun. But they'd have picked her up at security if

282

she was packing any weapons, wouldn't they?' he said, having assumed that there would be metal detectors as part of the check-in routine for the Eurostar.

'In an ideal world, yes,' Tobe said.

Alex looked at the two armed-officers in front of him.

'We are still going to see if she's on there, aren't we?'

'Sure, but it pays to be prepared,' Joe said, his fingers slipping to his belt and touching the butt of his gun. 'Right, here's what we're going to do,' he said addressing Alex. 'You and me will get on the train at this end of the platform and flush this woman out, while Tobe here and this fella,' he said, gesturing to Bob, 'stand guard on the platform and get her if she tries to make a run for it. That okay with you Tobe?'

'Sure, we can head down to the mid-section and I'll mark you from there.'

'Great. Let's go,' Alex said, eager to get started.

Joe laid a restraining hand on his arm.

'Wait. Before you get on, you need to understand how this is going to work. We'll get on the first carriage and work our way down. I'll be behind you. If you see her, say clearly which side of the carriage she's on and roughly how far down. Use whatever visual prompt you can to help me to home in on her. Once you've done that step aside, away from the side she's on, and I'll isolate her. You got that?'

'Sure.' Alex said, moving towards the train.

'One last thing: no running. We don't want to set off any panic. We take it nice and easy. The train's going nowhere. If she's on this thing then we've got her. She's got nowhere to run.'

Music to Alex's ears.

The first set of doors glided open with a hydraulic wheeze, sounding like a garage mechanic sucking air between his teeth as he considers the price of a job. Alex stepped into the carriage. He walked slowly, checking out the occupants down both sides of the aisle. It was surprisingly difficult to get a good look at them. He found he had to almost be on top of them before he could see them properly. Many had their heads buried in a newspaper or book, others were gazing out of the window, watching the comings and goings of the people on the platform. He grew more nervous with every step; stupidly worrying that Jenny wasn't even on the train, or, if she was, whether he'd be able to make an ID – and quick enough – given that she might see him a lot sooner than he'd see her. Annoyed for being so negative, he pushed his reservations aside and continued to walk forward slowly, taking his time, making sure to look carefully at everyone. He knew how easy it could be to be misled by something as simple as a hat or sunglasses. With every step he expected to be seized by a sense of recognition but they reached the end of the first carriage and nothing. Before going on he looked back at Joe and shook his head. He turned to face the door to the next carriage and drew a deep breath. He made a mental note to breathe slowly and steadily before pressing his hand onto the door pad, causing the hydraulics to open the way into the second carriage.

Even though the Eurostar's customers were perhaps more cosmopolitan than those travelling on the domestic services, as Alex advanced, he noticed that they all fitted into one of just three categories. Business people, wearing the city's uniform of a dark suit and light shirt, sat po-faced, the train's delay screwing up their schedules. In their lesser numbers were the tourists, brimming with plans to visit the many attractions of Paris: The Louvre and Eiffel Tower at the top of their lists, as well as those returning home full of tales of the Tower, Tussauds and Buckingham Palace. And finally, the romantics: couples old and young alike, who hoped to drink in the heady atmosphere of one of the most amorous cities in the world. Carriage after carriage it was the same story.

At the entrance to the twelfth and final carriage, Alex was

fighting a mounting sense of defeat that had grown with every car they had cleared. Behind the last set of doors would either be the end of what had been a slow and trying investigation or the beginning of a long and tiring search. Realising he could put off the inevitable no longer he stepped through the doorway to repeat the slow walk and search.

To his left an elderly couple, motionless and silent, sat waiting patiently for their journey to begin. On the right two sharp-suited men continued about their business; one talked loudly into a mobile phone whilst the other tapped away at the keyboard of a laptop that rested on the pull-down table in front on him.

Alex moved forward a step.

A couple of young women sat twisted in their seats talking animatedly to one another. The woman sitting nearest to the window looked up at Alex as he passed by. She turned back to her neighbour and resumed her conversation. Opposite them were a middle-aged couple; the woman sat with her head bent, engrossed in a novel, while her husband noisily shuffled a large broadsheet newspaper. A half-empty bottle of coke sat wedged between them, getting warmer as the minutes ticked by. The breadth of the next row was taken up by a family of four. Mum and dad straddled either side of the aisle as the children stood on the seats, noses pressed to the windows.

And on it went. With every step forward he sneaked a fleeting glimpse into the smallest portion of other people's lives.

And then he saw her.

She was in the corner towards the back of the train, near to the door. She was gazing out of the window, looking down the platform. She wore her hair loose. It fell across her face and could have made identification difficult – but not for Alex. He realised then that he would have known her no matter what. He wondered if she suspected anything, whether she had any idea that she was the cause of the delay, but he couldn't see any outward sign of anxiety or nerves. He took a step closer and she looked up. As with other passengers, maybe she expected to see a train official or maybe a fellow traveller trying to find their way to the toilets, but as soon as she saw him, there appeared to be no doubt or confusion; she recognised Alex as fast as he had her. And just as quickly Jenny launched herself at the train door. Forcing herself through the tiniest gap as it opened, she stumbled out onto the platform. She quickly regained her footing and began to run.

Alex instinctively gave chase, followed closely by Joe. Alex was about to call out and demand that she stops, when events overtook him. As he opened his mouth, he heard words that sounded alien to his ears fill the air. He looked down the platform to where Tobe was standing, legs set wide, gun poised, with Jenny Black firmly in his sights. She skidded to a stop on seeing the armed officer standing between her and freedom. She spun around. Joe was on the platform behind her, his gun already aimed. Alex stood beside him, a simple observer of a series of events no longer in his control.

Alex watched as she desperately looked for a way to escape, like a cat cornered by a fox. He could see her frantically weighing up all of the options. He thought at first, she was going to try to run for it but then her shoulders sank and her head bowed. Tobe started to advance and called at her to drop to the floor. Beads of sweat had broken out across her brow. Tobe was barking instructions at her now, demanding that she lie down but she wasn't listening.

Alex saw Jenny cock her head towards the adjacent track. He did likewise and listened. That's when he heard it. The wind whooshed through the tunnel, growing slowly louder; a dull click-clacking set the background beat.

Alex grew rigid.

'There's a train coming. Make her get down. Now!' he shouted urgently to Joe.

But they had already run out of time. The train glided into

view. The brakes sighed as they brought the train to a crawl until it eventually groaned to a stop. The doors slid open and suddenly there were people pouring out onto the platform, oblivious to the drama they were unwittingly walking into.

Jenny, like Alex, recognised an opportunity when she saw one, and a crowd of people spreading across the platform was exactly that. Maybe she saw it as her only chance, or maybe even in the few seconds that passed she was able to weigh up the risk. Whatever her reasoning, Jenny appeared to channel every ounce of her strength into her last dash for freedom and launched herself towards the emerging masses.

Twenty-Seven

'What! They shot her on the spot?'

Cat tried to ease herself up on her pillows, wincing as her stitches pulled, her side still heavily bruised from the trauma of the attack.

'Stay where you are,' Alex said. 'It doesn't get any more exciting the more vertical you get.'

'Okay, okay.' Cat flopped back down. 'Well, what happened next?'

'Well they didn't shoot her. Can you imagine it – taking a pot shot with a platform full of people? No, Joe ran after her and took her out in a flying tackle. I'd have him in my squad any day. No messing. He took her off at the knees. She didn't stand a chance against a young fit guy like him.'

'And?'

'Within seconds there was a crowd gathering. But Bob, Tobe – the other armed guy – and a guard that had appeared from nowhere ushered them away. That left me and Joe to deal with Jenny. It was all over fairly quickly. It was weird. At first she just lay there. I guess she was winded from the fall. But then she started to scream. Christ, she's got some lungs on her. And well... that was that.'

'Has she confessed yet?'

'Yeah. She spilled the lot in her first interview, hoping to get a more lenient sentence. She more or less admitted it just after I'd cautioned her anyway. Well, as soon as she'd stopped the hysterics. She was writhing around on the floor making a right bloody meal of it. I was restraining her until she calmed down enough to let us get the cuffs on. I know I shouldn't have but I couldn't help myself. I said to her "You're lucky they didn't blow your brains out". She looked me square in the face and said, "I wish they had. I'd rather be dead than in prison." Can you believe it?'

'I bet she meant it too,' Cat said.

It made sense. Everything Jenny had done was to get a bigger and better slice of life. There were so many more questions she wanted to ask but she knew they would have to wait for another day.

'I'm so gutted I wasn't there. After all that so-called leg-work, I go and miss out on the catch.'

'Don't worry about it. You'll still be the hero. I'm the bad guy in all of this.'

'What are you talking about?'

'For letting you go in to the house on your own. If I'd have done the right thing you would have been the one watching her sink a knife into me, not the other way around.'

'Oh Alex, that's just not true. We discussed it. I went in on good grounds. If anything, it was my own fault. I should have kept my guard up.'

Alex looked at her, his face unmoving.

'At least we'll both know better for next time,' Cat said. 'Though I'm not sure Mike will find a stab vest quite as appealing as my normal choice of underwear.'

Alex gave her a surprised look and laughed.

'Anyway, I'm looking for a nice easy time of it when I get back,' she went on. 'I must be able to stretch my recuperation out for at least a couple of weeks, don't you think?'

'You take as long as you want.' Alex looked at her, his brown eyes smiling warmly. 'Joking apart, when I saw you go down I thought you'd, well, you know. I don't know what I'd have done if...'

And for the first time the seriousness of her situation seemed to strike Cat. She took a slow, deep breath, before saying in a quiet voice, 'Let's not think about that. I'm just glad you were able to come tonight. It was so nice to see you sitting there when I woke up.'

Alex gave a smile.

'No problem. I know it's little consolation but at least we closed the case and you get out of having to do the paperwork.'

She put a hand to her mouth and stifled a yawn.

'Oh good, that makes it all worthwhile then.'

'I should leave you to get some sleep. You look tired.'

'You don't look so hot yourself.'

Alex put his hand to his face and touched his fingers to the rough stubble on his chin.

'But you're right, you should go,' Cat said. 'You've a long drive ahead of you.'

He gave a nod and after digging around in his coat pocket pulled out a bulky set of keys. He stood up and lifted his jacket from the arm of the tubular steel framed chair that he had been perched on.

'I feel bad about leaving you here on your own.'

Cat looked around her and took in the sights and smells of the post-operative recovery suite she was settled in.

'Don't worry. I'll be fine. I'm in good hands and to be honest I really do need to get some sleep. Besides, I'm sure Mike will be here soon.'

Alex took the cue and left. Tired and without any distractions, Cat soon sank into a deep slumber, faintly aware of a feeling of relief that Mike had yet to make an appearance.

Twenty-Eight

Cat pushed the door open more slowly than usual. She paused at the threshold and watched everyone going about their normal business. Spencer was on the phone taking scribbled notes. Bob had a newspaper open, probably the sports pages. In front of him sat a plate of buttered toast. She smiled. Coffee rings and grease spots on official documents were par for the course.

It seemed quieter than she remembered, but then, as Alex had reassured her countless times over the phone in the last couple of weeks, there were only a few routine cases running. She hadn't missed anything exciting. All of the cases she had been working on were out of their hands now. It was down to the Crown Prosecution Service to make the charges stick.

She let the door close quietly behind her and walked to her desk. Spencer glanced up as she pulled out her chair. She saw him stand. He gave her a wide grin before bringing his hands together enthusiastically. Soon the whole office was joining in with the applause, even Bob. Although Cat thought that the fact he did so only after rolling his eyes called into question his sincerity.

She could feel herself flush pink with embarrassment. Any hopes of a quiet return were gone, and as keen as she was to slip seamlessly back into the routine, everyone else wanted to hear her account of events leading up to Jenny Black's capture.

Maybe it was because of all of the attention, or just the effects of her first day back at work – the doctors had warned her that the first day back in the office would wear her out – but by the afternoon she was flagging.

'Bob, did Alex say what time he's due back?' she asked the untidy detective as he happened past her desk.

'He didn't say anything to me. Look on the board.'

'I already did. It's not on there.' Cat had already checked the movements board. 'I'm going to have to head home. I'm knackered. Will you tell him Hi from me?'

'But it's only just gone four,' Spencer said. 'Can't you stay a bit longer?'

'I suppose I could just about manage another cup of coffee.'

When Alex did eventually make it back, he made straight for her desk.

'Sorry. I couldn't get here any sooner. Sod's law I got called out. Some inconsiderate bastard turned up dead in St Martin's but I can tell you all about that tomorrow. Welcome back.' He produced a badly wrapped potted gerbera. 'I thought it might cheer your desk up a bit.' Cat took the gift and ripped off the wrapping. She cleared a space for it next to her coffee mug.

Alex took off his coat and threw it roughly in the direction of his desk. It missed both the desk and his chair and landed in a heap on the floor. He left it where it had fallen and turned back to her.

'How's your first day back been?'

'It's been a bit strange, to be honest. Everyone's been making such a fuss of me. Don't get me wrong, it's nice that they have but I feel a bit of a fraud. It's not like I did anything special. I mean I got myself stabbed by a middle-aged woman.'

'A murdering middle-aged woman,' he said.

'True.' She smiled.

'But you're feeling okay now?'

'A bit tired but otherwise fine.'

'Good. Call home and let Mike know you'll be late for dinner. We're going over to Mickey's for a quick drink to celebrate the end of the case and to welcome you back.'

Cat started to say something but Alex put a hand out, gesturing to her to stop.

'No excuses, not tonight. Please, just one drink. I promise I'll walk you back to the car myself.'

'I wasn't going to make an excuse. I was just going to say I don't need to call anyone. Well... Mike, I mean. It's over between us. Hell, if we don't go out for a drink, I'll be disappointed.'

'What are we waiting for? Grab your coat.'

The pub was busy when they got there. They crowded into a corner close to the bar while Alex got the drinks in. After making sure that everyone had a full glass, he lifted his pint and cleared his throat loudly.

'I won't beat about the bush. You all know why we're here. Thanks for all your hard work and commitment. We've got not two but three people facing charges for the death of those poor women. At one point I feared it might have been one more.' He cast a glace in Cat's direction. He lifted his pint and everyone followed suit. 'Welcome back Cat. To everyone – good health.'

And for a short while cheers and excited chatter filled the room and Cat found herself feeling flushed with a feeling of wellbeing. Soon everyone separated into their cliques and she found herself sharing a table with Alex, Bob and Spencer.

'I take it the third person facing charges is Steve Berry?' she said. 'Did Jenny drop him in it?'

'She tried to but between them we think we've got the complete picture. He's given a detailed account of the death of his wife,' Alex said. 'He reckons that Caroline died as the result of some freak accident. He says the night before she was due to fly back to England there was some sort of tussle between her and Jenny, which ended with Caroline falling from the roof terrace of their home. She cracked her skull on the patio below and died instantly. He says he wanted to report it but Jenny convinced him not to, because if no one believed them she'd be facing a prison sentence and he'd be court martialled. According to him the whole thing was so traumatic, he was in shock and couldn't think straight, so he just went along with whatever Jenny suggested.'

Spencer cut in excitedly, 'It was her idea to hide the body and take Caroline's identity. She masterminded the whole thing.' He looked sheepishly at Alex. 'Sorry boss, you carry on.'

Alex resumed his telling of the story. 'Berry somehow convinced himself they weren't really doing anything wrong. It was an accident and, with Caroline dead, her father's inheritance would have gone to him anyway. So when Jenny suggested she accompany him back to England, to take her place as his wife, he was happy to go along with it.'

'An accident eh?' Cat said.

Alex nodded.

'You're right. Anyone with any sense can see it doesn't stack up. Berry says Caroline got a call from the solicitors with news of her father's death earlier that day. By the time she told him she'd already booked a flight back to London for the following morning. She said she wanted to get back quickly to start on the funeral arrangements. He admitted they both knew she wouldn't be back. Their marriage had been failing for some time. Berry reckons Caroline only married him because she was sick of doing what her family expected.'

Cat thought of her relationship with her father during her late teens.

'It's a bit extreme but could be true I suppose.'

'Anyway, according to him, they agreed to go their separate ways,' Alex said. 'Caroline said she'd see him all right financially and they agreed to try and work something out so he could see the kid. And that was that, so he says. With everything sorted he went for a drink and left Caroline to her packing. Jenny was at the pub, as usual. He told her what had happened. He said she seemed over the moon with the news. He stayed at the bar until around nine and then went home. By the time he got back Caroline was all packed and had even prepared them some dinner. So far so good.' Alex took a drink before continuing,

'This is where things get a little hazy. According to Berry, after dinner they took a bottle of wine to the roof terrace for some sort of farewell drink. They hadn't been up there long when the doorbell rang. He answered it and was surprised to find Jenny there, reeling drunk. He says he tried to convince her to leave, reassuring her that they'd soon be together, but she pushed past him, ran up the stairs and launched into a verbal attack on Caroline.'

Cat screwed her face up.

'Saying what?'

'She accused Caroline of denying Steve his dues, money-wise. Caroline retaliated, accusing Jenny of splitting her marriage up. This continued for some time until Jenny had worked herself into such a frenzy that she hurled herself at Caroline, pushing her off the roof and to her death.'

'And then he behaved like a well-trained soldier,' Cat said.

'That's right. Good at obeying orders, resourceful, flexible and physically fit,' Alex recited the comments made by Steve Berry's old commanding officer. 'He'd have been able to carry a sixty-kilo dead weight across woodland without too much difficulty.'

'What about Megan and Jane?' Cat asked. 'What's he said about their deaths?'

'He's sticking to his guns there,' Alex said. 'He's adamant he knew nothing about them. Had never met them and had nothing to do with their deaths. To be honest, given what we now know, I think he's probably telling the truth. Remember how Jenny – acting as Caroline – said she was ill in bed with a migraine when Megan was attacked?'

'Yes,' Cat said. She had half an idea what was coming next.

'Not true. We've got CCTV footage clearly showing her driving her car in the direction of the station shortly before Megan's train was due in. As far as we can tell, there was no one else in the car with her. No she did it on her own, I'm positive. I also think we've got enough to nail her for Jane Francis' murder as well. Steve Berry told us – and a nurse at the hospital has since given a positive ID – it was Jenny who took Jake for his appointment that time. She had intended to continue the pretence of being Caroline, but Jane must have said something, making it obvious she knew the real Caroline. I can imagine it must have come as a bit of a shock to Jenny. She would have had to think on her feet but, quick thinking as ever, she just made out to be a friend of the family, helping out while Caroline was unwell.'

'So that was why they were both so cagey when we asked them about that appointment,' Cat said. 'It makes sense now. And after having already met her, Jane would have had no qualms in letting Jenny near her when she was out walking her dog. She only needed to get close enough to Jane to throw the wire around her neck.'

'But how did Jenny know that Jane would be in the park when she was?' Spencer asked.

'They would have been chatting during the appointment,' Cat said. 'We know from Jane's husband that she returned home that day all excited about the prospect of meeting Caroline. It wouldn't have been too difficult for Jenny to have prised that information out of her.'

'So that's everything,' Alex said. 'Obviously we've still got a ton of work to tie up all the loose ends for the CPS but I'm pretty confident we'll get there.'

Cat took a sip of her drink. A nag at the back of her mind left her feeling that there was still something unaccounted for.

Bob stood to go, knocking back the last of his coke. He put the empty glass on the table.

'Sorry I've got to run. The missus is expecting me back.'

As he left, Spencer rose to his feet. Cat noted the almost full bottle of lager in his hand.

'If it's alright with you two, I'll disappear as well. Got some mates I want to catch up with,' he said, looking in the direction of a couple of women police constables hovering nearby.

'Bob seems a little more, how shall I put it... agreeable,' Cat said to Alex, as soon as they were on their own.

'I think he's finally realised how crap it is when you have to deal with someone else's prejudices.'

Cat adopted her best quizzical look, hoping that he'd elaborate, but Alex simply reached for his pint. Casting her mind back she remembered Bob's sudden absence from the office following his afternoon pub crawl.

'Oh,' she said, clicking her fingers, that elusive loose end jumping to mind. 'Did you get anywhere with the missing guy?' she asked. 'The ex-boyfriend of Megan's. Did he turn up?'

Alex took a drink of his beer and returned the glass to the table.

'Anthony Stewart. Yeah, he called us a couple of days after we'd arrested Jenny. Turns out he'd been in rehab the whole time.'

'Ahh, no phones, no TV.'

It made perfect sense.

'Needless to say, he was devastated. He'd only checked himself into the clinic on the back of Megan's advice. He's back with his wife now, determined to make a go of it.'

'No wonder Bob had a hard time finding him,' she said.

'He didn't think outside of the box, that was his problem. You should always put yourself in the shoes of the other person. Don't assume they'd do what you would in the same circumstances. Remember that and there won't be a crime you can't solve. So anyway, that's all of our news. So what about you?' he asked, looking her square in the face. 'How come you finally gave Mike the heave-ho?'

'It had been on the cards for a while. I told you in Cyprus I'd do something about it once the case was solved.'

'Yes, but...'

'You didn't think I'd do it?'

'To be honest, no. You were under a lot of pressure with work and going through a rough patch at home. I figured once the case was over, you'd settle back into the routine.'

'Oh, come on Alex, the guy was a complete arse. He treated me like I was there at his disposal. I lost count of the number of times when he didn't come home after a night out, or when he'd come in on a Friday afternoon and announce that he was going to Brighton or Southend, or some other place with his mates and wouldn't be back until Sunday night.'

'So, what happened this time?'

'Well it started at the hospital. You know he didn't turn up until the morning after I was admitted? And even then, he didn't seem too concerned for me. What bothered him more was the fact you'd been there before him.'

'Maybe he was in shock. You know how people react differently when they find something difficult to deal with.'

'But it didn't stop there. Once I was back home, he kept going on and on about it. He wanted me to raise a complaint against you. He told me to request a transfer – *told*, not suggested. I would have chalked it up to worry or concern if he had appeared to have any. And to cap it all he didn't change any of his own routines. They only let me go home because I said he'd be around to help me, only he wasn't. Even when I needed a lift to the hospital to get my stiches out, he said he was too busy. Yet every time he got a call from one of his mates, off he trotted. After a week or so it became blatantly obvious that whatever made Mike hang around it wasn't his undying love for me. I guess it was fairly obvious to everyone else, wasn't it? I must have looked a right bloody mug staying with him.'

'Not at all. No one knew what you two were like in private. Things always seem worse once you've broken up.'

'But you must have known something.'

'What do you mean?'

'That night, when you punched him, he must have done something to provoke you.' Cat waited, expecting him to confirm her suspicions. Sensing his reticence, she added, 'I know I believed him when he said it was your fault but I should have known better. What was it? Did he say something about me?'

'It doesn't matter now.'

'What did he say? Come on Alex, what was it?'

'I can't remember exactly. I'd had too much to drink, obviously. I'd never have touched him if I'd been sober.'

'Bullshit.'

'Okay, okay. He was dancing with another woman. Provocatively.' He looked down and began to swirl the last inch of his pint around the bottom of the glass. 'Anyway, he knew I was there and had seen him. I tried to ignore him but he came over. He was in a worse state than I was. He started to talk about this woman he was with. Stupidly I rose to the bait and asked where you were. He told me to mind my own business. I should have walked away then. And I did start to, but he made some parting shot.' Alex lifted his glass to his lips and drank the last few drops of bitter. 'Well, it doesn't matter exactly what he said, he was only doing it to wind me up and I'm ashamed to say it worked.'

Cat looked at him, trying to read between the lines. He looked sad. She gave him an encouraging smile.

'At least you did it for the right reasons. You'd be amazed at how many of my so-called friends have told me how he was always messing around behind my back, yet not one of them thought to mention it to me before. I feel pretty stupid I believed him. It just goes to show I made the right decision.'

'Is that what happened? You found out he was messing around?'

'No. Well, not then. It was actually the stupidest thing. He came home one lunchtime; he'd got the afternoon off and had arranged to play golf with some friends. So, anyway, he breezed in and headed straight for the kitchen. Five minutes later he wandered back into the lounge carrying a sandwich. He sat down and turned the telly over. Not a single thought of whether I was watching what was on, or whether I might want some lunch as well. I think I made some sarcastic comment but it went straight over his head. In fact, if I remember rightly he had a go at me for whinging. He said he didn't complain when he had to make his own lunch despite the fact that I'd spent all morning sitting on my arse. I just flipped. I grabbed his coat from the hallway, went back into the lounge and threw it at him. He started laughing and told me not to be stupid. I don't know if he was being patronising or really did think I was joking. But somehow, I managed to stay calm. I told him I wanted him and his things out of the house before dinner.'

Alex raised his eyebrows.

'And he went without any argument?'

'I wouldn't say that exactly. To cut a long story short, he sent his mates around to pick up the rest of his stuff a few days ago.'

'So that's it?'

Cat nodded.

'Yep.'

'And how do you feel about it? Are you okay?'

'I'm fine.'

Alex's eyes roamed over her face, scrutinising her expression.

'Are you sure?'

'I'll get over it.' She could hear the uncertainty in her voice. 'It's not like it was ever going to go anywhere. And at least now I feel like I've taken charge of my life.' She paused before lifting the Pinot Grigio to her lips. 'So anyway, how are you doing? How's Cody?'

The lines faded from around Alex's eyes.

'He's good, thanks. They say he'll make a full recovery.'

'That's fantastic news. And how about you – how are you doing?' Cat asked again.

'I'm okay,' Alex said, shifting in his seat. 'But let's not talk about me. We're supposed to be celebrating your return.'

'You get me another drink and I'll do some celebrating.' Cat passed him her empty glass. 'Unless you've got to go?'

'Don't worry about me. I've got a late pass.'

He stood and picked up his empty pint glass.

'If we're staying, do you want to grab something to eat?'

'Actually, now that you mention it, I'm starving.'

Alex laughed.

'You're always starving. Do you want to stay here or go somewhere else?'

Cat checked her watch. It was almost nine o'clock.

'I vote we stay here. Unless you've got somewhere in mind?'

'No, here's fine. I'll bring a menu over.'

Alex walked over to the bar and handed the barmaid their empties. Cat watched as he reached for a large laminated menu from behind a yellow plastic collection tin in the shape of a cute puppy with big pleading eyes. The menu caught on the coin-filled container. It tipped onto its edge and then toppled over the bar. Alex thrust out a hand and managed to catch it just in time. He looked over to Cat and rolled his eyes. She could see him exhale through pursed lips. He rooted around in his pocket and dropped a handful of coins into the slot on the top of the tin between the puppy dog's ears. More careful this time, he tucked the menu under his arm and picked up their fresh drinks.

Just then Cat noticed a guy, tall with collar-skimming blonde hair, take a couple of loping strides around the bar, approaching Alex from behind. He said something, causing Alex to turn. With his back to her, she watched him return the drinks to the bar and clap the other man on the shoulder while the two of them shook hands.

Alex pointed towards Cat. A minute later the two men approached, their hands full of drinks and a menu. Cat took her wine and looked at the man hovering behind Alex.

'Cat, this is Dan, a mate of mine from Vice. You okay if he joins us?'

'Of course.'

'I won't stay long. I only popped in for a quick pint.' Dan set his glass down and pulled out a stool. 'Good to meet you,' he said, shaking her hand. 'Cat is it?'

'Short for Caitlin,' she said.

'Irish?'

'Good guess. I'm named after my grandmother on my mother's side. She was Irish. But just to confuse matters my father's family are all Scottish.'

'It was your red hair and green eyes, gave it away.'

'It's auburn,' Alex said. 'She'll never forgive you if you call it red.'

Cat opened her mouth, about to take Alex to task but just then he gave her a subtle wink and she let it go. This time.

The chat flowed easily and for a change it was nice not to be known as Pete McKenzie's little sister. Nothing was said about the fact that Dan's single pint turned into several or that he joined them for something to eat.

'Well, someone made quite an impression,' Alex said, as they stood at the pavement's edge waiting for the taxi to draw to a stop. Cat was still looking down towards the end of the road, to where Dan had disappeared into the shadows.

If it wasn't for the dark, Alex would surely have noticed her cheeks flush.

'I don't know what you mean,' she said, breaking off her gaze. 'Besides, I'm not ready for a new man in my life. Not just yet.'

'Well, whatever, it was a good night. We should do it again,' he said, holding the cab door open for her to climb in.

'Just tell me when and where.'

She stepped into the car and pulled the door closed behind her.

Before you go...

If you enjoyed this book, please think about writing a review. The support of readers is invaluable and very much appreciated. Reviews mean an awful lot to me, as well as to readers looking for their next book.

If you'd like to know more about me and my work, check out my website www.susanhandley.co.uk, where you can join my exclusive readers' club. By joining, you will be kept in touch with news on up-and-coming publications. It will also enable you to access FREE exclusive offers. To join costs nothing. Simply provide details of your e-mail address (no spam, I promise). That's all there is to it.

Don't forget, you can also follow me on:
Twitter @shandleyauthor or Facebook @SusanHandleyAuthor

Acknowledgements

Writing can be a long and lonely road, but it's only by sharing your work with others that you are able to breathe life into it. I am lucky enough to have great family and friends – including my long-suffering husband – who have had drafts in various stages foisted on them for their opinion, some more than once! I'm even luckier in that their feedback was always encouraging. For that I will be forever grateful. Special thanks must go to those who took the time and trouble not only to tell me what they liked but also what they didn't.

I'd especially like to thank Sally Payne and my sister, Debby Bratt, for their eagle eyes; Kath Middleton for her insightful feedback and invaluable comments; and Andrew Barrett for being so approachable and generous with his advice.

Finally, I'd like to thank Julie Platt for her excellent editorial work, kind comments and patience in dealing with my shortcomings, all of which made publication possible.

Printed in Great Britain
by Amazon

38834244R00179